Moriah snapped her head to the side, too frightened to remember to breathe. Powerful hands locked onto her arms and pulled her off her feet. Dazed, she was on her back and pinned beneath him before she could rally for a second charge.

Royd's hands clamped over her mouth, and she felt his lips touch her ear. "Guards!" he hissed.

Moriah did not move. She heard footsteps. Her mind refused to function. She was unable to figure out why Royd Camden did not want to alert the guards, but her body sent messages to her brain that startled her senseless. One of Royd's hands was entwined with hers and his pulse beat against her fingertips. Long muscles molded against her limbs, and she could feel the rapid beating of his heart against her chest.

The iron door rattled before the footsteps moved on to the next cell yard. Then Royd's hands slipped around her wrists and caressed her scars. She looked up at him, surprised by the serious expression on his face.

"It's time to keep up your end of the bargain," he whispered . . .

Evergreen

Delia Parr

ST. MARTIN'S PAPERBACKS

EVERGREEN

ISBN: 0-312-95376-3

Printed in the United States of America

St. Martin's Paperbacks edition/February 1995

10 9 8 7 6 5 4 3 2 1

Dedicated to my sister,
Carol Beth,
whose love and encouragement is *Ever Green*
and
my critique partner,
Linda,
who does so much more than make tea every other
Thursday!

Prologue

T he stern-faced, middle-aged man took a deep breath, apparently concluding his half-hour monotone lecture to an audience of one. "The routine here is quite simple. Absolute silence at all times. Labor six days a week from sunrise to sundown. The minister visits on Sunday. He'll assign Bible readings for the week. Do you have any questions?"

Moriah felt her bottom lip quiver. "Ruth. Will I be able to see her?"

She flinched when his eyes narrowed with obvious vexation. "Haven't you been paying attention? Other than Reverend Beecham, for the next four years you'll see no one. Speak with no one. Write to no one. Especially your sister."

A loose-fitting, head to shoulder hood, nothing more than two pieces of leather stitched together with holes cut out for her eyes, not only covered Moriah's face to protect her from being recognized, but also hid silent, salty tears. Sniffling, she inhaled the sweet scent of

musty leather that brought back comforting memories of
Uncle Jed's cobbler shop.

"B-but she's here, isn't she?"

"Against my better judgment," he admitted as he rose
and walked around his desk until he stood inches away
from her. "We don't coddle women and children here.
You'll get no extra consideration from me or any of the
staff even though you're only thirteen and your sister
barely a year older. Use your time here to repent and
beg for the Lord's mercy and forgiveness."

Cowed by the man's awesome size, Moriah sank back
against the hard planes of the wooden chair. She shivered, wondering if Ruth was afraid, too.

Harsh hands gripped her upper arms, pulled her to
her feet, and turned her about-face. "Go with Keeper
Jones."

A pock-faced man, no less intimidating than the first,
appeared in the doorway. "Keep your eyes down, your
tongue still, and your steps quiet," he ordered brusquely.

Weak-kneed, Moriah followed him into a large rotunda. Defiantly, she dared a few furtive glances, noticing six or seven arches that led to separate, isolated
wings of the massive building. The walls were window-
less, but dismal, minipools of argentine light filtered
through a mosaic of overhead skylights onto the stone
floor beneath her feet.

An eerie silence hung like a thick mist in the air,
broken only by the heavy echo of the keeper's footsteps
and the jangle of keys that hung from a worn belt which
passed over his shoulder. He stopped abruptly at the
first door, made of thickly scarred oak, solid except for a
small trapdoor at the bottom.

She waited as he selected a key and casually unlocked
the door. He swung it open, and she stifled a gasp of
surprise when yet another door appeared. She stared at
the crisscrossed strips of galvanized iron that were

welded into squares large enough to give anyone a full view of the room within.

The keeper unlocked the second door and stepped aside. He bowed, a mocking grin revealing scum-covered teeth as he swept an arm in front of his chest and motioned for her to enter.

She scurried past him, nerves raw, eyes darting to the four corners of the room. A small cot, a chair, a worktable, a curious wooden stall, and yet another door, although it was low, barely four feet high.

A loud, clanging sound jolted her, and she spun around. The keeper locked the iron door. "Probably better than you deserve," he spat, as though he heard her unspoken whisper of despair. He pointed to a Bible that lay unopened on the table. "Tomorrow, you work. For the rest of today, you pray. First bell you hear is dinner. No sleeping until the next bell."

She nodded, grateful for the door that now separated them.

"You can use the exercise yard at your pleasure. Till tomorrow."

She cocked her head and hunched her shoulders.

"Through the back door," he snickered.

Turning about, she placed her back to him, anxious to escape the contempt in his eyes and the perverse pleasure her situation seemed to give him. She stared at the elf-sized door and a small glimmer of hope filled her spirit.

As soon as the outer door slammed shut, she tugged at the leather hood until it slid over her head. Tossing it aside, she wiped the perspiration from her face and smoothed her hair. She walked over to the back door, opened it cautiously, and stooped beneath the frame to step outside. Precious few patches of scraggly grass and weeds dotted a dirt yard which was surrounded by stone walls at least ten feet high. She kicked off her slippers and lifted her coarse skirt to step onto the closest green mound and lifted her face to the sky. The hot summer sun warmed her, almost chasing away the emptiness in her heart.

She sank to her knees and folded her hands. "We'll be together again, Ruth. It's only for a little while. Be strong. Be brave. It doesn't matter what other people think. We both know why we helped Uncle Jed. And so does God."

She was still outside when the bell rang.

Later, when she inspected the food tray sitting just inside the trapdoor, her heart fluttered to a halt. They had taken away her freedom. They had separated her from her sister. And now this. Trembling fingers traced the crudely etched lettering on the tray. For the next four years, she wasn't even allowed to be Moriah Lane.

She was simply inmate Number Seventy-nine at Apple Knoll County Penitentiary.

Quietly. Gently. In the silent winter of her mind came a beloved voice. She closed her eyes and saw her uncle again, frail and broken, reading the Bible.

Daughter. I have called you by name. I will not forget you. Take my yoke and put it on you, and learn from me because I am gentle and humble in spirit; and you will find rest.

She smiled.

They could not take away her memories or her faith. But would they be enough?

One

1828

"Not now, Bandit."

Moriah burrowed deeper into the cot and covered her head with the pillow to escape the cold, wet nose that nuzzled her awake in the middle of the night.

Undaunted, the raccoon sauntered across her back sending chills down her spine. When he reached the end of the cot, he clawed at the covers, found her feet, and licked the soft underside of her toes.

Groaning, Moriah gave up, scooped the critter into her arms and carried him back with her beneath the covers. "Need some company?" she whispered, scratching absently behind his ears as she attempted to go back to sleep with her discontented companion perched on her chest.

He nipped at her fingers.

"Beastly animal," she growled, resignedly throwing off the blanket. Sitting up, she leaned against the wall and plopped the bothersome creature onto her lap. Complements of a full day's labor binding shoes and an extra tour of scrubbing the corridors, every muscle in her body rebelled.

She stared into the darkness. She needed no light to

study her surroundings. Every nook and cranny of her small cell was etched in her mind. Each crack in the walls, the precise spot where she occasionally stubbed her toes on a loose stone in the floor, the warped board in the outer door that let frigid blasts of winter wind and cooling summer breezes into her cell.

Nearly four years ago, she welcomed the silence and solitary isolation it offered, although she missed Ruth terribly. She needed time alone to grieve for Uncle Jed, to erase echoes of harsh accusations and condemnation, and to find solace in her faith. She embraced her daily labor, devoted grueling hours to transforming the exercise yard into a garden, and studied the Bible until her vision blurred. Yet what good did it do to make shoes, to grow fresh vegetables, or to find joy in a Bible verse if you could not share it with someone else?

The rigid schedule at the prison, marked by the dreadful clanging of bells and enforced by harsh, judgmental keepers quickly shifted from novelty to boredom, surpassed monotony, and eventually became just another unbearable form of punishment. An illusion of perfect order and quiet repentance to visitors. A constant reminder of freedom lost and dignity denied to inmates.

She sighed, pouring out her miseries to the only one who could listen. "It isn't humiliating enough that the penitentiary is a morbid curiosity for the self-righteous who pay twenty-five cents to stare at us, is it? No. Now the state legislature is sending a committee of investigators to see the virtues of the Pennsylvania system first-hand. That means only one thing, Bandit. More work."

Moonlight trickled through the overhead skylights, and she inspected her red, work-roughened hands. Weekly scrubbings of corridors, cells, and water closets recently doubled. The vigilance of the keepers who enforced the rules increased to the point of absurdity. Begrudgingly, Moriah had to admit that there was one positive aspect to the entire situation: the food became edible.

A pang of conscience also reminded her that the arrival of the legislative committee was fortuitous. Although she preferred to wait until after her release to reveal the atrocious treatment of women at Apple Knoll, she had been led through prayer to believe that the committee would read her diary and act swiftly. She depended fully on God's guidance to direct her to the right person on the committee, but at the moment, her exhausted body took fleeting priority over her faith.

Bandit stirred and stretched his body up the front of her chest, kneading the soft flesh at the base of her throat. Hugging him, Moriah caressed his head with her cheek. "What would I have done without you?" she murmured, grateful for his company, but still mourning the loss of her sister's companionship, the sound of her voice, the touch of her hand.

Shortly after Moriah's arrival at the penitentiary, one of the keepers tossed the orphaned raccoon into her cell. Meant as yet another bizarre form of torture that went a step beyond the keepers' daily taunts, jeers, and insults, the wild, mask-faced animal was a far cry from the gentle kitten she had wanted. Desperate and lonely, she nursed the baby coon into survival. Like her, he was smaller than average and slender with an indefatigable spirit in his soul. He was her only friend and companion, and for the last year, her co-conspirator.

With a jolt of belated understanding, she lifted Bandit away from her and removed his collar. Made of scraps of leather she hoarded at the end of each day, the collar often contained messages from other inmates. She smiled. In an ironic twist of fate the keepers would never believe possible, Bandit turned out to be the perfect pet for her. With his sharp claws, natural climbing ability, and nocturnal habits, he scaled the garden walls at night, easily passing from one cell yard to another with ease. It seemed almost fitting that as a result of Bandit's evening forays, the very keepers who gave him to her would be discredited as malicious and deviant men. As she undid the supple folds, a single leaf fell out.

Sophie.

Unable to ignore the coded signal, Moriah hurriedly changed into a pair of patchwork leather breeches and a tight-fitting shirt and gloves she kept hidden in the straw of her mattress. From beneath her cot, she took a pair of oddly designed leather slippers, put them on, and laced them securely at her ankles. After removing her hood from a peg on the wall, she piled her long, blonde braid onto the top of her head and pulled the hood into place before belting a burlap bag over her chest. Stopping to shape the blankets into a form that might satisfy a keeper's cursory glance, she patted the now-sleeping raccoon on the head.

Her pulse beat rapidly, then slowed to a deliberate beat as she sat on the floor next to the iron-grated door. Waiting. Listening. Expecting the sound of heavy-booted footsteps as the guards followed their nightly routine. Once they went by her cell and continued down the long corridor, she knew from past experience that she would have thirty minutes between rounds.

Seconds stretched into minutes. Her breathing grew shallow with anticipation. Sweating hands clenched into fists, then flexed as she stretched the tight-fitting gloves. The sound of footsteps passing by her double-doored cell sent her into action and she left quickly through the back door.

A quarter-moon hung limply in the late July heavens, casting just enough light to guide her steps through the private walled exercise yard. Beams of light from the sentry tower at the closest corner of the outer walls stopped just short of her cell since it was the closest to the main body of the building. The lanterns in the central guard post, hovering above the rotunda, were just as helpful.

Opening the burlap bag, she removed two long leather ropes and lassoed the twin eye hooks that were bolted into the stone wall. Tugging to secure them, she attached a make-do leather ladder, each step hand-crafted to the width of a single foot.

She tied a thong from the last step around her ankle before taking a deep breath. After rubbing her gloved palms on her thighs, she started her climb, surrounded by the scent of wild honeysuckle that hugged the walls alongside of her. Her slight weight and physical agility were an advantage, and she quickly reached the eye hooks, grabbing them for solid support. She paused, took several deep gulps of air, and urged her complaining muscles, one leg at a time, to thrust her body upward until the soles of her feet rested on the eye hooks and the palms of her hands clutched the top of the stone wall.

She rested her protected cheek against rough stone and waited until her breathing became less ragged. Calling upon a reservoir of strength she dared to hope still remained, she hoisted herself upward, plopping belly-first to straddle the width of the wall.

The wind was nearly knocked out of her, and she twisted sideways until she lay full-length and facedown along the wall. She clenched her mouth shut to muffle soft pants caused by the physical exertion her escapade required. Without wasting another precious second, she untied the thong at her ankle, pulled up the collapsible ladder, and stuffed it back into her burlap bag.

Hidden in the shadows, she squinted and focused all of her attention on the guard in the tower. When he turned his back, she crawled along the perimeter and over to Sophie's yard. Resenting the occasional sharp-edged rock that jabbed at her knees and palms, she tried to ignore the bright light that made her an easy target.

Crouching in a position that mimicked one Bandit used, she jumped down from the top of the wall, landing inside Sophie's exercise yard with a dull thud. She froze, waiting for the sound of running footsteps, but silence prevailed. Satisfied that none of the guards or keepers heard her, she moved stealthily along the wall and bent low to tap lightly at the rear door of Sophie's cell. When it swung open, she crept inside and worked her way to the water closet.

Sophie placed her finger on Moriah's lips before yanking the chain that sent the water pipes creaking and moaning—noises which would help to cover their whispered, but forbidden, conversation. The towering woman bent over and greeted her friend with a sturdy hug. "I'm sorry. With only three weeks left to serve, I know you stopped visits..Just to be safe. But I had to see you," she whispered urgently.

Moriah nodded. "Is it Ruth? Do you have any news?"

"No, I'm sorry. She must be in the opposite wing. Don't worry. If your sister is as headstrong and resourceful as you are, I'm sure she's fine. You'll be together soon."

Moriah swallowed a lump of disappointment. She had spent the last year searching every cell in the woman's block on the east side of the prison. To no avail. One of the few women assigned to deliver the day's completed work to the west wing, Sophie had promised to be alert for any sign of Ruth. That, too, apparently had been futile.

"Then what is it?"

"The committee is arriving tomorrow. I overheard the warden bragging to Keeper Jones. It's a sham. Senator Williams is sending his representative to make sure the report is favorable to his cronies. Be careful, Moriah. Don't trust anyone with your diary. Especially him. You have to wait until you're out of here."

Confused, Moriah shook her head. "What about the

representative from the Pennsylvania Society for Prison Reform? You said he was accompanying the committee."

"You think he wants the report to contain anything damaging? Not by half. Construction of Eastern State Penitentiary is almost complete. Advocates of the Pennsylvania system can't afford to have Apple Knoll embroiled in controversy. It's one of the models that they used to convince the legislature to adopt the Pennsylvania system there, too. Wasn't the society part of the planning committee?"

"I suppose. But how do you know all this?"

Sophie bent closer to Moriah's ear. "Keepers have a loose tongue, especially after they're pleasured. Damn sure of themselves, too, spreading confidential information to folks they're sure can't repeat it."

A heated blush worked up Moriah's neck and covered her face. Fallen angel that she was, Sophie had no qualms about using her body to obtain information for Moriah. According to the lifelong prostitute, if she did not assuage the keepers' lust, they would only force less compliant inmates to accommodate their needs more frequently than either one of them dared to admit. It was Sophie's self-proclaimed mission, and Moriah was reluctant to find fault with her.

Moriah rubbed her wrists as though she could chase away awful memories. "It's not the system. It's Warden Figgs. He's evil and vindictive. He has to be stopped. What about Reverend Beecham?"

"Oh, he's coming with the committee, but he's not really able to help you."

"But he—"

"He likes to have heated Biblical debates with you. You're a challenge to him. No matter how hard he tries, he can't convince you that you've sinned against God. In spite of your conviction. In spite of his weekly Bible lessons. Your faith puzzles him." She put her arms around Moriah. "You were so young when you arrived. He protected you from suffering at the hands of these lecherous deviates. You know that. But he won't sacrifice his ministry for you."

Moriah paused, more puzzled than ever. "You're right. He can't help me. If he makes the problems at Apple Knoll an issue, they'll just replace him. He's so old . . . he'll never find a real congregation." She sighed, wondering what would have happened to her and Ruth if Reverend Beecham had been their pastor instead of Cummings Glenn. Would Reverend Beecham have understood what she and her sister had done? Or would he have wrapped his heart with strait-laced dogma and condemned them like Reverend Glenn did and forced them to accept society's punishment? She chased away thoughts about the past and concentrated on the present. "I prayed and prayed, asking for guidance. I was so sure that God sent the committee here to help us." She took hold of Sophie's hands. "Maybe He wants me to wait. I'll pray harder. Open my heart more fully to Him. But I promise not to forget you or any of the others."

"Don't you worry none," Sophie responded. "It's not so bad here for me. But for the younger ones . . . the senators need to know that the women suffer indignities no man can fathom."

Moriah could only imagine them, but she saw unspeakable horrors, violated bodies, and broken spirits mirrored in the eyes of the women she had visited for the past year. "They'll know. I have my diary. Names. Dates. Details of all the wrongdoings. I'll take it to Harrisburg. Ruth will help me."

"I know she will, darlin'. You're sure the diary is safe?"

"It's hidden well."

Moriah hesitated, reluctant to tell anyone else where she had secured the remnants of leather, each lettered with painstaking care with the tip of the awl she used in her work. Forbidden access to paper and pen did not prevent her from recording her findings—it only made her more creative.

"You best hurry now or the guards will catch you for sure."

Together, they tiptoed out to the exercise yard where Sophie easily boosted Moriah to the top of the wall. After taking a few crawls forward, Moriah stopped and turned her head around. "What's his name? The senator's representative?"

Sophie's whispered response came quickly.

"Camden. Royd Camden."

♣
Two

One step ahead of the others, Royd Camden scanned the perimeter of Apple Knoll Penitentiary. Medieval turrets posted the corners of the outer stone walls. He half expected the sun to bounce off guards plated in armor. Instead, men in blue uniforms, outfitted with rifles and spyglasses, kept silent watch in solitary, bell-topped towers.

Lonely duty.

Was his any better?

Warden Figgs stepped around him and walked quickly to the front of the group, pausing to catch his breath. "Not a single escape. Not over those walls." Beaming, he mopped beads of perspiration off his forehead.

George Atwood, the only state senator on the four-man committee, grinned. "Granite and slate. Too smooth to mount." He raised one hand and gestured over his shoulder, pointing behind them. "These the only gates?"

"Better for security." Figgs nodded then motioned for the tour to continue.

Dense green grass covered all but the cobblestone walk that led to the main doors of the building and hugged two wings that spread at odd angles from either side. A dozen saplings, planted in measured distances along either side of the walk, cast little relief from the sultry heat.

Damp with perspiration, Royd's shirt clung to his back. Resisting the urge to use common sense and dress as casually as his companions, he had worn the full dress of a gentleman. He rebuttoned his waistcoat and adjusted his limp cravat, refusing to let the midsummer heat mock his decision.

Prescott Darlow, the young legislative aide to Senator Harris, nudged Royd's elbow. "Exciting, isn't it? Do you think we'll actually get to go inside one of the cells? I've never been this close to wretches, profligates, and whores."

Disgust soured the taste in Royd's mouth, and his jaw tightened. His eyes flashed briefly before they shuttered his scorn for the man's callow attitude. "I'm sure the warden can arrange it."

"I hope so. Senator Harris said we would have access to just about anything we wanted."

Royd glared into hazel eyes twittering with superiority and flecked with bizarre curiosity. "You'll give me a copy of your report when we finish. I'll prepare the official findings for Senator Williams." Leaving the immature pup to recover from his cold reprimand, Royd followed the others into the building.

As he stepped inside, cool draughts of air, laced with the pungent odor of lye soap, doused the fire in his veins. Turning away from the sight of the corridors that led to the inmates, he shivered. He was too close to what might have been. Quelling his discomfort, he accepted the hand thrust in front of him.

"Marley Young, sir. Pennsylvania Society for Prison Reform. Senator Williams introduced us several months ago when your betrothal to Alexandria was announced. How is the senator's daughter?"

"Well," Royd replied, totally at a loss to remember meeting Young before. Not that the man had a single distinguishing quality to trigger Royd's memory. Of average build and nondescript coloring, Young could easily escape anyone's attention. But not his, and Royd studied him closely, putting a face to the name that triggered a mental alarm.

"You're a lucky man, sir, if you don't mind my saying so. Alexandria is an exceptional woman."

"Indeed." Royd turned away, unwilling to be less than gallant and discuss his fiancée's qualities with a total stranger.

Young grabbed his arm and leaned close. "Senator Williams has been a good friend to the society. I'm sure he shared our mutual concerns with you."

"The society's? Or yours?"

Young's face reddened, and Royd regretted his outburst immediately, perplexed by his lack of self-control. Without a doubt, the society deserved support and Royd had made substantial contributions. Anonymously. Through his influential contacts, however, he had learned that Young was atypical of the men and women who earnestly sought to protect prison inmates from vile or deranged wardens, keepers, and guards. Young was an opportunist who had hitched his future to the powerful Senator Williams several years ago.

You're different?

Grimacing, Royd recovered quickly and clapped the stunned man on the back. "Senator Williams is counting on you. I trust I can do the same?"

The tension drained from Young's expression. "My last visit here turned up minor problems. Nothing that would spark more than casual interest in the legislature. The warden is cooperative, his reputation exemplary."

Spoken in a whisper, Young's reassurance quieted Royd's nagging conscience. He was expected to deliver a positive report on Apple Knoll, refuting rumors of deviant discipline and the exploitation of female prisoners. Recalling Senator Williams's overt instructions made the remnants of a hasty breakfast churn in his stomach. Trusting no one with the dilemma he faced, Royd battled his own private memories, his conscience, and his carefully laid plans for the future, unable to reconcile them.

The warden's echoing voice interrupted his mental reflections, and Royd rejoined the others as they gathered in front of a framed ink-sketch mounted on the wall.

"The design of Apple Knoll is quite unique and is being replicated in county penitentiaries throughout the state." The warden pointed proudly to the center of the drawing. "We're in the rotunda. Here. It's like the hub of a wheel, with six wings extending like spokes, each containing twenty individual cells, each with private exercise yards. Access is controlled inside with double doors to each cell. Outside, solid iron doors secure the yards."

Tracing the outline of a seventh corridor facing the east yard, Figgs continued. "This wing contains administrative offices, a physician's examining room and sick bay, a laundry and kitchens. The other wings are strictly reserved for inmates. Currently, there are a hundred and twenty-six."

Darlow edged forward. "How many females?"

"Thirty-five. Separated from the men, of course, in two wings. One on the east is directly behind the offices; the west wing faces the front yard. Notice, if you will, that both of the women's cell blocks are nearest the offices. According to Senator Williams, these are the focus of your interest."

Hope grew, and Royd let it blossom. He could find no fault with the physical layout of the penitentiary. If the rest of the tour was as easy, his dilemma would evaporate.

The warden continued to drone. "Isolating prisoners is a direct result of the work of the prison reform movement which Mr. Young will be quick to remind you.

Previously, inmates were grouped together in large rooms. Regardless of age, gender, or crime. Our system protects the sensitivities of the young criminal, especially a first-time offender."

Young nodded in agreement. "The purpose behind incarceration is not to punish but to allow each inmate, in the privacy of his or her cell, to pray and repent before returning to society."

George Atwood pressed forward eyeing the diagram at close range. "The Auburn system employs group labor. I don't see any workrooms." His mouth formed a grin that spread only to the corners of his mouth, apparently satisfied that he had demonstrated that he had done his research before arriving.

"Labor is performed individually to prevent contact between inmates and contamination of some of the younger convicts, a disadvantage of the Auburn system. The number of guards required is also significantly less. Several businessmen have contracted for piecework, primarily shoes. They provide the materials; convicts provide the labor. Busy hands breed profit for the businessman, reduced costs for the penitentiary, and a skilled trade for the inmate. No one loses."

Royd knew better, but kept silent. Admittedly, exploiting convicts with forced labor had more benefits for the system than drawbacks, particularly when it nearly paid for the operation of the penitentiary.

The warden stepped away from the sketch. "If you'll follow me, gentlemen, we'll start with a quick tour of the wings before we adjourn for dinner with Reverend Beecham."

Moriah placed the awl and needle on the worktable next to a pile of precut leather pieces waiting to be fashioned into shoe uppers. Shifting the shoe clamp until it was balanced against one thigh, she arched her back and stretched her bunched muscles before lifting the hood to wipe her face and rub the strain from her eyes. Perspiration trickled between her breasts.

Dratted visitors! Blasted hood!

She couldn't decide which was worse, although the former always dictated the latter. At least the outer wooden door was open, and occasionally, a soft flutter of cool air drifted into her cell.

A bevy of distant voices, their words muted, broke the eternal silence, and she slipped the hood back into place. She hesitated, took a deep breath, then stood abruptly.

The committee had arrived.

The shoe clamp fell to the floor, but she ignored it for the moment, too intent upon turning her chair around to face the iron-grated door. By the time the conversation became intelligible, she was fast at work with the shoe clamp hugged between her knees and her skirt arranged properly. Head bent, she stitched the soft leather with intensity, wishing she had been able to get a message to the others to reverse their usual positions and face the door instead of the wall.

If Royd Camden meant to conduct a false investigation, he would make a travesty of the pain women endured here. At least he would have had to confront their eyes instead of their backs, knowing that each of them memorized his face and silently condemned him with the only weapon they had—their spirits.

Heart pounding, she held her position.

She wasn't afraid to be the only one.

Voices quieted to a murmur. Footsteps halted at her cell.

She looked up, prepared for the shocked expression on the warden's face. She blinked it away, concentrating instead on each of the four men who stared back at her. A lump of surprise lodged in her throat. Her chest tightened. Facing these visitors, seeing contempt and perverted curiosity in their expressions, hurt more than she cared to admit.

She was accustomed to listening to visitors as they traveled through the cell block. Occasionally, parents dragged their whining children over to her door, threatening similar punishment if they continued their evil ways. Some giggled nervously. Others, cloaked in puritanical fervor, knelt and prayed for her blackened soul.

Face-to-face contact was difficult for her, yet the men who stared at her now seemed to enjoy it.

No. Not all of them. One man, taller than the rest, looked different. His expression was hard to read. Was it fear? She bent forward and looked more closely. No. A mask of interest. Then pity quickly cloaked with detachment.

Royd Camden.

Her eyes darted, sketching his countenance indelibly in her mind. A mane of unruly, blue-black curls framed strong angular features set with large, winter green eyes. His image evoked determination. A strong will. A touch of arrogance. A dare?

Powerfully handsome, his riveting gaze locked with hers. Challenged, she tilted her head and squared her shoulders, too obstinate to back down and call back the gauntlet she tossed to him.

Judas.

He broke eye contact and stepped out of view before the warden ushered the others away. Shame seeped slowly through her veins.

Judge not.

She couldn't help it, but she should have. Seeds of doubt took root, strangling her faith which demanded forgiveness and understanding. How could she be sure it was Camden?

She knew.

As sure as she knew that Sophie's information had saved her from making a terrible mistake. She couldn't trust Camden or anyone else on the committee. The fate of too many women weighed heavily in the palm of her hand. She had to wait . . . just a little bit longer.

Shaken, Royd tried to erase the blazing censure that sparked in the depths of those pale blue eyes. They bored a hole straight through all of his defenses and left him feeling vulnerable.

Stop it, he argued silently as the tour continued past the doors of other inmates. She couldn't know. No one here knew, except for Young and possibly the warden.

Despite the warden's claim otherwise, Royd knew that the penitentiary reeked of unusual cleanliness and order. No doubt the menu improved considerably. He wasn't a fool. Neither was Figgs. Royd guessed that inmates had been worked hard and long to make sure that a sparkling institution met the committee's arrival.

By the time Royd reached the last cell, he felt better. Little Miss Pale Eyes merely resented the intrusion of the committee, probably with good reason. Exhausted by extra work and unable to voice her complaint, she chastised him nevertheless. Surprisingly, she had found the wherewithal to fling it in his face. None of the others seemed to have the courage to confront the committee openly, and not a single other inmate faced the outer doors. Blurred images of hooded women, their bodies draped in brilliant colors of orange, brown, and red—one overlarge woman wore deep scarlet—created a colorful collage of order, steady labor, and obedience.

Except for one petite woman with eyes the color of a spring sky at dawn.

The sound of Darlow's animated voice interrupted Royd's mental distraction and brought him back to the task at hand. "Why are the women in different colors? Are they coded . . . by crime?"

Figgs shook his head. "A first-time offender wears

orange; the second time, brown. Regardless of the nature of her conviction."

"And red?"

"Repeat offender. Fortunately, there's only one at Apple Knoll, but she's never served a sentence here before. Served twice, no three times, in the Walnut Street Jail in Philadelphia for whoring. She's something of a challenge, a test to see if we can have an impact on the hardened criminal."

Miss Pale Eyes wore orange, Royd noted before he pressed a question. "If the women are isolated from one another, what purpose does color-coding their garments serve? I assume the records indicate their criminal history."

Nonplussed, Figgs answered quickly as he steered the group back down the corridor in the direction of his office. "Once a week, pairs of women scrub the corridors. Although the guards maintain strict silence, we also try to keep the first-time offenders away from the bad influence of the others."

"And the hoods?"

"To protect their identity. From each other. From visitors. Once they leave here, they've made their peace with God and society. They deserve a fresh start without fear of being recognized."

Atwood endorsed the idea wholeheartedly, his head bobbing in time with his steps. "It should also prevent the inmates from banding together after they're released. Good idea. I'm sure the legislature would endorse the custom. What do you think, Camden?"

"It's satisfactory." Royd couldn't help but wonder if hooding their faces didn't also have an unexpected benefit for the inmates. With their faces covered, they were free to indulge their frustrations at being viewed like caged animals in a circus or branded as the devil's handmaidens. The hood was a queer touch, yet offered a tangible defense against man's nature which demanded perfection and found the reflected image of failure an obscene obsession.

He almost wished he had one himself. It might make his job here easier. Deep in the recesses of his soul, however, he knew that no hood, even if fashioned of heavy, plated steel, could protect him from the glitter of condemnation in those penetrating pale eyes.

It had been thirteen years. Half a lifetime. He remembered. Only too clearly.

He closed his eyes as he passed her cell—a cell that could have been his. He felt her stare, cold and demanding, prying open the door to his boyhood.

He felt shaky.

Perhaps he remembered too little.

Three

For the duration of the afternoon, Moriah continued to work, finishing two shoe uppers before spending an hour in prayerful reflection. She glanced at the now closed wooden door, grateful that the committee had gone and left them all in peace.

Closing the Bible, she hugged it close to her heart, ashamed of her abrupt fall from grace by being willful and defiant. Her mind began to wander, and she thought of Ruth. Loving, ever-faithful Ruth. "I've spent my whole life trying to be like you," she whispered softly, knowing that she had failed again to emulate her sister's calm faith and reason.

She frowned, trying to picture her sister's face and form. It was hard, and she felt a flush of guilt stain her cheeks. Fuzzy at first, Ruth's smiling image became clearer, and she wondered how much Ruth's appearance had changed. After nearly four years, had she changed as much as Moriah had?

Moriah entered prison as a child, but would leave as a woman. She glanced at her body. Soft curves replaced the angular lines of her childhood, although she hadn't grown much in height. Small, firm breasts filled out her tattered chemise, hidden by an ill-fitting, gaudy gown. Her straight, blonde hair had grown so long that her braid touched the base of her spine. She tugged it, thinking about how different she and Ruth were in appearance.

Ruth's hair, a mass of tight brown curls, always fought control, with soft ringlets escaping to defy Ruth's attempt to style it. Built like their sturdy German father, Ruth had a solid bone structure and a strength of character to match. By now, Moriah imagined that she was rounder and even more amply curved. Petite and slender, Moriah was a replica of their Irish mother although her pale coloring indicated distant Nordic blood.

The two girls were more alike in their character, although Moriah always felt she had to play catch-up. Ruth was a paragon and had a faith that was natural, almost inborn. Moriah, on the other hand, struggled to imitate the teachings of the Bible, using Ruth as a flesh-and-blood model. Strangely, it had been easier to build her faith here, isolated from society, although she missed Ruth's companionship desperately.

Close in age, the sisters grew even closer when their parents were killed in a carriage accident. Injured slightly, both girls recovered, thanks to the doting care and attention provided by Uncle Jed.

Dear, sweet man.

Tears swelled and trickled down her cheeks. It hadn't been easy for him. A smile tugged at her lips and they trembled. Instant fatherhood, especially for a confirmed bachelor, had been difficult, yet the two rooms over his cobbler shop were crowded with love and patience.

Four years ago, when he reached out to his nieces asking for help, neither one of them hesitated. For both girls, breaking the law didn't matter. God's commandments were harder to violate, but in the end, they each found their decision blessed by a quiet inner peace.

A rumbling growl, deep in the pit of her stomach, ended Moriah's timeswept memories. Famished, she set

the Bible aside, tidied her cot, and washed her face and
hands.

The sound of the bell coincided with the creak of the
wheels on the meal cart. Kneeling, Moriah caught the
food tray as it slid through the wooden trapdoor. Tantalizing odors made her stomach growl again, and she carried her supper to the table, her mouth watering with
anticipation.

Stew! She could almost taste it, and she lifted the
cover of her wooden bowl, daring to hope for a chunk of
lamb.

A scream bubbled out of her throat, and she clamped
one hand over her mouth. With the other, she shoved
the bowl away from her. The raw clatter as it hit the
floor sent Bandit in a mad dash through the back door,
but Moriah barely took notice. She watched with horrid
fascination as the stew splattered across the floor.
Greasy, shiny gravy, spotted with brown lumps, oozed
down the walls.

Cockroaches! Dark brown, long-legged, creepy-eyed
roaches! Half a dozen of the disgusting bugs lay listlessly
in the remnants of her supper.

Bile stung her throat, and her whole body shook. Nervous perspiration dotted her upper lip as she backed
away from the table. One insect stuck to the hem of her
skirt, and she brushed it away with a trembling hand.

Retribution. Swift and silent.

Did she expect her little performance today to go un-
checked? The presence of the committee would not stop
the warden from penalizing her for her impudence. She
should have expected him to devise a subtle but powerful form of punishment that would be difficult if not
impossible for the members of the committee to discover—if they cared.

Thinking about the committee took her mind off the
horrid bugs, and brought Royd Camden's image into
focus. Deep, green eyes flashed with victory. She

groaned and closed her eyes, chanting a prayer faster and faster to make them go away. Why wouldn't he leave her alone? Hadn't she prayed long and hard just a short time ago for the Lord's forgiveness?

Moriah's stomach growled again, pulling her back to a more pressing problem. Accepting her punishment as justly deserved but disgusting and gruesome, she found it compatible with Keeper Jones's penchant for embellishing the warden's orders. She tiptoed past the globs of inedible stew. At least she had a few scraggly vegetables that she cultivated in her yard to supplement her meager diet. She would have to eat the vegetables raw, but they were better than nothing! As she neared the back door, she heard footsteps before it slammed shut, startling her. As the bolt squeaked into place, she almost cried.

Not my gardens, too!

To compound her misery, the flow of fresh air that drifted into her cell halted abruptly, and she felt the air grow close. Hungry and shaken, she finally admitted defeat. Grabbing a pail of water, she moistened a rag and knelt down to clean her cell. Offering her efforts as additional penance, she welcomed the opportunity to make amends, although handling the insects made her skin crawl. When she finished, she stripped down to her chemise and lay on her cot, staring up at the skylights.

The blue-velvet sky, studded with diamonds, soothed her brittle nerves. Sleep tiptoed softly into her consciousness and carried her away, but not before those devilish green eyes winked at her maliciously, making her sleep fitful as best.

Following a light supper, Reverend Beecham led his guests outside to a wraparound porch. Hydrangeas, covered with snowball flowers lace-petaled in white, pink, and blue, cuddled the whitewashed railing. He motioned for them to take a seat. "Mr. Camden. As head of the committee, I wanted to meet with you earlier, but it seems that the Lord had other ideas. Death, like life, has its own calendar. Fortunately, the poor soul made his peace with God before drawing his last breath."

Royd nodded, noting the sincerity that underlined the elderly man's words. "I understand. Completely." Choosing to stand, Royd watched the others settle into paint-chipped wicker chairs and waited for the minister to continue.

"Lester Figgs tells me you're all here for another two days."

Out of the corner of his eye, Royd caught Darlow's look of disappointment, an emotion foursquare with his own. Royd dreaded the next two days and looked forward to them as much as he would enjoy standing naked in a snowstorm. "Senator Williams thought it would be time enough. Do you agree?"

" 'Twill be enough." Pole-bean thin, the graying minister posed thick-veined hands in a V on his lap. "How can I help?"

Atwood fidgeted in his seat while he took a small tablet and a finger-sized pencil from a pocket in his jacket. "I think we all need assignments. When Senator Montgomery asked me to join the committee, he mentioned specific areas to be investigated. Perhaps it would be best . . ."

"Senator Williams is the real head of this committee, and I'm aware of what he wants." Royd cleared his throat and set his features in a firm expression. "I don't need to tell any of you how important our work is. The rumors that have reached Harrisburg damage more than just the reputation of Warden Figgs or the penitentiary. The Pennsylvania system has been approved by the legislature for Cherry Hill and other locations. It's important to make sure there are no scandals."

No one blanched when he used the common name for Eastern State Penitentiary in Philadelphia, although he caught the minister's momentary confusion as it fluttered briefly then disappeared. "Female inmates draw the most concern, naturally. They are more vulnerable and their exploitation a more explosive issue."

Darlow blushed, but Royd did not miss the resident glint of interest in his eyes before he continued. "As Chairman of the Senate Committee on Prisons, Senator Williams accepts responsibility for the inmates. It weighs heavy on his shoulders. As his representative, let me assure you that the senator will not be satisfied with anything less than a forthright and thorough investigation."

Although his words flowed smoothly, Royd felt a knot twist in his chest that nearly choked the breath out of him. Williams was a hypocrite and a master of political chicanery who pledged his allegiance to several cronies who sponsored Apple Knoll and profited from the inmates' labor. Mistreatment of female inmates, whether real or alleged, was not important.

Royd discovered the dark side of Williams's character only when it was too late—after his betrothal to Alexandria. His marriage to Senator Williams's daughter was supposed to lock his place in genteel society. Instead, Royd found himself mired in political intrigue and an ethical dilemma that turned his lifelong ambitions inside out. Unless . . .

George Atwood pushed Royd to issue a directive. "How do we start?"

"By dividing the tasks. Reverend, your knowledge of Apple Knoll is firsthand. I'm counting on you to add anything important that I overlook."

Beecham nodded approvingly.

"Atwood. We need to document the number of female inmates, past and present, health records, deaths, et cetera. Make an appointment to speak with the physician as soon as possible."

While Atwood scratched a few notes, Royd added a deliberate chill to his voice. "Darlow. You can inspect the kitchen and laundry areas. Document the menus, methods of food preparation, availability of clean garments, et cetera."

"What's that have to do with rumors about physical abuse?"

"Being forced to eat tainted food can be unhealthy if not deadly. It's a form of abuse as clearly as being beaten."

Thoroughly rebuked, Darlow pouted. Beecham placed a hand on the young man's shoulder. "Every facet of an inmate's life is important, son. Your work can make a difference." Beecham looked up at Royd. "I assume you'll want me to give an account of my ministry?"

"Please. I'll want to meet with the keepers and guards, and if you wouldn't mind, I'll need the names of several women to interview."

Darlow shot Royd a look of contempt which Royd wanted to toss back at him. Instead, he smiled benignly, but the corners of his mouth quickly turned into a frown that matched the minister's.

"Names are impossible. I can only give you numbers."

"Numbers?"

"All of the inmates receive a number when they arrive. It's . . . it's tattooed high on their left arms so that it's normally hidden from view. It's also stamped onto their personal possessions—garments, work tools, food kids. Women have numbers beginning with seven while the numbers beginning with one through six are reserved for the men."

The minister leaned forward in his chair. "It may sound dehumanizing, but the motive behind the system is well-intentioned. It's meant to maintain the inmates' right to privacy in just the same way that the hoods protect their identity. Anonymity, one hopes, preserves dignity."

Beecham's eyes grew darker as though troubled. "It's

important to remember that sometimes the system fails. Inmates do not always repent or reform, and they return to society only to repeat their mistakes. The tattoos make it quite simple to identify a convict as a repeat offender no matter where time was served before."

Royd shuddered as an icy finger of disbelief trickled down his spine. The inner flesh along his upper left arm tingled, and he fought the urge to scratch it.

"Numbers, then," he said quietly through gritted teeth. "Do you suppose the warden will have any argument against the interviews?"

"Not at all. I prepared a list and showed it to him last week anticipating your request. I'll send it over to your room at the inn later."

Royd took a deep breath. "That leaves you, Mr. Young. I'd like you to prepare a financial summary. I'm sure the warden has records to help you. Get names of business contractors, inmates' work output, net cost of maintaining the prison, and the like."

"I have preliminary data based on my visit last year."

"Update it," Royd said, perhaps too firmly, judging by the man's hurt expression.

Atwood rose and flecked a paint chip off his sleeve. "If there's nothing left to discuss, I'd like to retire."

"No. I have nothing more. Reverend Beecham?"

"You've covered everything, Mr. Camden. If I think of something you've missed, I'll leave a message at your hotel. I—I must apologize. Mildred and I are disappointed that we couldn't provide accommodations for all of you."

"Your sister couldn't have been more gracious. Thank her again for supper; it was delicious. It would be unreasonable to expect both of you to entertain the full committee."

"Still . . ."

Royd flashed a genuine smile. "Darlow and I will be quite comfortable at the Dew Drop Inn. It's only a few

minutes' walk from here. We can meet Young and
Atwood here in the morning and ride to the penitentiary
together. The warden said he'd send a coach about
eight."

"Then both of you come at seven. Mildred insists you
take your meals here. She says the cook at the inn has a
heavy hand when it comes to grease and twice as heavy
where dirt is concerned, although Mildred's eyes are
failing so quickly I'm not sure how she knows." He
laughed out loud when Royd started to protest, his smile
softening the aging effect of the wrinkles that lined his
face. "Don't argue. Mildred already laid in stores. Besides," he said as he escorted Royd and Darlow to the
steps, "once you taste Mildred's apple fritters, you'll get
a glimmering taste of heaven."

Unable to mouth further arguments, Royd returned
to the hotel, ignoring Darlow's sullen face and studying
the small town that had sprung up just four miles from
the penitentiary.

Weather-stained, clapboard cottages, similar to the
one Reverend Beecham shared with his sister, clustered
close together. They lined the single dirt road that led to
Apple Knoll in the east and the Ohio border some miles
to the west.

Neither man spoke, and as they approached the business square, Royd made quick study of the dilapidated
mercantile, two pubs, a granary, and a livery that sat
farther back from the street than any of the other build-
ings.

Excusing himself, Royd headed toward the livery. A
pair of towheaded boys nearly bowled him over when he
reached the stable door, and he jumped aside just as the
tall, barrel chested owner, presumably the boys' father,
charged after them. "Young-uns! Gotta get 'em back
here. Your stallion's in the back pasture. Gave him oats
and rubbed him good," he shouted over his shoulder.

Royd chuckled as the man disappeared in a cloud of

dust. He walked around to the back and found his horse charging the gates, retreating, then recharging, each run shaking the ground. He whistled, then grinned when the horse's ears pricked forward. The horse nickered softly and pranced over to Royd, nipping at Royd's waistcoat until he found the lump of sugar hidden in its usual spot. The amber-colored horse, his body glistening with sweat, quieted as Royd scratched the white diamond that nature painted on the animal's face.

"Relax, Brandy. It's just for a few days."

The horse stomped with both forelegs.

Royd closed his eyes. "I want to leave, too. Hell, I didn't even want to come, but there's a job to be done."

The horse nudged Royd's chin until he opened his eyes.

Laughing, Royd uncharacteristically gave in to a wild impulse. He walked back into the barn, stripped down to his shirt and trousers, and grabbed Brandy's bridle. Scoffing the extra time it would take to saddle his mount, Royd was astride bareback and galloping through the countryside not five minutes later.

Royd gave his steed full rein, enjoying the rush of cool, early evening air that replaced the midday heat. He concentrated on his body and the feel of powerful horseflesh straining beneath his thighs, closing his mind to anything else. When they crested a hill, he pulled hard on the reins. Brandy reared, snorting and pawing the air with his forelegs. Quieting the stallion, Royd urged him into a slow canter until he had a better view of the valley below.

Surrounded by orchards, Apple Knoll looked like a relic, a vestige from another time and place. A time when kings ruled courts, troubadours carried epic tales of bravery and sang of courtly love, and knights in shining armor jousted for ladies' favors.

A bitter laugh tore from his throat.

Not quite.

Somewhere behind those walls there was a nameless woman with pale blue eyes and a number tattooed on her left arm. She was an inmate in a penitentiary, tried, convicted, and found guilty of crime. It didn't matter what she had done. A social outcaste, Pale Eyes was assuredly no lady!

He pictured Alexandria. Well-born, proper, and refined, although he was disappointed by a jealous and selfish nature she skillfully hid from others. Nevertheless, she was the perfect mate to fashion a socially prominent future. All he had to do was sell his soul to keep her.

He turned away and rode the horse hard, galloping away from the sight of the prison. The faster he rode, the more he became aware of the invisible armor he wore. Ambition and drive, linked together with emotional detachment and single-minded purpose, encased his heart and protected his secret.

Shame and embarrassment raged through his frame.

If Pale Eyes was a lady, he was a knight, all right.

A knight in tarnished armor.

Four

Moriah rose before dawn and started her daily work. A dull ache in the pit of her stomach kept painful track of the time. She shuddered, remembering the cockroaches. As the breakfast hour passed without the arrival of her food tray, she didn't know whether to be relieved or angry.

Late in the morning, the turn of the lock in the iron door startled her. Her fingers froze in midair. Did Keeper Jones or the warden come to gloat?

"I'm to stay, sir. Warden's orders."

The keeper's voice, oddly high-pitched, sounded a bit strained. Curious, she turned around, half expecting to see Reverend Beecham's kindly face. Her heartbeat accelerated as soon as she caught a glimpse of outrageous black curls. She swung back to her work, but her fingers refused to stop shaking. She dropped the awl and fumbled with the needle which pierced her index finger. Plopping the tip of her finger into her mouth, she closed her eyes, praying for her heart to stop racing.

"Stop working, Number Seventy-nine. You have a visitor. Mind your manners. The warden expects you to answer Mr. Camden's questions the best you can."

She envisioned the diary hidden behind a loose stone in her yard wall. *I wouldn't get fed for the next three weeks if I did that,* she answered silently. She forced herself to relax. None of the staff would believe what she had uncovered and documented. Except for an infraction of the rules shortly after she arrived, she was a model prisoner. Until yesterday. Still, she was proud of her ability to leave her cell and visit with other inmates without ever getting caught. The only thing she lamented was not being able to find Ruth.

Nevertheless, today she had been given the rare privilege of having a conversation with someone other than the minister. She was so excited and anxious to hear another human voice that the fact that her visitor was Royd Camden didn't matter.

Almost.

She reminded herself that she had been blessed to uncover Camden's subterfuge in time; she left judging him to another. Besides, there was nothing to stop her from making his job anything but easy.

"Please come in," she said softly as she rose to her feet, placed the shoe clamp on the floor, and turned around. Embarrassed that her voice cracked, she cleared her throat.

Her visitor stepped back then straightened slightly before standing in front of Keeper Jones, blocking Moriah's ability to make eye contact with anyone other than him. She stared straight ahead, but her eyes only focused on the middle of his chest. Feeling smug about having correctly identified him yesterday, she stared at him.

He towered over her, even at a distance of several feet. Impeccably dressed in exquisitely tailored attire, he was the image of monied success. His chest and shoulders were broad, but not overmuscled. A businessman, she decided. Well-connected and powerful enough to represent Senator Williams. She avoided looking up at his face, reluctant to be intimidated or chastised by him again.

"I'll need a chair."

His voice was deep and strong, his words issued like a man used to having others follow his orders. Jones pulled a chair into her cell and stood like a sentry beneath the door frame, legs apart, hands clasped behind his back. Camden set the chair on the opposite side of her worktable. He pointed to her chair. "Please be seated."

She sat down and stared at her hands which were nearly covered by the overlong sleeves of her gown and folded on her lap. His chair squeaked when he leaned back, and she felt his eyes examine her closely. He didn't say a word.

Moriah knew she looked plebeian compared to the women who shared his world, and she toyed with the folds of her skirt. Did anyone in society ever wear such an outlandish color? She felt like a stuffed orange! One of the seven deadly sins, vanity, surfaced almost too naturally, and she shivered.

"You're not cold, are you?"

Her head snapped up. "Not likely in this heat."

"Afraid, perhaps. There's no need."

She tilted her chin. "No. Curious."

He smiled. "As I am. Would you tell me your name?"

She chewed on her lower lip and shook her head. "Not unless I must."

A flicker of disappointment crossed his face before he answered her. "No." He took a sheaf of papers from his pocket and spread them on the table, pushing her work aside. He ran a finger around the inside of his shirt collar as if it were too tight and nodded. "You may remove your hood."

Her hands flew instinctively to her cheeks. Eyes wide, she blinked several times. Except for the guard who escorted her from the courthouse to the penitentiary, no one—not even the warden—had ever seen her without her hood. Perhaps Keeper Jones had since he was responsible for her during the day and occasionally surprised her after visiting hours, but she doubted it.

"I think not," she whispered, hesitant to remove the first line of her defenses.

"It's hard to have a conversation with a woman when you can't see the expression on her face. I find it odd as well to give you the advantage."

She grinned, but when she felt the supple leather move ever so slightly, molding to her smile, she set her lips in a firm line. "It's probably the only advantage I'll have."

He cocked his head and stared deep into her eyes until she shifted uncomfortably in her seat, waiting for him to issue a command that she would have to obey. His eyes glowed like emerald coals, and Moriah returned his gaze, very much aware that she would have to hide the fact that she knew anything at all about the committee or its purpose. "Who are you? Why are you here?"

"I head a committee convened by the state legislature to examine conditions at Apple Knoll. You've been here, let's see"—he bent his head and referred to his papers—"almost four years."

She nodded, catching a glimpse of his long, slender hands. *Large enough to hold thirty pieces of silver?*

"Have you any place to go when you leave here?"

His question about her future surprised her, and she had no intention of divulging her plans to travel to Harrisburg and go public with her diary. Not to Judas. "I thought the committee wanted to know about the penitentiary. Where I go or what I do once I'm released is my concern . . . and beyond the realm of your investigation."

"Not if you are left destitute and subject to the vagaries of street life. You'll wind up here. Again. One of our concerns is the lack of any structured programs to resettle inmates after they've served their time."

Moriah took a breath. "Three dollars and a suit of clothes will be enough."

"For a day, perhaps. What then? How will you return home?"

He pressed into murky waters, and she resented the sensation that she was in over her head. "You presume I have a home to return to. Begging your pardon, Mr. . . . Mr. . . ."

"Camden."

Moriah gulped, finding it hard to even say his name. "Mr. Camden. I have a skilled trade and a strong constitution. I have faith in the Lord. He'll guide and protect me. Even provide for me. He always does."

Let him argue with that, she thought as she notched the verbal skirmish in her favor. She dismissed the look of genuine concern in his eyes as disappointment that he had been unable to pin her down to answer his questions more fully.

Royd couldn't understand how he could have been so wrong. Miss Pale Eyes was docile and . . . what else? The word *serene* came to mind, despite the clever way she avoided his questions and held her ground. If someone read a transcript of their conversation thus far, her words might be interpreted as flip or arrogant. Was it her tone of voice or the calm, peaceful luster in those transparent, limpid eyes that made the difference?

Damn! He resented her, and it made his pulse pound in his head. He expected to be uncomfortable with her, although he could have avoided coming face-to-face with her quite easily. When he argued with the warden about seeing inmate number Seventy-nine, whose number had been crossed off Reverend Beecham's list, he had no idea that it was *her.* If he had any sense at all, he would have turned around the instant the keeper stopped outside of her cell. But something . . . Pride? Curiosity? Or stubbornness? Something forced him to follow through and interview her as planned.

"I yield," he murmured, noting that her shoulders dropped just the merest bit, and her hands stopped fiddling with her skirt. "Let's pursue another topic," he suggested as he picked up a finished shoe upper and inspected it closely. "The craftsmanship is remarkable. Did you learn your trade here?"

"No. My uncle was a cobbler. My sister and I helped him in his shop."

The tremulous quality of her voice intrigued him as much as the hint of an answer to the question he had tried to get earlier. "Then you'll return to your uncle to work with him again?"

She sighed, her voice almost wistful. "No. I can't."

"Why not? Did he disown you after your . . . er . . . well . . ."

"He wouldn't do that. I just can't go back," she said defensively.

"Too proud to ask for help or too ashamed?" he whispered, remembering how it felt to disappoint someone who loved you. The possibility that she was also an orphan was an uncommon link between them.

"He's dead."

Royd blushed with embarrassment. "I'm sorry. I didn't mean to bring up unhappy memories."

Her blue eyes paled and became almost translucent, exuding forgiveness and understanding which made him even more uncomfortable. He much preferred the spit and fire she hurled at him the day before.

He turned the shoe upper in his hands and placed it back on the table. "You'll have no trouble finding a position. You're fortunate."

She didn't answer, but when her stomach growled, he responded intuitively. "You're hungry. Don't you get enough to eat?"

"N-no. I mean, yes. The food is plain but ample."

She was lying. There was no mistaking it. Her eyes darted left to right, and he caught the subtle movement the keeper made to set off the jingling of the keys on his ring and the way she kept trying to look over her shoulder.

"Ample. That's the best you can say?"

She nodded her head, then pointed toward the back of the cell. "I have a garden. I'm permitted to grow whatever vegetables or fruits that suit my taste. Would you care to see it?"

He followed her outside, finding he had to nearly bend in half to get through the doorway. The keeper stepped inside the cell to guard them. Once outside, Royd blinked several times in the bright sunlight to make sure he wasn't imagining what he saw. He was Adam, standing in the Garden of Eden. With Eve? He looked for a bloody apple tree, half expecting to find one, but there were no trees at all.

Vines nearly covered the stone walls, and he spied wild, golden honeysuckle blossoms nestled in deep green foliage. The smell of fresh mint came from an herb garden on the left. Cobblestones lined an S-curved walk which led to the iron door at the far end of the yard. On the right, rows of tomatoes competed for space with vines loaded with squash.

He couldn't hide his awe. "You did this?"

"Reverend Beecham helped. His sister sent me some seedlings. Flowering weeds just seemed to pop out of the ground."

She bent down, pointing to miniature, purple pansies that tickled the edge of the walk. "They're not found in formal gardens, but I love them. Do you know what they're called?"

He shook his head, unable to speak.

She shrugged her shoulders. "Neither do I."

"It seems almost idyllic here. I never imagined that accommodations for each prisoner would resemble a country estate rather than a dungeon."

She glared at him. "A country estate?" Her laugh was

brittle. "Appearances can be deceiving. Imagine what it's like to spend days, even weeks, without hearing the sound of another human voice. Or without feeling the touch of someone . . . anyone . . . that isn't brutal or fiendish." She shook her head, her expression pained. "To have every moment of your life regulated by others. To lose your privacy and your dignity. To lose touch with your family. This is no small version of paradise," she whispered. "It's a pastoral imitation of hell."

Before he could respond, a flash of movement triggered Royd's reflexes, and he jumped backward. Her laughter, pure and sweet when just moments ago it was bitter, filled the air as she caught hold of an animal just as it was about to dash past her. "Oh, no, you don't. Be good, Bandit."

Royd's eyes widened, and his palms grew sweaty. She was holding a full-grown raccoon!

She laughed again. "You don't usually wake up until evening, do you, fella? I guess we disturbed you."

The mangy animal curled into her arms!

"He's . . . a pet?"

"A friend," she countered. "Reverend Beecham says that some of the inmates have cats, even a rabbit or two. It helps to break the loneliness. I asked for a kitten once. I got Bandit, instead. I guess it was supposed to be a joke, but it turned into a boomerang. He's perfectly tame, except to keepers and guards."

Royd edged closer. "Put him down."

"He'll bite you."

"Put him down."

The minute the black-masked critter touched the ground, he loomed straight for Royd. Teeth bared, he skirted Royd's boots and sniffed at his trousers. The woman appeared nervous, but Royd remained very still. Eventually, the raccoon rolled onto his back and wriggled his legs. Royd accepted the animal's invitation and leaned down to scratch his belly, but he never took his eyes off the woman.

"H-how did you do that?" she murmured.

Royd shrugged his shoulders. When his fingers touched an odd texture, he turned his attention to the animal and inspected a leather collar around the raccoon's neck.

Without warning, the woman stomped back into her cell, body rigid, eyes straight ahead.

"What the . . . ? Sorry, Bandit. Guess we both made a mistake. Mine was forgetting what I was here for," he muttered as the raccoon scampered away. Royd followed the woman back inside, and Jones immediately went back to his original post. The woman stood by her cot facing the wall. Her sudden mood shift sobered Royd. He acted like he was courting a lady instead of questioning a convict! He sat down again and distanced himself emotionally and physically.

"Your sentence seems harsh. What was your crime?"

She did not turn around to face him, but he thought he heard her whisper a response. He resisted the urge to pound his fists on the table and force her to look at him. Instead, he repeated his question.

The keeper snickered and answered for her.

"Murder, man. Cold-blooded murder!"

Five

Startled, Moriah swung about quickly and lost her balance. She stumbled and pitched forward, landing with a thud on her knees. As pain shot up her thighs, she inhaled a scream of protest.

Jones swaggered forward, his ring of keys bouncing on the soft folds of his belly. "Murdered the uncle. The two of them!" Ignoring Moriah, he spoke directly to her visitor. "Maggots are feastin' on the man's body and not a splinter of regret! Even the minister can't crack this coldhearted bitch!"

Royd Camden stood abruptly, and his chair crashed to the floor. Moriah caught her breath again and every muscle in her body stretched taut. Her eyes slammed shut instinctively, but she did not cower. Forcing herself to take measured breaths of air, she opened her eyes.

Royd Camden stood in front of her, but he turned his face toward the keeper. "Enough!"

An order. Sharp, cold, and demanding.

Jones tripped backward, but his face purpled with rage. "The devil's own, she is. Studies the Word and twists it into somethin' unholy."

"I said enough!"

Royd's body stiffened. Was his face flushed from the heat or with anger? If anger, was it directed at the keeper or at her? Moriah was not sure, but she didn't dare move.

"Get up."

She trembled as she accepted Royd's outstretched hands. His fingers were as cold as the expression on his face. When she leaned on his strength to get back on her feet, her sleeves slid up to her elbow. She shook her arms until the fabric dropped back to cover her hands to midknuckle.

Too late.

Royd encircled each of her wrists with one of his hands and pushed the sleeves back. His eyes narrowed. The dimple in his cheek deepened and then froze. The hard, fearsome look on his face gave her a solid case of gooseflesh.

During their interlude in the garden, hadn't she glimpsed gentleness and compassion in the man? Impossible. The man before her now looked as hard as granite. Perhaps she was too inexperienced with men to read them correctly. Keepers and guards, even the warden, were easy to understand.

Royd Camden was different. He was soft and tender with her in the yard; now he was harsh and condemning. Sophisticated and handsome, he could turn any woman's head. Or use her?

Moriah needed to collect herself. Regardless of his nature, Royd Camden was not going to pacify his conscience by claiming he had moral superiority over her. Assuming he had a conscience! What kind of man was he if he could accept a position on the committee in good faith and deliberately plan to undermine the results?

Moriah yanked her hands away. He let go without saying a word. She walked unsteadily back to her chair and sat down. Her pulse pounded in her ears as she waited, wondering which question would come first.

"Murder is usually a capital offense," Royd remarked as he upended his chair and casually reclaimed his seat.

Relief swept through her frame, cooling her anxiety and restoring her reason. She met his gaze and spoke slowly. "The charge was voluntary manslaughter."

"Either way, your uncle is dead."

"Yes, he is," she whispered, wondering if anyone other than Ruth would fully understand how thankful she was that Uncle Jed was no longer alive. If only . . .

Royd bent forward until his face was mere inches away. "By your hand?" His eyes narrowed. "Or was it an accomplice? A lover, perhaps? Were you too greedy to wait for your inheritance?"

She smiled. "I was only thirteen. My uncle was a simple cobbler. Not a man of wealth."

His eyes widened. "And you loved him . . . enough to see him dead?"

Her gaze softened. How could she make him understand? And why did she care what he thought? "Thou shalt love thy neighbor as thyself."

Royd's lips twisted into a sardonic grin. "You're right, Jones. She's got the serpent's tongue. She hasn't the slightest bit of remorse, either." He bent so near she could feel his breath. "Can it be you're not guilty?" He looked over her head to the keeper. "How many inmates here protest their conviction and cry out their innocence, Jones?"

The keeper's gritty laugh sent chills down her spine. " 'Bout all of 'em, sir."

"About all. Hmm . . ." Royd paused and lifted one brow. "Are you innocent, then?"

She shook her head.

"No? You admit it. You murdered your guardian. Your own flesh and blood?"

"Under man's law? Yes."

Royd shoved himself away from the table and crossed

his arms over his chest. "You were judged well, but per-haps too leniently."

She sighed. "I have no quarrel with the court's judg-ment, although it doesn't matter to me what it decreed."

"Why not? The court sent you here!"

"I only care about His judgment," she murmured, glancing at the Bible that rested on her pillow. "I've made my peace with Him. Should I spend the rest of my life trying to convince society there are times when the law is wrong?"

His derisive laughter rumbled in his chest before it burst out and echoed in the cell. "She's not Lucifer's disciple, Jones. She's an anarchist!"

She tilted her head and frowned.

"A rebel. Someone who balks at people in authority."

"Oh-h. Yes. I guess I am."

Royd's expression seemed to soften, and his eyes twin-kled with amusement. Then it was gone, and she watched as he masked his thoughts with a bland expres-sion. "Be a good man, Keeper. Bring some water. My throat is parched."

"The warden said I should stay."

Royd glowered and started to rise.

"Guess it won't do no harm. Watch her careful."

Royd nodded, his smile solemn. The minute the keeper left, Royd rose and walked around the table. Standing behind her, he reached down and stretched both of her arms out flat. One at a time, he lifted an arm and rolled the fabric back until her wrists were bare.

Frozen in place, Moriah tried to ignore the heat of his body as it pressed against her back. Her breath seemed to hopscotch. She felt dizzy. Why was he doing this to her?

"Was this punishment for rebelling once too often?"

She shook her head. "Only once."

His fingers traced the thick scars that encircled each of her wrists like bracelets etched into her skin. His touch was gentle, almost reverent. She closed her eyes, allowing a ripple of whisper-soft sensations to spread up her arms.

"Will you tell me what you did?"

The words blurted out before she could stop them. "I was only here a few months. I-I forgot one of the rules. I was only thirteen, but they . . ."

"What did you do?"

She opened her eyes and titled her head back until she could see him. "I sang a song."

Royd stared into her face searching for some hint of guile. But her eyes were clear, sparkling with innocence and a haunting sadness that touched him in a way he had long feared. He felt himself drowning in limpid pools of cool, calm water, unchurned with either hatred or shame. He couldn't devise a more intriguing paradox if he tried. A convicted murderess with the aura of an angel!

The keeper's approaching footsteps broke the spell, and Royd stepped back from the woman. He brushed past the keeper and left him standing at the door to her cell with a pitcher sloshing water down his chest and a puzzled look on his face.

Royd had to get away from her. Fast. Before he lost his mind completely. He turned the corner and practically knocked George Atwood off his feet. He did, however, manage to send Atwood's pile of papers flying to the floor.

Atwood scrambled to pick up the papers. "Camden! I was just coming to find you. Do you have a minute? I've found some rather interesting information."

Royd's hands balled into fists. He wanted to leave. Saddle Brandy and ride back to his firm in Hampton and forget he'd ever heard of Apple Knoll. Alexandria wasn't the only woman he could marry. Damn her father to hell! Atwood could give his information to the next man who would be willing to sugarcoat his weak character with social respectability. It wasn't like he had fallen in love with Alexandria. Love? He didn't know how. His chest tightened. Yes he did. He just didn't want to risk it. It was easier this way. Knowing the good senator, however, Royd knew that if he did not cooperate, Williams would ruin his name so thoroughly that no woman of worth would agree to carry his name and his clients would scramble to his competitors.

Fool! Throw everything away he worked for these past eleven years? Why? Because a seventeen-year-old, blue-eyed murderess made him feel guilty and forget his goals? Or made him remember what it was like to be young and alone?

Not a whisper of a chance.

"Sorry, George. Let's take a look." Royd led Atwood to a small office that had been set aside for the committee and motioned for him to join him at a conference table.

Atwood took a few minutes to put his papers in order before he removed his coat and rolled up his sleeves. "From the records, I've been able to discover a disturbing pattern."

Atwood handed Royd a list of numbers set down in two columns. "On the left I've recorded the numbers of male inmates disciplined since Apple Knoll opened. Females are listed on the right."

Royd scanned the list quickly, noting that the number of females was nearly equal to the number of males. At a second glance, his eyes skidded to a stop at number Seventy-nine, and he felt his pulse quicken. "It doesn't seem that females are disciplined more than the males," he said, glancing up at his companion.

Atwood's expression hardened. "Not at first. But if you consider that males outnumber females here by four to one, it doesn't take a mathematician to calculate that a female is four times as likely to be disciplined as her male counterpart. And that's not all I found."

Surprised, Royd nodded. "Go on."

"The method of discipline is different. Look." He handed Royd yet another document. "Ducking seems to be the preferred method of discipline for females; for males, it's flogging. Occasionally," he added grimly, "they use an iron gag. It also must be reserved for the men since I can't find a single instance where it was used on a woman."

Atwood paused and took a deep breath. Furrows of confusion lined Royd's forehead. "You've lost me, George. I understand your point about the females being more vulnerable to discipline. Still, I can't find fault with the discipline except that I have no idea what 'ducking' is."

Atwood smiled. "I came across the term when I gathered some research. It's a fairly well-known and commonly used form of prison discipline. The inmate is shackled to a wall and a keeper stands on the ledge above and douses the inmate with water, preferably iced water if it's available." He shuddered. "The goal, I suppose, is to get the inmate's full attention."

"That it would," Royd commented. Not to mention the perverted pleasure keepers would find in staring at a female whose wet garments clung provocatively to her body, he added silently, wondering if the keepers taunted and leered at the women as well. "It's not excessively cruel."

"It is when the inmate is stark naked and hanging several feet above the ground and the punishment is carried out in the dead of winter. Then the inmate is left outdoors hanging from eye hooks for days at a time afterward."

Royd's head snapped up, and he glared at Atwood. "That's documented?"

"I think so. If you match the date of discipline with the physician's records. In almost every case, the inmates were punished and later treated by the physician, although the connection between the two is never made. In fact, it's almost as though the physician is trying to cover it up. Look at this." He slid a paper over to Royd.

December 28, 1824. #79 Illness: Lung fever.
Severe lacerations on both wrists.
Diagnosis: Attempted suicide.

Royd's throat began to burn, and he had a hollow feeling in the pit of his stomach as it dropped. Picturing the vine covered walls of an exercise yard that looked like the Garden of Eden, he had the awful feeling that if he searched hard enough he would find two eye hooks hidden beneath the wild honeysuckle. His eyes misted briefly. His breathing became ragged. How long had they left a thirteen-year-old girl hanging from hooks for singing a song? At Yuletide?

"Are there more?"

"At least four, but I haven't finished studying the log for the sick bay. Should I continue?"

Royd took a deep breath. He could end it here. Now. Direct Atwood to help Darlow or assist the minister. Walk away. Pretend he didn't know.

Pale blue eyes tugged at his conscience.

"Document everything you can find, but say nothing to anyone else. When will you finish?"

"It's growing late. We can't expect Miss Beecham to hold dinner. Probably early tomorrow. I'd like to interview the physician, too. He may be able to explain his notes further. Maybe . . . maybe it's just coincidence."

As likely as a knight in tarnished armor?

"Find out what you can," Royd responded, lost in his own thoughts. No. It wasn't just coincidence. Inmate Number Seventy-nine had the scars to prove extreme cruelty. She may have committed murder, but she certainly did not attempt to take her own life. She was too . . . too comfortable with her conscience and too damn aware of His punishment for people who committed suicide.

Unless it took a desperate act that left her balancing on the precipice between life and death and four years of penance to achieve the inner peace that was so apparent now.

Royd stood and walked out of the room. There was only one way to find out.

Moriah poured her frustration into her work. She stitched until her fingers were stiff and her back ached from staying bent in the same position for too long.

Yet no matter how hard she tried to concentrate on her labor, she could not get Royd Camden out of her mind. She hated him and then prayed for forgiveness. She detested his cold, aloof questioning and then prayed for understanding and patience. She resented the way he made her pulse race when he stood close to her and stitched harder as penance for her impure thoughts.

But most of all, she despised him for pretending to care about the scars on her wrists and the look of mock compassion in those startling green eyes.

"I hate him. I hate him not," she whispered with every fevered stitch she made.

Each jab of the needle or puncture with the awl did not pass through leather—it pierced his treasonous heart! Fiend! Liar! Who was he trying to fool? He did not care. Not about her or any of the others. He was toying with her. Did he find it amusing? The prominent businessman and the murderess . . . who did he really believe had the advantage?

Royd Camden was so clever, trying to come down to her level. How he would enjoy entertaining his associates with that story!

She drove herself to the point of exhaustion. When dinner arrived, she left it untouched. She was beyond hunger now. She was too tired, too hurt, and too confused to eat. Despite the fact that the wooden door was still open and Keeper Jones could easily report her for breaking the rules, she removed her hood, threw herself on the cot, and curled into a ball.

She wrapped her arms around herself, wishing Bandit had come back. He had deserted her, and she felt bereft and hungry for something to hug and hold and cuddle. She started to drift asleep when loud bells tolling the alarm jolted her awake.

Footsteps charged down the corridor, and she knew that Keeper Jones would take off and join the others. She crawled out of bed and knelt down to pray. The alarm meant only one thing—an escape attempt. She had heard it only twice before. On each of the following days the warden had every inmate assembled in the outer yard to witness the administration of punishment.

Punishment? It was legalized murder! Both men had been flogged until their lifeblood puddled at their feet. She shuddered and prayed harder. Maybe this time the prisoner would actually scale the walls and escape.

Suddenly, she froze in place, unable to breathe. Her pulse began to zigzag and her palms grew moist.

She was not alone.

"Quickly. I need to speak with you."

Her head snapped up, and she bolted to her feet, recognizing his voice immediately.

When she turned around, she came face-to-face with the one person she did not want to see.

Six

The edges of the iron grate bit into the palms of his hands, but Royd gripped them even harder. He edged closer until the door pressed hard against his cheek. Swallowing hard, he took back a curse when he saw inmate Number Seventy-nine without her hood.

Those damn blue eyes were so big! They almost seemed too large for her thin, heart-shaped face. Her cheeks were flushed and looked a bit hollowed, but her lips were full and sensuous. The longest braid he had ever seen lay across one shoulder. Pale, pale blonde, the color of a midsummer night's moon.

He gulped, unable to speak until she spun around and presented him with her back.

"What do you want?" she whispered.

"I need to speak with you before the keepers get back."

She shrugged her shoulders. "Why aren't you with the others? I'm sure it's great sport watching the guards and keepers corner an inmate like an animal. You'll enjoy tomorrow even more when they flog the desperate soul to death."

"Tarnation, woman! Get over here and talk to me. I didn't set off that alarm so we could argue!"

That did it! She spun around to face him again.

Victorious, he smiled.

She twirled away before the smile reached his eyes.

"Keep it up and you'll get dizzy," he drawled, quickly scanning the corridors for any sign his ruse had been discovered.

"I don't think there's anything more I care to say to you."

"I need an answer. Just one. You're the only person who can give it to me."

She laughed. "You don't need information from me. Talk with the warden or Keeper Jones. They'll tell you everything you've come to hear."

He smacked the door. "I need you!"

He watched her closely as a shudder passed through her frame. She turned around slowly and walked over to him.

"Why?"

He reached through the grate and laid his hands on her wrists. "Tell me what happened."

She closed her eyes for a moment and then opened them. Her unspoken question turned her eyes a fascinating shade of blue.

"I need to know."

"So you can do . . . what? Satisfy your morbid curiosity? Have yet another tale to tell to entertain your friends at the next soiree? I think not."

Royd swallowed hard. The evidence Atwood had uncovered was only circumstantial, and Royd suspected that none of the prison records would provide absolute proof that female prisoners had been subjected to barbarous punishment. Atwood himself suggested a planned cover-up which meant that Royd needed firsthand testimony from the woman who stood on the other side of the grated door. If she confirmed Atwood's suspicions, then Royd faced a dilemma that would shake the very foundation of his existence. If not . . .

The bells stopped ringing, and Royd knew there were

too few moments before the keepers would return. "Please. I just need to know if . . . if your wounds were self-inflicted or . . ."

She blushed and pulled out of his reach.

"Were they?"

Her eyes started to glow like sapphires trapping a beam of sunlight. "Suppose I make you an offer, Mr. Camden. You're a businessman, I presume?"

"What's that got to do with it?" he snarled.

"You're used to making deals. Business deals."

He did not like what she was intimating, but he nodded for her to continue.

"I'll tell you about . . . about the scars if you'll do something for me in return."

Conniving wench! "Anything."

Her brows furrowed and suspicion danced across her features. "You haven't given me a chance to tell you what I want."

"Name it," he said, "or we'll both be in trouble. The keepers will be back any moment."

She walked back to him but stopped just beyond his reach. If he was telling the truth, she had only seconds to make up her mind. Should she trust him? Concern for Ruth was greater than her distrust. After she peeked up and down the corridor, she grabbed onto one of the grates and stood on tiptoe to whisper into his ear. "I want you to find an inmate for me. Make sure she's all right. Her name is Lane. Ruth Lane. I-I don't know her number."

Royd turned to face her. "That's all?"

"Well . . . no. If . . . if I write a letter, will you take it to her?"

"And?"

"That's all. Except I have no paper or pen. They're forbidden."

"I'll bring them later. Write your letter and slide it under the iron door to your yard. Tonight."

She grinned. "Then you'll do it?"

"On one condition," he responded, curious to know why she would barter a simple letter and news about another inmate for details that were clearly painful for her to discuss. "Tell me why contacting Ruth Lane is so important to you, and I'll agree to your bargain."

Indecision clouded her eyes, and she chewed on her lower lip. "Ruth Lane is my sister."

"Your sister!"

"Hush! Someone will hear you," she warned, breaking away to check the corridor again.

Small pieces of the puzzle began to fall into place, and the picture that was emerging was even more heinous than he had previously imagined. "Your accomplice?"

"I haven't been able to see her since we first arrived. We're being released in a few weeks and I . . . we need to make plans."

Royd nodded, not quite sure if he wanted to think about what two convicted murderesses might have in mind once they were freed.

"I'll need your name," he suggested.

She gasped. "Why?"

"When I check the records, I'll have to make sure I don't wind up right back here. I can't exactly saunter into the warden's office and ask him for the information you want, can I?"

"You have my number. Hers will be different."

"Look, Pale Eyes, I haven't seen the official prison register yet. What if the numbers aren't put next to the name? What if they're on another list? I don't have time to jump from one record book to another while I'm watching my back. Either give me your name or the deal is off."

He held his breath. Knowing her name seemed important somehow, and he did not quite know why. Her face skewed into an odd expression as she appeared to give his line of reasoning some thought.

She dropped her eyes to the floor. "My name is Moriah," she murmured before she turned away and walked back to her cot.

Moriah knew the instant he was gone. Oddly enough, she didn't hear his footsteps as he left. She didn't need to—she could sense the moment he slipped away.

She got up and walked unsteadily over to the wooden stall and opened the door. Leaning against the door frame, she reached inside and retrieved a small cloth hanging on the wall. She bent over and dipped it into a pail of water. She nearly swooned. Trembling, she ran the damp cloth across her face then hung it back on its peg.

Feeling refreshed but still light-headed, she walked slowly over to the table where her food tray sat untouched. She flipped the cover off her bowl and jumped back in the same motion.

No cockroaches. Thank you, Lord.

Famished, she sat down to eat, swallowing each morsel without even tasting it. By the time she finished, the meal laid in her stomach like a puddle of hot lead, and she realized she had eaten too quickly. Groaning, she took to her cot, sitting with her back to the wall.

An hour later she was still in the same position when Bandit darted through the back door and ran in circles at her feet. Laughing, she dropped down to her knees and tried to catch him. He raced to her table, jumped up, and stood on his hind legs. "I thought you'd be curled up somewhere sound asleep. Where did you spend last night, my fickle little friend? I missed you."

He cocked his head and swished his tail.

"I wish you could talk," she whispered. Grinning, she got up and walked over to him. "No, I don't. We'd get in trouble for sure. 'Absolute silence.' Remember?"

She patted him on the head and sat down on her

chair. He jumped onto her lap and licked her face. "You missed me, too," she giggled.

Hugging him close, she wondered what it would be like to be held close in a man's arms. Uncle Jed was always affectionate, calling her *Leibchen,* the German equivalent of loved one, and if she tried real hard she could almost remember how she and Ruth would sit on his lap—one on each of his knees, his arms draped around their shoulders. Ruth was always quick to hug and cuddle, too, especially after their parents died. Night after night, Ruth would lie with her in bed and hold her close, promising to take care of her.

A man's touch would be different. Unbidden, the image of Royd Camden materialized in her mind. There was something missing in the smoldering green embers that stared back at her. It was like he kept a piece of himself locked up, afraid to share it with anyone else. Oh, he knew how to share pleasure with a woman. She could read that in his eyes even if she didn't quite know what it meant to share physical intimacies. There was a void in the depths of his eyes that told her he would not cuddle.

Not hug and hold and cuddle? Her arms tightened around Bandit. The man didn't fathom what he was missing!

Bandit squirmed free and headed out the back door. Moments later he returned, dragging a small canvas pouch. He dropped it proudly on her lap.

When she loosened the drawstring and turned the pouch upside down, a stub of a pencil plopped onto her lap. She shook the pouch then reached inside. Sure enough, she found a single leaf of paper.

Stunned, she gave Bandit a stern look. "Well? How did he convince you to be *his* messenger? You're well trained, but there isn't a loyal patch of fur on your body, is there?"

Was that a grin on the critter's face?

"Oh, never mind," she muttered. Grabbing the pencil, she pulled the single piece of paper from the pouch and scribbled a quick note to Ruth. After folding it carefully, she slipped from her cot and made her way out the door and through her garden.

She knelt at the iron door. Letter in hand, she stopped, unable to slide it beneath the door. Her fist closed around the letter. She was so excited by the prospect of contacting Ruth that she hadn't even given her impulsive bargain a second think-through. Suppose Royd Camden did deliver her letter? At least she would rest easier knowing that Ruth was well and ready to help her take her diary to Harrisburg.

For the first time since the committee arrived, the suspicion that Ruth had somehow perished like other inmates brought tears to Moriah's eyes. She had given her word, though, and Royd Camden would expect her to tell him the truth of what had happened to her. But she would not tell him until after she and Ruth had been freed. He could not accuse her of lying or backing out on her end of the bargain, either. After all, she did not tell him when she would answer his questions. She only told him that she would.

He deserves to be tricked, the cad!

A second alternative slammed into her head. What if Royd Camden took her letter to the warden and used it to prove how easy it was to breach the guard system? Punishment would not be as light as a cockroach-infested meal.

Moriah gnawed on her lower lip with her teeth. It didn't matter. She had to do it. A sad sigh escaped her lips. Why was she doing this? To protect other inmates? Hardly. Royd Camden had no intention of including anything damaging in his report.

"Lord forgive me," she whispered as she slid the paper under the door. It would probably require an extra-heavy penance, but she couldn't back away or deny her intentions any more than she could decide which alternative was worse.

Let Royd Camden betray her to the warden if he must. And if he did? Then he would know, beyond any doubt, that every word he wrote in that cursed report was a lie. Let him imagine the horrid punishment that Warden Figgs would order for her. When Royd Camden closed his eyes at night and drifted into sleep, he would have her image dancing in front of his eyes and haunting his dreams. Assuming he slept deep enough to let the gentle spot in his heart listen.

Judas took his life when he realized what he had done. She didn't want that to happen to Royd Camden. She just wanted him to suffer enough to make him listen to his heart.

She tilted her face up to the heavens. If she prayed very hard, He would listen. He would soften Royd Camden's heart just enough to fell the prick of his conscience. Hopefully, He would also forgive her for stretching the truth.

With a sigh, she walked back to her cell. She was not particularly proud of herself, but she'd simply have to deal with that matter . . . tomorrow.

Royd slipped along the outer walls of the exercise yards in the east wing. Why the blazes was he here? It took thirteen years to rebuild his character and to create a new life. In less than twenty-four hours, Pale Eyes had cracked the armor that held his past captive and protected the image of the man he had become.

One single day, and the man who owned a highly successful printing business, calculated every step up the ladder to social respectability which included a politically advantageous betrothal, risked it all.

He wished he understood why.

Long-dormant skills came back so quickly it only took a second try before he had picked the lock to a secret door hidden in the outer walls of the penitentiary. The lock on the warden's office door would be just as easy. Even if the records Royd needed were locked in a safe, he had no doubt that he could crack it just as quickly and effortlessly as he had picked the locks.

Anticipation trickled through his veins. Damn! He'd been a fool! No amount of respectability could change his bloodlines. He was the son of the Philadelphia Prowler and his equally talented wife.

Apparently, blood ran strong and true.

At the age of two or so, his father used to brag, Royd could pick the contents of the reticule of any woman foolish enough to stand too close to chuck him under the chin. By six, he could open a locked safe faster than his mother and play lookout as efficiently as most adults. Within two years, he joined his parents as a full partner. Six months later, he stood in the crowd and watched them hang.

His parents had not meant to kill the man, but the old jeweler had choked on the rags they stuffed in his mouth to keep him quiet while they pilfered the fortune he kept hidden in a safe in his bedchamber. Fortunately, Royd had escaped by convincing the softhearted constable that he was not a willing participant.

Lost in memories he could not change or erase, Royd made a concerted effort to focus on the present. When he reached the iron gate at the end of Moriah's cell, he crouched in the shadows. His arm shot out, and he grabbed the edge of her letter. His fingers froze in place.

There's still time to change your mind.

If not now, when? he argued silently. Sooner or later, everyone would know him for who he really was. It did not matter that he had tried to change. Blood never changed. The past could never be silenced, and when Alexandria or her father or anyone of influence discovered his real identity, the world he had built for himself would collapse like a house built on a weak foundation being battered by a storm.

Royd pulled the letter out from under the door and stuffed it into his pocket.

The eye of a storm, so he heard, was calm.

As he headed toward the warden's office, he wondered if it might also be blue.

♣

Seven

By midafternoon the following day, Royd had a hammer pounding in his head and thunder rumbling in his stomach. Double fool! He had gotten a scant three hours sleep and missed both breakfast and the coach escorting the committee to the penitentiary. Arriving long after the other committee members had started working, he nevertheless managed to interview the rest of the female inmates by skipping the midday meal. Atwood offered to help and took responsibility for interviewing the keepers and guards.

By the time Royd was finished, he was ready to strangle Moriah with his bare hands . . . if they would stop shaking long enough to wrap around her neck! Curse the twit! He could not get her out of his mind which was functioning at the moment somewhere between infancy and lunacy.

It was all her fault. Royd knew he would not be able to forget who he was or the life he had led before. His secret fear had been that he would never be able to extinguish his larcenous spirit and the frisson of adventure and spine-tingling thrill that accompanied a successful break-in. God's blood! He felt it surge the minute he agreed to their bargain.

The interviews had gone twice as badly. Royd tried to

make them brief and brusque, but the minute he gazed into the inmates' eyes, he had been lost. Blue, hazel, brown, and black. It did not matter. The curtain in those blank, expressionless eyes parted briefly and in that fleeting moment, he saw the same defensiveness, anger, and bitterness that once filled the heart of an eight-year-old boy.

The women were a motley group: thieves, prostitutes, an arsonist, and two women convicted of assault. None of them would utter a single word against their treatment at the penitentiary, and not one of them cared a damn about where she was going after she was released.

Pale blue eyes beseeched him to help.

"No! I have a life of my own to live. Ordered. Secure. Respectable," he muttered as he stormed back to the committee's room. Hell! He was unable to decide if he would give Moriah the news he had about her sister. Moriah's letter was still in his pocket.

"Pardon me, sir. Did you say something?"

Royd's head snapped up. He groaned and quickened his step. "Darlow. What is it?"

"My report is finished," he said as he trailed behind Royd like a pup on a short leash.

Royd skidded to a halt and turned around. Darlow slammed into him and backed off with his hands raised in surrender. "Sorry," he mumbled. "I-I finished the report this morning, but I've spent most of the afternoon working on something else."

Royd glared at him. "Is there anything you want to add before you leave? I assume you *are* leaving now that your report is finished?"

Darlow looked over his shoulder and then gave Royd a wink. "I found something you might enjoy seeing. It's not in the report. I didn't think you'd want anyone else to know."

Royd let out a deep breath. "What is it?"

"I'll have to show you."

Darlow turned around and led Royd to the laundry area. No one else was in the room, and Royd assumed that work for the day had ended. They skirted puddles of brackish, soap-scummed water and passed drying racks lined with damp garments. In the rear of the room, Darlow opened the door to a room the size of a small closet.

The minute Darlow opened the door, Royd felt the urge to gag. The air reeked of stale sex! Standing inside, Darlow motioned for Royd to enter. Once Royd stepped through the narrow opening, Darlow quickly closed the door. Streams of light poured through holes at odd levels. Royd held his breath and ran his fingers around the curved edge of one. The holes were not flaws in the wood; they had been deliberately drilled.

Following Darlow's lead, Royd leaned close to a hole at his eye-level and peered through. He blinked, swallowing a splinter of outrage, as he realized what had prompted the men to pleasure themselves in the privacy of the closet. He hauled Darlow out of there by the scruff of his neck. Royd slammed the door shut and took a deep whiff of fresh air before backing Darlow up against the wall.

"Explain yourself!"

The younger man frowned. "Why are you angry with me? The keepers or guards made the peepholes!"

"You spent the *entire* afternoon in there watching women strip naked and bathe? What kind of demented monster are you? Don't these women deserve privacy?"

"Wretches and whores, not women!"

Royd's laugh was bitter. "Nice Christian attitude."

Darlow shot him an angry glance. "They have free will. They choose lives of sin and depravity instead of righteousness! I don't see where it should matter to you. Senator Harris said—" He clamped his mouth shut and glowered.

"What did Senator Harris say?"

Darlow squared his shoulders and looked annoyingly confident. "Senator Harris told me the kind of report you'd be writing. You don't have to worry. Unless . . ."

Royd had the tempting urge to smash the idiot's teeth into the back of his throat. He nodded, afraid to make a move that would set his hands in motion.

"Unless you've changed your mind and intend to write a valid report." Darlow preened, his mistaken perception of advantage glaringly apparent. "I'm sure that Senator Williams would be fascinated by the idea that his future son-in-law had a soft heart for these . . . these social misfits!" He turned on Royd. "You think I'm a novice, don't you? Too inconsequential to warrant your concern. Bah! You're the fool, Camden! I'll leave my report in the room, but I won't be leaving. Not yet. Senator Harris thought it might be wise to accompany you back to Hampton so I can visit with his dear friend, Senator Williams."

Royd damned himself for being hoodwinked by Darlow. He had never given a second thought to the notion that anyone on the committee was watching him. Young Darlow was plain stupid to tell Royd what he was doing. Royd was older, but he had been cocky and careless. He remembered dismissing a brief nudge of disquiet when Darlow offered to stay at the hotel with him. Now Royd knew that it had been planned all along. Royd's entire body broke out into a sweat. What if Darlow had followed him last night?

Royd paused, wondering why he hadn't heard of any connection between Harris and Williams before. Williams had specifically named two other senators who expected a favorable report on Apple Knoll. Harris brought the number to three. How many others were there?

"Suit yourself," Royd snapped and stormed from the room. Darlow had the good sense not to respond or to follow.

Brandishing a folder of papers, Marley Young hailed Royd down before he took five steps along the corridor. "There you are! Have you seen Darlow?"

Royd suppressed a groan and nodded back toward the laundry area. "He's gathering research."

Young's eyes bulged in their sockets and a heated flush stained his neck.

So Darlow wasn't the only committee member to play Peeping Tom!

Young cleared his throat and handed the folder to Royd. "Everything you wanted is fully documented in my report. I planned on leaving it with Darlow, but that won't be necessary now."

Royd cocked a brow. "Leaving already?"

"The warden ordered the coach to take me back to Reverend Beecham's. If I hurry, I can catch the late afternoon stagecoach to Philadelphia. Problems at the Walnut Street Jail. I'll be a day late for the hearings, but they'll probably drag on for at least a few more. Let me know if you need clarification on the figures. I'll be in Hampton early next week."

"I'm sure everything is in order," Royd answered calmly. What was Williams doing? Gathering a militia in Hampton to stand guard while Royd prepared the official report?

"Give my warm regards to the senator and Alexandria."

They exchanged brief handshakes, and Royd watched Young as he left the building. Some committee. A conniving opportunist and a sleazy young watchdog. Poor, decent Atwood. He did not stand a chance in hell of convincing anyone to listen to him—assuming that he had been able to substantiate his suspicions.

After returning to his temporary office and meeting with Atwood for two hours, Royd's dilemma was worse than he had imagined. The list of female inmates whose corporal punishment required medical treatment now stood at sixteen. The thread connecting cause and effect was thin, but only an idiot would snip it off as coincidence.

Or a group of state senators?

Eyewitness testimony would strengthen Atwood's case, but none of the females Royd had interviewed would dare to give it. All had sentences remaining that ranged from several months to a year and a half. Fact: They'd never get to testify.

Except one.

"You've done an exceptional job," Royd commented as he placed Atwood's report on top of the others. He paused, choosing his words carefully. "Without positive proof, I'm not sure how seriously the legislature will weigh your findings. As of now, the evidence is circumstantial."

Royd watched Atwood's reaction closely, but it was hard to tell what the man was thinking. A lawyer's practiced specialty, he supposed.

"You're quite right," Atwood responded. "It's also rather curious. Eight of the women are no longer here."

"Released?"

"Transferred."

Royd's heart began to race. "Why were they sent to another penitentiary?"

"They were sent to Willow Valley. It's an asylum, not a penitentiary. I've heard rumors that prolonged isolation can lead to mental derangement. It's one of the side effects the Pennsylvania Society for Prison Reform doesn't want to recognize. Neither does anyone else dedicated to either the Pennsylvania or Auburn systems. I checked further. Eight females were sent there, but only four males. Four!"

The letter in Royd's pocket suddenly felt like a millstone.

"What are you suggesting?" Royd breathed, loosening his collar.

"I don't know." Atwood smiled and shrugged his shoulders. "More coincidence? There's a part of me that dares to hope it is. Women's brains are smaller than men's and twice as fragile. It's possible they simply cannot adjust to isolation."

"And the other?"

"That's not quite as naive. Truth to tell, I'd like to stop at Willow Valley. Talking with the women is probably useless, but maybe I can put it all to rest by meeting with the director. I'm just not sure if the committee has the authority to extend its investigation that far. I could go on my own," he added, glancing up over the rim of his spectacles. "If there is something awful happening to women here, I'd find it hard to rest knowing I could have stopped it."

Atwood's moral fiber was like a lasso that tightened around Royd's neck. Refusing Atwood's request to go to Willow Valley in an official capacity would only send the man there snooping around on his own. The better choice, obviously, was to authorize Atwood's trip. At least Royd would be able to find out what Atwood discovered before anyone else did.

Royd's dilemma was forestalled, but he had the feeling that it would rear up again soon.

"Go ahead. I'll prepare a letter of introduction," Royd suggested as he pulled a piece of paper in front of him. He picked up his solid gold pen, dipped it into the ink bottle, and stopped in midair. "When you've finished, come to Hampton. Regardless of what you find, share it with no one but me. Understood?"

"What about Senator Williams?"

"The senator gave me full rein to prepare the report," Royd said firmly. "Rather than jeopardize the entire report, we'll meet and discuss what you find first."

Long after Atwood left, Royd sat at the conference

table deep in thought. The circumstantial evidence Atwood discovered, combined with Darlow's discovery of a peep-closet, would lead a reasonable man to only one conclusion: Female inmates at Apple Knoll were physically and mentally misused. That was not good enough. He needed proof . . . proof that only Pale Eyes could give him. Tonight.

Begging the need to remain late, Royd paced the room until dark. He ate a tasteless meal the warden ordered sent from the kitchen. He reread the reports.

After the last bell, when all the inmates were abed, Royd slipped from the room and hid in the shadows of the rotunda. Within an hour, he had calculated the time between guards' rounds. The next time the guard passed by his hiding place, Royd waited precisely three minutes and made his way to the females' corridor in the east wing.

Thirty seconds later, Royd was inside Moriah's cell, pocketing the key he had taken from the warden's office. Excitement pumped through his body, but he moved slowly over to her cot. She lay buried beneath the covers.

One scream and the guards will be swarming over the two of us like termites on rotten wood!

Crouching low, Royd reached out to cover her mouth or at least where he best judged it to be. The other arm he positioned above her midsection to keep frenzied arms from thrashing out in terror.

With a deep intake of breath to calm his nerves, he sprung forward, hit a pocket of air, lost his balance, and fell sideways onto the empty cot.

Blast the woman! Where was she? Feeling rather foolish, he shoved the covers aside. On second thought, he reshaped them as best he could and proceeded to exit through the back door.

Obstinate female! She can't follow rules to save her soul!

The minute he stepped onto the cobblestone path and visually searched her yard, his temper flared!

Gone!

The troublesome female was gone!

Eight

Beams of light from the sentry tower flitted and bounced off the high yard walls in a frenzied dance. Calculating the distance between her position and the safe shadows that cloaked her yard twelve cells away, Moriah took a deep breath. Ignoring the pain in her left foot, she started the long way back along the ledge of the wall. Crouching low, she crawled forward as quickly as she dared without risking a topple to the ground that would alert the guards.

Not that getting caught at this point would matter much. By now the committee had left, and Royd Camden had never come back to see her. Moriah could draw only one conclusion: Royd Camden had baited her as easily as an unsuspecting little fish. All the warden had to do was to reel her in. He would not extend her sentence, but the punishment for attempting to contact another inmate would be severe.

Anger propelled her forward motion more than fear. How could she have been so reckless? She knew Royd Camden was at the penitentiary to cover up problems. *Dunderhead!* It should have occurred to her that he might also have been searching for weak links—women who would divulge the secrets that Warden Lester Figgs wanted to hide.

No! They would not stop her! Not the warden and certainly not Royd Camden. Tonight's foray to see Iona had been ill-timed, but served as a critical reminder of the importance of Moriah's diary.

As she neared her yard, Moriah nearly leaped into the shadows and dropped facedown on the wall ledge to catch her breath. Despite the leather gloves and breeches she wore, her hands and knees were sore. Her left foot throbbed, reminding her of a less than graceful landing in Iona's yard. She turned her head to the side and rested it on her protected cheek, waiting for her breathing to become regular.

Without warning, her heartbeat skidded to a halt. Ruth! What if they punished her for what she had done? Tears of regret trickled down her hooded cheeks. "Please, God. Don't let them hurt Ruth," she whispered as she lifted her face to the heavens and awkwardly pressed the hood against her cheeks to dry her tears.

She swung her legs over the ledge of the wall. Using her right foot, she groped blindly for one of the twin eye hooks. Nothing. Scooting down the ledge on her bottom, she tried again. There! And there! She planted the ball of her right foot on a hook, twisted around, and gripped the wall ledge with both hands. Resting nearly all of her weight on her right leg, she used her left knee and both arms to push away from the wall.

Landing with a soft thud, she gave a sigh of relief when the right side of her body took the brunt of her plunge. Pitching forward, she inched closer to the wall, turned around, and leaned back against its solid strength. Leaf covered vines cushioned her. Legs out straight and arms at her side, she closed her eyes.

Once Moriah caught her breath, she rose and limped slowly back into her cell. A quick glance assured her that her cot was still as she left it, and the outer wooden door let in enough light to guide her search through her tools. Gripping the awl with one hand, she selected a leather

remnant. Before she returned to the yard, she also removed the burlap bag that hung across her chest and
stored it behind the tank in the water closet.

Moriah returned outside, propping the back door
open to give her light. Ignoring the curving path, she
hobbled directly to the far left corner. Stooping, she
pushed aside branches of honeysuckle and loosened a
stone in the wall that was just above ground level. Using
both hands, she removed the stone and placed it at her
feet.

She reached inside the small opening and quickly retrieved her diary. It certainly did not look like the daybook she kept as a child, but it served the same purpose.
Long, thin remnant strips of leather were strung on a
thicker piece that served as a thong. Like keys on a ring,
each leather strip contained information much more
meaningful and important than anything she had ever
recorded in her little daybook . . . information that
would unlock the door of conspiracy that kept the
abuses against women at Apple Knoll a secret from the
outside world.

After replacing the stone and fluffing the branches
that covered her hiding place, Moriah removed her
hood and gloves and then sat down. Using the awl, she
punched a hole in the end of the new remnant, untied
the thong, and slipped the end of the remnant through
until it slid next to the others. After reknotting the
thong, she laid the makeshift diary, which resembled a
row of long fringe, on one leg and positioned the newest
strip of leather on the other. Using one hand as a cushion, she worked quickly and effortlessly to punch a series
of small holes that ended with the date: July 27, 1828.
Her well-honed skill with the awl and the supple leather
made the work easy.

Satisfied, she laid the awl down. Unable to resist the
temptation, she paused to enjoy the familiar chorus of
summer scents and sounds that surrounded her. Crickets

chirped in the damp earth and lush green foliage
smelled tropical in the humid air. Every once in a while,
she caught the sharp scent of apples which grew in the
orchards that surrounded Apple Knoll. Tonight's breeze,
although stinted by the high walls, brought a fragrant
whiff to her.

Her senses focused, sharpened, and then sounded a
mental alert. Body tense, she froze in place. Her eyes
darted about, searching for sign of any movement in the
yard. Nothing. Yet terror tickled her spine, and her
hands tightened around the diary.

She was not alone!

Before her heart stopped altogether, Bandit ran out
of the garden and plopped down beside her. Relief restored her heartbeat. "You frightened me." She sighed,
shaking her head as the raccoon nudged her arm begging for attention.

Laughing softly, she gave him a playful bop on the
head. "If you didn't wander off all the time like a scamp,
I wouldn't be caught off guard!"

Bandit rose onto his hind legs and licked her face.

"Just like a man," she giggled. "Desert a lady and
then try to sweeten her anger with a kiss. I'm busy. Settle
down." Moriah patted the ground next to her, and Bandit curled up and laid his head on her leg. A veil of
sadness surrounded Moriah as she recalled her visit with
Iona, but in no time she had punched several coded
words next to the date and put the awl on the ground.

She really should hide the diary and get back to bed,
she mused, absently toying with the leather strips. She
hesitated, wondering what it would be like to be free
again. She looked forward to her release and being reunited with Ruth. Using the evidence she had gathered
to help the friends she would leave behind was something she and Ruth would do together.

She would miss Bandit, knowing they would never let
her take him with her. Even if they did, how would she

and Ruth ever get rooms? Once a landlady spotted Bandit, she would slam the door in their faces!

"If only I could find a way to get you out," she murmured. "You should be free, too. You could find a mate, start a family. Go wherever you wished."

Bandit stood up and cocked his head.

"You'd like that, wouldn't you?"

"I think he would."

Moriah snapped her head to the side, too frightened to remember to breathe. She broke out in a sweat that chilled her to the bone. Following the sound of the voice, her eyes focused long and hard on the opposite corner of the yard. Bandit scooted away, and before Moriah could turn around, she felt the diary being lifted off her lap.

A whisper. "Let's see what you have here."

A sickening dread flip-flopped in her stomach followed immediately by rage with Royd Camden's name on it. She flew to her feet and attacked him like an animal turned rabid. Lowering her shoulder, she dove into him, snarling with fury.

Her offensive maneuver must have caught him off guard, and he fell backward. Powerful hands locked onto her arms and pulled her off her feet. Both of her legs kicked into the air, and her head smashed into his chest as they struck the ground.

Dazed, she was on her back and pinned beneath him before she could rally for a second charge. His weight made it impossible to take a breath, and she struggled to remain conscious.

"Hold still," he demanded in a muffled snarl.

She choked and tried to twist her head to the side, gasping for air, but her braid was caught beneath her and held her as captive as he did. "I-I c-can't breathe!"

The pressure on her chest eased enough for her to take gulps of air, but her head felt like it was about to burst. Small mewing sounds escaped from her throat.

His hand clamped over her mouth, and she felt his lips touch her ear. "Guards!" he hissed.

Moriah did not blink a muscle. She heard footsteps as they approached. Hour-long seconds later, the iron door rattled before the footsteps moved on to the next cell yard. Her mind refused to function. She was unable to figure out why Royd Camden did not want to alert the guards, but her body sent messages to her brain that startled her senseless. Long muscled legs molded against her limbs, and she could feel the rapid beating of his heart against her chest. Lord, the man was big!

Royd's breath tickled her ear, sending strange and confusing sensations through her veins. One of his hands was entwined with hers and she could feel his pulse beat against her fingertips. Locks of his hair brushed against her cheek, and his male scent overpowered the fragrant earth beneath her.

"I'm not going to hurt you," he whispered.

She nodded and he removed his hand from her mouth.

She moistened her lips and turned her head until she could see his face. Wicked emerald eyes laughed back at her.

"Get off of me."

He grinned and rolled away, but he kept her trapped by increasing the pressure on her hand. Lying side by side, he seemed even more threatening, but she was not sure why.

"Give it back," she demanded, expecting him to hand over her diary.

"Not yet. You have a lot of questions to answer first. Then I'll decide whether or not to return it."

"It's mine!"

"I don't have time to argue."

She pouted. "Good. Give it back without an argument."

"Why?" He chuckled, obviously enjoying his teasing game.

This isn't funny. "Thou shalt not steal," she spat, wishing she could make him eat dirt.

"Oh, no, you don't. You can't hide behind the Word when it's convenient. Since I seem to have the advantage here, I'll ask the questions. If and when I'm satisfied with the answers, I'll decide whether or not to return . . . this." He dangled her diary in front of her face, and the long strips of leather swayed in the air. He laughed when she tried to steal it away with a one-handed grab.

Frustration filled her eyes with tears as he stuffed it into his shirt. "Ready?"

"Do I have a choice?" she murmured as she inched as far away from him as she could. "Forget I said that," she muttered when he frowned. "What do you want to know?"

"Where were you?"

"I can't tell you." Her chin tilted defiantly.

He waited, staring her into a blush.

"Please. I can't tell you."

His eyes grew dark. "How did you get over the wall?"

She smiled weakly. "I—I have a . . . Wait!" she said, suddenly remembering their bargain. "Why didn't you come earlier? Did you find Ruth? Did she read my letter? What did she say?"

Royd's face softened, but his lips grew taut. "I get to ask the questions, remember?"

Disappointment was deep, but Moriah was too stubborn to let it bend her to his will. "I need to know. If you don't tell me, I'll . . . I'll call the guards myself. Maybe you would like to explain just what it is you're doing here in the middle of the night!"

His eyes flickered with anger, and he squeezed her hand so hard she blinked. "Don't even give it a second thought."

"Why? Are you afraid?" she argued, noticing the way

his body tensed. "Don't tell me the warden doesn't know you're here!"

"Of course he doesn't!"

"You're lying! You're only pretending to have slipped in here tonight, aren't you? Why? Are you trying to convince me that you're really trying to help me? I know. Do you hear me? I *know* why Senator Williams sent you! I know the report you'll give to the legislature is a sham!"

He shoved away from her and rose to his feet. He towered over her as she lay on the ground looking up at him.

"The bargain is off."

She grabbed his ankles as he started to walk away. "Please. Don't go yet. Tell me if you found Ruth or if you lied. Did you lie to me about trying to find her?"

"Let go."

She dropped her hands. "You never intended to try to find her, did you? All you wanted was to find out if I knew something that had to be concealed. You still aren't sure, but you're not man enough to face me, are you? You have a bright future in politics, Royd Camden, but you'd better practice lying to people and looking them in the eye while you do it."

Royd swirled around and dropped to one knee, his face contorted with anger. "You want the truth? Fine. I'll give it to you. Your sister isn't here. She left eighteen months ago. There! Are you satisfied now?"

Moriah scrambled to her knees. "What do you mean she's not here? Where is she? What happened to her?"

He did not answer her. He just knelt there staring at her with a queer look on his face.

"Tell me!"

"Your sister is at Willow Valley."

His words slapped her face. She flinched. "No!"

"I found it in the prison register."

"You're lying! Ruth wasn't . . . isn't . . . no! It isn't

true! Why are you being so cruel?" Despite her isolation, Moriah had heard enough about Willow Valley from the keepers and other inmates that just hearing the name of the asylum sent icy shivers down her spine. It was a squalid, miserable dump full of lunatics, its name synonymous with hell on earth for wretched, mindless souls!

Hugging her arms around her waist, Moriah started to rock back and forth, despite the fact that God had answered her prayers. Ruth had survived. But insane? Not Ruth! Ruth was strong and brave, her protector and guide. No! God, no!

Moriah looked at Royd and shook her head. "You're wrong."

"I fear it's true. Her name was listed several lines above yours. Ruth Lane. Inmate Number Seventy-five. Admitted August 14, 1824. Brown hair and eyes. Transferred to Willow Valley on February 28, 1827." He reached into his pocket and placed her letter into her hands. "I'm sorry."

Tears. Hot, blinding tears erupted quickly as a sob tore from Moriah's throat and echoed in the garden. She crumpled to the ground moaning Ruth's name over and over like a litany.

Royd lifted her into his arms, and she burrowed deeper into his embrace, too full of hurt to care what kind of man he was. She needed comfort, warm and human. His arms came around her, stroking her back, his voice murmuring soft condolences. Her cries of distress drowned against his chest, and she clung to him. Needing his touch. His strength.

Snippets of the past flashed through her mind, stored in a precious album of memories. Ruth—laughing when Moriah tried to trim her own hair and ended up shoring seven inches off the top. Ruth—telling Moriah stories about Mama and Papa. Ruth—holding her hand when they said good-bye to Uncle Jed. Now, Ruth . . . un-balanced! Ruth . . . a lunatic?

Oh my God, why have You forsaken me?

"Hush, Pale Eyes," he murmured as he carried her to the rear of the garden and settled them on the ground. She lay in his lap, limp and drained.

Moriah wiped her face with her hands and clutched his shirt. "Will they let me see her? Maybe I can get rooms for us, and they'll let her come home with me. I'll take care of her, and she'll get better. I know she will."

He smiled and rubbed her arms. "I don't know. The register doesn't list the physician's diagnosis. I suppose there's a chance . . ."

She sniffled and started to smile. "I'll pray. Day and night. He'll help me. I know He will. Ruth will get better. She's all I have."

His hands slipped around her wrists and caressed her scars. She looked up at him, surprised by the serious expression on his face.

"It's time to keep your end of the bargain," he whispered.

Nine

Royd watched Moriah as the impact of his words penetrated through her grief. Her body tensed and those eyes! They seemed to swell to the size of melons. She scrambled off his lap, brushing her arms and legs off as though she had been contaminated by his touch.

He never moved. Instead, he studied her as she turned away from him. Silhouetted by the light coming from her cell, every line and curve of Moriah's tiny figure was further accentuated by the shirt and breeches that clung to her body like a second skin. Her long braid had come apart and strands of hair as shiny as cornsilk fluttered in the air.

His mouth went dry with the sudden urge to swing her around and clasp her within his embrace. Lord! He must be crazy! Rationally, there wasn't a single damn reason why he should resent the fact that she was no longer in his arms. She was a convict. A murderess! A cold-blooded woman without a conscience. For the love of God, she murdered her own uncle!

His body, however, was weak. He liked the feel of her curled on his lap, the gentle curve of her back, and the swell of her buttocks when they pressed against his thighs. He forced his physical response to her to cool. It was bad enough that she had broken through the thin veneer that covered his inherited vices. To fall prey to the lure of her femininity would be ludicrous! Absurd!

He felt like he was being caught in a web. *Her* web, which left him totally at her mercy.

No! He was betrothed to Alexandria. He wasn't a naive or inexperienced youth! Moriah would *not* make his bloodlust surge with every wild beat of his heart. He was known as a calculating and shrewd businessman. He wanted answers, damn his soul, and he wanted them now! He stood up and approached her from behind. "I'm waiting for your answer."

Her head tilted upward just a bit and her shoulders straightened. He didn't have to see her face to imagine the defiant look in her eyes.

"You're entitled to an answer because I gave you my word," she murmured before she turned around to face him. "After I'm released, I'll be perfectly willing to come to Harrisburg to give my information at the legislative hearings."

Dammit. He did not have the luxury of waiting that long. He needed answers now! He narrowed his gaze. "Forget it. We made a bargain."

"The bargain we made did not specify *when* I would give you the information. Only that I would. I'm not breaking my word."

"Hypocrite!" he hissed, unwilling to accept the verbal sidestepping that seemed to be her specialty. "I need that information now, and you're going to give it to me."

He stepped forward, hoping to intimidate her, but she never even flinched. He was close enough to hear her breathe, and he could almost smell her stubborn determination.

"I give you my word . . ."

"Your word isn't worth the breath it takes to utter it," he muttered. He had never throttled a woman in his life, but he was close. His fingers tightened and flexed, but a better alternative occurred to him. He pulled the odd leather contraption from his shirt. If she took the trouble to hide it, then it may just be the leverage he needed. He had no idea what it was, but the look on her face confirmed that it was important to her. "I want your answer now," he said. When she lunged for it, he simply raised his arm and held it above her reach.

"That's mine. I want it back!" she pouted, her face flushed with frustration.

"No more deals, Moriah. Now you can have an ultimatum. Either give me the information I want or I'll be forced to report your little adventures tonight to the warden." He stared at her skin-tight, leather costume. "Just where *did* you go dressed like a snake?"

"To shed my skin," she hissed, tossing her hair over her shoulder and eyeing him warily as he secured the treasure on his person again.

"How utterly feminine," he growled, irritated by her flippant attitude. Her tight-fitting garments which outlined her very female figure made his loins ache. Some angel! She was a two-tongued vixen, and there was no way he would ever allow her to best him in any verbal skirmish.

To his astonishment, her eyes widened and filled with tears. She paled and he saw the blood literally drain from her face. She seemed taken aback and stared at him until the air became pregnant with tension. She looked like a lifeless marionette, and he felt responsible for cutting all of her strings.

Her lips moved, but no sound came out until she cleared her throat. "I thank you for telling me about Ruth. I'll make a home for her and care for her when I'm released. As for the rest, tell the warden if you must. Keep my . . . my trinket as a memento of your visit here. If you add bells to the tips of the leather, you can hang it around your neck. When the wind blows through the holes in your heart, the tinkling sounds can remind you of how you overpowered a woman and took away one of her few meager possessions. I'm certain that you will feel strong and powerful and manly, won't you? Well, you always did have the advantage, Royd Camden, whether or not you care to admit it."

Her wooden diatribe ended, Moriah turned away and started back to her cell, still favoring her left foot.

Reprimanded for his blackmail attempt, Royd felt like a bastard. If he even hinted that Moriah had left her yard, Lester Figgs would punish her severely. If he turned over her trinket to the warden, Royd would feel like a rat. In the past, he had done many things against the law and stolen from more people than he could count, but he simply could not do this to her.

Not when she looked like every ounce of strength and will had been drained from her spirit. He watched her as she hobbled slowly away from him. Head slightly bowed and shoulders set, she did not look defeated. She appeared to be . . . resigned, almost apathetic.

In the final analysis, it was her strongest weapon and it castigated him more effectively than anger or tears.

Royd caught up with her in several long strides. "I'm sorry. I didn't mean to . . ."

She answered him as she continued to limp ahead, but she did not look at him. "I'm tired," she admitted weakly. "Too tired to match wits with you. You're a man with a job to do. So do it. Right now, all I care about is Ruth. She needs me. She always took care of me. Now it's my turn to care for her. I don't expect you to understand love and loyalty, Royd Camden, but I do expect you to accept my word. When Ruth and I are settled, I'll find a way to get in touch with you. I'll give you the information that you want. Your conscience can dictate what you will do with it."

Royd felt utterly and miserably ashamed. Never once did he question his right to bully or intimidate her. Until this moment. He took her leather trinket and placed it into her hands, but she pushed it away.

"Keep it as a guarantee. You seem to think so little of me, you'll need to know that I'll keep my end of the bargain."

The lump in his throat made his voice husky. "I live in Hampton."

She nodded. "Then I'll come to Hampton. Keep my trinket safe," she said quietly and ducked back into her cell.

Her soft whimper of pain urged him through the door right behind her. He managed to get inside just as she toppled to the floor. He caught her before she hit the floor and carried her across the room. "How did you hurt your foot?" he grumbled as he sat her on the cot.

"Bad jump," she said through gritted teeth.

Royd unlaced her slipper and eased it off her foot. A single dark bruise covered the top of the instep which had already started to swell. "Snakes don't jump. They slither," he murmured, gently probing the contours of her foot. "Nothing appears to be broken. Stay off your feet for a few days," he added as he relaced the slipper and cupped her foot in the palm of his hand. "Keep this on. It will help to control the swelling. If it continues to bother you, ask the keeper to see the physician."

Moriah pulled her foot out of his grasp. "I don't need to see Dr. Welsh."

The instant defiance chilled his concern. "Fine! Nurse it yourself and become a cripple!"

Just as he got to his feet, Bandit ambled inside and sat down next to Moriah. Her arms reached out and she cradled the animal's head with her hands, stroking his fur. "When do you leave?" she asked without taking her eyes off the animal.

"In the morning. I have a final meeting with the warden at ten o'clock. I'll return to Hampton after that."

She bent and rubbed her cheek on the raccoon's head

before she looked up at Royd. "Will you take him with you tonight and set him free?"

Huge blue eyes simmered with emotion. She waited for an answer.

She couldn't be serious! He had to sneak out of here without getting caught and return to his hotel. In the dark. On horseback. With a raccoon?

"He'll try to get back to you," he said as he shook his head.

"Not if you take him far enough away. Past the orchards and out of the valley."

A ride in unfamiliar woods in the middle of the night with a domesticated raccoon and a skittish stallion made as much sense to him as the ridiculous extension he had given her to keep her end of the bargain. How could she even begin to think that he would . . .

Moriah removed the collar from around the critter's neck and lifted him up to Royd. He grabbed the raccoon, pulling his own head back when Bandit tried to lick his face. "Stupid critter," he mumbled.

She smiled as she tied Bandit's collar around one of her wrists. Muttering an oath, Royd took the key out of his pocket and walked to the iron-grated door.

"Mr. Camden?"

He shot her a frustrated look.

"Thank you."

"I'll send you a bill."

She wiped away a tear. "A bill?"

"That's right, Pale Eyes, a bill. I'll probably break my neck doing this, not to mention laming my horse. I'll have to hire someone to oversee my business while I recuperate. The way I total your account, you owe me. A lot."

"You have collateral to make sure I pay you. I assume you always collect your debts?" Her smile drooped into a frown.

He cocked his head and opened the door. "Without a

doubt," he whispered before he disappeared, carrying Bandit with him.

Moriah waited until Royd Camden's footsteps faded into soft, muted echoes she heard only with her mind. She sat on her cot, eyes closed, one hand curled around Bandit's collar that was still wrapped around her wrist.

In her mind's eye, she traveled with her furry friend, through the main gates, down the dirt road past the orchards to the town, and up and over the rolling hills covered with endless acres of wooded land. She watched Bandit as he charged off into the woods, following new and intriguing scents and sounds.

Out of her life.

Home.

The loss of Bandit's company for the next few weeks was something she sacrificed without a second thought. She stored the love she had for him deep within her heart where it was safe. Trusting Royd Camden and accepting his help, although it was given begrudgingly, bothered her into much deeper concentration.

Royd Camden was a scoundrel of royal proportions. He resorted to blackmail and intimidation without hesitation, yet he did have a tender spot in his heart—for animals. Tender? He was raw and hard, ruthless and motivated by his own self-interest. Countless women would continue to suffer because of him. He was an abominable man, she decided as she undressed and climbed into bed. By morning the warden would know . . . what? How much would Royd tell him? Would Royd withhold her diary and wait for her to come to Hampton?

Maybe.

It was just as likely that he would tell the warden everything to protect the interests of Senator Williams and others who controlled the investigation.

It was useless to worry. She could not change the man

nor control what he would do, she decided as she tossed in her cot. Her overriding concern right now was Ruth. She had to find a way to get to Willow Valley and convince the physicians to let Ruth come home with her.

Home? Where was home? They could not return to the cobbler shop. After their conviction, the shop and its contents as well as the furnishings in the rooms above it were sold. As the girls's appointed guardian, Reverend Glenn claimed the proceeds for the church as tangible atonement for the sin she and Ruth had committed. Indeed, he was the man who contacted the authorities and made sure that Moriah and her sister would be disinherited and sent to prison.

Moriah sighed as she folded her hands in prayer. She needed a position and a home for Ruth where her sister could get well. Moriah also needed a way to help the women inmates at Apple Knoll. Sophie. Iona. So many others. In order to do that, she needed the courage to confront Royd Camden and get her diary back. She needed funds to travel to Hampton and to Harrisburg, funds for lodging and food. The list seemed endless!

What I need, she groaned silently, *is a good night's sleep.* Tomorrow would be soon enough to make plans—plans that ultimately would depend on Royd Camden. He held the key to her future, and one question nagged at her as she drifted off to sleep.

Would Royd Camden keep the key or give it to the warden?

♣

Ten

By the time Royd arrived for his final meeting with Lester Figgs the next morning, his nerves were stretched taut and brittle. His body fared even worse. Bloodshot eyes, gritty from lack of sleep, made it difficult to see and a series of deep scratches on his left cheek made his face feel like it was on fire. To add to his misery, every step he took sent shooting pains up his spine.

He could not decide what hurt more—his body or his pride. He had been thrown rather ignominiously from his horse not once, but three times on a single outing! Cursed raccoon! The stupid critter followed him back to the inn anyway!

When Royd entered the warden's office, he forced his expression to hide his surprise. Despite his understanding that he would have a private meeting with Figgs before leaving, Prescott Darlow was present and chatting amicably with the warden. Their conversation halted abruptly in midsentence, and Royd had the nagging suspicion that he had been the topic of their discussion.

Royd nodded to both men and sat down next to Darlow, refusing to be baited by the man's rude snicker.

"Rough night, Camden?"

Royd shot him a warning scowl that cost him dearly. He wanted to send the man to Hades, but he was afraid that Lucifer himself would send the man back. He shook his head and grunted. "Nothing that couldn't have been avoided. My horse stumbled and pitched me into a patch of brambles. It was my fault," he said as he gingerly cupped his injured cheek. "I guess I was overtired. I shouldn't have worked so late last night."

Figgs pitched his round body forward in his chair and leaned across his desk. "Nasty looking wounds. You'd better let Dr. Welsh look at them."

"It can wait," Royd replied as he shifted in his seat to find a more comfortable position. "I'd like to conclude our business as quickly as possible, though. I have a long ride home."

Darlow laughed. "Might take a little longer than usual. It's a pity your dedication couldn't be rewarded better. I'm sure Senator Williams appreciates your late night efforts, although I'm afraid Alexandria might swoon when she sees your face."

Royd couldn't miss the undercurrent of sarcasm that laced Darlow's words. His pulse quickened as he glanced from the warden to Darlow. There was a sense of camaraderie between them that chilled his blood. Royd could handle almost anything the two of them plotted against him, even if they suspected he had visited Moriah Lane more than once. But Pale Eyes was extremely vulnerable. There was no way Royd could protect her if the warden got wind of her activities. If either Figgs or Darlow had Royd followed last night, Moriah's secret had been told.

Royd wracked his brain trying to remember anything that would have alerted the guards to his presence in Moriah's cell yard last night. Had someone overheard them? Last night Royd was certain that they had been unobserved, but now he wasn't so sure.

The warden smiled. "We all appreciate your work,

Camden." He leaned back in his chair and folded his hands. "How soon do you expect the official report to be ready?"

Royd cocked a brow. "The findings will be given to Senator Williams in about two weeks, but they won't be made public until the hearings in the fall session. You'll be attending?"

"Of course." Figgs sat up and squared his shoulders although the attempt did little to change his egg-shaped appearance. "Perhaps you'd make a few suggestions before you leave."

Testing the waters, Royd responded cautiously. "One of my recommendations will be to seal the hidden door in the outer wall." He watched as the warden's face registered surprise. Feigned or real?

"What hidden door?" Darlow's high-pitched question gave Royd some comfort. Apparently, neither man knew that Royd had discovered the secret entrance and used it to breach prison security.

Figgs sputtered. "That door is secure! It hasn't been used since I became warden."

"You said the main gates were the only entrance," Royd reminded him.

"Indeed they are. No one has used that door!"

"I did."

Royd grinned. Figgs and Darlow both looked like roasted pigs waiting for someone to pop an apple into their gaping mouths. "You really should seal the opening permanently. I'm not the only one who has used the door recently, either. The hinges are well oiled and there's nary a bit of rust on the lock. I'd hate to think that there's a basis for the rumors here, but it's certainly plausible that access to the female inmates is possible—from the outside. It's something of which you might be totally unaware. Nevertheless, you are responsible for the well-being of every inmate at Apple Knoll."

Darlow reddened and glared at Royd, but the warden

snatched the opportunity to escape censure, apparently more concerned with covering the penitentiary's lack of security than questioning Royd as to why or how he managed to discover the door. "I'll see that it is sealed immediately. By the Lord's Word, I'd forgotten about it. Do you really suppose it's been used by . . ."

"It would be a shame to see Apple Knoll's reputation tarnished by rumors that have any basis, especially if the problems are coming from the outside. If the door should be sealed, however, I see no need to mention it in my report."

"As good as done, sir."

"There's also the matter of the women's bathing area." Royd stared at Darlow while he continued to direct his words to the warden. "You owe a debt of gratitude to Mr. Darlow. He uncovered a rather curious room in the laundry area."

Darlow looked like he wanted to tar and feather Royd and march him back to Hampton!

Royd nodded. "Would you care to share your discovery with the warden?"

Darlow dismissed Royd with the back of his hand. "The warden and I were just discussing the matter when you arrived."

Figgs bobbed his head in agreement. "Quite right, Mr. Camden. I'm appalled that any of my staff would stoop to such depravity."

"Apparently, they didn't have to stoop. I fear there are enough peepholes to accommodate a man of almost any height so that he can enjoy the view fully standing. Even your height."

Figgs's eyes narrowed as he apparently decided whether or not Royd was mocking his short stature, then he relaxed when Royd gave him a one-cheek smile.

"Never underestimate a man's cunning. Some will take outrageous measures to assuage their lust. They have violated the women's right to decency. What do you think, Darlow?"

"I think it's time to leave," he snapped and stood up, offering his hand to the warden. "I'll give your regards to Senator Williams," he said confidently. "I'm sure Camden will mention your dedication and expertise which make Apple Knoll the fine institution that it is. Are you ready, Camden?"

"More than you can imagine," Royd mumbled under his breath before following Darlow from the room deep in thought. In the time Royd would take to return to Hampton, George Atwood would have concluded his visit to Willow Valley. It would only take a few more days for him to reach Hampton and report his findings directly to Royd.

Not that the information that Atwood had already uncovered couldn't stand alone and raise enough of a public outcry to demand better conditions for female inmates at Apple Knoll as well as demand further investigation. Spying on women as they bathed was inexcusable, but physically tormenting females until they lost their minds, regardless of their crimes, was an abomination that no man could tolerate.

Senator Williams could not possibly know the extent of the problems at the penitentiary. When Royd told him, the senator would have to reassess his commitment to serving the public good rather than private interests. *There was no dilemma!*

Royd walked through the outer gates as though a heavy burden had been lifted from his shoulders. Senator Williams would have to issue a report that would leave his integrity intact as well as his own. Royd's future was assured. He would marry Alexandria in late fall and continue his life as a prominent businessman connected to the elites in society permanently. Surrounded by men and women of the proper sort, his character would not be tested again.

Royd stopped and turned around, taking one last look
at the prison. Behind those walls, women were abused,
molested, and Lord knew what else.

Not for long.

Royd turned and walked away, unable to get one particular inmate out of his mind. She was temptation. Eve.
A serpent. She was a murderess!

Perhaps his brain was addled from too many falls from
his horse. He did not know why, but the thought of
seeing Miss Pale Eyes again made him anxious for the
time to speed by quickly. He did not like the fact that
she had misjudged him and pulled him down to her
level, although she clearly felt morally superior to him.

He almost let it happen.

He could not wait to let her know that she was wrong
about Senator Williams and the committee. Wrong
about him. He was a man of character and ethics. To
prove it, he would not even inspect the damn worthless
pieces of leather she seemed to prize!

Rash judgment. Pure and simple.

He would throw that at her and see how she could use
the Word to defend herself, the conniving little tart! The
sooner he saw her, returned her little treasure, and sent
her packing, the better off he would be. And she had
better take the bloody raccoon with her!

Royd needed to surround himself with people of quality. Alexandria respected him and saw him as a gentleman of the first order. He would be safe with her. His
past would remain buried, and there would be no crisis
that would unleash the wickedness that flowed through
his veins.

Moriah peeled away his armor and unleashed the man
he used to be.

Never again, he vowed.

Pale Eyes was not ever going to do that again!

Eleven

Lester Figgs paced the length of his office and back again. Hands clasped behind his back, he stared at the floor seeing more problems than there were stones inlaid beneath his feet. He paused as he passed the man seated to his right and lifted his head. "You're sure she said it was Number Seventy-nine?"

"That's the one." A hint of sarcasm laced Tamin Jones's answer.

The warden digested the keeper's affirmation, annoyed when Jones popped each of his knuckles, breaking the silence that filled the room. "I can't begin to fathom how she did it."

"*How* don't seem to matter much now," Jones argued. He turned sideways in his chair to face the warden. "Brash little strumpet that she is, Number Eighty-six couldn't spill out the words fast enough once the guard persuaded her that he heard her talkin' to someone last night."

Figgs came to full attention. His head snapped up, and his hands balled into fists. "It matters to me!"

"The bitch is clever and learned enough to make you listen to me and hang your concern for the reverend. Seventy-nine is gonna make trouble. Heaps of trouble.

Seems the reverend's pet inmate has plans to go to Harrisburg and testify at them hearings."

"And say what? She doesn't know anything."

Jones snickered. "I warned you about maybe settin' some dogs free in the yard at night, didn't I? Be better than the sluggards at the towers. She's been visitin' other inmates. Got a whole lot to tell the committee. Promised Eighty-six she'd make sure everyone knew what's been happenin' here."

Sweat broke out like a rash on the warden's body. "How? Damnation! Somebody had to let her out of her cell. When I find the guard or keeper who helped her . . ."

"None of 'em would do that."

Figgs's anger was choking the breath out of him, and he sat down behind his desk to take several deep gulps of air. Jones was right. Every one of his men was reliable, especially with the reward system in place. One questionable move by any of the men, and one of the other keepers or guards would turn him in. But how did Number Seventy-nine get out of her cell? Unless she had wings, there was no way over those high yard walls. Hah! An angel she wasn't. The question of "how" still remained.

"Camden saw her. You were there. Did she say anything to him that would indicate they were planning something together?"

Jones squinted his eyes and leaned forward. "I told you they didn't talk 'bout nothin' important. She baited and debated the sucker till he bolted outa there convinced she was the devil's serpent. I thought you said Senator Williams would make sure Camden's report was favorable."

"What the senator promised hasn't been delivered yet, has it? Maybe Camden is going to play a tune on somebody else's fiddle. Atwood spent considerable time with Camden. Atwood was too bloody thorough, and I

don't think he was so diligent without prodding from
Camden. I don't like it. Any of it! If Seventy-nine could
get out to visit inmates, maybe she met with Camden,
too. He admitted he used the rear gate."

Jones shrugged his shoulders, setting off the jingling
of his keys. "Easy enough to remedy. Do what we done
before, and don't forget about Eighty-six. That one
knows too much. Gonna drop a brat before the end of
the year unless you tell Dr. Welsh to do somethin'."

"I have to think this through," Figgs countered. "Reverend Beecham has to be considered. He's an old fool,
but he'll be suspicious if Seventy-nine disappears too
suddenly. Is Dr. Welsh here yet?"

"Just arrived. My guess is he's tendin' to Eighty-six."

"I want to see him as soon as he's finished."

"What about Camden and the senator?"

"Can't afford to let fate run its course without a little
help, can we? I'll take care of Camden and alert the
senator. Maybe I'll just notify Senator Harris and the
others, too. If Camden isn't cooperative, they'll handle
him. As for Seventy-nine, meet me in her cell in an hour.
By then I'll have everything worked out."

Tamin Jones stood up, his eyes gleaming with anticipation. "Seventy-nine is mine, right? I been waitin' an
awful long time to take a swipe at that one."

The warden nodded. "In due time. I have to be sure
that she's guilty and not a scapegoat that Eighty-six
named to protect someone else. Once I'm convinced
Eighty-six wasn't lying, Seventy-nine is all yours. Just
make sure you don't . . . well, never mind. I'll be there
to supervise. You went too far with the last one."

Long after Jones took his leave, Lester Figgs remained secluded in his office. All he needed was another
year. Twelve short months. Was that too much to ask? By
then he'd have enough funds to retire to a nice country
estate with a few carefully selected maids to service his
needs. Young innocents like Seventy-nine weren't prac-

ticed enough, and he was getting too old to waste time training them. He'd tried that with her sister, but that had resulted in a debacle he would just as soon forget.

Problems like this just weren't supposed to happen. When Figgs was approached by several select members of the legislature to run Apple Knoll, he accepted with the proviso that he be given full rein to handle the inmates. As long as the profits for business contractors remained high and the penitentiary was close to being self-sufficient, no one interfered—even if they suspected what was going on.

Just how the rumors started were of little consequence now, although Figgs suspected that one or two jealous contractors who were outbid for the inmates' labor were responsible. Figgs wasn't worried. He had clout with the right people, and he was relatively confident this whole hearing business would be carefully orchestrated. The public would be satisfied when the legislature noted several small problems. As for the rest, he could undermine Royd Camden at this end while the senators added a little pressure of their own.

Figgs rose, fully satisfied that he was competent enough to see this problem through and left to confer with the physician before meeting again with Jones in the women's east cell block. By nightfall, Seventy-nine would be silenced. He sniggered. By the time the hearings convened in the fall, no one would give more than a moment's credence to anything Seventy-nine had said to Camden or anyone else.

Moriah heard the iron latticed door creak as it swung open. It was long past tour hours, and she reached across the table to grab her hood. It was quickly snatched from her fingers, and she felt a fleeting quirk of anxiety before she bent over the shoe clamp and continued her work.

"You won't be needin' this either," the keeper

drawled as his meaty fingers grabbed the clamp and tossed it aside.

Moriah bit back a question and folded her hands on her lap. She stared at the keeper and saw a lascivious glint in his eyes that made it difficult for her to swallow. Before fear laid absolute claim to her, the warden entered her cell and stood next to the keeper.

"You'll remain as you are, Number Seventy-nine."

She had not seen the warden for several years. He had gained considerable girth around the middle, but the hard-shell look in his eyes was exactly as she remembered.

"You do not have permission to speak unless I ask a question. Is that clear?"

She nodded and lowered her eyes. Her mouth became dry, and she moistened her lips. *It didn't take very long for them to come for me,* she decided, wondering if the dust had settled yet from the departure of the committee.

"Do a thorough search," the warden commanded as several more keepers entered her cell.

Moriah closed her eyes and started to pray for strength and for some semblance of mercy. She could not find it within her to pray for Royd Camden. Maybe that would come later, but Lord! It was not easy to love her enemy enough to pray for him or to forgive him at the moment of her betrayal.

Royd Camden was Judas reincarnated, and she was frightened by the searing hatred that singed her spirit. He was as evil and wicked as the devil himself. What kind of man would be this cruel and duplicitous? He promised to help and then smashed her dream of caring for Ruth. He stomped on her plans to help the inmates. He was vile and contemptible, a coldhearted man whose lack of compassion and talent for guile made a mockery of her own trusting faith in human nature.

Her thoughts about Royd Camden were interrupted

when two keepers carrying shovels entered her cell and quickly ducked through the back door to her yard. She could hear them outside digging up her precious garden. What were they looking for . . . buried treasure? Only her cherished vegetables and flowers were in her yard. She did have a brief flash of gratitude that Royd Camden carried her diary with him when he left. There! She could be grateful to him for that, unless he had turned that over to the warden. She wondered if either one of them had discovered the nature of the entries or dismissed them as simple decorations on a worthless trinket.

A shout of victory from within the water closet made thoughts about the diary fade in importance and warned her that her leather ladder and ropes had been discovered. Keeper Jones took them out of her burlap bag and handed them over to the warden who threw them in her face.

Instinctively, Moriah raised her arms and caught the leather pieces as yet another man brought the warden her shirt and breeches from beneath her mattress. Her eyes locked with the warden's fierce look. She held his gaze but remained silent.

"Did you really think Royd Camden wouldn't tell me?" He grabbed her things out of her hands and tossed them to the floor. "I know how you got over the walls. I want to know why."

If the warden didn't know, she hoped that meant he did not know about her diary.

"Answer me!" he thundered.

Moriah blanched and shuddered as a chill spread through her body. The warden laughed demonically. "The senator was right. Camden is a man who can turn a lady's head. Now we know he has a real flair for it if he can convince the likes of you to trust him!"

Figgs took a step closer to her. "So what have you been doing out of your cell? Playing Angel of Mercy?

Not likely. You're too coldhearted a bitch for that. Were you selling your favors? Tsk. Tsk. If I had known you were experienced, I'd have savored some of your charms myself. What do you think, Jones? A bit too peaked for a harlot, but you think she's hiding a fair set of tits under that gown?"

Moriah clasped her hand around the collar of her gown and blushed as the keeper fondled her breasts.

"Naw. Not like some of the others. She's a bit scrawny." Jones snickered and tweaked both of her nipples with a brutal twist of his fingers.

Tears sprang to Moriah's eyes, and she caught the inside of her lower lip between her teeth. Horrible possibilities made her head swim. Were they going to rape her? Here? Now?

The keeper stepped back and disappeared behind her, and Moriah felt a surge of blessed relief.

Too short and too sweet.

Without warning, Moriah's head snapped backward as Jones yanked on her braid. A halo of pain made her catch her breath. Just as abruptly, her head lunged forward as his hold was released, and she blinked, trying to comprehend what had happened. The warden leered at her as her shorn braid came flying over her shoulder. He caught it and dangled the plait in front of her face.

"Quite a unique color. It's a trophy I'll add to my collection with great pleasure."

Moriah's hand flew to her head. The blunt stubby ends of her hair tickled her fingertips, and she gazed at the warden with a horrified expression. He ordered her hair cut to keep as a trophy? Her stomach lurched and bile stung the back of her throat.

Before she could take another breath, Jones pulled her to her feet. Aided by two other men, he forced her into a strange sort of jacket that locked her arms at her side. She did not even try to struggle for fear it would give him a reason to strike her. When he finished, Jones shoved her backward, and she plopped awkwardly back into her chair.

The warden cocked his head and raised one bushy brow. "No comment? No complaints?"

Moriah lifted her chin and glared at him.

"Answer me!"

She clenched her jaw.

"Last chance," he hissed, standing so close to her that his sour breath fanned her face. He spoke in a whisper now, but a shout or a scream would have frightened her less than the cold timbre in his voice. "No one will ever listen to you again. No matter what it is you think you can do, it's a phantom of your dreams. Royd Camden did what he was sent here to do and no one, especially you, can be permitted to interfere with the hearings."

The warden's deep-set, black eyes were so close to her that Moriah could see her own face reflected in their evil depths.

"Come now. You must want to say something!"

Moriah closed her eyes and listened to the pounding of her own heartbeat. She knew she should not hate the warden or the keepers, but she did not seem to be able to extinguish the loathing for them that seared her soul. "Father, forgive them," she whispered. The words sounded hollow and hypocritical to her ears, and she wondered if saying them aloud would help her to actually forgive these men for what they were doing to her.

The warden's laughter echoed in her cell. Then pain, sharp and vibrant, pierced her lips. Her eyes snapped open and began to water as Jones and another man began to gag her. They pried her jaw open and shoved something metal into her mouth. At the same time, a man behind her pulled on something that sounded like a chain and two bands of iron molded against her cheeks. She retched and a firm hand grabbed her chin.

"Put your tongue on the rest!"

Moriah tried to pull away, but the metal bands bit into

her cheeks and ripped the corners of her mouth. The image of a horse being fitted with its first bit flashed through her consciousness, and she stilled. Incredibly, the chains were tightened, and the iron bands became more indented in the flesh of her cheeks. She gulped, nearly retched again, and quickly found the tongue rest as the chains were secured at the back of her head with the tell-tale snap of a lock.

Moriah could not think beyond taking one breath at a time and trying to swallow her own bloodied saliva without choking. She lifted pained eyes to find the warden smiling with satisfaction.

"Can't talk to anyone else now, can you?" He grunted at the question she could not verbalize.

"The iron gag is reserved for especially difficult cases, my dear. As I said, you won't be talking with anyone else here. As for later, well, it's a pity, isn't it? With only a few weeks until your release, I'm sure the doting Reverend Beecham will be greatly saddened when he learns what happened to you. Mental derangement does seem to run in the family, though. You're fortunate to be sent to Willow Valley. Maybe you'll be reunited with your sister. Royd Camden agreed it was best to send you there."

Moriah's eyes widened. Royd Camden agreed to this? No! He could not be that wicked. Where was the man who held her and comforted her when he told her about Ruth? Until that moment in the garden, she did not believe that the man had a single redeeming quality. But then he held her, cuddled her in a way that made her cringe at her earlier assumption he did not know how. He must have thought it wonderfully ironic that she would be sent to the same institution as her sister. What a fool she had been, rattling on about how she would take care of Ruth when all along he knew she would be locked away. *He knew!*

All she wanted to do was let the bubble of a scream

escape her chest, but she knew that she could not utter a sound without tearing apart the inside of her mouth.

"The gag will remain until you're safely ensconced in your new institution. Dr. Welsh wrote the orders this afternoon. The gag will help to prevent your biting your tongue when you have your 'seizures.' I'm sure it will be removed . . . eventually."

Numb with the awesome realization that all of her efforts had been for naught, Moriah barely noticed the men leave. She did not have to look any further than herself for the root cause of her downfall. She should have been patient enough to wait for the day of her release to find out what happened to Ruth. She never should have trusted Royd Camden. Never!

Moriah sighed as the full impact of her error in judgment sank in. She failed Ruth. She failed Sophie, Iona, and the others who were counting on her. She failed herself by being selfish and trying to manipulate Royd Camden.

She wasn't God! It wasn't her place to try to change anyone or to prick his conscience. She had overstepped the boundaries of her own humanity and conceitedly used her faith as a way to assert her superiority over Royd Camden.

In the end, Moriah judged herself harshly but vowed to find a way to reverse her situation. She was not crazy! She had to convince the staff at Willow Valley that she was sane. Once she did that, they would have to release her. Ruth, too.

A surge of hope filled her heart. Royd Camden would *not* destroy her hopes and dreams. She would surprise him. She would surprise them all. And before she was finished, heads would roll.

Lord willing, Royd Camden's head would be the first.

Twelve

Armed with a copy of his final report which unfortunately lacked any substantiated link with Willow Valley, Royd Camden approached Senator Fithian Williams's study. Renewed confidence in himself and his ability to keep the chains of his blackened past from manacling his future increased with every step he took.

For the past ten days, Royd had divided his time between running his business and preparing the final report for Senator Williams. In the evenings, he and Alexandria resumed their courtship, although she disliked the full beard he sported to cover his face until the scratches Bandit had scored across his cheek had healed. He basked in her youthful adoration and the unqualified acceptance given him by the social elites who curried his opinions and extended more printing contracts than he could dream of handling.

Not unexpectedly, the militia Williams assembled to reinforce his stand and add pressure on Royd to prepare a favorable report on Apple Knoll appeared. Prescott Darlow spent several days fawning at the senator's side all the while devouring Alexandria with his lascivious eyes. The man made Royd's skin crawl, but he managed to remain civil although he was confused by Alexandria's apparent fascination with Senator Harris's aide.

Marley Young stopped briefly in Hampton en route to yet another conference. He arranged to have several hundred pamphlets printed by Royd's firm which Royd supposed was his way of encouraging Royd to stay within the fold. Royd, however, refused to discuss the precise contents of his findings with anyone, including Senator Williams.

With his ego restored, life for Royd was almost as sweet and secure as it had been before he accepted the senator's bid to go to Apple Knoll. Once he spoke with Williams, Royd felt his dilemma would be resolved. Then perhaps Pale Eyes would finally give him rest. She haunted him incessantly, and whenever he sat down to write his report, he could almost feel her hands guiding his pen. It was no small wonder then that the report was a glaring exposé of conditions at Apple Knoll. He could hardly wait to see the expression on Moriah's face when he confronted her with it—when and if she showed up to claim the little leather treasure he had stored in his safe without more than a cursory glance. He also had a surprise waiting for her. Bandit had followed him back to Hampton, much to the chagrin of Royd's housekeeper who quit immediately!

As Royd opened the door to the senator's study, he realized how much he counted on Williams being as repulsed by the report's contents as he was. Senator Williams, looking relaxed but powerful behind an impressive, mahogany desk, gestured for Royd to enter. After shaking hands, Royd settled into a high-backed, leather chair and placed his report on the desk within reach of the senator. He watched as a slight frown covered his future father-in-law's face.

Fithian Williams made no move to open the report. Instead, he lit a cigar, leaned back, and toyed with one end of his mustache. He took a deep puff until the tip of the cigar glowed orange. Smoke quickly separated the two men before dissipating, leaving the pungent aroma of tobacco in the air. Royd tensed, but resisted the urge to begin the discussion.

The senator cocked his head and pointed at the report. "I didn't expect you'd be finished so quickly."

Royd cleared his throat. "I didn't want to let my impressions of Apple Knoll fade. Neither did I mince words, sir. Once you read the report, I believe you'll agree that something needs to be done. The rumors scarcely do justice to reality, and the legislature must take steps to stop these vile practices against female inmates at Apple Knoll."

"My instructions were quite clear."

"I don't think either one of us considered the possibility that the rumors of sexual perversion might be true. Notwithstanding the physical punishment doled out to these women that far exceeds decent standards, the female inmates are routinely harassed by lewd remarks and licentious treatment. There is evidence," Royd continued lowering his voice, "that females are routinely raped. I can't prove it, but it also appears that if a female gets pregnant, she's forced to abort. For the keepers and guards, Apple Knoll is naught but a harem. The warden—"

Williams held up one of his hands and shook his head, interrupting Royd's carefully chosen words. "Lester Figgs runs an excellent, self-supporting institution."

Royd snorted. "Figgs is a whoremonger with his own personal brothel!"

The senator tapped the ash off his cigar, narrowed his gaze, and leaned forward. His expression was curiously paternal. "What the warden does with murderous thieves and harlots is not an issue I care to address. I daresay that if the conditions are as you describe them, they are still a sight better than the way these women lived on the outside. Their basic needs are met far beyond what they are entitled to expect."

"These women, sir, are violated most cruelly!"

The senator smiled benignly. "Your gallantry is admirable, son, but misplaced. While I expect a gentleman of your caliber to be outraged if a gently bred female is abused verbally or physically, I also expect you to mark the difference between her and her unfortunate unwashed sisters. These inmates are not like Alexandria. They're women of the street accustomed to harsh treatment. They're born and bred on it. It's their heritage and their destiny."

Royd felt his pulse quicken as he remembered his mother and the way of life she clung to for survival. "Perchance," he admitted slowly, shifting to a different tact. "On the streets, however, these women have a choice. Limited, perhaps, but they do have a choice. As inmates, they can hardly refuse the advances of their keepers or return the keepers' taunts in kind. The women are more vulnerable in the penitentiary. Isn't it our duty to protect them and to extend some measure of decent treatment?"

"They are protected—from hunger, disease, the elements, and even from themselves. I think you've probably exaggerated a few isolated incidents of indiscretion."

Royd picked up the report, opened it, and pointed to specific cases Atwood had uncovered. "*These* are not exaggerations or figments of my imagination. Read them before you make any further assumptions."

When the senator sighed, Royd tossed the report back on the desk. "You're not going to read it, are you?"

"I want the report to reflect—"

"I don't believe this!" Royd stood abruptly. "Don't you care about these poor unfortunates? Even if they did commit heinous crimes against man and God, they have an opportunity within the penitentiary system to learn a trade and reform. It's unconscionable that we permit—" He halted in midthought, taken aback by the grin on the senator's face. "You . . . you find this amusing?"

The senator ignored Royd's question. "Reform? Their blood is tainted from birth. They can't reform any more than a snake can defy its nature. The prison reform movement is nothing more than a passing fancy. What this society needs is a return to the gallows for offenders. That would stop crime, not a system that pampers the wicked."

Royd swallowed hard, trying to forget the image of his parents as they swung from the gallows. A cold sweat broke out on his forehead. He would never forget that sight for as long as he lived.

The senator's grin changed into a benevolent smile. "You wear your idealism like a knight in shining armor. You don't perhaps have a white horse as well?"

The blood in Royd's veins chilled and his expression turned cold. The irony of the senator's mocking metaphor hit closer to the mark than Williams could possibly have imagined.

"As I see it, son, you have two options, one of which is too ludicrous to be considered." The senator sat up straighter now and reassembled the report before handing it back to Royd. "I'm counting on you to be as astute in this matter as you are in business. You must know how pleased I am that Alexandria has accepted your offer of marriage. You have a promising future. As sole printer for the legislature, your income is substantial. I don't think I need to mention that contracts from many of my friends have come your way as well. Every businessman knows that financial success can be as fickle and fleeting as a woman's favors. Senators Whitcomb and Flanders have a substantial investment in labor contracts with Apple Knoll. If the penitentiary is mired in scandal, their names will be sullied in the process. Their support for your state contracts, of course, would be withdrawn."

Royd threw his hands up. "Their contracts aren't threatened, particularly since they bid fairly for the inmates' labor!" He took one look at Williams's face and knew beyond any doubt that what he just said was not true.

Fool! Marley wrote that section of the report, and the man himself hinted that he had a vested interest in seeing a favorable report for men who could enhance Marley's future. "The food contracts?" Royd asked, knowing before the senator responded that anything Darlow wrote was a cover-up endorsed by Senator Harris.

"Never mind," he muttered before Williams could answer. Royd felt like he had been backed into a corner and there was no escape route other than the one pre-ordained by men more powerful and influential than himself. He shrugged his shoulders. "And if the report remains as written?"

"You're young and idealistic, but you're not a fool." The senator's comment was laced with mild esteem. "You've worked very hard to achieve a certain level of financial success and respectability. Force this issue and you'll be ruined. I've already discussed this matter with Alexandria. She's not prepared to spend the rest of her life with a man branded by poverty and social ostracism, especially when she has been placed in that situation because you care more about low-life females than you do for her. Quite simply put, Royd, without a favorable report, there will be no contracts and no marriage."

Royd's laugh was bitter. "I suppose I don't have much choice, do I?"

"There's always a choice. The question at hand is what yours will be. Will you write the report I want or shall I assign that task to Prescott Darlow?"

Royd took a deep breath and looked at the senator eye to eye. "I'd like to see Alexandria."

The senator rose without answering him and walked to the door. "I'll leave the two of you alone. I'll be in the parlor. Alexandria will let me know when you're finished," he said quietly before opening the door.

Alexandria entered the room, her face flushed with an

odd blend of excitement and irritation. "I don't know why this is so important to you," she gushed as she approached him.

Royd studied her carefully. Her tall, lithe figure was impeccably gowned to perfection. Her honey-blonde hair, richly coiffed, had not a curl out of place. Only the flashing of her brown eyes revealed irritation and her cold disregard for the female inmates whose fates apparently mattered less to her than the weather.

He rose and welcomed her with a brief peck on her cheek. "I don't think you have all the facts," he argued gently.

"My father told me everything I need to know. Really, Royd, this is most tiresome. I'm ready to leave for Philadelphia to visit Victoria. If you had done what my father wanted, you might have been able to come with me." Pouting her lower lip, Alexandria narrowed her gaze. "You didn't find someone else more interesting at that awful place, did you?"

Royd gulped, the intriguing memory of Moriah coming instantly to mind. "Of course not, darling. No woman can compare with you."

"Certainly not any of *those* women," she snickered with a toss of her head. "To think we would be having our first disagreement over whores and thieves! It's simply resolved, Royd. Listen to Father. He knows what's best. It wounds me to think you disagree with him. After all, he has much more experience in these matters than you do. In time, I'm sure you'll agree he was right. You *do* agree with me, don't you?"

Royd swallowed any attempt to reason with her. Her mind was made up. "I suppose," he murmured, deeply disappointed.

"Then I shall be off!" she announced gaily, with no more thought about the seriousness of the problems at Apple Knoll than she gave to selecting the color of a new gown. "It's terribly exciting to be traveling to Philadelphia," she droned. "Hampton is so . . . so dull. Do you think we might buy a town house in the city after we're married?"

Royd nodded absently. "I should think I'd prefer the country."

"Ugh! How terribly quaint. But absolutely out of the question," she responded, her face skewing into a frown. "I detest the country. Perhaps Father will purchase a town house for me," she whispered as she kissed him good-bye. "I wish you were coming with me."

At that precise moment, Royd wondered if he had been mad to consider marrying Alexandria for longer than it took to brush his hair. "We'll talk about it when you get back," he answered dully.

After Alexandria left the room, Royd sat deep in thought.

He did not love Alexandria madly and passionately as he knew most men beheld the woman they were about to marry. He also recognized the fact that Alexandria had agreed to become his wife because of his ability to support her in as grand a fashion as her father had rather than any heart-pulling emotional infatuation. Still, Alexandria's allegiance to her father instead of to her future husband was a bitter blow that made Royd's blood simmer.

Alexandria was barely eighteen, and although Royd could understand that she was still dependent on her father, he had hoped she would be more loyal to her fiancé. Royd would not tolerate such betrayal after they were married, and he wondered if she would ever challenge her father. If forced to take sides, would Alexandria *ever* choose Royd over her own flesh and blood?

Now that he thought more about Alexandria, her quick dismissal of the female inmates as inconsequential should not have surprised him either. She had been pampered all of her life and sheltered from the harsh realities many women faced when they were born into the lower order of society.

When Royd chose Alexandria to be his wife, one of the qualities that made her stand apart from any number of eligible women was her ability to conduct herself with grace and flair at the many social functions he attended. She was also a superb hostess who could make any man feel important, regardless of his looks or his age, with just the slightest touch of coquetry that inflated a man's ego.

Tidbits about Alexandria's nature that he had perhaps pushed to the back of his mind allowing for her youth suddenly became clearer. Alexandria's ability to keep a maid no longer than a few months may have been due to his fiancée's selfish and strident expectations rather than the ineptitude of the young women who served her. Once, when Royd had taken Alexandria to the theater, he remembered how aggrieved she had been when he pressed a few coins into the hand of a young flower girl whose entire basket of paper flowers had been ruined by a runaway carriage.

Royd's mouth went dry at the thought that maybe he had been blinded by ambition and had made a terrible mistake proposing to Alexandria. Marriage to her might be a whole lot less satisfying than he had hoped.

There was more at stake here, he chastised himself, than his choice of a life partner. The fate of dozens of women depended on what action he would take. As the senator returned to the room, Royd rose. "I don't know what to say. Naturally, I thought . . ."

Williams stood and walked around the desk to clamp a reassuring hand on Royd's shoulder. "You're young, Royd. No apology is necessary. Sometimes it's necessary to look at an issue from several vantage points rather than stay focused on only one. The females at Apple Knoll are released eventually. How many of them re-form? Not many. They don't merit our concern. Lester

Figgs does the best he can, but he can't monitor the keepers and guards every minute of every day. These women are a temptation that not many men of their ilk can resist. I know it's hard for a young man like you to understand that."

Royd's head pounded and his heart thumped in his chest. He felt like his whole body was about to explode. He understood these women's plight because he had lived in their world. His own mother had been a woman of the streets before she married his father. True, their life of crime was unacceptable, but Royd wondered now if they had been born to a life of luxury like Williams and his wife how different his parents' lives would have been —not to mention his own. "You don't think it's possible for these women to reform?" he asked, thinking now of Moll and Jack Clayton who had assumed the role left vacant by his parents' deaths.

The senator laughed. "Hardly."

Royd shrugged his shoulders and reached for the report. "I suppose I can have a preliminary draft ready within a day or two."

"Splendid!" The senator beamed. "I knew you would listen to reason," he drawled as he retook his seat. "As a matter of fact, I received a missive from Lester Figgs just a few days ago. He's concerned about where your interests lie. Apparently Atwood took his task to heart and the warden was worried he might persuade you to ply your findings elsewhere."

With a nonchalant laugh, Royd dismissed the concern that etched the senator's features. "I met with Atwood a few days ago. He won't be a problem."

"Good. I want you to deliver a draft of your report to me by Friday. With Alexandria away visiting her sister, returning to Apple Knoll shouldn't be a problem for you. I want Lester Figgs to have a copy of the report first thing Monday morning. I'm afraid he's got Senator Harris and the others a bit skittish. There's also been a breach of prison security. Apparently one of the females has been able to escape her cell and prowl about. You interviewed the woman—Number Seventy-nine, I believe."

Royd forced a look of disinterest although his heart skipped a beat as his worse nightmare suddenly loomed straight out of his dreams and slammed into his chest. He did not mind making a mistake when he was the one who would suffer, but this error jeopardized a woman who was subject to punishment the likes of which he did not dare to think about. Damn Figgs twice to hell!

Royd made one mistake, but he was not about to compound it by letting the senator know how much this news upset him. He shrugged his shoulders. "I really can't remember numbers unless I refer to the report. Did Figgs mention how she escaped? The walls in the cell yards are almost ten feet high!"

Williams shook his head. "It doesn't really matter. Figgs has everything under control now. He transferred the inmate to Willow Valley. He was afraid you might have discussed . . . well, it's not important. Once you meet with Figgs you can give him your personal assurances that the legislative hearings will not be problematic."

Willow Valley? Royd's mistake had not threatened Moriah. It had destroyed her. She was not mad. He was certain of it. After having two conversations with the woman, he had no doubt that she was as sane as he was. For obvious reasons, however, the warden had exiled her to an asylum where she would spend the rest of her days. Even a murderess did not deserve that fate!

"Can't I send the report with someone else?" Royd held his breath hoping his ploy would work as visions of Moriah in an asylum made him slightly dizzy.

The senator waved his hand in the air. "Figgs is much too upset to be placated by a messenger. Take the report to the man and talk to him. Convince him you're not about to upset the proverbial apple cart." He paused and gave Royd a chastising look. "It's important, Royd, or I wouldn't ask you to go."

Biding for time to completely reassess the dilemma that he thought was resolved not half an hour earlier, Royd responded cautiously. "I can be at Apple Knoll by Monday. Stevens can handle the printing contract for Marley. Since Alexandria will be away, I think I might extend my visit to the western counties. Land there would be a good investment." He paused, remembering an estate he had secretly considered purchasing through an agent a year ago. He dismissed it at the time as an extravagant dream, too costly to renovate, too far from Hampton to be practical, and located so far into the country that Alexandria would detest it sight unseen. He shook his head, shaking away the memory. "Is there a problem if I delay my return for a few weeks?"

"Not at all. You're quite right to invest in land. It's ever faithful, unlike the business world. I'll write to Alexandria at once. She'll be very relieved to know that all the plans for your nuptials in November can proceed."

Royd left the senator's home in a quandary. He could not dismiss what he had learned at Apple Knoll. Despite Senator Williams's low opinion of the inmates, Royd knew that other members of the legislature would be sympathetic to the women's plight. George Atwood, for one, would be willing to help him, although committing financial and social suicide was not particularly appealing for either of them. If Atwood had been able to meet with the director of Willow Valley, he might have gotten irrefutable proof of his suspicions. Unfortunately, the director was ill and unable to see anyone.

Royd also felt guilty about what had happened to Moriah. He remembered how adamant she had been that her sister could not possibly have gone mad. Now that Moriah was also confined in the asylum, Royd knew he would have to go there himself. He hoped that the answers he found there would not possibly be as horrid as the ones he imagined.

It was all his fault! Someone must have followed him the night he waited for Moriah in her cell yard, or perhaps their conversation had been overheard. In either case, Royd's visit had resulted in the discovery of Moriah's forays to other inmates.

He had to do something.

By the time he reached his home, Royd had several plans rolling side by side in his mind. Somehow he had to reconcile his shaky allegiance to Senator Williams, his upcoming marriage to Alexandria, his need to expose the problems at Apple Knoll which included the rescue of one blue-eyed vixen whose fate lay totally within his control, and the survival of his business.

Years ago, Royd thought he had left the sordid world of crime for a respectable life among the upper classes. Somehow that dream seem tarnished now, and he began to reassess whether or not the two worlds were more alike than they were different. Did he really want to spend his life kowtowing to men of power and influence? Could his own sense of right and wrong survive the dictates of others? What would marriage to Alexandria be like if he spent the rest of his life pleasing her father in order to safeguard their marriage?

There might be a way to free Moriah, alert the legislature to the real problems at Apple Knoll, and still maintain his social standing although it would take a miracle to pull it off. Before he could make any plans, however, he had to write a new report. He placed the original report in his safe next to Moriah's leather treasure. He closed the safe, closeted himself in his study, and began to write.

It galled him to think that Senator Williams actually believed Royd would acquiesce and write a report favorable to Apple Knoll. As he wrote lavish praises for the county penitentiary and lauded the performance of Lester Figgs as warden, unequivocally rejecting the rumors as falsehoods, his hold on the pen tightened. It was possible that his plan would fail, but he knew that the loss of his reputation was almost inconsequential compared to the price that Moriah would pay. Gritting his teeth, he signed the report, only too aware that he had no choice but to proceed with his plan. There was no turning back.

In the morning, he would deliver this new report to Senator Williams, give instructions to his assistant concerning Young's contract, and leave for Apple Knoll.

There was one stop he would make along the way.

He only hoped he was not making the biggest mistake of his life.

Thirteen

Royd sent the revised report to Senator Williams late Thursday afternoon. The following morning he arrived in Sweetwater, a small settlement just half a day west of Philadelphia. He approached the door to a ramshackle cottage on foot after tying Brandy to a decaying hitching post close to a large oak tree and a patch of weeds. Bandit, the ever-present pest, climbed the tree and hunkered down for a rest.

It was as though Royd had stepped back in time. He felt like he was sixteen again, looking over his shoulder for a last glance at the house that had been his home for nearly four years. Instead, today he was coming home, and he wondered what kind of welcome he would receive. He lifted away a tree branch that had fallen on the steps and knocked on the door. When it opened a crack, he removed his hat. "Moll? It's Royd. May I come in?"

A small, heavyset woman pushed straggly gray wisps of hair away from her face. She opened the door a bit wider and squinted her eyes. "Royd? Don't know no . . . Royd?"

The door flew wide open and she stood there trembling with disbelief. Tears rolled down her face and she wiped them away with the hem of her apron.

Royd stepped through the threshold and bent down to

embrace her. "I've missed you," he murmured as she clung to him.

Soft sobs shook her pillowed frame. "I told him you'd come back someday. Oh, my boy, he's missed you. He's just too stubborn to admit it. Come on in now, and let me get a good look at you," she said as she closed the door. She latched onto his hand and pulled him toward the back of the house. "Jack's been feelin' poorly. One look at you might put a spark back into the man."

Royd followed her into the kitchen, appalled by the run-down condition of the cottage. Sunlight streaked through several holes rotted in the roof and the floorboards creaked as he walked. As usual, however, Moll kept a well-ordered house. There wasn't a speck of dirt on the floor, and the kitchen was filled with the aroma of freshly baked bread. Royd swallowed the lump in his throat as she pulled out a bench at the hand-hewn wooden table.

"Are you hungry? I just made a batch of bread. There's no butter, but . . ."

He shook his head and laughed. "I didn't come to eat."

"Always had the appetite of a squirrel." She chuckled, dabbing at her eyes again. "Such a fine gentleman you are," she said, admiring the cut of his clothes. "Can you stay a bit?"

"I only have a few hours, Moll, but I hope we can spend more time together soon. Where's Jack?"

"Down to the creek tryin' to catch supper." She smiled. "You remember that old spot of his, don't you?"

He nodded. How could he forget? Whenever he thought about running away, he usually got no farther than there before he turned around.

"Go on down. Just be careful you don't scare him into fallin' headfirst into that creek. Can't be givin' him no excuse for not catchin' nothin'." She paused, and her eyes filled up again. "You'll stop back to the house before you leave?"

"I will. I promise," he responded, kissing her cheek before he slipped out the back door. He followed a dirt path down to the creek. Turning left, he walked along the water bank until it curved. He stopped abruptly the moment he saw Jack.

Moll's husband sat on a huge tree stump with a rod in one hand and a net in the other. He looked up, stared at Royd for a few moments, and then turned away. "Told you not to come here again," he grumbled as he flicked his wrist and toyed with the rod.

Royd walked over and stood next to him. He looked out into the clear flowing current and took a good whiff of cedar and pine that filled the air with memories. "I need your help," he said quietly. He picked up a pebble and threw it into the water.

"I'm trying to fish. You're scarin' them away."

"Moll warned me about giving you an excuse. You never did catch much here as I remember."

"Now you're talkin' and that scares 'em off, too."

"Come back to the house then," Royd suggested.

"Got nothin' to say to you."

Royd snatched the net and rod out of Jack's hands and laid them on the ground. "I want to talk to you, Jack. I stayed away for ten years. Isn't that long enough?"

"Some folks got memories fifty years long. Won't do you no good to be seen here. I told you when you left—"

"I don't care what you said then," Royd remarked as he kicked the rod farther out of Jack's reach. "I came back here because I need a favor. From the look of things, you could use some help, too."

Jack stood up and squared his shoulders, although his best effort could not change the fact that Royd now topped him by a foot. "I don't need your help, and I don't do favors no more. Gave that up," he grumbled as he extended his hands. The fingers on his left hand were twisted together like the roots of a tree. "Not much good one-handed, but even if these were as straight and young as yours, I still wouldn't do it. Gave up forgin' after you came to live here just to prove I could do it and to show you that people can change. Now get on outa here 'fore somebody knows you're here."

Royd shrugged his shoulders, picked up the rod, and sat down to fish. He ignored the fact that there was no bait left on the crude hook. "I did everything you asked me to do," he said, talking to Jack's reflection in the water. "I went away to school and made friends with all the right people. I don't suppose you'd like to explain where all the funds came from to pay for that." He chuckled when Jack started to mumble a denial. "I know you didn't have the money. Where did you get it, Jack? Forge one more bank draft?"

"That'd be none of your business!"

Royd recast the rod. "I bought a printing firm and built an honest fortune. Stayed away, too, just like you ordered." He waited for Jack to interrupt, but Jack stared out at the creek. "I learned something these past years," he added when Jack begrudgingly sat down beside him on the tree stump. "People are all basically the same. It doesn't matter what level of society you happen to land in. A man's character can be good or evil. You just don't notice it as quickly when the man is cloaked with upper-class respectability. Lord knows it's worked for me." A worried look etched his face.

Jack's chuckle softened his hard-set features. "Got a real scoundrel after you?"

"Damn near a whole militia. I've met my share of jackals in the past, and I've handled them. Honestly, too," he added when Jack started to interrupt him again. "This time it's different. Everything I've worked for is at stake. I know what I should do. I just don't know for sure how to do it unless you help."

"Always found it best to follow your gut instinct, son. It worked for me," Jack mumbled as he bent down and awkwardly picked up the net.

"My instinct for survival tells me to do what they want and be done with it," Royd whispered as a large catfish approached his line.

"And your gut?"

"Expose the bloody bastards for the parasites they are!"

Jack nodded. "Why can't you try to do both?"

Royd turned toward Jack, a quizzical look on his face. Jack nodded toward the creek and took the rod away from Royd, trailing the empty hook along the sandy bottom. The catfish followed the hook, and Jack quickly netted it from behind. Eyes glowing, he gave a whoop of victory as he hurled the net behind him and the fish flopped around on the ground.

"Sometimes approachin' a problem from a different direction works best. Since you're too stubborn to leave and too big for me to boot out, guess I'll have to hear this tale." He stood up. "Come on back to the house. Moll can cook this up while we talk. Then you're leavin'. Consortin' with ex-jailbirds ain't exactly good for your reputation."

"Jailbirds!" Royd muttered under his breath as he picked up the net and scooped up the fish before he followed Jack back to the house.

Jack stopped abruptly and raised his fist in the air. "Didn't you learn nothin' from Moll and me? A man's character is shaped by his own free will. It's not a bloody birthright. All a man needs is a chance to prove hisself. We took you in and gave you that chance. You done good till now."

Royd shook his head as they walked along together. "There are times when I miss the excitement and thrill of life on the streets. I've tried to deny it, but it's true. Maybe it's where I'm meant to be. The rest of my life is a thin facade of respectability that's downright boring if I'm honest enough to admit it."

Jack cast him a wary look. "Sounds to me like you just picked the wrong friends and the wrong business. If you own a printing firm, you're probably stuck in a room full of ink and presses. That'd be boring . . . unless you've a mind to do a little forgery."

"It pays honest," Royd countered.

"Humph! That's the best you can say? Looks like you're right. We need to talk. Then you're leavin', and you're not comin' back. Get that straight right now 'fore you go inside. Moll and me will help you if we can. We never let you down before, did we?"

Royd felt renewed hope. Moll and Jack would help him to make his plan work. He had sent a note to Atwood. After placating Lester Figgs, Royd would have nearly a month to follow through with a scheme that just might satisfy the conflict between his nagging conscience and his need for social survival. Yet he realized that even with help from Jack and Moll, he was taking a risk.

He only hoped he wasn't too late.

Two weeks later, Jack drove a rented coach over a deeply rutted trail through dense woods. He brought the coach to a halt in front of the gates to the Willow Valley Lunatic Asylum and jumped down to open the door for his passengers. He helped Moll out first and waited by her side for Royd to emerge.

Royd stepped out and brushed off his breeches and coat. He smiled at the couple who had fostered him and given him the opportunity for a respectable life. "Jack. Keep the horses ready and get that raccoon off the top of the coach! I don't expect this to take very long. Are you ready, Moll?"

She grinned and waddled over to him.

"Remember to let me do the talking. You're only here to make my story look authentic."

"Do I really look like a nurse?" she asked as she rearranged her cape and touched the brim of her hat.

"You look very competent," Royd responded, hoping that the director of Willow Valley would agree. He took her arm and escorted her to the gate while Jack saw to the horses.

The asylum was nestled in a small valley populated by more weeping willow trees than Royd had ever seen in one place. The institution was isolated, however, and there wasn't another dwelling for miles around which made the stone walls that surrounded the grounds almost ludicrous. They had spent hours searching for Willow Valley, and Royd reminded himself to chastise George Atwood for providing directions that had sent them in circles.

The gray stone building was massive with high, small windows that were barred. Royd reached out and pulled on a rope attached to a tarnished brass bell that hung just on the other side of the gates. Moments later, the main door creaked open, and a man dressed in a black shirt and breeches shuffled outside. "No visitors today," he said irritably and then turned to go back inside.

Royd called out to him. "I'm here to see Mr. Solter."

"He's busy."

"I'm an attorney," Royd shouted. "Randolph Crisham. I have orders here concerning two of your patients."

The man swung about and eyed Royd warily. "Mr. Solter expectin' you?"

Royd shook his head. "He'll see me. Tell him—"

"I know what to tell him," the man snarled as he went back inside and slammed the door. Half an hour later, he reemerged and unlocked the gates. He allowed Royd to enter but blocked Moll by closing the gate and locking it before she had a chance to slip through. "She stops here. Mr. Solter only agreed to see you."

With a reassuring glance at Moll, Royd followed the

man inside. It took a few minutes for his vision to adjust from the bright sunlight outside to the dark, dank interior. The director's office was located just inside and to the right of the main door.

A tall man with limp red hair stood up when Royd entered the luxurious, walnut panelled room. "Mr. Crisham? Herman Solter. How can I help you?"

Royd placed a packet of papers onto Solter's desk. "I've been appointed to handle the estate of Avery and Louise Lane. Judge Martindell has signed an order transferring custody of the Lane's two daughters, Ruth and Moriah, to me. I have a coach waiting outside and a nurse to care for them."

Solter paled, making the freckles that dotted his face appear even darker. "This is most unusual," he remarked as he spread the papers out on his desk and studied them closely.

Royd held his breath. Although the papers Jack painstakingly prepared looked proper and official to him, Royd was not sure if they would withstand too close a scrutiny.

Solter, however, appeared satisfied and folded the papers together again. "I'll need to keep these, of course."

"I expected you would," Royd answered with relief. "The judge prepared duplicates for my files."

"I'm afraid there's one slight problem. You say you administer the Lanes' estate?"

"I do."

"Then I assume you're prepared to settle the girls' accounts. The county supports the poor unfortunates who reside here providing they have no funds of their own. Since that's clearly not the case . . ."

Royd's expression hardened. "I can draw up a promissory note if you like."

Satisfaction swept across the director's face. "That won't be necessary. I'll have a statement prepared and sent to you. You're not related to the late Mr. and Mrs. Lane, are you?"

"The girls have no living relatives. Why do you ask?"

"A matter of curiosity, if you'll pardon me for asking. It was a celebrated case in this area. The girls were very young when they helped their uncle take his own life. To see both of them sent to prison and then go mad . . ." His voice drifted into a whisper as his face skewed into a frown of concentration. "I seem to recall a guardian. He's the one who alerted the authorities if I'm not mistaken. Terrible tragedy for the whole family."

"Suicide?" Royd murmured incredulously. "I thought he was murdered."

A skeptical look came into Solter's eyes. "I believe their convictions were for voluntary manslaughter."

Royd's chest felt like a band of steel was strapped around it making breathing hard labor. He had been quick to taunt Moriah about murdering her uncle during the first interview, yet she never once tried to explain what had actually happened. He felt like a total scoundrel.

Solter cleared his throat, catching Royd off guard. "You're not aware of the case?"

Royd apologized for his momentary lapse in attention. "I'm shocked. I've just relocated here from New York. I suppose you don't remember anything else that might be helpful to me or might perhaps let me talk with the physician who was treating the girls?"

Solter seemed curious but also concerned, and Royd did not like the look of suspicion now on his face. Solter picked up the packet of papers again and studied the order signed by the nonexistent judge. "You say you've just taken over the case. Didn't you get any files from the previous lawyer?"

"Mr. Landis was killed in a fire that destroyed his office and all of his records," Royd explained as calmly as he could, thinking of an excuse that Solter might swallow.

"That's too bad," Solter mused as he sat back in his chair. "How did you come to get the case then? Without any relatives, the girls may well have been forgotten."

Drat the man! Why couldn't he just buy Royd's story and be done with it? Royd hesitated using Senator Williams's name, but did he really have a choice? He gambled that Solter had heard of Williams. "My father is a good friend of Fithian Williams who has been very helpful to me. He arranged for me to take on Mr. Landis's cases. It hasn't been easy trying to reconstruct his files, but I was fortunate that he left a few of them at home. The Lane will was among those, and although it's taken some time, I was able to trace the girls here."

"Senator Williams?" Solter finally smiled and now appeared satisfied. He folded the papers together again. "There's not much else I can tell you. The uncle had a bad time of it. Some kind of dread disease. He probably wouldn't have lasted too much longer from accounts I read. It's just a real shame for the girls—orphaned twice before they even reached their majority." He paused and pursed his lips. "I'm sorry, but I have to add worse news. I—I didn't think it was necessary to notify anyone at the time. Ruth is dead. Since you're handling the estate, I assume you'll want a statement certifying to her demise?"

Royd felt the blood drain from his face. Moriah had been distraught when she found out that her sister had been sent to Willow Valley. He could only imagine how awful this news would hit her. "Ruth is dead? She wasn't even twenty when she was sent here!"

Solter shook his head sadly. "So very young, but there wasn't much to be done for her, I'm afraid. She was half-dead when they brought her to us. A terribly sad affair indeed. She lasted but a few days."

"What was the cause of death?" Royd asked quietly,

wondering why Solter would remember Ruth's death so vividly.

"Quite literally, the girl bled to death," Solter whispered. "I was so appalled by that man's butchery that I even wrote to the warden and Senator Harris. I think I still have a copy of my letters." He walked over to a tall cabinet in the corner of the room. After rummaging through several files, he found what he was looking for and handed them to Royd. "I have problems enough here at Willow Valley. I don't need castoffs from Dr. Welsh or Lester Figgs. Read them. Take them with you. Perhaps you'll have better luck bringing this matter to the authorities than I did."

Royd hurriedly skimmed the first page of one of the letters and his hands started to shake. "Dr. Welsh performed surgery?" His voice was cold with anger.

"You're too kind. The man is a butcher. He killed her. Given her youth and general appearance, there was no reason to perform an abortion on the girl. As dangerous as the procedure can be, there was no need for her to die if it was properly done. Dr. White's report is enclosed with my letters."

Royd expected to be surprised by the content of Solter's letters, but finding out that Ruth had been pregnant and then died as a result of a botched abortion left him speechless. This was the very proof he needed to nail the case against the staff at Apple Knoll, but his joy at having it in hand was overshadowed by the pain it would mean for Moriah.

"You never received a reply from the warden or the senator?" Royd asked when he found his voice.

"On the contrary. Both men assured me that steps would be taken to prevent this sort of thing from happening again. I saved their correspondence," he added when Royd lifted a brow in disbelief. Solter handed Royd two letters and brushed away Royd's look of disdain. "Lester Figgs should never have been given charge of Apple Knoll. Dr. White didn't record Ruth Lane's dying words, but one of the caretakers told me that she named Lester Figgs as the bastard who raped her."

Clenching his fists, Royd wished he could strangle Lester Figgs with his own hands. "There are legislative hearings in the fall. Will you be called to testify?"

"Take the letters I gave you and show them to anyone you like, but I won't be able to appear before the committee. I'm leaving Willow Valley next month to accept a position in England," Solter responded curtly.

Royd let the matter drop, preferring to waste no more time pursuing a dead issue. "I'd like to leave as quickly as possible. We have a long journey, and I'd rather see Miss Lane settled before nightfall."

"The aide can take you to her now, but before you see her, I'd best prepare you. She's violent at times so we've had to restrain her. It may appear cruel, but Dr. White tries to be as humane as possible under the circumstances. It's not like the patients understand what's happening to them. The physician did order the iron gag removed although Miss Lane's face is still badly bruised."

Royd shot up out of his seat. "They used an iron gag on her?"

"It's not that unusual. It prevents a patient from biting his tongue when he's suffering a fit. Dr. White removed it a few days ago, and so far Miss Lane hasn't had a single seizure."

Royd's mouth twisted in anger and he felt a dull pain knife through him as Solter got up and walked to the door. After summoning an aide, who turned out to be the same man who opened the gates, Solter shook hands with Royd and closeted himself in his office.

The aide headed straight down the corridor, and Royd followed him, his legs weak and his heart pounding. Walking past doors with small, barred windows, Royd could see some of the poor deranged souls inside small chambers as he walked by. Some seemed dazed and curled like fetuses on the floor. Others were manacled to their beds. The stench of stale urine grew stronger as they continued down a flight of stairs to a level just below ground.

Windows at ground level hugged the corners where walls met ceilings. The rooms here appeared to be larger, judging by the distance between doors. The aide, Jenkins, used a key to unlock the last door at the end of the hall. Royd stepped into the room and froze, unable to believe the sights that lay before him. Six waist-high, metal cages were lined up in rows of two. The smell of human waste, decaying food, and human misery made him gag. Outrage and horror nearly took his breath away as he peered from one cage to the other looking for Moriah Lane.

The patients started rattling their cages, moaning and screaming for attention. The aide walked over to the cage farthest from the door and crouched down to unlock the door. Royd was halfway there when the aide screamed out.

"Bitch!" The aide banged on the cage setting off a whimpering sound and then silence.

"Leave her alone!" Royd shouted as he charged forward to get to her.

"She bit me!" the aide whined as he gave the cage a solid kick with his booted foot. Royd shoved the man out of the way and knelt down to peer through the bars of the cage and the half-opened door. Shock held him captive.

He would never have known it was the same woman he had met just short of a month ago. This crazed, bedraggled creature simply could *not* be Moriah Lane. A mop of short-cropped, dirty hair lay matted against her skull. Her cheeks were blotched with bruises, yellowed and mottled various shades of pink and purple as they healed. Her lips, cracked and swollen, moved as though she were trying to speak, and the effort started a flow of blood which oozed from her mouth. Her gown, caked with dirt like a pumpkin that had been left to rot in the field, had slipped off her shoulders exposing emaciated flesh.

Her eyes made him tremble.

No longer sparkling with mischief or glowing with serenity, they were vacant and listless. Could anyone else have eyes that size and that shade of pale blue?

His hand trembled as he reached inside the cage all the while murmuring soft words to calm the fear that blazed back at him. She flinched when he lifted a torn sleeve, exposing the top of her left arm.

Royd stared at the numbers on her flesh and closed his eyes.

He had found Moriah Lane.

Too late.

The woman appeared to have gone mad!

♣

Fourteen

Huddled in the corner with her arms wrapped around her legs, Moriah was just barely beyond the stranger's reach. His gentle approach made her more curious than afraid, and she stole a quick glance at him to make sure that the aide was not with him. He was alone, and she saw the aide standing at the far end of the room. The stranger was large and dark with a full black beard that covered his face, but he did not frighten her as much as the others who had hauled her in and out of that despicable cage like a carcass of meat.

She tried to concentrate harder to make sense of the words that he was saying, but hunger and pain dulled her senses. Her vision blurred and her head started to spin from the effort. Then he was gone, only to return a few moments later. He was kneeling down in front of the door to her cage. What did he have in his hand?

It looked like . . . a cup of water!

The briny taste in her mouth created a longing that brought tears to her eyes. The stranger held the cup out to her, but in order to reach it she would have to move closer to him. Her mouth quivered, anticipating the cool liquid refreshment that would ease her dry, cracked lips that bled whenever she tried to speak. She continued to stare at the cup, torn between desperate want and terrified of getting near enough to the man that he would be able to grab her. If only he would leave the water and go away!

As though sensing her reluctance and recognizing her need, he placed the cup down just inside the door and backed away. She would have ignored his overture except that no one else had ever considered that she was simply frightened instead of bereft of all reason. The caretakers at the asylum treated her like she had no mind at all—as though that could excuse their fiendishness! By offering her a cup of water, this man touched a part of her that was as desperate for human kindness as her driving thirst.

Using the palms of her hands for support, she edged sideways in an awkward crab walk that took most of her strength. When she was within arms reach, her fingers wrapped around the cup and pulled it back so quickly that the precious liquid inside sloshed over the rim.

Trembling, she brought the liquid treasure to her lips using both hands to steady the cup. She tilted the cup and sighed as dollops of water coated her lips and trickled down her chin. Her tongue was swollen, as dry as a log of old firewood and as heavy as if it were carved out of rough stone. She could feel a strange sensation tingle in the back of her jaw as it tightened. Seeking more relief, she opened her lips just enough to try to take a sip and ignored the stitches of pain as the corners of her mouth split open again. As the water flowed into her mouth, she started to choke, incapable of using her tongue so she could swallow. Dipping her head down with sudden urgency, the water dribbled back out and she gasped to catch her breath.

Frustrated and exhausted, she determined to try again. She repeated her feeble attempts to quench her thirst and relieve the parchness in her lips until the cup was empty. The front of her gown was soaked with brackish stains, a mixture of the water and her own blood, but her efforts had paid off. She felt better than she could ever remember since arriving at Willow Valley almost two weeks ago—except for the moment they removed her gag.

The cup lay abandoned on the floor of her cage now, and although less than a few swallows had trickled down her throat, she felt indebted to this stranger. He started talking to her again. His voice was low and comforting in an oddly familiar sort of way. Kneeling at the entrance to her cage, his arms stretched out to her now, beckoning for her to come to him the way a concerned parent would reach out to a frightened child.

How she wanted someone to hold her and make the pain go away! She thought of Uncle Jed and what he had done the day she fell and cut her knees. She must have been only six or seven years old. Afraid he would punish her for ripping her new gown, she had taken refuge in her closet. He had come to her just like this strange man, offering his unconditional love and the comfort of his embrace when she was ready to accept it. But she did not know this stranger. Could she trust him not to hurt her?

His voice grew louder and more insistent which frightened her. She shook her head when he moved closer and gasped when pain tore through her mouth. Misty-eyed, she leaned back against the metal bars and listened to the sound of her own erratic heartbeat and took one shallow breath at a time.

Now he was acting just like the others did whenever she failed to obey them. She grew defiant and her body tensed. She knew it would do no good to resist. The first time someone tried to make her leave the cage, she wrapped her fingers around the bars and tried to hold on, but they just pounded viciously on her hands until she let go before they could break them. She curled her fingers into fists and closed her eyes. If he wanted her to leave the cage, she would not make it easy for him. He would have to upend it and spill her out the same way the others had done.

"Moriah? I won't hurt you."

Did she hear what she thought she had? Her eyes snapped open and she looked at him again, cocking her head and squinting her eyes. She was not surprised that he knew her name. So did all of the others, but they usually called her bitch and other names too horrid they were not worth the effort it would take to remember them all.

This man did not force her to move, however, and something about him made her believe that perhaps she *could* trust him not to hurt her. The other men always threatened and bullied her, using viciousness to force her to obey them. He was different, his voice gentle again as he patiently waited for her instead of relying on brute force to bend her to his will. Soft understanding lined his expression, and she sighed.

Merciful God! How she needed someone to be kind to her. She was so scared and weak and tired of fighting to survive that she had almost stopped praying for help. She could not speak, but she had tried valiantly to get someone to understand that she was not mad! She was not daft! Didn't anyone care enough to try to understand that she did not belong here . . . that there had been a terrible mistake?

She simply had to convince someone to believe her because she did not know how much longer she would last before slipping into a world that would make her confinement here necessary.

Was he the someone she prayed for to deliver her from this horrible nightmare?

A feeling deep within her urged her to take a risk. Just take one more chance—before she gave up completely and admitted defeat. She thought of Ruth and knew that Ruth would never give up. Ruth was stronger and bigger than she was, but Moriah knew that if she tried to imitate her older sister, she might be able to save them both. What choice did she have but to trust this man?

With a silent prayer in her heart, Moriah bunched her gown up around her thighs and crawled to the door. As she approached the opening, she watched him with wary eyes. When he inched backward, giving her space enough to exit, she felt reassured. Emerging from the cage, she leaned back on her heels, acutely aware that he was only inches away from her.

Compared to her, he was a giant of a man. His legs were sturdy and his shoulders were broad. She lifted her chin to gaze up at his face. He was smiling and his deep-set eyes gazed at her tenderly. She was so close to him that she could actually see how oddly colored they were.

Green. The color of winter evergreens.

Royd Camden!

Recognition shot through her like a bolt of lightning that made her shake. Fury flowed through every pore of her skin. There was no conscious thought. No prayerful reflection. Only hatred and vengeance thundered through her mind and her body. For herself. For Ruth. For all the women he betrayed. May he rot in hell for eternity!

Before his Final Judgment, however, she would have her pound of flesh. She lunged forward instinctively, and she fought him like a cornered animal gone mad with one supreme effort to survive before relinquishing life. Ignoring the pain and the cramps in her legs, she attacked him with every ounce of strength she could muster. Deep, guttural sounds came out of her throat as she raked his face with her nails. Locked together, they toppled to the side. She continued to fight him as his arms wrapped tight around her, trapping her flailing arms. She brought her knee up sharply, and he groaned. His hold loosened a bit, and she broke free, her reach long enough to grab handfuls of those outrageous curls that covered his head and a cheekful of his beard. She yanked and pulled as hard as she could, and his muttered curse of pain was a victory that fueled her waning strength.

Suddenly and without warning, pain exploded in the back of her head and bright colored lights danced in front of her eyes. Then darkness began to descend, and she could feel her body collapse against him. Her face landed hard against his chest, and the fabric of his coat felt like sandpaper. Before the pain could register, however, a curtain of oblivion fell and ended her attempts to vindicate her betrayal. Her last conscious thought was that she had not been strong enough to make him fully regret what he had done to them all.

Royd pulled the girl's limp body against his chest and glowered at the aide. "You didn't have to kick her!" he snarled, carrying her with him as he got to his feet.

The aide grinned. "Looked to me like she was gettin' the best of you. Got to act fast when they go wild. They're mighty strong when they have a fit."

Royd stared at Moriah, and he knew that if she had not been in his arms, he would have pummeled the aide senseless for kicking her. The girl's head lolled against his shoulder, and her feet dangled over the crook of his arm. Her face was battered but looked peaceful. The aide was wrong. She had not been having a fit. He saw the look in her eyes when she attacked him. They were furious and spitting liquid blue fire—but they were not crazed. She recognized him, he realized as he shoved past the aide and out the door.

He did not think that anything could make him feel worse than he did when Senator Williams told him that inmate number Seventy-nine was transferred to Willow Valley. He accepted his guilt as justly deserved, but finding Moriah here, caged like an animal, compounded his guilt. Seeing the condemnation and hatred in her eyes speared his heart, and he knew that he would fight an uphill battle to even have her trust him again. He needed her trust and so much more. Everything he had planned depended on Moriah's willingness to believe that he wanted to help the inmates at Apple Knoll. Judging by her reaction when she finally recognized him, however, that seemed as likely now as being able to catch a falling star.

Royd heard the aide following behind him, and he knew that he had to get out of there before she regained consciousness. If she did start another fracas, Herman Solter might discover exactly who he was. If he had not been carrying such a precious burden in his arms, he would have taken the steps two at a time. Afraid to jostle her, however, he worked his way back upstairs slowly, watching for any sign that he was causing her distress.

Her eyes were closed, and her forehead was pale. Soft shallow breaths fanned his throat and he was almost relieved that she was not awake. He walked down the main corridor with his eyes riveted on the door straight ahead. Just as he reached it, wondering how on earth he was going to open the door with Moriah in his arms, the door swung open.

Jack stood on the other side of the threshold. He took one look at Royd and the girl in his arms and then swung about. He ran ahead of them, opened the main gates, and called out to Moll, who was sitting on a huge rock beneath a willow tree. "Get in the coach, luv."

Royd got to the coach before Moll even got to her feet. With Jack's assistance, he climbed into the coach without jolting Moriah any more than he could help. He settled onto one of the cushioned seats and cradled Moriah on his lap, tenderly pushing locks of matted hair off her bruised face.

The first time he saw her without her hood, he had been mesmerized by her loveliness. He remembered thinking that she had the aura of an angel, but now she looked like she had fought St. Michael himself. And lost.

Breathless, Moll heaved herself into the coach and

plopped down across from him, her hat askew and beads of perspiration rolling down the chuff of her cheeks. "Whew! What took you so long. Me and Jack were gettin' worried. Where's the other girl? I thought you were gonna get both of them."

Royd's expression was grim. "She's not coming, Moll. She died a few days after she arrived at this hellish place." He did not know how he was going to tell Moriah about Ruth, but he knew it would not be until she was stronger.

"Is this . . . I mean . . . which one is she?" Moll asked quietly as she nodded toward the woman in Royd's arms.

"This is Moriah. It was her sister, Ruth, who died. I don't know what I would have done if anything happened to Moriah. It's all my fault she's here."

Moll smiled as she patted his arm. She leaned closer, her eyes softening with pity when Moriah groaned and turned her head. Moll took one look and gasped. "Oh-h-h! Dear God! What happened to her?"

Royd swallowed the lump in his throat and gave her a plaintive look. "You can't even begin to fathom," he whispered, shaken more by his own wild imaginings than by what he had witnessed with his own eyes. "I didn't think . . . I mean . . . Moll, how could anyone do this? She's just a young woman. She couldn't possibly deserve what they have done to her."

Even as he said the words, Royd realized that in spite of her size, Moriah packed enough of a whallop to make his groin ache even now. He had the feeling that if he checked carefully, he would find part of his scalp bald, too. Had she really gone mad and attacked him or was her mind lucid, compelling her to make him pay for being careless and alerting the authorities to her nighttime travels?

Remembering how brutally the guard had kicked her, Royd felt the back of her head. He took a deep intake of breath when he felt a large lump at the base of her hairline. God's blood, what if the bastard killed her? She was as pale as a corpse, but when he pressed the lump she moaned. Relieved, he realized that for a few moments his heart had almost stopped beating.

Moll clucked like a mother hen whose chick had been attacked by a marauding wolf. "The poor dear! What are you going to do?" she asked as she took one of Moriah's hands and clasped it between her palms.

"We can't stay at the inn," Royd commented. Thinking aloud, he looked at Moriah. "David's Crossing is only a small hamlet. I don't want anyone to see her like this."

Moll touched his sleeve, and he looked up to see her face bright with an idea. "Remember that property we passed a few miles outside of the town?"

Royd was not likely to forget that property. It was the estate he considered the previous year. He shot her a look of pure disbelief. "That's a bloody castle, not a property!"

She grinned. "Jack asked about it when you were renting the coach. A count from somewhere, Germany or some such place, built it for his bride. She was royalty, too. She died in childbirth, and he was so grief-stricken that he committed suicide. It's even got some furnishings, and we could probably move right in. Jack says that some lawyer in town is handling the sale, but no one has even looked at it. Me and Jack could work real hard to clean it up. We might even be able to hire a few local girls to help us. It'd be real private, too. There's probably a stable for that princely beast of yours, and there'd be plenty of room for all of us."

"There's enough room for forty people! I need a cottage, not a cursed relic large enough for King Arthur!"

"Have you got a better idea? If you do, spit it out. From the looks of that girl, you'd best be quick about it," she pouted.

"It'll cost a fortune!" he argued, although he was certain that Jack could get a price below the one quoted to his agent last year. "I don't have that kind of money," he added when Moll shrugged her shoulders. "I'd have to sell my business, and even then . . ."

"You hate running a printing house. Besides, if you didn't own that boring business, you wouldn't have to worry about cuddlin' up to crooked politicians anymore. Seems like that would help to solve more than one of your problems."

"Jack talks too much," he grumbled. Moll looked so sure of herself that Royd found himself actually warming to her idea. Instead of buying it, he could probably get Jack to convince the lawyer to rent it with an option to purchase it later. If Royd was really clever, he could make sure that there was a loophole that would make it easy for him to back out of the deal and not lose his business.

Royd looked down at Moriah again, and he was consumed with guilt for worrying about finances. He owed her the chance to recover without garnering undue attention. Lord knew she had suffered enough already. He started thinking about the property. Set on top of a hill, it was isolated enough to give Moriah privacy. It was also secluded enough that no one would hear the explosion when she woke up and recovered enough to realize that she was in his custody.

"We'll stop and look at it," he said quietly.

One thing about this whole bizarre idea appealed to him. There might be a place inside the castle where he could hide when Pale Eyes decided to skin him alive.

Fifteen

Several hours away from Willow Valley the coach stopped abruptly. Royd tightened his hold on Moriah and held his breath waiting to see if she would wake up again. Her eyes fluttered open and shuttered closed in almost the same motion. He relaxed, grateful that there would not be a repeat of what had happened earlier.

When Moriah had roused earlier from her unconscious state, the look of confusion on her face quickly turned to horror the instant she recognized him. They rode for several miles locked in a silent battle of wills before she gave in to his superior strength and fell asleep.

Royd was not proud that he had been able to win the preview round of their final battle which was bound to make Waterloo look like a skirmish. He was satisfied that she was sleeping peacefully now and had the sense to realize that she could do nothing but cause herself further injury if she fought him.

With his feet braced on the edge of the opposite seat and his knees bent, he created a safety barrier so that if the coach stopped suddenly like had just happened, the girl would not be pitched onto the floor. The rhythmic, rocking motion of the coach as they traveled back to

David's Crossing seemed to finally lull her into a deep sleep. She was curled onto his lap with her head on his shoulder and the palm of one hand pressed over his heart, almost braced in position so she could push away from him when she awoke.

Royd gave Moll a quizzical look which was mirrored on her own face. Before he could voice a question as to why Jack had halted so unexpectedly, Jack opened the coach door, popped his head inside, and looked at Royd with disgust. "Got a broken noseband on one horse and throatlatch on the other. I knew I should have checked the bridles and harnesses before we left. The livery in David's Crossing don't get much business. You bother to inspect 'em?"

Royd grimaced. "It never occurred to me," he admitted. Anxious to get to Willow Valley after several days' delay in Apple Knoll, Royd was too concerned about Moriah to give the condition of the coach much thought. It had taken nearly two full weeks before Jack and Moll arrived in David's Crossing where he waited for them. "I guess I assumed everything was in order."

"Guessin' and assumin' things are attached and hooked up proper can cost a man more than he's willing to pay. Any ideas 'bout what we're gonna do now?" he said.

Reproach was written all over Jack's face, and Royd felt like he did the November day he lowered a bucket into the well behind the cottage in Sweetwater only to discover that the rope had rotted. It had taken two hours and six attempts before Royd retrieved the bucket. The whole episode cost him his pride as well as a week in bed nursing lung congestion.

Moll edged forward and glared at Jack. "It's not the boy's fault. He was worried about this poor young thing." Her frown turned into understanding as she held her arms out to Royd. "I'll hold her for you. If the two of you can stop fixin' blame long enough to think, you should be able to figure out somethin' temporary to solve the problem so we can find somewhere to stay."

Royd hesitated, reluctant to leave Moriah out of his sight. Thinking more about it, if Moriah did wake up, seeing Moll might be better than if she found Royd staring at her. After getting several hours' rest, she just might try to fight her way out of the coach.

With a sigh of exasperation, he transferred the still-sleeping girl into Moll's capable arms and climbed out of the coach. After removing his coat and waistcoat, he rolled up his sleeves and inspected the damage himself.

The leather straps were worn thin and appeared to be dry-rotted. It was a miracle that Jack noticed the damage before any more of the riggings snapped. Wearing a weak smile, he turned to look up at Jack who was in the coachman's seat. "Got any ideas?"

"I don't usually carry extra riggings in my waistcoat pocket," he snorted.

"When was the last time you wore a waistcoat?"

" 'Bout the same time you turned yourself into a gentleman!" Jack tossed back angrily.

"It's not going to help the situation if you wake the girl up." Royd nodded toward a copse of trees that sat back from the road a few yards ahead. "Let's move into the shade. I have an idea, but it might take a little time to repair this. It's too hot for Moriah and Moll to be cooped up in the coach."

Jack held the reins steady with his one good hand while Royd gripped the bridles and urged the horses to go forward. Once they were alongside the canopy of trees, Royd carried Moriah to a soft thatch and laid her on the cape that Moll placed on the ground. Bandit descended from his throne on top of the coach and curled up next to his mistress, placing his head on her thighs.

"I'll stay with her," Moll offered.

"Bandit won't let anything come near her. I need another pair of hands," Royd said as he led Moll back to the coach. He climbed inside only long enough to find the brown-wrapped parcel that had been on the seat. He found it wedged in the corner, tore off the paper, and carried the contents outside.

Moriah's little treasure, which Royd took with him rather than leave back at the inn, was now worth its weight in gold. The leather remnants that dangled from the thong were not as wide as the straps he needed, but they were certainly long enough. Using a small, gold pocketknife that hung from the fob of his pocket watch, he cut the thong and dumped the remnants into Moll's waiting hands. Using two and three remnants at a time, he measured and cut them until he was satisfied. When they were tied in place, they made an acceptable replacement for the throat guard.

Sitting up high on the driver's seat, Jack held the reins slack. "Check the harness on that one, too," he ordered as Royd moved to the opposite horse and started removing the noseband.

"Want the horses' shoes checked, too?" Royd grumbled.

"Checked the shoes while I was waitin' for you back at Willow Valley. They're worn, but I don't think they'll be a problem."

Royd saved an acidic reply for later. After tying the ends of the nose guard in place, he reached back for the harness. His vision caught an odd pattern in one of the pieces of leather that lat flat against the bridge of the gelding's nose. Pausing to look closer, he could see that the series of holes actually formed three letters: BGS followed by a date: Nov. 6, 1827.

Bitterness cooled his curiosity about the rest of the letters, and he looked away before he could decipher them. Whatever Moriah Lane recorded on those leather strips was private, and he remembered his vow not to inspect her little trinket. A vow he had kept until now.

He had felt so damn noble safeguarding it for her and
waiting for the opportunity to use it to prove that he was
an honorable and trustworthy man.

Trustworthy?

He felt so laden with guilt for inadvertently helping
the warden discover that Moriah had been leaving her
cell yard that he had risked everything to rescue her.
Now that he had been successful, he was not going to
take advantage of her condition to break his word.

Royd ignored the look on Moll's face that invited him
to share the thoughts that made him scowl and concentrated on repairing the harness. By the time he finished,
there would not be a piece of her leather keepsake that
wasn't reused as part of halter or harness except for the
thong, which he would save as a blank but poignant
reminder of the woman's confinement and his promise
to keep her trinket safe.

Moriah watched the trio of people gathered at the front
of the coach through her lashes. Royd Camden, the
Prince of Darkness, looked like he was repairing the
riggings for the coach. The other two people, whom he
referred to familiarly as Moll and Jack, looked like
plump little trolls straight out of a fable.

The coachman was as round and plump as the nurse
who held her for a while in the coach. He had a large,
bulbous nose and bushy white eyebrows that probably
would have matched his hair—if he had any. He was the
strangest looking man she had ever seen, but he appeared to be a gentle sort who enjoyed provoking Royd.
She liked him for that if for no other reason.

The woman called Moll was so chubby that when
Royd put Moriah onto her lap, she felt like she was
resting on a pile of pillows. Moll seemed to be helping
Royd, and Moriah wondered why such a kindly woman
would even associate with the likes of Royd Camden.

Feigning sleep ever since Royd carried her outside

and left her alone, Moriah waited for the opportunity to slip away. Bandit's unexpected presence nearly caused her to cry out with joy, but she did not dare say a word or move a single muscle for fear of alerting Royd that she was no longer asleep.

The late afternoon sun filtered through the treetops, and Moriah basked in its warmth. It seemed like the whole world had gone underground for the past few weeks. Earth smells, moist with the heat of the summer sun, chased away the foul-smelling memories of Willow Valley. The sight of yellow and white daisies and lavender wild flowers was balm for her eyes which had seen only darkness. A gaggle of geese meandered noisily nearby, chasing away the echoes of scurrying rats and marching insects in her mind.

Despite the heavy ache in her head and the ever-present pain on her face and in her mouth, Moriah felt strong enough to make an escape attempt. With Bandit for company and the Lord's help, she would do everything in her power to get beyond Royd Camden's reach or collapse trying.

Royd Camden's arrival at Willow Valley had shocked her. Wasn't it enough that he had made sure she would be locked away? What did he plan to do with her now? At least when she was at Willow Valley she was close to Ruth, although she had to admit that she had little hope of finding Ruth as long as she was confined to a cage unable to speak intelligibly enough to convince anyone that she was sane.

Once Moriah's mouth healed, she knew she could convince someone to let her see Ruth—sooner or later. Once Royd Camden placed Moriah in a different asylum, she would never be able to see Ruth again since he would undoubtedly make sure that the authorities paid no attention to her claims of sanity.

Moving to a new institution made no sense at all to her unless Royd meant to keep her hidden even further away until after the hearings. But where else could be worse than Willow Valley?

The only thing that could possibly be worse than being rational in an asylum for the deranged was death. If it weren't for Ruth, Moriah would have welcomed it. To be reunited with Uncle Jed and her parents was a part of eternity that she dreamed about, but she could not and would not leave Ruth alone. Why else would she have fought so hard to stay alive?

When Royd and Moll disappeared on the other side of the coach, Moriah got to her knees and crawled away as fast as she could until she was well-hidden in a clump of bushes. Bandit ambled alongside her, and she welcomed his company. Her head felt like it was made of lead, but she felt a surge of energy now that she was out of sight.

She looked around and decided to go deeper into the woods rather than try to circle back to the road. It would be too easy for Royd to track her, and she knew that Royd would suspect she would try to get back to Willow Valley to find Ruth. Going into the woods would hopefully send him in the opposite direction.

Moriah wasn't foolish enough to try to get to Ruth until she devised a plan which at the moment was impossible to formulate. Crawling through the brush, which ended in a small clearing bounded by dense forest, she decided to make a run for the forest some thirty yards away.

"Come on, Bandit," she whispered as she got to her feet. The raccoon ran circles around her legs and then bounded ahead of her. With a lilt in her spirit, she started to run toward the woods. Her gait was heavy and awkward after being confined for so long. Panting with exertion, she forced herself to concentrate on making her legs move one at a time.

She stumbled twice and fell to her knees. Run? She could barely stay upright, but with only a few yards to go she could not think of anything other than finding cover before Royd discovered her missing. Through tear-filled eyes, she caught a glimpse of brown fur and a striped tail as Bandit scampered back to greet her.

"Good boy!" she murmured although her words sent a painful reminder to her brain to keep silent. When she finally made it past the clearing, she hugged a nearby tree trunk for support. She cocked her ear and listened for the sound of shouts or running footsteps. All she heard was the rustle of treetops as they swayed in the breeze and the sound of swift, running water.

Water!

She looked around and picked up a small stick that would serve nicely as a cane and with Bandit at her side, she worked her way through the forest with her direction guided by the sound of the gurgling water. The underbrush grabbed at her gown and scratched her legs, but there was little else she could do but ignore the obstacles and travel more slowly.

The ground cover grew moist, and she felt her heart begin to race as the woods began to thin. She could smell the water now and practically ran when she spied the shallow rapids of a small brook.

Bandit was already there, stone-stepping neatly as he hunted for a fish. Moriah plopped down onto her stomach at the edge of the moss covered bank. Using both hands, she cupped the sparkling cold water and splashed it on her face. Her fingers numbed almost instantly, but she felt absolutely refreshed. Edging forward, she bent down and let the water run over her lips and trickle into her mouth. The pain was chilled away in a matter of seconds, and she stared down at the froth and foam as she said a prayer of thanksgiving. She never appreciated the many sweet qualities of water as much as she did at that precise moment. She could have stayed there for hours, but the thought of Royd Camden and his accomplices reminded her that her flight would be momentary unless she put a whole lot more distance between her and them.

Nevertheless, she was going to wash the dirt from her body!

Gathering the tattered remnants of her skirt around her hips, Moriah sat on the bank and dipped her feet into the brook. Resting the soles of her feet on the rocky bottom she ripped a bit of cloth from her gown and washed her legs and feet. What she would not give for a sliver of soap! Dismissing that thought as an absurd luxury, she pulled a few briars from her toes and calves, grateful that the cold water numbed her flesh even if it was only a temporary respite.

After wiping her arms and chest, she crossed the brook and scooped Bandit into her arms. His little mouth reeked of his fishy catch, and she wrinkled her nose, although she was excited that he was able to hunt so well after being raised inside the prison. Moriah was more than a little curious to know how Bandit wound up with Royd Camden, but decided it was probably some kind of ploy on his part to convince her that he was trying to help her. The kind of assistance he planned would more than likely imprison her for the rest of her days, and she chided herself for being foolish and wasting time at the brook.

Tossing Bandit to the ground, she looked about trying to decide which direction to take when she heard something that broke the natural sounds of the forest. Engulfed with fear that turned her bones to solid ice, she swirled about.

Lounging lazily on the other side of the brook, Royd Camden held a piece of her skirt as he pointed to his right. "That direction will take you to the road where the coach is waiting for us." He shrugged his shoulders when she glared at him. "Go left and there's a magnificent waterfall. Would you care to see it? I'll venture to say there's probably a shallow pool where you can bathe more properly."

Royd stood up and draped his shirt over his shoulder, holding it in place with the crook of his thumb. Moriah's eyes widened. The man was half-naked! The muscles on his bare chest glistened with perspiration and rippled with power. A fur of dark curls that matched the color of his hair covered his chest. His broad shoulders tapered to a narrow waist with nary an ounce of spare flesh. Moriah's mouth went dry and she grimaced when she tried to lick her lips. He was the most virile man that she could have imagined, and her pulse began to race until she looked up at his face. The dastardly bloke was smiling at her!

"I had a long and tiresome task of repairing the harness. If you're ready, perhaps we can continue our journey," he said softly.

Fiend! How dare he look at her with such concern? She picked up a rock and threw it at him. He ducked out of the way. When she threw two more stones, they missed their mark so wide he never had to move, and he looked so much the martyr that she wanted to scream.

Furious, Moriah was torn between wanting to smash the look of concern on his face with a boulder or gouge the unveiled distress in his eyes with a rake of thorns.

"Are you finished?" he drawled as he started to cross the brook.

Moriah stepped back and looked around for a way to defend herself. If she only had her makeshift cane, she could hit him over the head with it. Worse luck! She had left it on the other side of the brook. Fear turned to panic as he drew closer, and she grabbed a chunk of rotting log and heaved it at his head. It struck him in the chest and landed in the brook with a splash. His eyes widened. "Whatever happened to loving your enemy?"

Moriah felt her conscience respond and stamped it out by hurling a handful of pinecones at him that bounced off him like flower petals which disappeared in the fast current.

"How about loving your neighbor?" he mused as he stepped onto solid ground. He stared at her so long that Moriah felt a heated blush crawl up her neck and cover her cheeks. Clutching the top of her gown, she tilted her chin and gave him a look that would have shriveled the devil himself.

But not Royd Camden.

He advanced slowly, one step at a time, until he was right in front of her. He frowned when she tapped her foot on the ground in irritation and crossed her arms in front of her chest. Insufferable monster! If she could talk, she would match his taunts with a tongue-lashing that would require a year of penance! What she obviously could not do was to talk or to attempt to run away with any hope of being fast enough to escape for good. She was not, however, going to fall at his feet and beg for mercy. She'd rather eat slugs.

Royd was so close to her now that she noticed the scratches on his face from her earlier assault. Unfortunately, he did not seem to be missing a single one of the curls that covered his head although she thought she had yanked hard enough to leave a bald spot.

"Such pale-colored eyes," he whispered, and she was shaken and confused by the soft admiration in his voice. When he reached out to touch her, she flinched and he dropped his hand.

"How far did you think you would get?" he asked without forcing her to look directly at him.

She shrugged her shoulders and her breath started to come in soft spurts that she took to stop the tears that welled in her eyes from trickling down her cheek.

"I'm sorry. I didn't mean for any of this to happen. You scared me when you ran off. It's not safe, and you're in no condition to wander very far. Let me help you.

There's a lot that needs to be said, but I think you need some time to rest and recover first."

Moriah was not sure if she could hear another lying word without gagging. He sounded so sincere that if she had just met him, she would have sworn he was baring his soul to her. Fortunately, she knew him for what he was—a spiteful, conniving man of the world who was determined to destroy her by trickery, brute force, and now thoughtfulness.

As much as she wanted to believe him, she was grateful that she was smart enough to outwit him. Feigning understanding, it took all of her courage to give him a tremulous smile that brought fresh, anguished tears to her eyes.

The moment their eyes met, she could see hope in those deceitful green eyes. He actually believed she would trust him . . . again? After what he had done to her? He was a nidget, but she played him for all he was worth and let the tears roll down her cheeks.

Anguish etched his face. "Will you let me take you back to the coach?"

Moriah twisted her hands in front of her and played with Bandit's collar that was still tied around her wrist. She nodded slightly as her heart started to pound. If he believed she would go with him, she might have a chance to catch him off guard.

"Can you walk or would you allow me to carry you?" he asked with a worried lilt in his voice.

Squaring her shoulders, Moriah turned toward the brook. With longing written all over her face, she stared at the water and licked her lips.

As if taking her cue, Royd smiled. "Let me get you a drink before we leave." He knelt by the water's edge and motioned for her to join him. "I'll cup my hands so you can drink," he suggested. When she nodded again, he bent over and positioned both hands in the water.

Taking a deep breath, Moriah approached him from

behind. Her legs felt like they were made of jelly, but she inched forward with her eyes squarely focused on a rock just inches from his boots. As she knelt down beside him, she hesitated for a brief moment and then grabbed the rock.

Royd tilted his head slightly and looked up at her with an odd look on his face. She closed her eyes and cracked the rock against the top of his head. She watched him as he lurched forward and then she bolted away as a mumbled curse died on his lips.

Blinded by desperate terror, she scrambled away as fast as her legs would carry her. Her mind raced ahead of her feet, and she felt like she was moving in slow motion.

Suddenly, her forward motion stopped. Something was holding her back! She turned around, horrified to find Royd Camden holding onto the back of her skirt. Blood oozed out of a wound on his head and trickled down his forehead. His eyes were glazed with pain, but his hold was strong.

"N-n-no!"

Moriah's scream ripped through the air, and she pummeled his fist, trying to loosen his hold.

Using his other hand, Royd easily captured her flailing hands and pulled her toward him until they were only inches apart. Her breath came in ragged spurts that created excruciating shock waves of pain in her head as she fought to free herself from his grasp.

"Hold still! I'm not going to hurt you. Dammit, woman! I'm trying to help you."

Her head snapped back, and she hissed at him, her vision blurred by fear and anger. She turned her head from side to side, allowing him to see what his help had cost her. "Y-you!" she mumbled.

"Yes," he answered, his expression oddly sad and remorseful.

Moriah's rage melted into confused curiosity. Was it

possible that the man had a conscience after all? Did he really expect her to accept his acknowledgment of guilt and forgive him before her injuries even healed?

"I didn't tell the warden," he offered.

Moriah smirked in disbelief.

"This is not the time to discuss the details. The situation is complicated enough to explain, and I'd rather wait until you're able to ask as many questions as you wish. For now, it's important for you to understand that I didn't mean for this to happen to you. I left Apple Knoll and returned to Hampton without mentioning you to Lester Figgs."

At the sound of the warden's name, Moriah's foot shot out and connected with Royd's shin. "Wicked man," she spat, remembering how the warden had gloated over her suffering.

Royd paused, but did not indicate that her attack had done more than halt his confession. When she caught her breath, he continued. "Figgs contacted Senator Williams questioning my loyalty and mentioned that your visits to other inmates had been discovered. I can only conclude that someone followed me to your cell, raising Figgs's suspicions about both of us. I'm sorry," he whispered. "I never wanted to see you hurt."

Moriah's eyes narrowed as he relaxed his hold. After all Royd had done, she simply could not accept his word that he was an innocent, although irresponsible party. Stepping back, she noticed the slump of his shoulders and dismissed his penitent stance as yet another ploy to gain her trust.

Royd had done more to her than just endanger her physically, whether he betrayed her or not. He had made it impossible for her to have Ruth released so she could make a home for her. Thinking about her sister, who was still confined at Willow Valley, refueled her anger. She had to make him understand the full extent of his treachery. "Ruth," she whispered, hoping to jolt his memory and remind him that it was concern for Ruth that tempted Moriah to trust him in the first place.

His eyes flashed briefly and then dulled with remorse before he bowed his head: "I intended to bring your sister with you."

Puzzled, Moriah waited for him to continue as her heart began to pound. If he was being truthful, then where was Ruth? Why wasn't she with them? When he raised his head, Moriah wished she had never mentioned Ruth—not if the answers to her unspoken questions were the ones reflected in his eyes.

"I'll tell you everything I know about Ruth," he began, wondering how he would find the courage to tell her that her beloved sister was dead.

Royd studied Moriah as she sat by the brook, her fingers trailing in the water. She hadn't spoken a word for the past hour, and he was worried. Moriah had not reacted to the news about the death of her sister the way he expected. Instead of collapsing into hysterical tears after he described all of the horrid events that led to Ruth's demise, Moriah simply walked away from him and retreated behind a wall of silent isolation. He respected her need to grieve privately, but he was concerned that finding out that her sister was dead had sapped her own will to live.

He had approached her twice, speaking softly and gently, trying to convince her to return to the coach with him. Both times, she ignored him and continued to stare at the rushing water, her eyes dry and expressionless. Although he suspected that she was lucid, his greatest fear was that after the horror of being confined to Willow Valley for several weeks, Moriah's fragile hold on reality had snapped after hearing the news about Ruth.

He had to do something soon, or Moriah might never emerge from her private world of grief. Taking a deep breath for courage to do what was necessary, he stood beside her and held out his hand.

"It's time to leave," he said firmly, studying her face for some kind of response.

There was none.

"Moriah?"

She ignored him.

He lifted her to her feet and placed both hands on her shoulders. He shook her gently, trying to make her aware of his presence. Her eyes flashed angrily, and she pushed him away, trying to get back to her place by the brook. He grabbed her shoulders again and forced her to stay standing. "No. It's time to go," he said forcefully.

Startled by her quickness, he rebounded from a stinging slap to his face as she sat down with her back to him. He tried to pull her up again, but she refused to stand on her feet. He let her down and stood over her, holding onto one of her hands to make sure she did not try to run away again.

"You can stand and walk, or I'll carry you back to the coach. Either way, you're coming with me."

The girl started to tremble and shake. When she lifted her face to him, her eyes glistened with hatred as she spat at him. "Judas!"

Before he could utter a response, a voice rang out that caused both of them to freeze in place.

"Royd Camden, you touch that young girl and I'll whelp you good!"

Sixteen

For one brief heartbeat, Royd was tempted to laugh when he caught sight of Moll and Jack as they tottered hurriedly toward him looking like a couple of human prickle pears. One look at Moll's fearful face and Jack's furious expression made him realize that neither one of them was in a state to appreciate humor. Moll and Jack should have known that he did not intend to harm the girl, but his surrogate parents looked like they expected him to rip Moriah to shreds! Moriah was trembling so hard that her teeth chattered, and her eyes were twin pools of pale blue terror. Although Royd was grateful that the girl was merely frightened instead of deranged, he also felt that it would not take much to send her over the edge.

Royd dropped his hold on Moriah and stepped back from her. When she got to her feet and twirled away from him, Moll caught the girl in her arms and pressed her to her heaving bosom. "There now, darlin'. He won't be touchin' you," she crooned as she patted Moriah's back and glowered at Royd over the girl's shoulder.

Jack moved alongside his wife and gave Royd a hard look. "You scared the poor wee girl to death! What's wrong with you?"

"Other than having my head split open by the 'poor

wee girl' after traipsing through the woods because she decided to run off, when she'd more than likely collapse and die unless I found her, I'm perfectly fine," Royd grumbled. He swiped at the blood that kept trickling down his forehead and into his eyes. What did she hit him with—an axe?

A thunderous pain in his head made him scowl. "She's not exactly defenseless," he commented when neither Jack nor Moll seemed overly concerned about him. With the two of them hovering around her, Moriah was certainly the center of their attention, and he was loathe to admit to himself that he felt slighted.

"Maybe she knocked some sense into that thick, educated head of yours," Jack remarked. "All you had to do was follow her until she gave out. How far could she have gotten? Besides the fact you're twice as big as she is, you're healthy and strong. Look at her, Royd! She was unfair game and you know it. Now apologize for frightenin' her so she'll calm down."

Royd's mouth dropped open as Jack braced his legs and crossed his arms in front of his chest. "I told her I was sorry," Royd spat. "In return, she tried to kill me!"

"Now there's a mighty threat," Jack snickered as he gazed at the slight girl. "Must be eighty or ninety pounds of holy terror packed in a battered body that looks like somebody took turns poundin' on her face."

"Hush up, you two!" Moll admonished. "This child's weak and tremblin' like an hour-old fawn, and you're not helpin' her none by gripin' at each other."

Jack's expression turned sheepish, and Royd blushed like a street bully caught taunting a beggar. Moll was right. Moriah seemed to grow more agitated as he and Jack traded barbs. The girl was sobbing now, and Royd felt his chest tighten. They needed to get on their way without upsetting Moriah any further. He wondered if Moriah would even agree to go with them after refusing his heartfelt offer to help her. As much as he resented the girl's apparent trust in Moll and Jack, he had no choice but to be glad that Moriah was not fighting them, too. Maybe once they were in the coach with Moll acting as the girl's protector, Moriah might be calm enough to reconsider what he had told her.

When Moriah quieted, Moll took one of the girl's hands. As Jack took the other side, Moriah reached out and placed her other hand into Jack's crippled one. Slowly, they started the walk back to the coach. Royd cocked a brow, uncommonly touched by the fact the Moriah was not repulsed by Jack's disfigurement which was something that would probably send Alexandria into a swoon. When the raccoon emerged from the brook, Royd was not surprised that he scampered straight to Moriah and left Royd to walk by himself.

Royd kicked at a stone and followed after them, donning his shirt as he walked. When they reached the coach, he stepped around them and opened the door. Moll needed a boost to get inside, and the instant she let go of Moriah's hand, the girl huddled closer to Jack. The old man whispered something into her ear that made the tense look on her face ease into a shy smile before he lifted her into the coach and closed the door when Royd tried to follow.

"Moll and the girl need some time alone," he explained when Royd questioned him with a glance. "You can ride up top with me. You'll have plenty of time later to sweet talk Moriah into forgivin' you. Right now she needs a woman's touch, and you need time to practice bein' less of a bear."

If Jack had not been right, Royd would have climbed over hell's gates to get into that coach. Why couldn't he make Moriah realize that he wanted to help her? He did not want to terrorize the girl when he went after her, but his good intentions were obviously not enough to erase the fact that she had been brutalized or misused by nearly every man she had come near in the past four years.

Including him, he realized with dismay.

He thought he could not hurt her any more than he had by being careless and not realizing that he had been followed one of the times he visited with her at Apple Knoll. Forcing her to talk with him now would just be intimidation with a new face, and he could not afford to have her turn against him permanently. Moll and Jack prevented that from happening and he was truly grateful for that although he would probably wait a while before he admitted it to either one of them.

Once the two men settled onto the coachman's seat, Royd's mood lightened. He gave Bandit a playful tap and an order to lie down on top of the coach. The stupid creature was supposed to sleep during the day, but he was sure following his own schedule today. Royd reached for the reins, but Jack grabbed them out of his hands. "I'll take those," he said with a chuckle. "Even with one bad hand, I'm better at this than you are. Ever handle a team of horses?"

Royd smiled as Jack clicked the reins and the coach groaned into motion. "I usually hire a coach and a driver in Hampton when I need one. I can handle mules, though. You and Moll can be ornery and stubborn when you set your minds against me."

Jack rubbed away the sweat that was running down his face from the top of his head. "Might be because you need a pair of keepers from time to time." Changing the subject, he nodded toward the sun setting low in the horizon. "Might be dark by the time we reach David's Crossin'. You have a mind to stop at that house Moll suggested? We should reach it before the sun goes down."

Royd took a sideways glance at Jack before he answered, ignoring a feeling deep in the pit of his stomach. "You sure it's empty?"

"Lawyer said it's been empty for almost five years. No takers, though. It's a shame. Looks like a mighty fine house. Two hundred acres of land, too. A man could live like a king with that much property. The lawyer's eyes seemed to light up like a dozen candles when I mentioned you might be interested."

Royd turned around to face Jack, his fists clenched. "You . . . what?"

"Don't get your claws out," Jack said matter-of-factly. "I just wanted to see if the price was written in stone." His eyes started to dance. "Number dropped twice before I even started to play with him. People are superstitious nidgets to let that property slip through their fingers."

"Fools," Royd agreed, although he felt a bit reticent about staying at the house himself. "That house will be inhabited with nothing but sadness, not to mention a goodly amount of dirt after five years."

"Houses can't be sad or anything else when they're empty. It's people who make it a home," Jack said quietly. "They can fill it with love and laughter."

Royd swallowed hard as he remembered the love that warmed the tiny cottage in Sweetwater. It was not as run-down when he lived there with Jack and Moll as it was now, but it had never been what he wanted for his surrogate parents. The money he sent them later was always returned, and when he saw the cottage just a few weeks ago, he was angry that they never told him how bad things were for them. With Jack unable to find work, Moll earned their keep by taking in laundry. Her hands were red and chafed, and she seemed embarrassed when Royd chided her for not letting him help out.

If Jack and Moll were so set on staying at this place, Royd owed it to them to at least meet with the lawyer before dismissing the possibility that he could buy it for them. Besides, Moriah would be able to recuperate easier if she was not the daily topic of conversation in town.

There was no place in David's Crossing where she could go without arousing curiosity, especially with her face so bruised. Isolated in a country setting, Moriah could heal while Royd convinced her that he was not the devil in disguise.

Moll and Jack had helped Royd to survive the loss of his parents and chipped away the bitterness in his heart. They did not breathe life into his body, but they restored his soul. He felt sure that if anyone could help him to reach Moriah, it would be them. "We'll need supplies," Royd suggested, looking at Jack for his reaction.

Jack smiled and puffed out his chest. "Got the general store to send out a wagonload along with our trunks from the inn. Just in case we needed 'em," he added when Royd's brows furrowed.

"Don't you think we should have discussed this first?" Royd asked, wondering if he was in for any other surprises and not quite sure if he really wanted to find out.

"You were too busy rentin' this fine coach," Jack countered.

"It was the *only* coach. I hesitate to think it, Jack, but we'll have to keep it for a while if we do stay outside of town."

Jack grinned.

"I said *if*," Royd repeated. "Rats and vermin have probably moved in to that house along with Lord knows what else. Moll won't step inside any place you can't take supper off the floorboards."

"By the time we get there, the beds will have new linens and there'll be a meal bubblin' on the hearth. Don't know how much else will be done, but—"

"That's it!" Royd slammed his fist on his thigh when he realized that his first instinct had been correct. "Spill it all out, Jack. Tell me you bought the place behind my back without consulting me first and I'll . . ." Royd tightened his jaw and glowered at Jack who was grinning like he had suckered the Pope. "You don't have enough funds to buy a jug of cider!"

"I didn't buy nothin'," Jack sniffed before he started to laugh. "You did. Made a right smart investment, too."

"You're not serious. You didn't . . . Damn! You did! You forged my name, you cursed dog!" Royd grabbed the reins out of Jack's hands and clicked the horses into a trot. "I can't believe that you did this to me. And to Moll! You gave up forgery, remember? What kind of example are you setting?" he growled. "If I'd even mentioned picking a lock you'd hog-tie me to the bed, remember?"

"Sometimes a man has to take control of a situation usin' whatever skill he's got."

"Hah! This isn't the first time you took a convenient backslide, is it? Admit it! You forged a bank draft to get the funds to send me to school!"

"I ain't admittin' nothin'! You needed a chance to make somethin' proper of yourself. Me and Moll got it for you."

"On stolen money!"

"Figured it was a good cause. You kept to the straight and narrow, too, 'cept for what you did at Apple Knoll. Seems to me that pickin' a few locks and breakin' into places you shouldn't be got that girl into a real fine mess."

"And I'm sure you'll remind me every opportunity you get," Royd spewed. Wasn't it enough that he was sleepless with guilt? He did not think he could stand it if Jack tossed it in his face, too.

Jack laid his hand on top of Royd's. "You wouldn't be a man I could be proud of if you didn't try to help them women in that prison. It wasn't your fault that the warden found out what the girl was doin' and misused the girl. Me and Moll love you like you was our own flesh. We're only tryin' to help you the best way we know how."

Royd felt a well of tears in his eyes. Unaccustomed to displaying his emotions, he blinked them away. "I hope you settled on a decent price for the place."

"Got the lawyer to hold your note for sixty days to make sure you like it, but I had to promise him you'd print some wretched book of poetry he wrote."

Royd chuckled. "How many free books does he want?"

"Fifty, but I told him he'd have to settle for twenty-five now and the rest when the sale was final. You shudda seen his face. He was so happy you'd a thought I gave the man a promise to get rid of his ugly wife." Jack shivered. "Must be somethin' sorry to be married to a woman who looks like a hairy black spider."

Royd burst out laughing, picturing this bald little midget of a man haggling with a country lawyer for a property that no one else wanted and sealing the bargain with a promise to print the man's bloody book of poetry! It made as much sense as a former thief trying to convince an ex-convict and escapee from a lunatic asylum that by working together they could make life better for female inmates.

Moriah sat inside the coach and held onto Moll's hand for dear life. Whatever the relationship the older man and woman had with Royd Camden, they were certainly able to control him and keep him at bay. As long as Moriah stayed close to either one of them, she was sure Royd would not get near enough to hurt her. Jack promised to make Royd ride with him, and sure enough, Royd had done it!

If Moriah were honest, she would admit that she had surely given Royd plenty of provocation to hit her, yet he never raised a hand to strike her—oddly failing to fulfill her expectations. After being pelted with sundry useless, but stinging objects back at the brook, he never lashed out at her. He just turned the other cheek.

Judging by the amount of blood on his face, Moriah must have really gashed his head open when she hit him with that rock. She was not simpleminded enough to believe that Royd could not have hit her and tossed her over his shoulder when he caught up with her. Still, he hadn't, and although she credited Moll and Jack's warning with preventing Royd from doing just that very thing, something about the way Royd looked at her tugged at her conscience.

Sorrow and pity were mixed with a plea for understanding that she saw in his expression back at the asylum when he urged her to leave her cage. They were the same emotions that made his deep green eyes grow darker at the brook when she rejected his explanations and attacked him. Even then he never struck her, and Moriah realized for the first time that the blow to her head in the asylum had come from behind and not from him. She could not blame him for Ruth's death, either, and she sniffed back the tears that filled her eyes.

He should be sorry anyway, she mused, refusing to acknowledge how gently he had treated her. It was his fault that she had been sent to Willow Valley, and she would not give him the opportunity to take advantage of her again. How many times must she forgive him?

Seventy times seven.

Moriah bit her lip, wishing Ruth could be here to help her. It was so hard to imagine what life would be like without her. She glanced at Moll, who opened one eye and shook herself awake.

"I thought you were restin'," Moll apologized and tucked Moriah's arm protectively under hers. "I guess I can't blame you for bein' fitful. It's a dreadful thing they done to you, and you must have thought we were part of it. Poor Royd was near out of his mind when you ran off."

Moriah stiffened and pulled her hand away. Were Moll and Jack simply playing roles that Royd Camden

assigned to them? Were they trying to fool her into believing that Royd Camden truly wanted to help her?
Why?

Moll and Jack looked too sincere to be part of Royd's
wicked world of lies and deception. Yet thinking back
over her last few weeks at Apple Knoll, Moriah realized
that she had grown a tad cocky. It was foolish to tempt
fate by continuing her visits to the inmates with her release so imminent. Sophie and Iona, however, were her
friends. They would never ever tattle tales to the warden
unless . . .

Moriah closed her eyes and took a deep breath. Lester Figgs and Tamin Jones had more than one brutal
method of forcing a confession. Why hadn't that possibility occurred to her before? Reluctantly, she admitted
that there was a remote chance that Royd hadn't handed
her over to the warden. That thought made her want to
retch when she considered how awfully she had treated
him. If only she knew for sure! One way was to ask him
to return her diary. If he still had it, that meant that he
did not give it to the warden. It was the only thing she
could think of to test his loyalty—or confirm his betrayal.

Moll sighed as she squeezed her, and Moriah looked
up into her face. "Royd brought us with him to help
you," Moll said quietly. "I'm feelin' a little guilty myself.
I've missed the boy. So has Jack, but we thought it best
. . . When Royd showed up a few weeks ago and told us
what happened, I didn't really care what was happenin'
to you or why. It was just so good to have him home
again." Moll's eyes filled with tears, and her chin started
to quiver. "I didn't know how bad it was for you till I saw
you and Royd told me what it was like at Willow Valley.
Will you forgive an old woman for bein' selfish?" she
whispered.

Moriah was so confused she could not begin to sort
out fact from fiction or truth from fable. She could no

sooner refuse Moll's heartfelt request than deny her own need for an ally. She wiped a tear off Moll's cheeks and slipped her hand back into Moll's as she attempted a small smile.

"You settle back, darlin' and let me hold onto you," Moll crooned.

Moriah laid her head on Moll's shoulder, grateful for the comfort the woman offered. Her eyes drooped closed as the sway of the coach and Moll's tenderness lulled her to sleep with plans for escaping Royd Camden fashioning her dreams.

♣

Seventeen

The horses turned onto the winding path that led to the estate and shied away from the scraggly branches of overgrown evergreens and pyracantha that turned the once-manicured hedgerow into a maze of thorns decorated with orange-red pomes. While Jack concentrated on urging the horses forward, Royd strained his eyes to see what lay ahead at the top of the hill, beyond the trees that obscured his view. Smoke billowed in the sky, and the smell of roasted mutton filled the air with an aroma that made Jack's belly rumble. Royd laughed as his empty stomach echoed a similar hunger. Jack's suggestion to stay here suddenly seemed like a good idea, although Royd would not be quick to admit it to him. Neither would he even consider buying the manor house that started to take shape when they rounded a bend, despite Jack's apparent fascination with the place.

Royd studied the mansion as it came fully into view, his breath catching the same way it did the first time he had seen it. Standing against a backdrop of low, green-covered mountains in the distance and wispy white clouds that dotted a summer blue sky overhead, it was massive, but picturesque. The sun was just beginning to slip into a promise of another hot day tomorrow and cast brilliant streaks of fuchsia and orange across the sky that created an aura surrounding the building that almost made it glow.

Round twin turrets on either side of the imposing fieldstone manor house lent a medieval touch to the stately, three-storied structure. The hip roof, made of bronze-colored tiles, sloped inward at an uncommonly steep angle. Four paneled glass windows too dirty to catch the light jutted out at equal distances from each other in the roof.

As the coach neared the front entrance, Royd's attention was centered on the front door, arched to match an unusual curved entry cover and set with a band of stained glass windows. Massive pairs of Romanesque windows on either side of the door, which repeated on the second and third stories, were nearly obscured by overgrowth from gardens that had been left untended for far too long.

"Grand, isn't it?" Jack murmured after bringing the coach to a halt.

"Fit for a king," Royd muttered as he climbed down and stretched his legs. "You'd better pray that the inside is a sight more ordered than the grounds or you're going to answer to Moll. This was all your idea, although why you'd even think about living in a miniature castle is beyond my imagination."

When Jack ignored him and continued to stare at the house, Royd decided to let the matter drop. He was hungry, bone-weary, and covered with a day's travel dust. Truth to tell, he was more worried about Moriah than he was about the house. "Take the coach around to the rear and see if there isn't a stable or something for the horses. I'll see Moll and Moriah inside," he suggested.

Jack barely acknowledged him, and Royd shook his head as he walked back to the door of the coach wondering if he could convince Jack that the house and its upkeep were a bit too grand for his purse. Even if Royd could afford to buy the property, he certainly would not be able to furnish it, let alone heat the huge relic in the winter!

For now, however, Royd had to agree that it was the perfect hiding place to mend a girl's broken spirit. With a touch of luck, he might be able to convince Moriah to let him help her. With a second dose of good fortune, they would all be off the estate before the first frost.

Royd had sixty days to reclaim his note. Feeling magnanimous, he thought he might even agree to print the last twenty-five copies of the lawyer's poetry book. How big could it be, anyway? Keeping the lawyer satisfied would also ease the twinge of guilt Royd knew he would have when he rescinded his offer to buy the property.

Moll and Jack would be disappointed, but he would find them something more suitable if they would not agree to come and live with him—something he fully intended to insist upon. No one in Hampton knew about his surrogate parents, but Royd was growing less concerned about answering to his acquaintances than he was committed to staying close to Moll and Jack.

The coach door opened before Royd reached it, and he had to step quickly to help Moll as she backed out of the door, causing the coach to tilt to one side under her weight.

"Thank you," she gushed as her feet touched the earth. "It's good to be on solid ground," she said between gasps as she caught her breath and tried to fan the heated blush from her face. "Now help the girl. She's every bit as anxious as I was to breathe fresh air."

When Moll stepped aside, Royd looked up to see Moriah waiting timorously for the offer of his hand. Wrapped in Moll's cape with the deep hood covering her head, her eyes seemed to swallow up her face. When she leaned forward and out of the shadows to place her small hand in his, Royd noticed that her eyes were red

and puffy and her cheeks were tearstained as though she
had been crying. He felt another stab of guilt when she
looked at him as though he were a beast about to devour
her in a single gulp. Her hand was cold and clammy, and
he could feel her trembling as she alighted from the
coach.

"We're going to stay here," he explained gently when
she pulled out of his grasp and gazed nervously at the
house. "No one knows where you are so you'll be completely safe. When you're well enough to travel, you'll be
free to leave. I'll help you to relocate if you'll allow me
to. I hope we can talk and settle the misunderstandings
between us, but I'll leave that to when you're feeling up
to it. Would you like to go inside now?"

Moriah looked at him and then her eyes darted to
Moll who was standing a few feet away.

"Moll and Jack will stay here, too," he said reassuringly as he placed his hand on the small of her back. He
felt her stiffen and saw her shoulders square, but she let
him lead her toward the house and up to the door. He
was glad that Moll walked alongside the girl for added
encouragement, although the girl's steps still seemed a
trifle hesitant.

A square brass doorplate seemed to catch Moriah's
attention, and he watched with interest as she moved
closer and traced the letters of a foreign word with her
fingertips. A tiny smile played on her lips. *"Leibchen,"*
she whispered and turned around to face Moll while she
pointed to the doorplate, her eyes glowing with pleasure.
"Loved one," she repeated in English, grimacing slightly
and touching the side of her face.

The tension seemed to ease from her shoulders, and
her earlier reticence seemed to dissipate. Royd wondered if she spoke a foreign language. The word seemed
to please her. Was it a term of endearment that meant
something special to her? It was good to see something
other than fear on her face, and he was reluctant to

upset her with a question. Instead, he tried the handle to the door, not really expecting to find it locked. He was surprised when Moriah walked through the portal without waiting for either Moll or himself. He heard her gasp and quickly stepped inside after her.

The foyer was splendid enough to take anyone's breath away, and he realized that the agent's report on the interior of the house did not do justice to its magnificence. He relaxed when he saw that Moriah's reaction was one of pleasure and not of fright. A magnificent, ornate crystal chandelier hung above a gleaming marble floor the color of pale buttercups in a room that no doubt was every bit as large as a formal ballroom. Thick carved mahogany envelope doors on the right and the left led to closed off rooms that Royd could only assume were drawing rooms or parlors. At the far end of the room, a dramatically wide staircase with marble pillars at the bottom led to the second floor.

Moll edged next to Royd and clapped her hands. "I knew it would be beautiful! I'm so glad this house got cleaned up. Jack said he'd arranged everything, and he did a fine job." She blushed when Royd cocked his head. "I had nothin' to do with it," she said with a saucy toss of her head.

Royd laughed softly. "I know better than to swallow that fairy story. You and Jack plotted this together, just like you did when you selected a school for me and pretended you didn't know how fine it was." He looked over to Moriah and then nudged Moll to look at her, too.

Moriah appeared to be absolutely bedazzled by her surroundings. Her eyes were wide with wonder and there was a look on her face that Royd wished he could paint and keep forever. The haunting sadness he had detected earlier was still reflected in her eyes, but so was astonishment and joy. It was the second time Royd had seen her look almost radiant—like she looked when she had shown him her little garden. Amidst such opulence, however, the girl looked even more like a bedraggled waif, and Royd looked at her appearance with deep regret and anger toward the men who had treated her so harshly.

Moriah self-consciously pushed her matted hair from her face when she caught him staring at her, but Royd was relieved to see that she also appeared to be less afraid of him. Moll took the girl by the arm and steered her across the room and up the steps. "Let's see about a hot bath and then it's supper in a nice, soft bed for you, young lady."

Royd chuckled as he watched them go up the stairs, remembering how he fought against taking a bath when he first came to live with Moll and Jack. If he recalled correctly, his first bath had been in the creek, not too far from Jack's favorite fishing spot, where Jack dumped him and tossed him the soap with orders to wash himself or be washed!

He had the feeling that Moriah would not squawk at all. Poor Pale Eyes probably had not had a bath since . . . His pulse began to pound when he thought of the peepholes that intruded on the women's bathing area at Apple Knoll. How many men had spied on Moriah when she bathed? Dismissing that destructive thought, he turned to tour the rest of the first floor.

By the time she followed Moll to the top of the steps, Moriah stopped and clutched her chest. Her heart was pounding so hard she thought the sound would echo throughout the huge foyer. Grief, shame, and exhaustion clamored at her weakened defenses. Her emotions seemed to be ruling her body, especially since learning that Ruth was gone, leaving Moriah utterly alone in a world that seemed bent on destroying her.

Royd did not really shock her when he told her that Ruth died at Willow Valley. Deep in the sweet, secret part of her spirit that she kept private even from herself most of the time, Moriah realized that Ruth's death was not a sudden reality that jolted into her consciousness even though Royd was the one who had the courage to tell her.

Moriah suspected Ruth was dead a long time ago. Last year, the closeness she felt for her sister, a sort of invisible bond that she could sense even when they were apart, had faded away. Maybe that explained why she had begun a frantic search for her sister. Her visits to the other inmates were perhaps an attempt to deny her suspicions and to keep Ruth's memory alive with an ever-faithful prayer that she was wrong. As time passed and the date of their scheduled release approached, her fears grew but remained unspoken. She wondered why Reverend Beecham stopped coming to visit. Did he know about Ruth and simply could not tell Moriah that she was dead?

Moriah had grieved the loss of her sister's companionship for nearly four years. When Royd told her why Ruth died at Willow Valley, her resolve to make Lester Figgs pay dearly for his debauchery reached a fearsome intensity. When they had finally come, Moriah's tears were not for herself. After experiencing the terror of confinement at Willow Valley, she wept because she had not been able to comfort Ruth when she needed her the most.

Royd Camden's role in this whole sick scheme of things was hard to ascertain. Was he really innocent of deliberately betraying her? Probably not. Maybe he simply felt guilty about what he had done. To salve his conscience, he must have decided to help her. What about the others at Apple Knoll? They needed help, too. Would he really agree to tell the truth in his report? Moriah had to admit that rescuing her from the asylum took courage, and she was touched when Royd told her that he intended to take Ruth with them. He risked his own future by coming to her aid, and she found herself beginning to respect him just for that alone. It was just so confusing!

She finally decided to reserve judgment of his motives for later when she could figure out a way to discover the truth. Turning around, Moriah glanced at the foyer below. In spite of herself, she could not quite believe that Royd had brought her to this wondrous place. When she read the doorplate, she was stunned. *Leibchen.* How many times did Uncle Jed call her that when he tucked her into bed at night when she was still a little girl? It was almost like a sign that her uncle was watching over her, and suddenly she did not feel quite so abandoned or alone anymore. For hours on end these past few weeks, she had prayed to God to send her an avenging angel to rescue her and wreak justice on the wicked men at Apple Knoll.

Royd Camden was the least likely angel she had ever expected God to send. She shuddered. Did David feel a little unsettled with God's plan when he faced Goliath?

Moriah blinked as Moll shook her gently out of her reverie. "What's the matter?" Moll whispered, her face etched with concern.

Moriah attempted a weak smile and squeezed Moll's hand.

"You scared me. Didn't you hear me tellin' you to follow me?"

Moriah shook her head and frowned with embarrassment.

"You probably knew I was headin' in the wrong direction," Moll suggested with a grin. "Your rooms are the other way. Give me your hand, and we'll discover them together."

Moriah laced her fingers with Moll's, and they walked down a wide hall that seemed like it was more appropriate for a museum or a fancy hotel. On the left, pictures draped with heavy cloth dusted with spiderwebs hung on

the wall between richly carved doors. Moll opened a
door on the right and quickly closed it before Moriah
could peek inside. When they reached the second door,
however, Moll whisked Moriah inside and closed the
door behind them.

Moriah took a quick double look about the room before she gasped aloud. Her eyes watered with longing at
the sight of a large copper bathing tub that had delicate
blue flowers painted on the rim. Fresh linens and a
sculpted cake of scented soap lay on a stool at the side of
the tub. The fragrance from the soap seemed to fill the
closed room with just a hint of lemon. Several buckets of
fresh water sat on the floor by the tub ready for use.
Although there was no telltale steam rising from the
buckets, Moriah felt so filthy that she would have bathed
in ice water and been eternally grateful!

As Moll went to draw apart the heavy drapes at the
far end of the room and open a window, Moriah slipped
the cape from her shoulders and laid it on a chair next to
the door. Walking as reverently as she did when she was
in church, she approached the tub and ran her fingers
down its sleek surface. She peered inside and gave a
horrified cry when she saw her own pitiful reflection. She
covered her eyes with her hands. Merciful God! She did
not even recognize the creature she saw staring back at
her!

Moll rushed over and tugged at Moriah's hands until
Moriah had no choice but to look at the woman. "Now
don't you get yourself all upset," she scolded. "All you
need is a good soak in that tub and a few more days to
let those bruises heal 'fore you'll be good as new."

Moriah swiped at her hair and felt the tears well in her
eyes again. A bath and a few days of rest would not
make her hair grow. There were so many knots and
tangles in her hair she just knew they would never come
out, and she felt her bottom lip quiver.

"I can't promise to give you a mane of hair, but we'll

put a shine on your hair that will put a dainty smile on your face again. Now strip off that ugly orange rag you're wearin' while I see if there's any hot water ready." Moll tilted Moriah's chin up for her. "Where's that mettle I saw in you when Royd tried to catch you, girl? Don't seem right you'd be losin' it now."

Moriah sniffled and straightened her backbone. She never really gave her appearance much thought until now, and she did not want to disappoint Moll who was trying to be so nice to her.

"That's the spirit! I'll be back in a few minutes," Moll said with enthusiasm that was hard to resist.

Moriah cast a worried look at the door, wondering if Moll was going to lock it. Although the room was larger than her prison cell, Moriah could not bear it if she heard another lock click—now or ever again.

Moll's face twisted into a frown when Moriah squeezed her hand. "Are you worried someone will come in? Royd and Jack have strict orders to stay away."

Moriah shook her head and led Moll to the door, opened it, and pointed to the key that rested in the brass lock beneath the crystal knob. Moll smiled, pulled out the key, and placed it in Moriah's hand. "You keep this," she murmured, then disappeared into the hall. When she returned a few moments later, she handed Moriah two more keys. "One's for the sittin' room and the other's for your bedchamber," she said as she closed the door to show Moriah a bolt on the inside. "You can latch this if you want to feel more secure, but no one is ever going to lock you in your room. Ever," she added with a stern look for emphasis.

Moriah sighed with relief. "Th-thank—"

"Don't try to say anything, darlin'. Just you rest easy now and before you can peel them crusty clothes off, I'll be back to help you bathe."

Moll opened the door and slipped into the hall. After Moriah closed the door, she listened to Moll's footsteps as Moll scurried away. Moriah forced dark memories of the past four years to the back of her mind. Determined not to wear that wretched orange gown any longer than another minute, she shed the tattered thing and rolled it into a ball. On impulse, she put on Moll's cape and carried what was left of her prison gown over to the opened window and tossed it outside. She would never wear anything orange again!

Leaning her elbows on the windowsill, she looked out at the countryside and felt a surge of excitement quicken her pulse. She had been too scared when she was running through the forest to escape from Royd to even notice that her worldview was so different from what it had been for four long years. Trees! She could actually see the tops of trees again. She marveled at the different colors that ranged from the deep evergreen of the pines, the pale, wispy green of the willows, and the verdant maples and oaks. Pale pink blossoms on a nearby mimosa tree looked lovelier than she remembered, and deep orange berries on the pyracantha along the drive added unusual color to the view.

Branches swayed in the wind, looking as though the trees were bowing to the majesty of their Creator. Folding her hands, she bowed her head to pray—for herself, for Uncle Jed and Ruth, for Moll and Jack, and finally, for Royd Camden. It was time to start over, and she was grateful that God had answered her prayers and given her a second chance. As she turned and walked toward the bathing tub, she felt a new sense of energy that washed away her fears. She did not know what the future held, but she was certain of one thing: She was not getting out of that bathing tub until she had scrubbed away every trace of Willow Valley and Apple Knoll from her body!

After bathing and eating a quick supper, Royd took a tour of the entire house, with the exception of Moriah's suite of rooms which Moll guarded like a seasoned sentry. His first glimpse of the inside of the house had melted his earlier suspicions. His tour, however, only confirmed his agent's report and his own business-sided intuition that made his initial misgivings appear to be just on the shy side of brilliant. With the exception of that magnificent foyer, a comfortable library, and a hotel-sized kitchen, every other room on the first floor was a mere shell! There was no plaster on the walls let alone a stick of furniture. The second floor was no better. Except for a pair of suites, no doubt intended for the master and mistress of the house, the only other rooms decently finished were a nursery and a servant's chamber. Every door he opened revealed rooms as unfinished and unfurnished as the rooms on the first floor! The third floor was nothing more than an attic, with wooden studs starkly outlining the owner's intentions to have half a dozen additional bedrooms at some point in the future.

Any ideas he had about Jack hoodwinking the lawyer quickly evaporated into irony, although he calculated that even with the cost of finishing off the house, the property was worth nearly twice the price of the estate which Jack assured him was agreed to by the lawyer. Returning to the kitchen, he found Jack nibbling on the leg of lamb left from supper with a contented look on his face.

"Got a real bargain, didn't you?" he muttered between bites.

Royd held out his hand, and when Jack looked at him questioningly, he took a deep breath. "I want the note you so proudly forged my name to."

Without interrupting his feast, Jack nodded toward his waistcoat which was hanging on a peg by the back door. "It's in my pocket. I can't believe you don't trust me," he complained as he wiped his mouth with his sleeve. "No sense lyin' 'bout it. Read it for yourself.

Everything's included that's in the house, 'cept the food.
You owe Mike Finnegan for that. I told him you'd be
back in David's Crossing tomorrow to settle up the account at the general store before you stop at the livery to
get your horse. Word spread pretty fast 'bout your bein'
the new owner, and he didn't seem to mind extendin'
credit for the supplies. Moll made another list of things
we'll be needin'," he added as Royd started to read the
note. "I asked the girl who made supper to come back
tomorrow. Moll's plum exhausted, and she'll be needin'
extra hands to get this place fixed up."

Royd stopped reading and raised a brow. "What girl?
I didn't see anyone else here besides us."

"Said her name was Anna. She was leavin' through
the back when I brought the coach around. She lives
with her widowed mama and half a dozen sisters. They
worked all day sweepin' and washin' with a few others
who were more anxious to earn a meal and a few coins
than to be worried about what happened here. Guess it
wouldn't hurt to have 'em come back till—"

"Stop a minute," Royd grumbled, thinking about how
much it would cost to support the entire family. "There
are only enough rooms for us to use. The rest of the
house isn't even finished off."

Jack waved his argument aside with the greasy bone
still in his hand. "Poor girl lost her papa. Lost the farm,
too. Her mama is strugglin' real hard to make a livin' for
her girls. Can't hurt none to help 'em out, and we could
use the extra hands. Thought they might stay on the
third floor. It'd be easier than goin' back and forth to
that lean-to they live in."

Royd threw his hands up in the air. "Seven females?
The third floor is nothing better than a garret. They're
probably better off in the lean-to. Don't I have enough
problems on my mind as it is? Moriah needs peace and
quiet. With that many people here, the house will be

nothing short of bedlam! This isn't a home for waywards or unfortunates, dammit!"

"Eight if you count the mama," Jack corrected as he picked a piece of meat out from between his front teeth.

"No!" Royd thundered.

Jack looked at him like he had marbles for brains. "Sure it is. There's seven girls and the mama—"

"I'm not going to argue about the number, you old fox!"

"Good. Then it's settled. I didn't think you'd mind. I'm glad I told the girl to bring them all here as soon as the sun's up." He looked at Royd and hedged. "I don't want nothin' to hurt Moriah, either. I'll ask 'em to come back in a week."

Royd ran his fingers through his hair and decided to read the note instead of arguing with Jack. Royd would let the woman bring her seven offspring to work next week and then pay her off at the end of the day.

Sitting across from Jack, Royd laid the note on the table and leaned on his elbows, propping his head in his hands. When he finished reading, he shook his head. "You really didn't exaggerate, did you?" he said, his voice an odd blend of disbelief and admiration.

Jack beamed. "Sorta like dancin' in a fairy ring." He chuckled. "Can't quite believe it myself."

"I suppose you'll credit the charm of your magical presence for getting this price, although it's not unusual for property this valuable to sit for a few years until a suitable buyer comes along."

"The bargain is signed and sealed," Jack pouted. "You're not thinkin' 'bout leavin' already? You haven't even seen the land that goes with the house. Be a shame to change your mind till you do."

"I have sixty days to do that unless someone challenges my signature," Royd said as his mind raced with a dozen reasons why he should not even consider buying the property and settling here. He was city born and bred and knew next to nothing about living on a country estate. For all his braggadocio, Jack could not possibly know enough about farming to fill a fairy's thimble. Royd had a business to run in Hampton, a betrothed who thought that country living was only one notch above hell, and a scandal at Apple Knoll that needed to be resolved without destroying the reputation he worked so hard to build, despite the coterie of men like Fithian Williams.

Deep in thought, Royd mumbled a cursory good-night to Jack and headed toward his rooms. His first concern at the moment was getting a good night's rest before tackling the biggest challenge of his life that had eyes the color a man could spend the rest of his life admiring.

Eighteen

Moriah woke to the delightful warbling of thrush and starlings as the first hint of dawn warmed her face. Snuggling beneath a soft, lightweight blanket, she stared up to admire the filmy, pale gold fabric draped elegantly between the four corner bedposts. The featherbed felt so luxurious that it was almost sinful, but after a week of recuperating, Moriah was anxious to stretch her boundaries beyond her three room suite.

Despite Moll's insistence that she rest inside a few more days, Moriah felt strong enough to resume some kind of normal routine. The problem was that she did not quite know what normal was supposed to be. She lay in bed for a few moments toying with the ribbons at the top of her gown and glancing around the room. With the bed set up high on a platform that required a three-step riser, she felt like a bird looking out from its nest.

The bedchamber, which reminded Moriah of a room designed for a princess, was painted pale gold with small green leaves stenciled in a border at the top of the walls. Thick gold carpet trimmed in emerald green covered the floors and matched the heavy brocade drapes that were pulled back to let in both light and air. A tall cherry wood wardrobe, with a matching dresser and bed table, had the same heavy scrolling as the ornate headboard on the oversized bed.

A chaise lounge which sat near the fireplace was more comfortable than the cot Moriah slept in for the past four years at Apple Knoll. While Moll altered the clothing that curiously had been in the room, Moriah had moved from the lounge to the bed and back again as she regained her strength.

Now she was ready to do more than that although she had one last thing to do before she ventured beyond Moll's watchful eye. Slipping out of bed, she lifted the hem of her gown and descended from the platform. Padding barefoot across the room, she opened the door to the adjacent dressing room. Closing the door behind her, she was careful not to make a sound. With her heart beating wildly with anticipation, she approached the dressing glass. Before she lost her courage, she whipped off the sheet that Moll discreetly put over it to prevent Moriah from being distressed by the sight of her injuries.

Moriah blinked her eyes, gaped at her image, and stepped closer to the glass. Her hand reached out to touch her image in the mirror and then stopped in mid-air. Pleasure curled her lips into a smile that did not hurt anymore. The bruises on her cheeks were gone, although her cheeks still looked pinched from the weight she had lost. The circles under her eyes had faded to a faint bluish tint that made her eyes look even larger.

Her hair, tousled from a night's sleep, looked as shiny and clean as it felt. The ends, lovingly trimmed by Moll, barely touched her shoulders, but the knots and tangles were gone thanks to Moll's patience.

It was a miracle, Moriah decided, and so was how quickly her mouth healed. Although she still had a few tiny ulcers, she could eat solid food and she could even talk without pain!

Now that she was confident about her appearance, she went into the bathing room to wash her face before returning to the dressing room. Dressing quickly in the mauve gown Moll had laid out the night before, she sat down at the dressing table and brushed her hair. She wrinkled her nose as she tried to figure out what to do with it. It was too short to put into a single braid like she used to do. Until her hair grew a few more inches, she would have to let it fall naturally.

After much thought, she made a center part and braided the section of hair on either side of her face, tying the ends with bits of ribbon she found in one of the drawers. She pulled the braids to the back of her head and tied the ends together. Humming softly as she worked, she wondered if Moll would be surprised or scolding when she arrived expecting her to be abed.

Satisfied there was nothing more to be done with her hair, she tidied the bed linens, but she was too excited to sit and wait for Moll. Poor woman, she thought as she paced the room. She had spent every hour tending to Moriah since they arrived. Last night she finally agreed to let Moriah sleep alone and abandoned the chaise lounge to join her husband in a room across the hall.

Judging by the light that streamed into the room now, it was still very early. Moriah decided to quell the curiosity she had about the door in the corner of her room while she was waiting for Moll. Opening the door slowly, she was surprised to see a circular series of steps in a small, rounded chamber no larger than an ordinary closet. Recognizing this as the turret, Moriah quickly lit a candle and climbed the narrow steps while holding onto a slim railing. She was nearly out of breath when she finally reached a door at the top. She twisted the handle several times until it caught, and the door squeaked open.

Moriah stepped through the doorway onto a sunny terrace and blew out the candle. The panorama was nothing short of spectacular and she walked over to the low stone wall to get a better view. Facing out the front of the house slightly above the level of the third floor, the vista was almost identical to what she had seen from the window in her bathing room. From this vantage point, however, she could see even farther and the view was even more majestic.

Turning around, she saw the mountains far in the distance behind the house. Pillowy white clouds seemed like dollops of whipped cream that capped the mountain peaks. She dropped her eyes and surveyed the estate, noting several empty pastures and fallow fields as well as numerous outbuildings near the main house all connected by a maze of dirt roads. Sunlight danced across a small lake, and when she looked closer, she could see what appeared to be an abandoned cottage nestled on the far shore.

Eden.

Lush and green, bursting with peaceful serenity and the sweet smell of nature.

Moriah sighed. How she yearned to wander outdoors —without fear or restriction. It had been such a very long time! Moistening her lips, she made a decision that brought a smile to her heart.

Her first thought was that Moll or Jack would disapprove or that she would encounter Royd, but none of them was likely to be up yet. She had not seen anyone other than Moll for the past week, although she heard the men's voices from time to time. What could it hurt to take a walk around the grounds? She could look for berries to have with breakfast, and her mouth began to water. She could cook breakfast today, too, and have it ready for everyone as a way of showing them how much she appreciated what they had done for her.

Retracing her steps, she had to go slowly and resented blowing out the candle. She returned to her room, glad to escape the dark stairwell, and looked around for a basket to hold the fruit. Finding none, she settled on a scarf that she could fashion into a makeshift pouch. After checking to make sure all the keys to her rooms were still safely hidden underneath a corner of the carpet, she slipped out of her room and made her way back to the foyer.

Dismissing the idea of trying to open either of the large sets of doors on either side of the room, she walked down a hall toward the back of the house which led, fortunately, to the kitchen. It was fit for a hotel, she mused, as she noted a large cooking stove as well as a hearth lined with several ovens. A large wooden table with six chairs sat at one end of the room; at the other end, an opened door revealed a well-stocked pantry with yet another door she decided to leave for another time to investigate.

Crossing to the back door, she slipped outside and headed toward the woods beyond the barn. She had not taken more than a dozen steps before an old friend came around the corner of the barn.

"Bandit!" she cried and ran to greet him. The raccoon scampered to her outstretched arms and nuzzled her hands as she petted him. "Moll told me you've been exiled outdoors. How do you like this place, fella?" Moriah had not quite gotten over the shock of finding Bandit the day she left Willow Valley, although Moll told her that try as he might, Royd simply could not get rid of the pesty critter.

"I'm going berry picking," she announced as she pointed toward the woods. "Want to come?"

The raccoon followed her as far as the edge of the forest and then settled down to sleep, much to Moriah's dismay.

"I guess you're getting back to normal," she said, sighing. "At least instinct tells you what to do. I wish I knew what was normal for me." She patted the raccoon on the head. "I'll see you later tonight," she promised, trying to figure out a way to sneak him up to her room.

As she walked down a narrow path, Moriah kept her

eyes focused on the lush foliage. Before long, she spotted a patch of wild raspberries, but got no more than a handful which she plopped right into her mouth! Tart and juicy, she rolled the raspberries on her tongue and savored every last bite.

Encouraged, she moved on, envisioning the look of delight on her hosts' faces when she had breakfast on the table when they came downstairs. And in the middle of the feast, she would set the biggest mound of raspberries she could find!

Royd jumped out of bed, dressed hurriedly, and tore down the hall taking the back steps to the kitchen two at a time. It sounded like an invasion was taking place directly behind the house, and he was going to strangle Jack the minute he found him! What the bloody hell was going on?

When Royd opened the back door, he blinked, muttered an oath, and bolted outside.

"Mighty neighborly of you," Jack said to a man who had a wagonload of crates filled with squawking chickens, squealing pigs, and several bleating goats. Perched on top of a pile of feed sacks sat a boy of about fourteen who stared at two dairy cows tied to the back of the wagon. Jack turned and grinned at Royd.

"Royd, this is Jonathan Gates. He's got a farm a few miles to the other side of David's Crossing. He's been carin' for some of the animals. Now that the estate's been sold, the lawyer told him to bring 'em back."

"Mr. Camden." The man doffed his hat and smiled nervously toward the house. "Got a list here just so you'll know everything has been returned. 'Course, they're not the same animals. Not after five years. But the count is right. I could use some help unloadin' if you've a mind. Brought my boy with me, too, but it'd be quicker with some extra hands."

Royd shook his head and pointed toward the road. "I

don't want the animals," he said firmly and gave Jack a scowl.

"You have to take them. The lawyer said so," the farmer argued. "Everything that was on the estate when the count died goes with the sale. To you. I got my own farm to handle," he said, again glancing nervously toward the house.

Royd wondered if the man was afraid that the count's ghost was about to appear. The man's weather-beaten face looked ashen, and a tic in his cheek started to twitch faster. "We'll have no need—"

"Sure we will," Jack interrupted and rolled up his sleeves. "You take that wagon on back by the barn. We'll help you unload."

Royd pulled Jack aside and lowered his voice. "What in blazes are we going to do with . . . with those animals?"

Jack shrugged. "Raise 'em and slaughter 'em is my guess."

"Who's going to do that?" Royd muttered under his breath.

"We are."

"Like hell!"

"Keep your voice down," Jack scolded and waved reassuringly to Gates, motioning for him to move the wagon. "Jonathan Gates didn't come all this way to turn around and haul them animals back to his farm. He's only doin' what he was told to do. Besides, you'll hurt his feelin's."

Royd stifled a laugh. "Hurt his feelings? The man can't wait to get out of here. He'll be real pleased when I tell him to keep the damned things. I'll even write him a bill of sale, but I'm not going to start stocking this estate!"

"Moll sure would like fresh eggs." Jack sighed. "She could make butter, too. Reckon you can tell her why she has to do without."

"Bloody hell!" Royd ran his hands through his hair. "Who's going to milk those . . . those . . ."

Jack grinned. "Leave it to me. I'll take care of everything." He turned and started walking toward the wagon. "Bring it 'round here," he shouted, and Royd followed as they headed toward the other side of the barn. He did not know where to put the animals, let alone what to feed them or when. He was not a farmer! Damn Jack for playing on his feelings for Moll! He never could deny her anything when he lived in Sweetwater, and he sure could not start now.

By the time the animals were unloaded and placed in their new homes and fed, which Gates was quick to organize and explain, Royd felt like he had done a week's work. Gates had an older son who was willing to care for the animals as long as he did not have to stay on the estate after dark, and Royd gratefully agreed to hire him. "Tell William he can start tomorrow," he suggested and confirmed their arrangement with a handshake. "What do I owe you for today?"

"Everythin's been settled up," Gates answered. "Five years ago, after . . . well, the lawyer set it up so's I could keep the offspring in return for carin' for the lot of 'em. It gave me a good start. No need for anythin' more. Glad to have someone on the place. Maybe it'll chase away . . . well, good luck to you, Mr. Camden. You need anything—anything at all, you just tell my Will. He'll know how to help you along till you're settled in."

Royd nodded his thanks and watched the wagon until it pulled out of sight. It had been a long time, if ever, that he had felt beholden to another man. It gave him an odd feeling, and he felt something stir in his chest.

"Good man," Jack commented as he wiped his brow. "Lord, I'm hungry. What about seein' if Moll's got some breakfast ready? I doubt she's got any crow for ya, but some good, hot biscuits might do fine."

Royd chuckled. "Why did I let you talk me into this?

We're not going to be here that long. Then what? Jonathan Gates will have to come back and load everything up again."

"We'll see," Jack mumbled as they walked back to the house.

Royd placed his hand on Jack's shoulder. "We're not staying. This is temporary," he said firmly.

"Temporary. Sure."

"I mean it, Jack. It's a beautiful estate, and Lord knows the price was right. But I have a business to run. I can't stay here, and it's just too big for only you and Moll. Come back to Hampton with me. If you don't want to stay in town, we'll find a small farm nearby."

Jack looked up at him, his dark blue eyes twinkling. "Sixty days. That's all I'm askin' for. Then whatever you decide to do is fine with us. Can't see Moll and me, well . . . you got your sixty days. Why not enjoy 'em?"

Royd sighed. "Fifty-three left," he said, "but I'm not going to argue with you."

"Royd! Jack!"

Both men snapped to attention as Moll's worried cry rang out. Standing in the doorway, Moll waved for them, and they took off running.

Royd felt his heart start to pound faster and faster as he ran over to her. Her eyes were wild with fright, and she was wringing her hands nervously. "What's wrong?"

"Moriah's gone! I checked everywhere. She's not in her rooms. I even went up to that awful terrace, but I can't find her! What are we going to do?"

Royd felt like a band of steel tightened around his chest making it hard to breathe. Moriah was gone? "She must be in the house," he said as he bolted past Moll and ran into the house. "I'll check the second and third floor," he called over his shoulder. "Jack, you and Moll look on the first floor. And lock the doors!"

An hour later, after Royd searched every room on the two floors, he did not know whether to be frantic with worry or enraged that Moriah had slipped so easily out of his grasp. Although Moll assured him that the girl was nearly recovered, he had not seen Moriah since the day they arrived. Even if she looked only half as bad as she had then, she was in no condition to run away. Last night when Moll let the girl sleep alone, Royd knew it was a mistake. Every fiber of his rational being warned him that everything had gone too smoothly, but he never really thought the girl would actually run away again. He should have camped outside of her door! Even though Moll had turned over the keys to the girl, maybe he should have used the skeleton key he found in the study and locked her in.

No. He could not do that.

He should have! But he did not have the heart to keep Moriah a prisoner. If she did not want his help, so be it, he fumed, as he rejoined a worried Moll and Jack downstairs hoping they had had better success.

Moll and Jack shook their heads as Royd approached, and his heart sank.

"She couldn't have gotten far," Jack offered. "I'll take the coach and check the main road. Moll, you stay here in case Moriah comes back. Royd?"

"She won't come back," he said quietly, knowing that he would never have the chance to explain what had happened at Apple Knoll.

Moll wiped the tears from her face. "I'll just search the grounds close to the house. Royd, you can use your horse to cover the rest of the grounds. She might have tried to get away, but she does not have the strength to get far. She could be hurt or . . ."

As Moll's voice trailed off, Royd felt a knot twist in his stomach. If Moriah did run away—again—he did not know whether or not they would be able to find her. She had probably been gone for hours. She was also disposed to exploring at night, and he recalled how effortlessly she seemed to scale the cell yard walls. If she was

recovered, she had most likely left during the night and
was miles away by now. How many times did he have to
go after a woman who scorned his help?

He felt a surge of anger replace his despair. Didn't she
know that Moll would be worried, too? Even if she detested him, Moll had shown her nothing but kindness. So
had Jack. He did not deserve to be upset, either. As
much as he would have liked to simply forget about her
and return to Hampton, he knew that Moll and Jack had
grown too fond of the girl to make that possible. There
would be precious little rest for any of them until they
knew she was safe.

"If you find her, give her only one choice. Either she
comes back willingly or she can keep on walking, the
ungrateful wench." He nodded grimly before he headed
to the door. "There isn't a woman alive worth this aggra-
vation."

As he reached for the handle, the door swung inward,
and he dropped back a step. Stunned, his hands
clenched into fists. His jaw dropped open as he stared at
the figure in the doorway, his pulse quickening and his
eyes narrowing.

"Well, I'll be damned," he mumbled and stepped
aside.

Nineteen

aken by surprise, Moriah looked up into Royd's scowling expression, and the bright smile on her face quickly faded into a defensive frown. When he glared past her, she intervened before he could utter yet another oath. "It's all my fault that Mrs. Haskell and the girls are late. I met them while I was searching for berries for breakfast. Here," she said as she handed him the scarf full of overripe fruit that dripped juice on the floor. "We stopped to gather eggs, too. I didn't know how to do it, but little Rachel was good enough to show me."

A small girl, no more than seven or eight years old, curtsied and stepped forward with an apron half-full of eggs. Moriah put her arm around the little one's shoulders and caught a younger girl by the hand. "Her little sister was a big help, too. I'm so excited they're going to stay with us," she gushed as she led the entire Haskell family into the kitchen past Royd who looked dumbfounded as well as angry.

Moriah walked over to Moll and gave her a peck on her cheek. "I wanted to surprise you," she explained, her brows furrowing. Moll looked like she had been crying and Jack had a bewildered look of relief on his face. Realizing that she was the source of their distress dampened Moriah's gay mood. "I'm sorry. I didn't think I'd be so long. I—I didn't mean to worry you."

Moriah looked over at Royd, only to find him glaring at her. Feeling suddenly shy and embarrassed, Moriah smoothed back her hair and brushed at her skirts. Her eyes widened with horror. She had not noticed the red stains that trickled down the front of her bodice or the snags that pulled the delicate fabric of her skirt. She licked her lips and tasted the residue of raspberries.

"Isn't she a sweet little girl?" she said, urging the smaller child to come out from behind her skirts and trying to divert Royd's attention from herself. Poor little mite, she thought to herself. The child was just a miniature version of her poor mother and six older sisters. Thin and frail, with limp brown hair and lifeless eyes, the barefoot girl looked like a starved field mouse. The minute she saw the child in the woods, her heart constricted. The girl's dress was nothing more than a patched hand-me-down, clean but barely able to survive another washing. If anything would soften the harsh look on Royd's face, the plight of this little girl should.

When Royd ignored the youngster and stared at Moriah with a look that made her shudder, Moriah tried another tact. "I think we all need a solid breakfast," she announced, trying to cheer away the tense silence in the room. "Let me introduce everyone then we'll get started."

Pulling the youngest girl along with her, Moriah walked over to Royd who seemed annoyed by the crowded presence of an additional eight people in the room. She addressed herself to the matriarch of the Haskell family first. "This is Mr. Royd Camden. He's my . . ." She stammered for a moment and then smiled. "He's my guardian. Jack is the man Anna met last week, and this is his wife, Moll."

Ignoring the frown on Royd's face, Moriah started introducing the Haskell girls in age order. "I hope I can

remember your names. Let's see. This is Anna and her
twin sister, Sarah. They're fifteen. Then there's Naomi,
two years younger." She stared at the next girl for a
moment before continuing. "Deborah is eleven, Judith
is ten, and you've met Rachel. The youngest is . . .
Ruth."

Moriah paused, the sound of her own sister's name
bringing tears to her eyes, and she tightened her hold on
the child for moral support. "Mrs. Haskell told me how
hard they all worked to clean the rooms for us. I think
it's grand they're going to stay here."

Proud that she had not made a mistake in the girls'
names, and even more pleased that she had not started
to cry when she said Ruth's name, Moriah smiled. One
look at Royd's hard expression wiped the smile off her
face in an instant and made her pulse skip a beat. Why
was he so angry with her? Ignorant brute! He hadn't
even acknowledged the introductions she had made and
totally ignored the Haskells. Annoyed by his rudeness,
she put the eggs into a bowl herself and tried to grab the
raspberries out of his grasp.

"May I have a word with you?" Sparkling green eyes
darkened with unspoken rage that turned his expression
into a thundercloud about to burst. His hand tightened
on hers as they both clutched the raspberry-soaked scarf,
neither one relinquishing possession.

Moriah tilted her chin and smiled again, although she
felt more like smashing the berries in his face. Instead,
she looked away. "Of course. Ruth, you help your mama
to wash these. I'll be back in a minute."

Royd let go of the scarf, and Moriah handed the berries to Mrs. Haskell who took Ruth into her skinny arms,
her eyes full of questions that Moriah could not answer.
As he led Moriah from the room, she looked over her
shoulder and called back to Moll and Jack who had not
said a word. Obviously they were deferring to Royd this

time, and she wondered why. "I'll help make up the beds after breakfast. See if you can find some linens."

The pressure of Royd's hand on her elbow increased, and Moriah felt the first quiver of indignation. Who did he think he was to march her out of there like a child about to be chastised? When Royd led her to a large room lined with books and filled with furniture draped with cloths and closed the door, she swirled around. Escaping his grasp, she twisted her hands in front of her. "Would you care to explain yourself?" she demanded, following him as he walked around her. "You were rude and inconsiderate to those nice people. You're fortunate to find anyone to work here, and it won't help matters to scare them."

Royd stopped and turned around to face her. "Since when is it your responsibility to concern yourself with the people I employ?" His voice hardened. "Just what did you mean when you said that it was fortunate to have them work here? Assuming they can work. Not a one of them looks like she can labor more than a few hours without collapsing!"

"You know perfectly well what I mean," Moriah answered without backing down. "Mrs. Haskell told me all about the couple who lived here and how they died. If Mrs. Haskell and the girls weren't one step ahead of starvation, they wouldn't be here. Poor little Ruth was in tears, begging her mama not to make her live in a house with bad spirits. The mother is caught between fear and hunger. What would you tell little Ruth?"

Royd's expression softened just enough to give Moriah the courage to continue. "I finally convinced Ruth that there were no bad spirits here when you acted like a mean, arrogant . . . ugh! You didn't even give her a smile. How could you be so mean?" Nearly out of breath, Moriah paused, waiting for him to respond. She did not dare hope for an apology, but she would have an explanation if she had to stand there all day to get one.

"Sit down, Moriah," he said calmly as he removed the cloths from two chairs by the window, sat down, and patted the chair facing his.

The dolt totally ignored her pointed diatribe! "I can stand," she countered, although her legs felt like they were on the verge of buckling. She had not intended to be gone quite so long, but when she met the Haskell family, she could not resist spending time with them. Mrs. Haskell was doing the best she could under the circumstances, but the family was clearly in dire straits. Moriah's opinion of Royd Camden had improved considerably when they told her of his generous offer of employment and a place to live. That lasted no longer than a rainbow, she mused, noting his reluctance to have them now that they were here.

"Please," he added, although it was hardly more than a veiled command.

Despite her reluctance to give in to his dictatorial manner, Moriah took her seat. She refused, however, to be intimidated by his patriarchal, insensitive demeanor and sat up straight, folding her hands on her lap.

Royd leaned forward, his knees practically touching hers. "Do you have any idea what chaos you caused by your little escapade?"

"I went for berries. That's hardly cause to sound a general alarm," she sniffed. "I didn't know I was confined to my rooms." Her eyes narrowed, and distrust stiffened her spine. "Am I now your prisoner? You told me I could leave whenever I was ready. Have you changed your mind about that, too?" She held her breath as she waited for his reply.

"You're not my prisoner," he snapped. His eyes glittered indignantly. "Neither am I your legal guardian!"

Fire lit Moriah's spirit, and she spoke without thinking of anything more than wiping the supercilious look off his face. "What did you want me to tell them? 'This is the man who had me sent to a lunatic asylum. When he realized what he'd done, he kidnapped me to get me out. He's holding me here against my will, and I'm going to be punished for leaving my rooms. But don't worry—he's really a compassionate man. You'll enjoy working for him as long as you remember that he is the lord of the manor!' "

"Don't be melodramatic," he hissed with an impatient wave of his hand.

Moriah wanted to scream; instead, she closed her eyes and forced herself to take deep breaths of air. Her lips barely moving, she prayed, silently and hard, for patience and calm. If she could just cool her thoughts, she knew she could think of a way to make him understand how important it was to maintain a decorous appearance.

"Tell me," she said softly as she opened her eyes and gazed at him with such intensity that he actually squirmed in his seat. "How should I explain who you are without risking your reputation as well as my own? It's certainly improper for an unmarried man to live with a maiden."

Royd's eyes glimmered like twin emerald fires, and she could see him battling for control. His jaw twitched, and his hands tightened on the arms of the chair.

"Our relationship is not the issue, although I daresay it surprises me that you're worried about being accused of consorting with a man without the benefit of marriage. Considering your conviction, I hardly think you have any reputation to worry about."

Moriah's head snapped back, and her cheeks stung as though he had slapped her. How could he make such a cruel statement? Clearly, he considered her to be a cold-blooded murderess. No wonder he acted so righteous and sanctimonious!

She bolted out of her chair and clenched her teeth, trying to forestall an angry outburst that would only make matters worse—as impossible as that might seem at the moment. "I don't have to listen to this . . . this bold-faced condemnation from you, Royd Camden. I didn't ask for your help, remember? God only knows I would have been better off without it."

Eye to eye, they faced off, neither of them blinking back their stance. He was so close she could feel his breath fan her face and see the pulse beating furiously at his temple. He seemed so sure of himself and her lack of virtuous character it was more pathetic than outlandish. "Where is my leather diary?" she murmured, her voice catching when his eyes lit up.

Shrugging his shoulders, he smirked. "It's been put to good use."

"You had no right to use it for anything," she said, shaking her head. "It doesn't belong to you. I want it back."

When he laughed at her, she felt a cold sweat begin to form on her brow. What did he mean when he said he put it to good use? The diary was all she had left to prove her accusations against the wicked men at Apple Knoll. She had to get it back!

Moriah was still not sure she could trust him. If he knew what her entries were really all about, would he return the diary to her? Maybe he had already shown it to the warden, and Royd's mission of mercy was really a ploy to discover which inmates she had visited. Once she deciphered the entries, would he notify the warden? Royd's valiant rescue of Moriah from Willow Valley suddenly took an unexpected twist which could place her friends in jeopardy.

On the other hand, Royd seemed to enjoy her discomfort. He also appeared too agitated to listen to reason right now. Yet, it was clear that he was not moved by her anger, and begging for the diary would only give him an added sense of power over her. Drat! She simply had to get that diary back! "Well?" she said finally, trying to look innocent and pouting with her lower lip. "I'd like my diary. Please."

"As I recall," he said with a cold timbre to his voice, "we had a bargain. Until you fulfill your end of it, the diary stays where it is."

Royd lifted the cuff of her sleeve and turned her wrist so the scars were visible. She thought she detected a softness in his eyes when he looked at the leather collar tied around her wrist, but it was quickly replaced by an icy stare.

Pulling out of his grasp, Moriah slid the sleeve back into place and stepped back from him. Her heartbeat stammered, and she could feel the heat rise to her cheeks. She had assumed that she would never have to explain the source of her scars to Royd, especially after being sent to Willow Valley. Once he freed her, she knew it was only a matter of time before he broached the subject. She had hoped she would be able to stall him until she was sure he would use the information to help the other inmates, but the look on his face demanded an answer. Now.

She thought about appealing to his sense of compassion by saying that the scars were too painful to discuss. If the scars evoked pity, she could deal with that. The way he acted right now, however, she sensed that he would dismiss them as a reminder of just punishment doled out to a convicted murderess, instead of a sadistic attempt to force a young girl of thirteen to obey the rule requiring absolute silence.

Reluctantly, she realized that she was in no position to make him wait unless she was willing to forsake her diary. Unwilling to admit that she had been cornered, she tried to force him to give her the diary before she told him anything. No matter how he reacted to her explanation of the scars, she would at least have possession of the diary. "Give me the diary, and I'll keep my word."

His laugh was brittle. "I've played this game with you before, but this time you'll abide by the rules that I set. The diary stays in my possession until I've heard your explanation for the scars on your wrists."

The sardonic tone to his voice had cut through her resolve to be patient and her determination to keep a cool head. Tears sprung to her eyes, and she detested them as a sign of weakness that he would probably find amusing. At least she knew he had the diary here and had not turned it over to the warden, but at that moment, she was more concerned with escaping from the room before she lost her composure completely.

"When cows dance," she spat and stormed out of his reach to stand defiantly in the doorway. "I'm going to my room to freshen my gown. When you decide to be reasonable, you can let me know. Unless," she added before she lost her courage, "you decide to force me to keep my word. What kind of punishment do you plan to use?"

As tears started to trickle down her face, she laughed nervously as the prospect of having him use physical coercion relit memories she had tried to forget. "There isn't much you can do to me that hasn't already been done. If you need help, you could always ask Lester Figgs or Tamin Jones. They're far more experienced than you could imagine."

Royd wanted to stop her, but before he could utter a word, Moriah had fled and slammed the door behind her. He stared at the closed door, wondering if he could ever salvage the wreck he had created out of his attempt to be reasonable. One minute he was tearing the house apart, searching in every wardrobe and under every bed, hoping against hope that she had not run away. The next minute he found himself looking at her bright smile and treating her like a runaway slave! What was wrong with him?

His hands shook as he walked over to the door. He

could not face Moll or Jack right now. They were no doubt waiting for an explanation for his rudeness to the Haskell family. He could not follow Moriah and explain his behavior either—not when he did not understand it himself.

Wiping his hands over his face, he decided to stay in the library. Returning to his chair by the window, he sat down and stared at Moriah's now empty place. He rested his hand on the upholstered seat and touched the fabric. It was still warm with her presence.

He had been beyond livid when he came face-to-face with her in the door to the kitchen. She looked so damned happy when he was nearly crazed with the thought that she might be lying hurt somewhere beyond his help. Why couldn't he talk to her, explain that he was frantic with worry when she disappeared? Surely he could not resent the fact that she had recovered enough to venture outside. Or was it that she had exuded such healthy vitality when he had spent the past week worried that she might never be able to overcome the traumas she experienced?

Fool!

None of those reasons explained his abominable behavior, and he knew it. When he looked at Moriah—her lips stained red by the raspberries, the morning sunshine dancing in the highlights of her golden hair, and her eyes . . . Lord! Her eyes were sparkling with delight!—all he wanted to do was to kiss her breathless and beg her never to frighten him like that again.

Instead, he had acted like a miserable cur, demanding that she explain herself like he owned her. No wonder she was vexed with him. By rights, she should have dressed him down in front of Moll and Jack, not to mention the poor family who looked like they had walked into a lion's den. Even then, she had tried to cover up for his lack of manners.

Moriah was absolutely within her rights when she demanded an explanation when they were alone, but what did he do? Apologize like a gentleman and tell her that he was sorry for acting so badly? Explain that his worry turned to anger?

No.

He pushed her away, just like he shoved away the realization that he was more than just physically attracted to the woman.

Royd stared at the intricately woven design on the seat cushion and traced it with his fingers. A variety of multicolored threads, if separated, would be singularly attractive. When woven together, they created a beautiful design of breathtaking complexity.

Moriah was as intriguing as that design. Strong of faith, yet capable of displaying emotion that made her unfailingly human. Weak and vulnerable, she emerged strong and defiant, championing herself and others like her. Abused and violated, she was restored even lovelier than before although she acted like she was unaware of how attractive she was. Pitted against his formidable mood, she held her ground and castigated him for his cavalier attitude and made him realize how utterly wretched he had behaved.

She made every other woman he had ever known seem as dull and lifeless as a burlap sack. She challenged him, made him angry, made him feel emotions that he had long buried. Damn her! He wished he had never seen those blasted pieces of leather she called her diary! If she knew they were in the barn as part of the horses' tack, she would probably drive the bloody coach away herself just to reclaim them.

Royd got to his feet and stared out of the window. He did not have to tell her about the whereabouts of the diary. He could go straight to her room and demand that she keep her word. Explain the stupid scars and be done with it. If she had been abused, he would add that to his original report and hand it over to her. With the funds he intended to give her, she could go to the capital and present it at the hearings. With the information he had given her about what really happened to her sister, Moriah would lead a crusade that would shake Apple Knoll to its foundation—without needing any help from him.

He would be done with her. Once and for all. He could return to Hampton, resume his life, and disavow any knowledge about Moriah Lane or how she got the information she would give to the legislature.

There was only one problem as he now saw the entire situation.

Moriah was obstinate enough not to explain anything to him until she had that cursed diary. When she taunted him about physically forcing her to keep her word, he felt like she had put a stake through his heart. Yet hadn't he acted like a bully? What else could she have expected him to do when anyone who demanded her obedience had always relied on using superior force to make her comply?

Turning from the window, Royd realized that he only had one choice: take the harnesses and bridles apart, confront her, and send her away before he made an absolute disaster out of his previously well-ordered life.

He knew he was in trouble the first time he saw her. Scoffed at it. Denied it. Fought it. It was ludicrous and absolutely beyond the realm of reason. And today, he realized that he would be unable to resist it any longer unless he sent her away. The sooner the better.

God help him.

He had fallen in love with Moriah Lane.

Twenty

When Royd finally left the library, he went directly to the stables, using a door that led directly outside instead of passing through the kitchen. He was not ready to explain himself to Moll or Jack, and he certainly did not want to see any of the Haskell brood. At the moment, retrieving Moriah's diary was his sole interest, and he sped toward his destination without regard for anything else.

The stable door wobbled and creaked as he opened it, and he held his breath, hoping that the cursed hinges would hold. Leaving the door ajar to flood the interior with light, he spied the harnesses and bridles hanging from nails planted side by side on the wall to his right.

Anxious to be done with his task before anyone discovered what he was doing, Royd lifted one harness away from the wall, studied it closely, then dropped it back into place. After inspecting the second harness, his heartbeat began to accelerate, and his palms grew sweaty. Muttering an oath, he grabbed both bridles at the same time, but a cursory glance at the soft leather pieces sent the same impossible message to his brain. All the tack had been replaced!

Spinning on his heels, he charged back to the house and into the kitchen in a blind panic. "Where's Jack?"

he bellowed, disregarding little Ruth who was standing on a chair helping Moll by drying dishes.

The girl dropped a plate and burst into tears when it hit the floor and smashed into pieces. Moll placed her arms around the little one as she sent Royd a scathing look. "He's upstairs movin' furniture, but unless you're gonna keep a civil tongue, you can march right back outta here! Right now, I don't know whether I even recognize you!"

"It's my house, dammit, and I'll . . . oh, forget it," he grumbled and tore up the servants' steps taking three at a time. When he reached the second floor, sweat was dripping off his forehead. After wiping his face with his sleeves, he paused to listen and then followed the sound of wood scraping against wood until he found Jack in one of the rooms trying to move a wardrobe.

Jack looked up and gave him a relieved welcome. "Glad you're here," he panted. "Blasted furniture is too heavy for me, but don't tell Moll. Do you think you could lend a hand?"

"Forget the furniture. I want to know what you did with the old bridles and harnesses for the coach horses," Royd demanded without stopping to consider the tone of his voice.

Jack's spine stiffened, and his bushy eyebrows scrunched together as his eyes narrowed. "You talkin' to me?"

"Of course I am," Royd spat with exasperation.

"No, I don't think you are," Jack corrected. "Never let you be disrespectful when you was young, and I won't allow it now."

Royd sighed with frustration. "I'm sorry. I didn't mean to snap at you."

"Well, you did. Probably growled at Moll, too." Jack shook his head when Royd's shoulders drooped. "What's wrong with you, boy? You're actin' awful peculiar ever since Moriah came strollin' back lookin' so bonny fair." His eyes softened. "All of us jumped to conclusions this mornin', I guess. She gave you a real scare, too, didn't she? I suppose there might be more to your feelings 'bout the girl than just guilt."

Royd should have known better if he thought he could hide his feelings about Moriah from Jack even though he had been able to submerge them below his own awareness. "Why is it you were always able to read my thoughts before I was?" he asked, the wind knocked out of his fury.

"Kindred souls, you and me," Jack said quietly. "Both of us had rough beginnin's."

Royd leaned against the door frame. "It doesn't really matter how I feel. I can't fall in love with Moriah. She would never fit into my world. She wouldn't be accepted. Not once people found out about her background which she's not likely to hide. Neither would I if I didn't create a new identity for myself. Besides, I'm already betrothed to Alexandria. I can't break my troth."

Jack's eyebrows twitched. "You're right. A man should always weigh everyone else's opinion before he chooses a mate and never change his mind once he settles on a particular woman. It's better to spend a lifetime married to the wrong woman than to admit he's made a mistake before he makes a vow before God that he can't ever break."

"That's putting a rather pessimistic view on the whole issue," Royd grunted.

"I just restated what you said," Jack said defensively.

"I don't like the way you put it."

"Good. You're startin' to think clearly. If you break your betrothal, you'd be free to marry Moriah."

"It's not that simple." Royd exhaled slowly. "Do you have any idea what it's like, wondering if someone will find out who and what I am? I've a fair resemblance to my father. What if someone recognizes the similarity? My whole life's work is at stake. I'd lose everything and be ostracized. Moriah's been through enough. I couldn't do that to her."

"Then you'd rather have Alexandria suffer that fate?"

"Of course not! The situation would be entirely different. Once I've aligned myself with the senator, I'd be above reproach. Alexandria wouldn't believe anything negative about me, and her father would make sure no scandal ever touched his daughter or her husband."

"Moll would say you've got yourself tied up to somebody else's apron strings. Be careful, Royd. They can loosen without your knowin' it or strangle you—one breath at a time. Look at the problems you've got already with this report, and you're not even married to Alexandria yet."

Royd could almost feel the figurative apron strings tighten. Jack's assessment of his predicament was so logical that Royd was disgusted with himself for not being able to see the inevitable progression of Fithian Williams's control over his life.

Based on what had occurred in their first skirmish over Apple Knoll, Royd knew that Alexandria would habitually side with her father. His life would be a never-ending series of battles he was destined to lose until he had no identity or character left. He took a deep breath as his anger and disappointment quickly turned to regret. "No matter how hard I try, I can't seem to escape my past. It's all been for naught. The education, the years I spent building a good reputation . . . Everything goes back to my early life."

"You weren't born into one mold. You grow into the man you make of yourself. Moll and I are proud of you. Folks who don't appreciate you ain't worth worryin' 'bout."

Royd shook his head. "You don't understand."

"I know you have to make up your own mind. Just remember that life can seem pretty long when you're matched up with the wrong woman or livin' under another man's shadow."

"Alexandria is a respectable woman," Royd retorted, suddenly feeling defensive. He had thought about marrying Alexandria for a long time before he had asked for her hand. Despite his lack of emotional commitment to her, he was a man of honor. He could no more bring disgrace on the woman by jilting her than give up everything he worked for to become a country gentleman.

"Tell me where you want the wardrobe," Royd suggested as a way of changing the topic. "Then you can explain where you put the old tack."

Royd was grateful that Jack let the discussion die without further argument. After repositioning the wardrobe, Royd went after the tack, vowing to keep his feelings for Moriah under control. Pale Eyes deserved more than he could ever offer her, and he felt a profound sense of loss as he thought about what might have been.

When Moriah finally returned to the kitchen, Moll was sweeping up broken fragments of a dish. Ruth sat huddled on a chair, her tearstained face looking pale and wan. Lighting a smile to ease the child's obvious distress, Moriah pushed away her own troubling thoughts. "I've broken enough dishes to stock a hotel. Uncle Jed used to say I was like a bull in the kitchen," she said, laughing softly when Moll snorted. Ruth's face brightened considerably.

"This particular bull has black hair and green eyes and charged upstairs. I hope he didn't scare anyone else into breakin' somethin'. No tellin' what kind of damage he could cause there with the foul temper of his," Moll muttered. "Little Ruth shook for five minutes after he left." She looked at Moriah with fire in her eyes. "He didn't . . . I mean . . ."

"Royd and I had a civil conversation," Moriah lied. Moll was upset with Royd now. If Moriah told her how he tried to intimidate her in the library, she had the feeling that Moll would corner Royd and force him to apologize.

An empty apology was worse than none, although an apology was hardly enough to erase the man's hateful words and behavior. She decided that the best course of action was retreat. "Where are Mrs. Haskell and the girls?" she asked as she walked over to Ruth and sat down on a chair beside her.

"Upstairs with the bull," Moll replied irritably. Ruth started to giggle, and Moriah laughed with her. "You never did eat any breakfast," Moll scolded.

"I'm not hungry. I ate more raspberries than I brought home." Moriah could not eat anything. Her stomach was too tied up in knots, and she was grateful that Moll accepted her excuse. "What can I do to help you?" she asked, eager to have something to occupy her time.

"You should be restin'," Moll suggested.

"I promise to take a nap later, but I'd like to do something to help."

"Why don't you take Ruth outside? She won't take a step farther than the kitchen, not with Royd stomping around."

Moriah took the little girl by the hand and stood up. "I saw some lovely flowers today. Should we pick some?"

Ruth's hand tightened, and she nodded slowly.

"Good. We'll need baskets. One for each of us, I think."

Moll fetched two small, wicker baskets from the other room and handed them to Ruth. She gave Moriah a small pair of shears which she placed into the basket. "Take these outside and wait for Miss Moriah," she instructed the little girl.

Ruth hesitated and squirmed in her seat.

"Go on. I'll only be a moment," Moriah said softly,

wondering why Moll wanted to speak to her alone. If she questioned Moriah about what happened in the library, Moll would not give up until she had the truth.

When the girl finally climbed down from the chair and carried the baskets outside, Moriah stood up and looked at Moll.

"The poor thing is petrified," Moll whispered. "Her sisters are old enough to understand how bad off they are. They don't like stayin' in the house any more than their mama, but they'll do it. Ruth isn't old enough to be realistic. She's scared, plain and simple."

Tears filled Moriah's eyes. "I know what it feels like to be scared," she murmured, thinking back to long before Apple Knoll or Willow Valley. After their parents died, Moriah and Ruth clung to each other for support, but they also had Uncle Jed who was patient and loving. Ruth Haskell's family was busy trying to survive, and she could not fault them for expecting Ruth to simply adjust to the harsh realities of life.

"I'll see what I can do," Moriah promised, although she was not sure if she could ease the child's fears about the stigma attached to the house and Royd, too. "Will you speak to Royd?"

Moll puckered her lips. "I intend to, even if I have to swat him with this broom to get his attention. Maybe he needs a good cuff in the head!"

Moriah laughed. That was one confrontation she would like to see! When she stepped outside, Ruth was sitting on the bottom step. "Are you ready?" she asked as she took one of the baskets.

Hand in hand, Moriah and Ruth wandered past the barn. The day was hot already, and Moriah let the warmth of the sun's rays help to dispel the events of a dreadful morning. She had an important task in hand, one that would keep her busy while she tried to sort out her feelings for a green-eyed bull of a man who was safely penned in the house by a woman who had much more of a weapon than a straw broom.

Royd stared at the twenty-foot-square trash pit set deep in a clearing in the woods on the northern end of the estate. According to Jack, he had tossed the old tack into the pit a few days ago. Judging by the mound of damaged goods and discarded debris from the house and outbuildings accumulated in the past few weeks, there was a top layer of trash that would take hours to sort through to find the tack.

After rolling up his shirtsleeves, he climbed down into the pit. Standing on a pile of broken roof tiles which obviously had been there since the house was constructed, his shoulders were at ground level. He studied the contents of the pit and realized that recent debris had been tossed inside haphazardly. Damn! He would have to scour the top layer of the entire pit which meant he would be fortunate to finish before the sun set!

Characteristically, he decided to be systematic and start with the north end of the pit and work his way around the perimeter. With any luck, he would find the tack there. If not, he'd search every damn bit of the pit, inch by inch, but he *would* find it!

Two hours later, Royd was ready to strangle Jack with his bare hands. His back hurt, his clothes were drenched with sweat, and his mouth was dry with a powerful thirst made even worse by the blasted heat and the dirt that clouded the air every time he moved something. Stopping for the first time since he started his search, he removed his shirt and wiped his face. His muscles ached, and his hands were raw since he had forgotten to wear gloves. When his stomach growled, he leaned back against the side of the pit to take a breather.

Out of the corner of his eye, he caught the glitter of sunlight on metal. Turning his head, he looked closer and grinned. One of the bridles had slipped out of a canvas bag that he had kicked out of his way an hour ago! It never occurred to him that Jack might have bagged the tack, but he was too excited by his discovery to be annoyed. Opening the bag, he was relieved to see nothing other than tack inside, and he climbed out of the pit with the bag slung over his shoulder.

Although he was hungry, his thirst was greater. Recalling a small stream that fed into the lake, he headed through the woods. The umbrella of trees cast a welcome shade and cooled his skin and his earlier frustration. The distinctive odor of pine was a welcome change from the smell of decay in the pit.

Even though he apparently misjudged the distance to the stream, he continued walking, following the sound and smell of running water. When he finally reached the stream, he satisfied his thirst and washed his face, chest, arms, and hands before sitting beneath a tree, tossing the bag of tack at his feet. He sat back, chewing on a blade of grass, enjoying the solitude and the peaceful sounds of the forest.

Emotionally and physically drained, he allowed himself the luxury of relaxing now that he had accomplished his goal. Closing his eyes, his mind drifted back, skirting past the disastrous morning to focus on his life in Hampton long before he had ever even heard of Apple Knoll.

After talking with Jack earlier, Royd realized how long it had been since he reassessed his life and future with someone he could trust to share his thoughts with honestly instead of carefully measuring every word he used.

Somehow, the distance between David's Crossing and Hampton gave him a fresh perspective that jolted submerged realizations to the surface. Examined in a fresh light, Royd realized that he had survived and prospered in Hampton, but he never really enjoyed living there.

A town bustling with commercial life, the streets were

congested with the noisy traffic of wagons and coaches, hawkers and peddlers. The strict routine he followed at work kept him inside tending to one crisis after another with the presses or scrutinizing the galleys before the final production of the books.

The business was profitable and respectable. It was also boring and tedious, Royd admitted to himself with total honesty, especially now that the initial challenges of operating his own firm had faded into monotony. He learned very early to relieve his boredom by immersing himself in a round of social activities that provided recreation and intellectual diversion as well as opportunities to develop important contacts that kept him abreast of his competitors.

Taking a deep whiff of air, Royd opened his eyes and looked around him. The woods that surrounded the estate were like a natural barricade against the pettiness and the intrigue of the commercial world. The air was fresh and clear, the land untainted by greed or competition.

His mind wandered, trying to imagine the man who created this isolated, earthly wonder. Moll said he was some sort of German noble who fled to America. Was he running away from something, or did he come here lured by the same pastoral charm that tugged at Royd now?

He thought of the man's vision. The manor house was handsomely built and held great promise. Royd had the suspicion that the German was re-creating something he had left behind, although only a dreamer would imagine filling nearly fifteen bedchambers with his own progeny!

Poor bastard. His firstborn child died at birth, taking the woman who inspired such devotion that the man hurled himself from the turret so they could all be buried together. Was it love that drove the man to seek refuge in the grave, or was it the dashing of his hopes and dreams?

Dreams were always quick to turn into nightmares. No one could testify to that with more experience than Royd. It was folly to even consider picking up the pieces of another man's vision and claiming it for himself. Hadn't he been tempted by the dream of owning this property once before?

Dismissing his wistful musings as just another lapse in judgment, Royd stood up. The sound of voices made him tense, and he scanned the area looking for the source. Beyond the other side of the stream where the woods thinned into open pasture, he spied the blur of color and what appeared to be two figures kneeling on the ground. Lured by his curiosity, he decided to investigate. Crossing the stream and avoiding the path, he approached the pair cautiously.

♣

Twenty-one

Kneeling in the weeds, Moriah bent forward and pushed away the five years of overgrowth that obscured the front of one of two grave markers. Ruth edged a little closer on her knees and clutched Moriah's thigh.

"There's no need to be afraid," Moriah said softly. "Look. This stone is for the mama and her baby." Moriah pulled out some weeds by their roots so that the lettering was visible:

In Memory of
Katarina
Beloved Wife of
Wolfgang von Ottinger
1805–1823

In smaller print at the bottom, her newborn child was remembered with two simple words: Infant Son.

"Help me to make it pretty," Moriah suggested. Lifting the shears out of one of the baskets, overflowing with wild flowers, Moriah began clipping away the choke weeds until there was a two-foot patch cleared in front of the marker. Without being instructed further, Ruth carried the clippings away.

Sitting back on her heels, Moriah wiped her brow. Glinting her eyes against the noonday sun, she perused her work and nodded with satisfaction. The granite marker was now clearly visible.

Ruth approached the marker and touched it reverently. "Why do babies die?" Her voice was soft, her eyes downcast.

Moriah reached out and took the girl by the hand, tugging until the little girl sat down in front of her. She put her arms around Ruth's chest as the child leaned against her. "God has a plan for all of us. Sometimes it's hard for us to understand why little ones are called back to heaven."

Moriah felt Ruth's shoulders sag. "I had a baby brother once. He was real tiny. He died, too."

"Then your little brother is an angel now," Moriah said gently. "Do you miss him an awfully lot?"

Ruth squirmed out of Moriah's grasp. "He cried a lot. Mama cried, too."

Moriah felt her heartstrings tighten as Ruth began to talk. "My mama didn't die, but Papa did. Why did this baby's mama die?"

Moriah had the feeling that Ruth was worried about losing her own mother and remembered the double tragedy that took both of Moriah's parents away. "I wish I could give you an answer, sweetheart. When my mama and papa died, my uncle Jed told me that God needed some very special angels. Big angels who could take care of all the baby angels in heaven. I still miss them," she whispered.

Ruth turned around and looked at Moriah with big, wondrous eyes. "Your papa died, too?"

"I was only three," Moriah said, nodding her head.

"I miss my papa. Sometimes." Ruth played with her hair and looked at the ground.

"I miss my papa, too."

"Do you think he's in heaven with my baby brother?" Ruth asked, her voice hopeful.

"I should think he is."

Satisfied, Ruth gave Moriah a smile before her expression darkened. Pointing at the companion marker still half-hidden by weeds, her little mouth puckered. "He's not in heaven. Sarah says he's in . . . you know." Squaring her tiny shoulders, she parroted her elder sister. "He was a wicked man who broke God's laws. Nothing good will ever happen here."

Moriah flinched. The girl's voice was cold, and her body started to quiver. "He was a bad man. I don't like being here."

Moriah shook her head. "He must have loved his wife very much. It isn't our place to judge him."

"I want to go home."

Moriah did not want to give the girl the opportunity to explain whether she meant she wanted to go back to the manor house or to return to the home she shared with her family before coming to work for Royd. Instead, she quickly sheared the weeds from the second marker and pointed to it. "His name was Wolfgang, and he was just an ordinary man," Moriah said, hoping to dispel Ruth's fears.

"He's a wolf?" the child repeated as her face paled.

"No. He wasn't a wolf. His name was Wolfgang."

When the shadow of a man fell between Ruth and Moriah, the girl looked up and squealed with fright. "The bull!" she screamed and leaped into Moriah's arms as she burst into tears.

Goose pimples pricked Moriah's skin, and she looked up to find Royd staring down at them with a strange look on his face.

"I didn't mean to frighten you," he said, quickly hunching down to pat the girl's head.

Ruth's arms tightened around Moriah's neck, and Moriah squeezed her tightly. "It's Mr. Royd, *Leibchen,*" she murmured. "He's not really a bull. I think he looks more like . . . like a bear. What do you think?"

After a few moments, Ruth peered at Royd through tear soaked lashes. "A big black bear," she said, hiccoughing.

Moriah giggled. "I think he'd look less like a bear if he shaved off his beard."

Ruth eyed Royd suspiciously before her little hand reached out to touch his face. "My papa had whiskers. They tickled when he kissed me. I like them," she pronounced.

Royd chuckled. "Then I shall keep my whiskers just for you. I was just going back to the house for some dinner. Would you like to ride on my shoulders?"

Moriah observed the exchange between the man and the child with bemusement. The child responded quickly to Royd's gentleness—a facet of his personality Moriah assumed to be calculated for his own purposes. The warmth and compassion in his eyes, however, were not feigned, and Moriah was reminded of the few occasions when he had been as compassionate with her as he was with Ruth.

How could this be the same man who confronted Moriah in the library just a few hours ago? His entire demeanor had changed, reminding Moriah of a chameleon who altered color to suit its environment. Did Royd have some kind of ulterior motive by being kind to the little girl?

Ruth tugged at Moriah as though deferring to her for permission. Moriah saw the look of delightful anticipation in the child's eyes and nodded her approval.

After helping Moriah to her feet, Royd swung the slight youngster to his shoulders in a single swoop. After adjusting a canvas bag that hung over his shoulder, he smiled at Moriah. "Will you come with us?"

Moriah felt a tingle trip down her spine and pool in her toes. His smile was absolutely captivating, and she looked away before he could see her blush. Gathering a basket of flowers into each hand, Moriah walked along-side of Royd as they made their way back to the house. She suppressed a giggle when she noticed the girl's hands wrapped tightly around several locks of Royd's hair that Ruth used like a rider holding onto a horse's mane for support. He grimaced occasionally when the girl lost her balance and tugged his hair, but he did not utter a word of complaint. When the girl's head began to bob, Royd settled her into his arms where she promptly fell asleep.

"I'm surprised you found us," Moriah ventured, wondering if Royd had been searching for her. "Did I violate another boundary?"

When Royd stopped walking, Moriah looked at him expectantly. "I guess I deserved that," he admitted without sarcasm. "You're free to come and go as you please. It would help if you'd let someone know where you were going," he added as an apparent afterthought.

Moriah looked at him skeptically, not quite sure what to say.

"I owe you an apology for this morning. You had no way of knowing that we all spent an hour searching frantically for you. Moll was certain you were lying hurt on the road after trying to escape again."

Moriah blushed. "I had no idea."

"Unfortunately," he continued, his voice softening to a mere whisper, "when I opened the door and saw you standing there, I didn't know whether to strangle you for wandering off or . . ." His voice trailed off, and he gazed at her with a look that made her heart skip a beat.

Desire, pure and naked, glistened in his eyes. Moriah's body responded, her flesh tingling with a warm flush that left her breathless. A dark tendril of curly hair fell to the middle of his forehead, and she had the consuming urge to brush it away. One touch. That's all it would take, she realized, and wondered how she could respond to a man who had hurt her so deeply.

Royd looked so different, so much less fearsome now as he held the child in his arms. The image unsettled her, and the baskets of flowers in her hands began to shake. She forced herself to remember how nasty and judgmental he had been with her earlier. Was his desire fueled by the assumption that she was the kind of woman who would respond to the natural attraction that seemed to flare between them? It should not matter to her, but she found it hard not to blurt out her contempt that he would use a child and a few kind words to lure her into his bed.

The spell broken, Moriah turned and walked toward the house just yards away. When Royd caught up with her a few steps later, she tried to ignore him.

"Aren't you even a tad curious?" he asked, slowing his step to match her stride.

"Nothing about you rouses my curiosity," she said coldly and stared straight ahead as she tried to hurry her pace.

"Not even about the canvas sack I'm toting?"

Moriah peeked a side glance at the bag strung over his shoulder and shrugged. "Why should I give one whit about what you're carrying in the sack?"

When he chuckled, she quickened her step. The more she thought about his blatant display of lust and his playful manner now, the madder she became. If he thought she was in the mood for games, he could find someone else to play.

"You don't like me very much, do you?"

Stunned by his question, Moriah ground to a halt. "I don't trust you," she responded, her fury spiraling into an explosion of words. "You claim to want to help me and then you betray me. For some reason known only to yourself and God, you rescued me and then tracked me through the woods vowing your innocence. All the while," she added with pent up emotion that made her voice quiver, "you use your strength to intimidate me. When you finally ensconce me on an estate most people shun, you treat me like a prisoner and threaten me again. Just this morning, you refused to return something that belongs to me and demand that I keep my word when you have yet to act honorably with me."

Pausing to take a deep breath, she glared at him. "Did you follow me when I took Ruth outside? Were you afraid I would run away again?"

Moriah's breath came in gulps, and her fists clenched at her sides. "No, I don't like you," she said when she finally caught her breath. "I don't know why you're so concerned about my welfare unless you're making sure that I won't disrupt the precious hearings you and the other wretched excuses for gentlemen want to subvert."

Royd allowed her the freedom of attacking his motives without defending himself. She had every right to doubt his sincerity, although he found it painful to listen to the litany of offenses he had committed against her. Her eyes sparkled with distrust and anger, making them turn the shade of an angry sea instead of the color of a cool, spring sky that had mesmerized him the first day he met her. Her body was tense with fury she struggled to control, and he waited until she exhausted the charges against him before trying to speak.

"Do you intend to appear before the legislative committee?" he asked. Noting the way she squared her shoulders, her answer was given before she even responded with her voice.

"You can't stop me."

Royd shook his head. "I don't expect to stop you."

Surprise danced in her eyes, and he took advantage of her momentary confusion. "I made a promise to you when we arrived, and I intend to keep it. I won't offend you by offering excuses for everything that has happened, but I want to make a suggestion."

Her brows raised in suspicion, and he continued with just a glimmer of hope. "I want you to sit down with me and listen to me with an open mind. Ask questions. Weigh the possibilities. If you want to leave without accepting my help, Jack will take you wherever you wish to go. If you decide to stay, I'll help you to prepare for the hearings."

Moriah chewed on her lower lip, apparently considering his offer which was all that he asked—at the moment. She looked at him for a long time, but her thoughts were unreadable. Would she give him the chance to make amends or would she embrace this as an opportunity to flee?

"How can I be sure you're not trying to trick me?"

The distrust in her voice made him wince. At the same time, she seemed to be wavering, and he counted on her apparent resolve to testify at the hearings to sway her to accept his offer. Shifting the sleeping child to his shoulder, he removed the canvas bag and held it out to her. "This belongs to you."

The bag hung between them, but neither moved. She studied the sack for so long the muscles in his arms began to twitch. Just when he thought his arm would give out, she took the bag, although she seemed to deliberately avoid touching his hand.

Obviously unprepared for the weight of the bag, she let it drop to the ground. Peering inside, her brows furrowed, and she raised her face to him with nary a second glance inside.

"Dump it on the ground," he suggested.

When the bridles and harnesses landed in a heap, she kicked them. "If this is some kind of joke—"

"It's not a joke," he interrupted. "I'm returning something that belongs to you. Unfortunately, you'll have to put it back together."

When Moriah gave him a look of utter exasperation,

he started to chuckle. "It's the only way I can prove to you that I'm only half the fiend you think I am."

"Right now I'm beginning to think you're either addled or tipsy," she retorted. "Why bridles and harnesses have anything to do with me or you is beyond reason."

"Remember when the coach stopped just beyond Willow Valley?" he asked. "Jack noticed that several pieces of leather were broken. Since neither of us know much about it, we were somewhat at a loss about what to do. Fortunately," he added, noting her sullen interest, "I had brought something with me to Willow Valley that provided a temporary solution."

Moriah studied his face, glanced at the pile at her feet, and then looked back at him. Her eyes flared with a jolt of insight. "My diary?"

He nodded. "You'll have to take the tack apart, but all of the remnants should be there. I really did put them to good use."

Her lips shaped a tremulous smile. "You used my diary as . . . tack?"

"It seemed appropriate at the time. After our . . . our confrontation in the library today, I went to the stables to retrieve it only to discover that Jack had replaced this set. While you were gathering flowers, I was shoulder deep in the trash pit trying to recover it for you. I was resting at the stream when I heard you with Ruth."

A bubble of nervous laughter escaped from Moriah's lips, and she shook her head. "You were in the trash pit?"

"All morning."

"You didn't follow me?"

His expression turned serious. "I was too preoccupied trying to find the tack. You were right. The diary does belong to you, and I have no right to force you to keep your bargain by using the diary as leverage."

Being honest and admitting that he had made a mistake made him feel a lot better than he had felt when he lashed out at her that morning. Although he knew that the diary was important to her, he could not use that as a way to intimidate her again.

Judging by the rapt expression on her face, Royd knew he had made the right decision. She would never begin to trust him if he did not treat her fairly.

Moriah knelt down and stuffed the tack into the bag, folding the edges of canvas over the end. She hesitated, rubbing her wrists and staring at the ground. "Why must you know about the scars?" she murmured.

"I don't need to know. Not unless you feel you want to tell me. If the reason for the scars will have value at the hearings, you can testify before the panel. If not, you're entitled to keep the cause of the scars private."

When he heard her sigh, he walked over to her and placed his hand on her shoulder. "I'm not proud of myself for acting like a bully. Or for making accusations that were cruel and judgmental. Will you forgive me, Moriah?"

His heart held still as he waited for her answer. When she finally lifted her face and looked at him, he was surprised to see that tears were running down her face.

"I'll tell you about the scars," she whispered, "if you promise not to ask any questions about the entries in my diary."

Twenty-two

Before Royd could answer Moriah's soft-spoken plea, Moll opened the kitchen door and interrupted. Luscious smells wafted through the open door as she wiped her hands on her apron. "That lawyer, Evan Brockley, is waiting to see you," she announced, obviously surprised to see Royd cradling the sleeping child in his arms.

Royd watched Moriah as she lifted the canvas bag and adjusted its weight so she carried it in her arms the same way he held Ruth. Whatever tenuous gain he had made with Moriah would have to be enough until he and Moriah were able to speak privately again. Her face averted, she entered the house without saying a word.

Royd transferred the sleeping child into Moll's arms, contemplating the reason for Brockley's visit. He rejected the notion that Brockley had discovered a problem with Royd's alleged signature. "Where is he?" Royd asked.

"I let him wait in the library. Neither one of the parlors have any furniture and the library seemed more appropriate anyway. He brought his poetry." Moll eyed Royd with a look that he remembered only too well.

"I know how to behave." He chuckled and embraced her, although the child in her arms prevented him from lifting Moll off her feet and swirling her around until she squealed. The ploy always managed to get him restored to her good graces whenever she was angry with him in the past. This time, however, he settled for a gentle kiss which he pressed to her forehead. "Apologies seem to be the order of the day," he whispered. "You're fourth on my list thus far, but you'll always be first in my heart."

Moll sniffled. "Don't forget the Haskells," she reminded him gently.

"Ruth is the only one I've seen," he answered, lifting a strand of hair out of the girl's face. "I'll make amends to the others after I deal with Brockley. Has he been waiting long?"

Moll shook her head. "I promised him dinner when he got here about half an hour ago."

"Have a few of the girls set up a small table in the library for the two of us. You and the others can eat here. Make sure Moriah doesn't miss another meal."

Walking quickly to the library, Royd introduced himself to the country lawyer Jack had tricked so easily. Evan Brockley, however, was not at all what Royd expected. Dressed fashionably, his solid frame and firm handshake dispelled Royd's assumption that Brockley was a reclusive, self-educated lawyer who immersed himself in books and disdained contact with people. Intelligence and friendliness reflected in the depths of his warm brown eyes.

"I see you're gradually getting settled in," the lawyer commented with a smile as he set his manuscript aside.

"Very gradually," Royd agreed. "I'm sorry I can't offer more gracious surroundings. As you know, the dining room is nothing more than walls of framed uprights like most of the second and third floors," he explained as Sarah and Anna carried a small table into the room.

"This will be quite sufficient. Quite," Brockley added as the girls quickly set the table with china and heavy silver tableware. Naomi and Deborah carried in steaming bowls of fresh vegetables and a platter of beef, sliced thick and swimming in a pool of gravy.

"Shall we?" Royd positioned the two chairs that he and Moriah had used earlier on either side of the table. After the lawyer sat down, Royd joined him. In the course of their meal, both men exchanged pleasantries while satisfying their hunger. Royd found himself enjoying the man's easy nature almost as much as Moll's excellent meal. When the dishes were cleared away, Brockley opted for a fresh peach for dessert from the harvest which Royd had helped Jack gather just the other day.

"This estate can be quite bountiful," Brockley said, wiping his mouth and leaning back in his chair. He clasped his hands together and rested them on his stomach. "I envy you."

Royd cocked a brow. "Why didn't you buy the property yourself? As a point of fact, it seems rather odd that no one has snapped at the opportunity to buy it in the past five years. I can't believe that I'm the first to seriously consider purchasing the property even with the stigma attached to it."

Brockley smiled. "To be honest, I wanted to, but my wife won't step foot inside the house. Neither will most of the local folk, although I realize that for some, the choice isn't theirs to make."

"Mrs. Haskell?"

"She's a good woman. Unfortunately, not many men are willing to take responsibility for another man's family. Not one with seven girls, at least. Females aren't much good at harvest time and downright costly to marry off."

"They have the housekeeping skills needed here," Royd countered, "although with a few weeks of good food and a decent place to sleep, I'm hoping they're going to have the stamina to match the work that restoring the house requires."

Grateful that he had used an agent the previous year to remain anonymous, Royd pressed his advantage. "Why didn't anyone buy the estate before now?"

Brockley shifted his position, stared at the floor, then looked at Royd with genuine worry. "You're not considering changing your mind, I hope?"

Royd shrugged his shoulders. "I haven't decided one way or the other. That's why I requested sixty days to consider it. The move would require a drastic change in lifestyle, and before I make my decision, I intend to weigh every possibility. Including the notion that perhaps there is a good reason why no one else would buy it." Royd watched Brockley's expression change from concern to indecision. "Perhaps there is something you wish to tell me," he asked quietly. When Brockley remained silent, Royd nodded grimly. "Then I rescind my offer immediately." He rose, hoping the man would react to his bluff.

With a sigh, Brockley waved Royd back into his seat. His eyes darted nervously around the room as he shifted in his seat. "You appear to be a sensible businessman with a reasoned approach to making decisions, but I must ask for your word that you won't discuss what I'm about to tell you with anyone."

Royd hid his pleasure behind a mask of indifference. "Go on."

"When Wolfgang Ottinger first arrived in David's Crossing ten years ago, he retained my services. After he purchased the land he presented me with details for the estate including blueprints for this house. After depositing a sum of money in an account, he signed power of attorney over to me. As his agent, I hired the laborers and supervised construction and followed his instructions precisely. In general, I did everything he would have done as the owner, although he reserved the right to see the completion of the house. That's why it's only partially finished. I suppose he wanted to—"

His interest piqued, Royd stopped the man's explanation. "Why didn't Ottinger do it himself?"

"He wasn't here. He returned to Germany. The estate sat empty for several years until I finally received a letter from him advising me to expect household furnishings to arrive. Sure enough, over the next eighteen months, Ottinger shipped nearly everything you've seen in the house from all over the world. The china we used a little while ago came from Bavaria. The furniture in the master bedrooms from Austria. I saved the shipment invoices. You can read them yourself if that will help to sway your decision."

Royd dismissed that as unnecessary with an impatient wave of his hand. Brockley continued. "Ottinger arrived the following year, this time with a bride. Katarina was twenty years younger than Wolfgang, and she was exceedingly lovely. They were utterly devoted to each other, although when tragedy struck, I never dreamed he would . . ."

Brockley's voice trailed off, and he paused, obviously lost in memories that were painful to recall. "I handled his will, of course, and followed his instructions to the letter. They're buried together in the north end of the estate. The markers are probably hidden by overgrowth, but they are exactly as he proscribed."

"I've seen them." Royd remembered how important clearing the grave sites had been to Moriah. Although she was obviously using the opportunity to ease Ruth's fears, Royd wondered if in some unspoken way, Moriah was caring for the graves of her uncle and her sister who were buried in resting places Moriah would never be able to tend.

Although the background on Wolfgang Ottinger and his wife was interesting, Royd was growing bored. "What does this have to do with the reluctance of potential buyers?"

Worry again crossed Brockley's face. "It took two years to find out that there were no heirs. At that point, I began searching for buyers, none of whom wanted a half-completed estate tainted by tragedy. That's when disaster struck for the second time. One of the laborers was killed in a freak accident while repairing a section of roof damaged in a storm. The local folk claim the house is cursed and refuse to work here even by daylight."

Royd could feel his patience thinning. "That still doesn't explain why there haven't been any buyers. Curses and superstition are nothing more than hysteria and certainly are no reason to let a good investment opportunity pass by." He shook his head. The absolute and impossible irony that this magnificent property now housed a former thief, a twice-convicted forger, and a murderess because everyone else was put off by ridiculous superstition was so preposterous that Royd started to chuckle.

The lawyer puffed out his chest. "It's all very well for you to consider my predicament humorous, Mr. Camden. You don't have to listen to local gossip and watch helplessly as potential buyers swallow the tales and leave before the dust settles from their arrival."

Brockley's hurt expression sobered Royd's ill-timed humor. "Good business decisions are never based on idle gossip or superstition. The property is a solid investment."

Hope filled Brockley's eyes. "Can I assume you'll make good on your offer to purchase the estate?"

"Whether I buy the property or not, I assure you that you'll have my decision within sixty days," he answered sincerely. Rather than deflate Brockley's hopes completely, Royd turned the lawyer's attention to the manuscript that Brockley set aside earlier. "In the meantime, let's take a look at your manuscript. I believe I owe you the courtesy of printing it for you."

For the next several hours, the two men reviewed the manuscript which was twice as long as Royd expected. He was also pleasantly surprised by the quality of the man's poetry. Gallantly offering to print the full fifty copies in advance of making his decision about the estate, Royd escorted a placated Brockley to the door. "I'll be in touch with my assistant and alert him to expect your manuscript within the next two weeks. By the time I edit it and send it to him, the cover design will be completed, and the book can go into production once the galleys are reviewed."

Brockley's parting handshake was firm. "I appreciate your help. Send Jack for the invoices and blueprints. Maybe they'll help you to make up your mind in favor of staying."

Royd nodded and watched Brockley as he rode away. Actually, instead of being disconcerted by the lawyer's speculations, Royd's fine-tuned business instincts made the idea of turning foolish superstition to his own advantage more than appealing.

In the privacy of the turret, Moriah sat cross-legged on the terrace and nibbled from a dinner tray that Moll had sent to her room. She stared at the bridles and harnesses spread out in front of her. Deciding to start with one of the harnesses, she pulled a section of the riggings onto her lap and tried to untie some of the remnants from her diary. The knots were tight. Too tight to be loosened with her fingers.

Furrowing her brow, she stopped for a moment and then reached for her fork. Using the tip of a tine, she struggled for several minutes before the knot finally loosened just enough to encourage her to continue using the fork as a tool. After ten minutes of concentrated work, the leather remnants were freed at one end. After another fifteen minutes, the knot at the opposite end gave way.

Moriah set the two remnants, including the one documenting Moriah's visit to Iona, to the side. Pausing to take another sip of milk, she quickly assessed her remaining work. Assuming the rest of the knots were as difficult, it would take hours to free the dozen or so remnants that remained.

Stifling a yawn, Moriah started on yet another section of the harness. As she worked, her mind drifted back over the morning's events that all centered around the most complex man she had ever met—Royd Camden. It was disconcerting if not downright puzzling how easily her opinion of the man seesawed from one extreme to the other, all in a matter of hours!

When she went looking for berries, she was absorbed with the prospect of surprising Moll and enjoying her freedom and restored health, and she was not expecting to confront Royd in the process. Only after meeting the Haskell family did she begin to think about him with anything less than distrust, despite Moll's obvious defense of the man's motives.

While Moriah recovered, Moll was evasive about Royd's plans for Moriah's future. Moriah could not fault Moll's loyalty to Royd. It was his continued absence from Moriah's rooms that made it seem possible that he really did want to give Moriah time to heal and understand that he meant her no harm.

Although most of her time the previous week had been spent allowing her body to recover physically, she knew it would take much longer for her to recover emotionally. The trauma of her confinement at Willow Valley seemed like a nightmare, but finding out about the manner of Ruth's death made Moriah's own experiences seem less horrific.

She had survived.

Why?

Her only answer came after hours of prayer, and there was only one man who seemed to play a central role in deciding whether or not she could stop the wickedness at Apple Knoll: Royd Camden.

Again.

Was he truly trying to help her, or did he have an even more wicked design to stop her from testifying?

This morning, Moriah was certain that he was going to keep her isolated on this estate until she was forced to tell him everything she knew so he could do . . . what? If he meant for her testimony to be silenced, why hadn't he left her at Willow Valley? Why bring her here, allow her to recover in such grand style?

By the afternoon, after watching Royd with Ruth, her distrust began to crumble, only to flare up again when he pressed her to tell him exactly what she thought of him. He undermined her accusations with an apology that made her feel foolish.

The return of her diary was the final crack in her defenses. If Royd was really trying to learn whether or not the entries were a threat, wouldn't he have read them all instead of just one? Was it possible that he had a code of honor after all?

Leaning back against the terrace wall, Moriah closed her eyes and folded her hands in prayer. "Help me," she whispered. "I don't know what to do." As she meditated, she added prayers for forgiveness. The list of her sins for the day was a heavy yoke: anger, deception, more anger. *Please, Lord!* It was so hard to follow every command-ment, especially when so many people depended on her to keep them.

Moriah had a feeling that there was another sin she had to confess, although she barely comprehended her mystifying physical attraction to Royd. It was an abso-lutely bewildering experience that left her awed by the multitude of sensations that flowed through her body like liquid fire.

Feeling safe in her secluded terrace, basked in sunlight, the stress of the day combined with physical exhaustion to interrupt her prayers and her work. She drifted into sleep with the hope that when she awoke, she would find the answers to her prayers.

Twenty-three

Midafternoon several days later, Moriah stood in front of the cottage she had sighted from the turret. It turned out to be a square log cabin that sat scarcely fifty yards from the shore of a small lake which was fed by a number of streams that ran through the estate. Two shuttered windows on either side of the door and a bar of wood nailed across the door looked weathered but still solid enough to have kept the interior safe from the elements and marauding critters.

The plan that she had mulled over in her mind suddenly appeared possible, and she quickly went to work. Using a crowbar she had brought with her from a toolhouse behind the barn, she pried at the wooden bar. Her feet left the ground as she used all of her body weight for leverage. After several tries, the rusted nails gave way, and the wooden bar squeaked free at one end. Rotating the thick wooden bar like the hand of a clock, she used her waning strength to swing the bar aside while it still remained attached to the door frame at the other end.

After leaning the crowbar against the exterior cabin wall, she studied one of the shutters. Apparently, it was latched from the inside, and she turned her attention back to the door. Pulling carefully on a weathered latchstring, she sighed with relief when she heard the inside latch respond.

Encouraged by her luck thus far, Moriah pushed the planked door open. As fresh air and sunlight poured into the cabin, the odor of musk and mold that assaulted her face from inside the cabin made her step back. After waiting several minutes, driven by a growing curiosity, she ventured a peek inside.

Apparently, whoever had lived in the cabin had left expecting to return or else they did not own the furnishings. Although the large, multipurpose single room contained rustic pieces that were a marked contrast to the costly furniture inside the main house, the pieces were numerous and appeared to be sturdy.

Once her eyes adjusted to the dim interior, Moriah stepped inside and walked about the room. A long table with side benches sat in the far end that was obviously used for eating and cooking. An iron pot still hung in the open hearth, and wooden trenchers and cups sat open in a corner cabinet. Spiderwebs and dust made everything look like it was coated with gray clouds, but dirt and grime could be easily handled.

A rocking chair, a hand-driven spinning wheel, and several leather trunks were grouped together in the front of the room. Moriah was careful not to disturb anything as she walked past them and unlatched the window shutter, using her skirt to protect her hands. She shivered as a cobweb brushed her face and rocked back on her heels.

The added light and warmth, however, inspired her spirit of exploration. A quick inspection of two adjoining rooms revealed identical bedchambers. One was furnished with a double bed and a cradle; the other had three single cots. The beds, curiously, were still made up, but no clothing hung from the pegs on the walls.

The floor planks squeaked as Moriah walked between the rooms, returning to what appeared to be the parent's bedchamber. A cloud of dust made her eyes water and lodged in her throat making her cough. As she glanced around her, she wondered about the family who had called the cabin home. Her best guess was that it must have housed an overseer of some sort and his family. Instinctively, her hand reached out and nudged the cradle. As it rocked and creaked, she tried to imagine the newborn child who had slept within its wooden protection.

Failing to retreat from thoughts that jogged dreams for a family of her own someday to surface, she found herself trying to imagine the wonder of swaddling her own child and singing lullabies as she rocked the baby to sleep. Her eyes filled with tears. Would any man ever accept her background and love her enough to want to have her bear his children? Who would love a woman who had spent years in prison instead of perfecting her housekeeping skills?

The flesh on her upper left arm began to itch, and she scratched at it absently. Who was she kidding? Explaining her lack of homemaking skills was minor compared to trying to convince a suitor to disregard her status as an ex-jailbird!

She could never fabricate a lie, even if she wanted to —the numbers tattooed on her arm were an indelible testament to the truth. No man would ever want her for anything more than . . . A violent shudder made her whole body tremble. Was she condemned to a life in a chasm with spinsterhood or harlotry her only options?

Probably. Romantic dreams were a woman's domain. Sadly, Moriah realized that for women like her, romantic dreams would never be transformed into reality. With a shake of her head, she dismissed her distressing thoughts as self-pity. She was fortunate to be alive, and she had a mission of such great importance that she felt guilty for indulging in schoolgirl fantasies or drowning in regret. For the present, all of her efforts had to center on the legislative hearings.

Eventually, that meant she had to deal with Royd. Her feelings about him were still a collection of conflicting impressions that were even more confusing than she first imagined. Lately, her view of him had softened.

Royd did seem to go out of his way to make her feel comfortable in his presence, and he certainly conquered little Ruth. The child followed him around almost as easily as she shadowed Moriah. She bit her lower lip. Would he agree to consider the idea that had driven Moriah here to this cabin?

As Moriah reshuttered the window, her vision rested on a table that sat next to the rocking chair. The stub of a burnt pinecone, apparently used as a mock candle, lay next to a thick book. Heart pounding, Moriah used her skirts to brush away the accumulation of dirt and dust from its cover and the yellowed outer edges of the pages.

After flipping through the book, Moriah clutched it to her chest. A Bible! The front pages of the sacred book where marriages, births, and deaths were recorded were blank. Although she was disappointed about not being able to learn more about the family who owned the Bible, she was equally thrilled to have discovered one to read again.

"Thinking of moving in?"

The man's voice startled Moriah, and she spun around, still clutching the Bible. Royd stood in the doorway with his back to the sun, and his silhouette made her mouth go dry. Her dizzying heartbeat nearly stole her breath. "I—I didn't mean to trespass," she stammered. When he chuckled, her initial fright turned into mere nervousness as Royd slipped into the cabin and looked around.

"I've wondered about the condition of the cabin, but I just hadn't gotten around to investigate it." He held up the crowbar. "I assume this belongs to you?"

Moriah nodded, a guilty look on her face. "I borrowed it from the toolhouse," she admitted.

"Were you going to borrow the book, too?"

The Bible burned in her hands. "I—I . . ."

He laughed again, and her eyes widened as he flashed her a captivating smile. "You don't have to explain, Moriah. I told you to feel free to wander about the estate and use anything you like. How did you know about the cabin? I didn't expect you'd find it so fascinating."

As his expression softened, Moriah was mesmerized by the sincere look in his eyes. Her heart resumed its normal beat then curiously began to accelerate again. "I saw it from the turret. Since you won't let me help Moll, I decided to try to find the cabin for something to do. It's quite sturdy," she commented as Royd walked around the room. "It's really a shame," she said, hoping to interest him in seeing the cabin's possibilities.

"Why is that?" he asked as he poked his head into one of the bedchambers.

"The cabin is empty. It would make a wonderful home for a family who needs one."

Royd looked at her askance. "You have a specific family in mind, I suppose?"

Sighing, Moriah shrugged her shoulders. "It's not my place to tell you what to do with the cabin. It doesn't belong to me."

"It's not like you to be coy, goldilocks." He smiled. "The estate doesn't belong to me, either. Not yet. That gives you almost as much right to make suggestions as I have."

Moriah's brows lifted. She assumed that Royd owned the estate, but apparently he was only in the process of purchasing it. The entire purpose to her escapade today was to see if the cabin she had spotted from her turret was in any condition to be used. Now that her hopes had been confirmed, Royd's surprise appearance left her at a momentary loss for words.

Royd approached her, his quizzical look inviting her response. Once again, however, she was befuddled by his presence, and she felt her cheeks redden. "I thought perhaps the Haskell family could relocate to the cabin," she gushed. "They need to be together. Like a real family. Not like . . . like servants who happen to be related to each other." Taking a deep breath, she waited for him to respond with either a reprimand or a caustic remark.

He did neither. Cocking his head, he stared at her, and she thought she detected a flash of relief race across his features before he smiled. His eyes lit with interest, making them appear a little lighter green than when he was angry.

"You want the Haskells to live here? I thought you liked having them in the main house. Especially Ruth."

"Oh, I do like it," she gushed. "It's just . . ." She paused and stared at the floor. "If they lived here, Mrs. Haskell could be more like their mama. I know Moll needs help, but Sarah, Anna, and Naomi could do that. Deborah and Judith could help their mama with the two youngest ones here. It's been so hard for them to live with other people since Mr. Haskell died. Ruth should be spending time with her mama, not with me."

Moriah grimaced as she recalled the hurt look in Rebecca's eyes just the day before when Ruth balked at her mother's request but agreed to help Rachel sweep the floor when Moriah asked her to. Moriah realized that Ruth's lack of allegiance to her mother was beginning to cause problems. As much as she hated to distance herself from the child, it needed to be done. Besides, if Mrs. Haskell knew that Moriah had been in prison and a lunatic asylum, Moriah shuddered to think that the woman might even forbid the child from seeing her at all.

"I thought perhaps you might want to stay here yourself for the privacy." Royd's voice was low and his expression thoughtful.

Moriah giggled nervously. "I've had enough privacy to last a lifetime. I enjoy having so many people around."

"Except me," he murmured.

"N-no, that's not true," she countered, her pulse quickening with her lie.

He cocked a brow. "No? Then why don't you ever join me in the sitting room at night? We have a lot to discuss, and I hoped you would give me the opportunity—"

"I've been busy." Her voice cracked as he stepped closer, and she clutched the Bible so hard she could feel her pulse beating in her fingertips. He stood directly in front of her now, and she gulped as those beguiling eyes studied her face.

"Busy. What could you possibly do in your room every night after supper?"

"I'm still working on the harnesses."

"I can help. If you'll let me."

The thought that Royd would handle her diary again cooled the tingling warmth that danced down her spine. "The knots are tight, but I can manage. I only have a few more."

"Then what?" he asked. "What excuse will you have for avoiding my company?"

"I'm not avoiding you," she protested, although she knew what he said was the truth. The way he made her tremble whenever he was near was beginning to worry her. What was the matter with her? Had she been isolated for so long that the mere presence of this man sent her pulse racing and her thoughts swirling into a whirlpool? Still, she had promised to listen to his explanations and to reveal the cause of her scars. She was not ready to do either, and she frowned.

Royd smiled as he reached out and gently wiped a speck of dirt off her cheek. "I'm glad to hear that."

Moriah closed her eyes, trying to ignore the warmth of his touch. His breath fanned her brows which was like a gentle charge that made her pulse skip a beat and then accelerate.

"I'll expect you tonight."

Her eyes snapped open. "I still have—"

"Plenty of time to finish working on your diary this afternoon. In fact, I'll have Moll prepare a light supper and bring it upstairs to the sitting room that separates our chambers. While we eat, you can give me some idea how I can suggest to Rebecca that they all move out to the cabin. Without offending her pride, naturally."

The lump in her throat made it impossible for Moriah to speak. She nodded as he cupped her elbow and escorted her outside. While Royd closed the door and adjusted the latchstring, Moriah stared out over the deep blue waters of the lake. Surrounded by forest, the lake glistened like a giant blue diamond. The gentle lapping of the waves against the shoreline did little to calm her shattered spirit.

Tonight.

Seemingly, an eternity stretched between now and then, but just as sure as the sun would set in a matter of hours, Moriah would have to finally keep her word. Royd did not bring up the topic, but she had no doubt that he would do so.

Tonight.

Jack grinned. "Private supper, eh? How'd you get her to agree to that? Seems to me the little lady's been avoidin' you pretty regular."

"It must be my charm and wit," Royd muttered as his fingers fumbled with his cravat.

"Need some help?"

"I'm not sixteen anymore," Royd grumbled as he finally got the cravat to fall in place and started to brush his hair. "Don't you have anything more important to do than watch me dress?"

"Nope." Jack chuckled. "Good boy, that Will. He's

got everythin' runnin' real smooth. Took a fine look at Rebecca's twins and he's been spendin' the better part of each day cross-eyed, too, tryin' to watch both of 'em."

"What about the posting to Stevens?"

"Delivered it yesterday when I stopped to see Evan."

Royd's hand froze in midair, and he stared at Jack's mirrored image. "Evan?"

"That lawyer fella is one regular chap, even if he did hoodwink me. You get a chance to look at the blueprints yet?"

Royd resumed brushing his hair and gave up trying to make the curls do anything more than fall casually around his face. "I was busy doing something else today. I set them aside." Royd felt that same acidic churning in the pit of his stomach that only Jack seemed to be able to set loose with a single comment. It occurred to Royd that it might have been easier to keep the lawyer's speculations private rather than use them to tease Jack. "Why are you so interested in the blueprints?"

"I thought I might study 'em a bit. Look for hidden treasure, so to speak."

Royd exhaled slowly and turned around to face Jack. "You really think that there's something of value hidden on this estate?"

Jack shrugged his shoulders. "A man with wealth enough to build this mansion must have had a safe to store his valuables. Evan didn't seem too interested in the subject, though. Addin' jewels or other valuables might complicate the situation."

"There is no situation," Royd countered. "Not for us. In six weeks, we're leaving. Whatever you find or don't find is a moot point. It won't belong to me."

"Yes it will. I checked the agreement with Evan today. If I should find somethin', it might be valuable enough to let you keep your business and the estate, too."

Royd started laughing in spite of himself. "You don't ever give up, do you?"

Jack grinned. "Kept after you, didn't I? What would it hurt to look? Besides," he added, "if you really do intend to leave, it makes no sense to repair much else. Will is handlin' the animals. The Haskells are helpin' Moll. Not much else left for me to do."

Royd swallowed a lump in his throat. Jack could not physically handle chopping wood or other heavy chores. Maybe letting him study the blueprints and search the house for a hidden safe might make him feel useful. He gave his permission reluctantly, however, lest Jack think Royd's go-ahead was equivalent to a *carte blanche* approval. "Check with me before you start tearing down any walls. There are enough unfinished rooms as it is! And don't you breathe a word of this to Moll. She's already got enough to do without worrying that you'll get trapped on the third floor or some secret room."

"You have my word."

"The minute you suspect you've found something, come to me. We'll have a look together."

"Of course I will! I'll need the best crackster I can find to open the safe. Think you still got the touch?"

Royd's lips pursed. "Weren't you the one who blasted me for using my unorthodox talents at the prison?"

"This is different. It's not illegal to break into somethin' that belongs to you." Jack gave him a mock salute. "I'll report back to you, Cap'n, soon as I locate the booty. Are the blueprints still in the library?"

Royd nodded silently, the corners of his mouth twitching in amusement. "The penalty for disobedience is the plank, mate."

Jack broke into a full grin and hustled out the door whistling a nautical tune and limping like he had a peg leg. Royd closed the door before he let a hearty laugh rip loose. Being reunited with Jack and Moll, despite the circumstances, had rejuvenated him. Royd had not taken a respite from either his studies or his business for the past ten years. He spent every waking hour driving himself toward a goal, straitlaced by social conventions. Maybe that's why he had forgotten the zany nature of life with Jack and Moll Clayton. It felt good to laugh again. As he walked through his suite, he only hoped that the last laugh would not be on him.

Royd entered the private sitting room directly from his suite. The supper Moll had prepared sat on a table set for two in front of a large window overlooking the front of the estate, and filled the room with tantalizing odors. Moriah had not arrived yet, but Royd was certain she would come. Selecting a mutually safe topic such as the cabin presented an opportunity to spend time together without raising issues that would be painful—for both of them.

The sound of the doorknob turning made him catch his breath. He turned around slowly, anticipating his first glance at Moriah dressed in something other than a dirt-smudged gown that covered her from neck to toe. Would she wear the apricot gown he had privately asked Moll to alter for her?

His mouth watered at the prospect of seeing the swell of Moriah's bosom and the creamy flesh at the base of her throat. His heart began to pump faster.

When he finally came about-face, Moriah stood absolutely still just inside the door. His eyes widened then narrowed before a chuckle erupted from his lips.

The vixen!

She had outsmarted him again.

♣

Twenty-four

Moriah's greatest triumph was the look of wolfish anticipation in Royd's eyes that turned like quicksilver into pools of amused disbelief. When Moll suggested that the apricot organdy gown might be the right one for this evening, Moriah had no doubt that Royd had chosen it. The pale orange creation was daring, and Moriah suspected that there was more than coincidence at work. Although the color was far from the wretched deep orange prison gown she detested, the merest hint of orange made her skin crawl.

"I hope I didn't keep you waiting," she purred, trying not to grin.

"No doubt you were kept busy sewing this afternoon," he drawled as he pulled out a chair for her at the table.

"Quite busy. I trust you're not overly disappointed. The other gown was not my color," she murmured as she took her seat. She heard Royd's deep intake of breath and knew that the issue of the gown's decolletage was easily dismissed. When Royd sat down across from her, his cheeks were flushed. She almost regretted making him suffer for his obviously unintentional blunder, but it was safer than trying to convince him that she was not the type of woman who bared her breasts in the name of fashion.

"I'm not usually so thoughtless," he admitted as he poured fragrant red wine into elegant crystal glasses that sparkled in the late rays of the afternoon sun that poured through the windows. He cleared his throat and lifted his glass in a toast. "To justice and truth."

Moriah flinched at his words, her fingers tightening around the stem of her glass. Her eyes locked with his, and she watched him warily as he sipped his wine. "An odd, but touching sentiment coming from you," she said before she followed his lead and tasted the fruity beverage. She relaxed as she felt the liquid trickle down her throat and a delicious warmth spread through her limbs.

"Not as strange as your dinner gown," he remarked. His eyes twinkled mischievously. "Did you borrow that rag from one of the Haskells?"

"Certainly not," Moriah gasped. "Those poor girls have little enough to call their own without lending something to me. I suppose it belonged to Katarina. I found it in one of the trunks in the dressing room. It's quite serviceable for my needs."

Royd laughed. "You don't find it warm?"

"No." Moriah blushed. The fabric of the black wool gown was heavy indeed, but it was the high neck and long sleeves that added the most discomfort. While the gown would undoubtedly keep her as warm as a teapot in a cozy in the winter, it was suffocating in the summer's heat. A small price to pay, she mused, just to see the look on his face when she entered the room.

Royd smiled and tipped his glass toward her. "Then perhaps it's the wine that makes your cheeks flush so prettily. It's quite a pleasure to see how quickly you've recovered."

Moriah set her glass down on the table and toyed with her food. The last thing she expected was a compliment from him, and her hand shook as she tried to cut a piece of chicken. "You wanted to talk about the cabin," she reminded him as she concentrated on slicing the meat into bite-size pieces.

"I've given your suggestion a lot of thought," he responded as he started to eat. "How do you propose telling Rebecca to move her brood out of the main house?"

"You don't tell her. You ask her. Make it seem as though she would be helping you instead of receiving more of your charity." Moriah did not know if Royd would understand how important it was not to hurt Rebecca's feelings. The woman had a guarded presence as it was, and Moriah sensed that she had experienced enough pity to last a lifetime.

"Charity is a virtue, not a vice," Royd countered.

"Perhaps for those who can afford it," she retorted, surprised by the cold tone of her voice. Her heartbeat quickened. "Women like Rebecca need opportunities to keep their families together. It's difficult being a victim of circumstance when there's no chance to survive alone in a man's world. Not without depending on a husband or father or son. Rebecca apparently has no one."

"Your point is well made, Moriah. I'll see what I can do."

Silence sat between them like an uninvited guest for the rest of the meal. Moriah concentrated on satisfying her hunger, although she barely tasted the food. She did not even notice that the sun had set until a flicker of candlelight caught her attention. Had Royd lit the candle? When?

When Royd suggested they move to the settee, she glanced at its narrow width and opted to take a high-backed chair instead. Royd smirked, took to the settee, and sat in the middle, his long legs stretched out in front of him as he casually leaned back and folded his arms across his chest.

Moriah's knees were shaking, and she locked her ankles together to try to still her skirts. Unskilled in the social graces, she had no idea what to say or how to act. Staring at the floor, she was startled when she felt him place a sheaf of papers onto her lap. Her head snapped up, and she looked at him questioningly.

"It's time you knew the truth," he said quietly. His easy demeanor had disappeared, and his expression was markedly serious. His eyes riveted on her face, and she found it hard to imagine that he was being anything but absolutely sincere.

Moriah broke eye contact and looked at the cover of what appeared to be his report on Apple Knoll. As she flipped through it, she discovered that there were actually two reports. The second one, for some reason, looked almost twice the size of the first, although both were printed and bound and looked very official. Was he actually giving her a copy of his report? Why were there two? Confused, she shook her head. "I don't understand," she whispered as she lifted her face to look at him. "Why . . ."

Royd sat up and assumed a more formal pose. "I'd like to explain a few things before you start reading the reports. As you read, take notes on them if you like. I have additional copies. When you've finished, we'll talk again, and I'll try to answer your questions. If you'll let me, I'd like to help you to revise the second report. You can use it for the hearings."

Moriah gripped the reports tightly. "I have questions I'd like answered now."

He nodded solemnly, and Moriah tried to organize the multitude of questions that swirled through her mind like autumn leaves caught in a sudden gust of wind. Taking a deep breath, she caught hold of the biggest one and gave it voice. "Is it true that you agreed to help Senator Williams cover up the problems at Apple Knoll?"

As though taken aback by her blunt accusation, Royd's eyes widened. "I agreed to investigate rumors that prompted the hearings. Rumors too wicked to be true," he added, his mouth drawn in a tight line.

Moriah pursed her lips. "The other members of the committee. Did they participate in the scheme?"

Royd snorted. "Two. Marley Young, the representative from the Society for Prison Reform, is a lecherous pervert. Senator Harris's aide, Scott Darlow, is a self-righteous hypocrite. The only man who really took his job seriously was George Atwood. He's a junior senator from one of the northern counties. He was also the committee's conscience, although neither Young nor Marley know how outraged Atwood became by his investigation. As the head of the committee, I instructed Atwood to share his findings only with me."

"To destroy them," Moriah said bitterly.

"No."

His quick denial made her brows arch, and her breathing became shallow.

"Look, Moriah. I'm not going to ask you to take my word as gospel, but I don't have any reason to lie to you. Not now. Not after . . ." His voice trailed off, and he seemed to be lost in his own thoughts before he continued. "When Atwood told me he suspected that the female inmates were being brutalized, I urged him to dig deeper into the records. What he found gave a shadow of truth to the rumors—more than either one of us could believe. But there's no direct proof. It's all circumstantial. We need eyewitness testimony. An inmate's testimony. Yours," he whispered, his eyes pleading for her understanding.

Moriah's heart softened. "My scars?"

"None of the other inmates would talk to me. Not honestly. They were too intimidated by the possibility of retribution, I suppose. You were the only one who was strong enough to be defiant, even that first day. I counted on your obvious willingness to challenge the system. That's why I was willing to breach security and try to find out about your sister for you."

It sounded plausible. Even probable. Why then did Moriah want to cover her ears so she did not have to listen? Was she so bitter and hurt that she could not bear to find out that the man she assumed had betrayed her was guilty only of trying to help? Forcing herself to smile, she tried to avoid the possibility that she had misjudged him. "What role did Lester Figgs play in this scheme?"

Royd stared off into the distance. "The warden. What a fine specimen of debauchery! He has important friends in the senate whose primary interests lie in making a profit from prison labor. As long as Figgs fills their pockets, they don't care a whit about anything else. Unfortunately," he added with disdain, "the warden is more observant than I thought. Even though he seemed convinced that I would do the senators' bidding, he must have had me followed to make doubly sure I would be cooperative. It's the only way he could have found out that you and I were meeting in secret." Royd slammed his fist on his thigh. "I shouldn't have been so almighty cocky!"

Moriah had expected the explanation Royd gave her. What she did not anticipate was the pain and self-recrimination that etched his face. It unnerved her own belief that Royd willingly betrayed her to the warden, and she felt the seeds of doubt about Royd's honesty begin to wither.

Judge not.

Moriah allowed her previous condemnation to be questionable and offered her own suspicions as penance. "I could have been responsible," she admitted. "The guards were overly cautious during the committee's visit. I shouldn't have left my cell. They could have spotted me as I returned and overheard our conversation when they came to investigate. If they suspected that you were wavering, rather than take any chances, it was wiser to make sure that I was silenced."

What Moriah said was only half the truth, but she was reluctant to discuss her visit to Iona and the possibility that their conversation had been noticed. That would require an explanation he would most likely dismiss. Without using the information in her diary as proof, she was hesitant to bring it up until she was sure he would not misuse it.

With a soft heave of her chest, Moriah felt tears begin to swell. "Maybe it's not your fault," she murmured. "How . . . how did you know what they had done to me?"

Royd stood up and paced the room. "Figgs wrote to the good senators, explaining his fears that I was undermining the report. When I gave Senator Williams the version that revealed the rumors to be truth, he insisted that I rewrite it. In the process of threatening me with financial and social ruin, he mentioned that inmate Number Seventy-nine had been sent to Willow Valley."

The cold tone of Royd's voice made Moriah shiver almost as much as his admission that he had tried to reveal the truth about Apple Knoll. She glanced at the reports on her lap. "Are these copies of each of the reports?"

He nodded. "Read the smaller report first. That's the official version Williams will rely on at the hearings. At least you'll know what the opposition is using. The second report is the one Williams rejected. It's still not complete. Not without adding the information about you or your sister."

Poor Ruth. Thinking about what had happened to her sister made her chest tighten. She did not want to break down in front of Royd and swallowed her grief. What about the others? She thought about the women whose names and abuses were recorded on the remnants of her diary that were now safely hidden away. Surely what had been done to these women had to be added to the reports!

Moriah's trust in Royd Camden, however, was still tentative, and she reserved a decision about telling him the contents of her diary until she could be certain that he was worthy of her confidence.

When Moriah did not respond to Royd's statement, he approached her with a look of genuine concern that made her heart skip a beat. "Is it too difficult to share what happened to Ruth with the committee?" he asked, so softly that his words were like a gentle caress that left her bewildered.

It seemed ironic that the pain of knowing how Ruth died would be understood by a man she had labeled as Lucifer's disciple. The compassion and empathy that filled his eyes, however, made her tremble. "Ruth's death makes a mockery of a system meant to reform inmates, not abuse them," she said, too shaken to raise her voice above a whisper.

"And these," he murmured as he crouched before her and tenderly lifted her wrists, nudging the cuffs of her sleeves back to reveal her scars. His touch was warm as his fingers gently traced the thickened flesh on the inside of her wrists.

The moment Moriah dreaded for so long was at hand, yet she was distracted by the sensations that he aroused. Her hands rested in his palms, and as he massaged her wrists, she felt the tenseness ease from her body. As he turned her wrists over and studied the ugly scars that banded each wrist, she closed her eyes, unwilling to see repugnance or pity reflected in his gaze. Her heart began to pound, and she felt her palms begin to sweat.

When she felt the brush of his lips on one of her wrists, her eyes snapped open. The dark curls that covered his head obscured his face as he kissed the scars on her other wrist. Her breathing grew shallow, and her head started to spin.

"You didn't inflict these on yourself." It was a statement, not a question. His words, husky with emotion, demanded no verbal response, but Moriah would have been unable to find her voice even if she tried. Overwhelmed by his actions, she stared at him when he finally lifted his head to gaze at her. She nodded, silently acknowledging that her scars were the result of ducking.

"Pale Eyes," he murmured. "Do you know how your eyes have haunted me? You are the most intriguing nemesis I could have imagined."

Confused and shaken by the raw desire reflected in his eyes, Moriah licked her dry lips and pulled out of his grasp. Her physical response to his touch turned to ice and made her earlier assumptions about his motives seem premature. Is that what he expected in return for his help? An illicit liaison? Bile stung the back of her throat. The only difference between this man and Lester Figgs was a handsome face and a glib tongue!

Standing abruptly, Moriah reached the door before he could recover from her rebuff. "I'll read the reports. If I have any questions, I'll let you know," she informed him icily before disappearing into her suite.

Royd clenched his fist to prevent himself from punching a hole in the wall. *Stupid!* How could he have been so blatant about the beastly lust that surged the moment she stepped through the door and reared its ugly head the instant he touched her?

The little minx would have been safer if she had worn the apricot gown, although he was not certain he could ever forgive himself for selecting that particular color. Dressed like a novice, she had still aroused him. Instead of making her look like a spinster, the sober black gown complemented her pale coloring, and the heavy winter garment made her flush, adding a delightful tint to her cheeks. The virginal style of the garment cast an aura of subdued sexuality to her angelic persona, inciting his loins to the point of recklessness.

He tried to distance his physical attraction to her by making a concerted effort to be as truthful as he could be when explaining his role as a member of the committee. The experience was more humbling than he expected, but his sincerity must have cracked the barrier that she erected between them. She actually looked like she believed him. Until . . .

Damn! Touching her had been a fatal mistake. His pulse quickened the moment he felt the soft under-flesh of her wrist. The raised, toughened scars were like magnets that drew his lips to them. God's blood! A simple kiss had set a fire in his eyes that rebuilt the stone wall she erected as quickly as the old one had crumbled!

He snickered. No. It was more than just a touch. It was her eyes, enticing pools of pale, lustrous beauty that sent shock waves through his body . . . until they churned and darkened with anger when he kissed her. Moriah's sudden shift in mood was a personal rejection that still smarted.

Pensive, he tried to rationalize her behavior. Was she afraid he would use sex as a leverage, withholding his help unless she shared her body with him? Did she think he was that contemptible? That notion hurt him almost as much as the realization that he could never compromise her virtue, and he found himself trying to understand his own behavior instead of hers. Shame filled his entire being when he realized that he was no better than the other men she had met in the past few years. She had been victimized too often in the past, and she did not deserve to be treated with any less respect than he had given to Alexandria or the other women he had known.

He could not undo his rash behavior tonight, but he could try to convince her that he was sorry for not acting like a gentleman and for not treating her like a lady. Time. He needed to give her the time to read the reports and see for herself that he had already given her enough information to make the legislature at least investigate

conditions at Apple Knoll further. Time in which he had
to convince her that he could control his baser instincts.
He would finish editing Brockley's manuscript while
Jack played pirate searching for booty. The Haskells
would be removed to the cottage. Moriah would read
and revise the report.

Within a few weeks, he and Moriah would go their
separate ways. He would return to Hampton to his fiancée and his business while Moriah traveled to Harrisburg for the hearings the first week in October.

Refreshed in mind and body, Royd would face the
future a much wiser man. There was only one benefit to
being so wise, he mused as he returned to his suite. It
would take a lot of wisdom to help him to figure out a
way to take less than a lifetime to forget her.

＊

Twenty-five

Instead of spending the entire afternoon in the library working with Royd on the report as she had done for the past ten days, Moriah decided to visit Rebecca. After leaving a note for Royd, she slipped past the outbuildings and followed the path that led to the cabin. The four older girls were helping Moll do laundry today while Jack took charge of the three youngest for a few hours. She heard them plotting a surprise for Rebecca, although she questioned whether Rebecca would be as pleased with the butter they were going to churn as she would be dismayed by the unholy mess they would make of their garments in the process!

September was only a few days old, but already the first signs of fall had appeared. As she walked, she noticed some of the leaves beginning to change from deep green to pale yellow. The summer berries were as scarce as Bandit these days. How quickly he had reverted to his inborn, wild nature! She saw him occasionally in the early evening, foraging for food a bit too close to the house to suit Moll who swished him away with her broom.

The smell of pine faded as she approached the cabin, replaced by the fragrant aroma of molasses that made Moriah's mouth water. When Rebecca unlatched the door and swung it open, Moriah grinned at her. "You're making cookies!"

Rebecca smiled as she wiped a smudge of flour off her cheek. "It usually brings the girls running. It's my mother's recipe. Would you like a sample?"

"I shouldn't," Moriah groaned as she followed Rebecca inside. "My gowns are growing tight, and I don't dare ask Moll to let them out again!"

Rebecca handed her a still-warm cookie. "You look good and healthy to me."

The cookie melted in Moriah's mouth, and she closed her eyes, savoring every delicious morsel. "Delicious," she pronounced, unable to resist eating two more while Rebecca removed the last batch and set them on the table to cool. Moriah glanced around the room. "You've done wonders with the cabin. Are you and the girls happy here?"

Rebecca nodded as she scrubbed the baking sheet clean. "Mr. Royd made it sound like we were doing him a real favor by settling into the cabin, but I—"

The cabin door swung open, and Rebecca's mouth dropped. Her eyes bulged, and the color drained from her face. Fear stiffened her body, and she looked like she had turned to stone. Heart pounding, Moriah spun around, and her eyes widened as she gazed at the awesome figure of a man who had stepped through the door. His hands clutched a rifle which crossed in front of his barreled chest. His cold glare rooted Moriah to her spot, and she heard Rebecca gasp as he moved awkwardly toward both of them, dragging his right foot along the floorboards.

Moriah's only thought was escape, but he blocked the only exit. Curiously, he seemed to ignore her after a cursory glance and stared at Rebecca who was shaking from head to toe. He stopped just inches away from Rebecca who had covered her face with her hands.

When Moriah tried to take a step closer to the woman, the man growled at her.

"Don't move!"

Moriah froze. "What do you want?" she croaked, hoping to dissuade him from whatever wickedness he had planned.

"Want?" He snickered and nudged Rebecca's hands with the barrel of his weapon. "I want my wife, don't I, Becky?"

Moriah watched in horrified fascination as Rebecca's hands dropped to her side. Tears streamed down her face, and her lips quivered. "I—I thought you were dead," she stammered.

His guttural laugh sent chills down Moriah's spine.

"Tried to kill me. My own wife! It'll take more than a few stabs of your kitchen knife, bitch!" He cracked the barrel of the gun across Rebecca's face, and she cried out as she collapsed to the floor, grabbing her cheek.

"Leave her alone!" Moriah screamed as she scrambled to Rebecca's side. Clutching the woman's shoulders, Moriah shielded her with her own body.

"Get away from her, or you'll suffer along with her. I've waited a year to make her pay for what she did to me!"

Rebecca lifted her head and groaned. "You should have died. You're not fit to live and breathe! Now leave before Mr. Royd finds you here."

"I'm your lawful husband. No man can interfere with my rights. Where are my girls?" he demanded, jamming the butt of the rifle into Rebecca's stomach. She curled into a ball, crying hysterically.

"They're not here," Moriah lied, praying that none of the girls would come home to witness their father's brutality.

Rebecca gripped Moriah's hands and pulled into a sitting position on the floor. Hatred flared in her eyes. "You'll have to kill me before I let you near them again.

Son of Satan! You tried to defile your own flesh and blood! Bastard!"

With one kick to Rebecca's head, the monster knocked his wife nearly unconscious. She fell limply into Moriah's arms. Shaking with fear, Moriah cradled Rebecca's battered and bleeding face against her chest. If what Rebecca said was true, the woman had just cause to murder her husband.

Embittered by the man's unconscionable acts against his wife and at least one of his daughters, Moriah glared at him. "Get out."

He laughed at her. "I want my girls. You can have Becky. Ain't no good for breedin' anythin' but females, anyway. Sarah and Anna are ripe enough to take her place. They'll raise the younger ones for me, too."

Moriah felt her stomach start to contract, and she covered her mouth. What kind of monster would violate his own daughters? Rebecca stirred, her eyes fluttering open. The instant she regained her senses, she tried to stand. Her legs were too weak to support her, and Moriah clutched the woman around the waist to steady her.

Rebecca squared her shoulders in a feeble attempt to look defiant. Blood oozed from the corner of her mouth, and her bruised cheek had already started to swell. "I've made a new life for myself here, Raymond. The girls are happier now. Please."

He pointed the rifle at Moriah, ignoring his wife. "Get 'em. Now. If you're not back here in thirty minutes, I'll start breakin' every bone in her wretched body."

Moriah gazed into Rebecca's eyes. "I won't leave you."

The woman's lopsided smile was weak. "Do as he says. I don't want you to be hurt," she whispered, her speech slurred.

"I can't bring the girls . . . to him!"

"Got no choice," he snickered as he put the barrel of the gun at the base of Moriah's throat. "Either get my girls and bring them back to me, or I'll blow your head off. And don't get any fancy ideas about summoning help. The law says they belong to me. There's nothin' you can do to stop me."

Moriah gulped, and her throat brushed against the cold metal. Nervous perspiration bathed her body. After squeezing Rebecca's hands in an offer of silent support, she walked shakily to the door. Once she stepped outside and started walking away from the cabin, a band of steel wrapped around her waist from behind, and a hand clasped over her mouth.

Terrified, she held her breath as a voice whispered into her ear. "Go back to the house and make sure the girls stay with you. Get Will to help you, and send Jack here. Tell him to stay well hidden until I signal for him. Can you do that?"

Royd! Sagging against his chest, she nodded weakly as he removed his hand and spun her around to embrace her for a moment that was all too brief.

"Run!" he whispered as he turned her toward the main house. "I'll make sure Rebecca is safe."

Moriah could barely see as she tore back to the house. Tears streamed down her face. With every trembling breath she took, she prayed that Royd could save Rebecca from that horrid, miserable cur!

Royd flattened his body against the exterior cabin wall and listened, waiting for the right moment to enter. After finding Moriah's note, he had decided to join her at the cabin. Fortunately, He was at the edge of the woods when he saw a man carrying a rifle break through the door, and he felt a sense of outrage that was so fierce it frightened him.

His first instinct was to barge inside to rescue Moriah and Rebecca, but his better judgment urged caution. He carried no weapon, although he would kill the man with his bare hands if he dared to touch either of the women.

By the time he crept stealthily to the window and peeked inside, Rebecca was already the victim of the man's brutality. Moriah looked scared out of her wits, but unharmed. He had heard and seen enough to understand that Haskell, if that was his name, had relinquished any justifiable claim to his wife or to his daughters. Convincing the man to leave would be a pleasure, although Royd's first concern was getting Rebecca safely away from his grasp.

After ten minutes of tense silence, Royd ventured a furtive look through the window. The man had his back to the door, but Royd was dismayed to find the rifle still clutched in the man's fist. When the bastard raised it as if to strike Rebecca again, Royd reacted instinctively, quickly formulating a diversion that he prayed would work.

Walking boldly into the cabin, Royd cleared his throat as he crossed his arms in front of his chest. "I wouldn't do that if I were you," he said firmly.

The rifle froze in midair and then swung around to point squarely at Royd's midsection.

"Who the blazes are you?"

Royd's voice remained steady. "I'm Rebecca's employer. This is my land. Who are you?"

The man straightened his aim. "Raymond Haskell. I'm Rebecca's husband. That blonde bitch send you here?"

Royd glared at him. "Moriah is my ward. I came here expecting to escort her home. Where is she?" he asked, hoping to convince Haskell that Moriah had not tricked him or disobeyed him.

The man's expression changed from skepticism to arrogance in less than a heartbeat. "I sent her to fetch my daughters."

Royd relaxed his stance. "She must have used the path. I'm afraid your arrival is a bit unexpected. Rebecca told me she was a widow."

"Damn near came to be the truth," Haskell snarled. "She run off with my daughters and left me bleedin' like a stuck pig. You got a problem with my takin' the girls with me?"

Royd shrugged his shoulders. "Not if Rebecca identifies you as her husband and the girls' father. I don't want any trouble. The law gives you the right to your own children."

Was it his imagination or did Haskell lower the rifle just enough to indicate he believed Royd? Haskell turned his head briefly to the side. "Tell him, Becky."

Rebecca nodded, her pleading eyes wet with tears. Royd smiled and pointed to the gun. "You don't need to threaten anyone, Mr. Haskell. You're free to leave with the girls. Take Rebecca, too. I won't have a woman working for me who stole a man's family and denied him his rightful place as the children's father."

Haskell grinned and dropped his rifle to his side. He turned to Rebecca and spat in her face. Before he could take another breath, Royd leaped at him, knocking the man to the floor and sending the rifle sliding out of reach. Haskell outweighed Royd by several dozen pounds and used his superior strength to land a painful series of blows to Royd's head.

Dazed, Royd fought back as they rolled on the floor. He managed to land a few stunning blows of his own, but either the man had lost all sense of feeling or Royd was not as strong as he thought he was. The man scrambled to his feet and kicked Royd in the groin. Doubled over in pain, Royd saw the glint of a knife blade through a blurred, hazy mist. The weapon descended in an awkward arc when a sudden blast echoed in the cabin.

Ears ringing, Royd staggered to his feet. Raymond Haskell twitched, a look of surprise on his face, before he fell forward, a gaping wound in his back. Royd blinked twice before his eyes focused clearly on Rebecca, who slowly lowered the rifle, her chest heaving with wracking sobs that filled the room.

Light from a single candle cast her shadow on the wall as Moriah bent over Rebecca's sleeping form. Using a fresh, damp cloth, Moriah wiped the woman's face before pressing a cold compress to her bruised cheek. Little Ruth, near hysterics when Royd carried the child's mama back to the main house, slept peacefully now, her head nestled in the crook of Rebecca's arms.

Moll had taken charge of the other girls who accepted Moriah's explanation that their mother had been injured in a fall while cleaning the top of the cupboard in the cabin. Royd took credit for the sound of the gunshot, and Moriah was grateful that the girls believed his story about falling and tripping in the woods, discharging his gun by accident. Except for Ruth, the girls were all asleep upstairs. Moll had promised to relieve Moriah after she had helped Jack to clean up the cabin.

When the door creaked open, Royd tiptoed into the room. Moriah smiled weakly as he approached the bed.

"How is she?" he whispered, his gaze centered on Rebecca.

"Moll gave her a dose of laudanum. At least she'll sleep peacefully through the night."

Royd's eyes widened when the little girl squirmed closer to her mother as they both slept. "What's Ruth doing here? Rebecca needs her rest."

With a sigh, Moriah tucked the covers around Ruth's shoulders. "She's afraid her mama is going to die. It seemed to calm her when Rebecca told her to stay."

Royd nodded, his expression hardening. "You need your rest, too. It's been a long and frightening day for you."

"I'd like to stay a little longer," Moriah protested as she changed the compress. "It's all my fault," she murmured, her eyes filling with tears. "If I hadn't interfered,

Rebecca wouldn't have been in the cabin alone. Her husband would never have dared to burst into the main house."

"It's not your fault," he argued. "Rebecca wanted to move into the cabin. If you're set on fixing blame, try her husband."

Although Moriah knew he was right, she still felt responsible. "Poor Rebecca." Moriah sighed. "She's been carrying a heavy burden. Alone. Now that her secret has surfaced . . ."

"We all have secrets, Moriah. Rebecca's secret was just more awful than most."

Royd's compassion and understanding tugged at Moriah's heartstrings, but something in his voice made him sound almost vulnerable himself. "It won't be a secret any longer," she murmured.

Royd shook his head. "No one need ever know what happened here today. As far as anyone else in concerned, Raymond Haskell died a year ago."

Surprised by the vehemence in Royd's tone of voice and his willingness to cover up the murder of Rebecca's husband, Moriah looked at Royd quizzically. "You're not going to report what Rebecca did to the sheriff?"

"No."

"What about the body?"

"Jack and I buried the son of a bitch." He shook his head. "Rebecca suffered enough at that brute's hands. She acted to protect her daughters as well as herself. She also saved my life. Having her sent to prison or even enduring a trial where the bastard's vile actions against his family would have to be revealed would be more than unfair. It would destroy Rebecca and the girls."

Moriah swallowed the lump in her throat as she recalled Royd's quick contempt when he learned that Moriah had been convicted of murdering her uncle. "The law says it's murder," she murmured.

Royd cocked his head and smiled weakly. "Legally?

Yes, unless the jury believed it was justifiable homicide. I'd like to think they would take my word. Maybe they wouldn't. There's little if any proof that Haskell attempted to rape his own daughter unless one of the girls would testify. Even then, enough men in the jury would be afraid to condone Rebecca's actions, probably out of fear that other women would be encouraged to strike back at abusive husbands." His voice grew softer, although more resolute. "It's too risky. Rebecca and her daughters deserve to put the past behind them without adding more unpleasant memories." He paused, his eyes softening. "No one knows the fickle nature of the law more than you do, Moriah. Your imprisonment was a travesty of justice."

Moriah's hands began to tremble, and she clasped them together on her lap so he would not notice. "You know?" she whispered, her voice laced with surprise.

He nodded. "The director at Willow Valley explained the case to me. Why didn't your lawyer appeal the conviction?"

"I don't think there's an appeal when you plead guilty," she answered slowly. "Our guardian, Reverend Glenn, insisted." She looked at Royd. When his expression hardened, she smiled shyly. "It doesn't matter. The past is spent. It's the future that worries me more. How can Rebecca keep what happened secret from her children?"

"She will. For their sake," Royd answered softly as he gazed at Moriah. "We all have secrets."

"What secrets could you possibly have that could compare to Rebecca's or mine?"

Royd's eyes held hers for an eternity before he answered. "My parents were thieves who trained me to follow in their footsteps. I watched them hang when I was eight years old. I survived on the streets by stealing until Moll and Jack took me in. They gave me a chance to turn my life around, and I succeeded. If anyone were to learn about my past, my future wouldn't be worth much. That's why I need to keep men like Senator Williams placated. If not . . ." He grinned sardonically. "I can't even use my real name. I had to break all contact with Moll and Jack. Is that enough of a secret to measure up to yours?"

Spellbound, Moriah found it difficult to witness the pain etched in Royd's features and averted her gaze. No wonder he agreed to the senator's demands! His entire way of life was at stake, and for the first time, she understood how risky it was for Royd to help her. Guilt for judging him without knowing all the facts made her heart heavy with remorse. "I-I'm sorry. I didn't know." Thinking about how close Moll and Jack were to Royd, she found it difficult to understand why they had to break contact with one another. "I don't understand why you couldn't see Moll and Jack. They're such good people. Why?"

Royd laughed. "I told you we all have secrets. Jack was afraid my reputation would be ruined if anyone found out that he and Moll were my surrogate parents. Jack is an ex-jailbird with two convictions for forgery."

"No!"

"Ask him. He won't deny it. He'll even show you the numbers tattooed on his arm. It was Jack who forged the documents that convinced the director at Willow Valley to release you into my custody. You aren't my ward after all."

The room started to spin, and Moriah closed her eyes as she took several deep gulps of air to clear her head. Was nothing as it appeared to be?

Moriah gasped. "If the papers making you my guardian were a forgery, what about the papers from the judge that stated my prison sentence was completed even though I was sent to Willow Valley instead of finishing the remaining days at Apple Knoll?"

"I wouldn't risk having Jack forge something that im-

portant to you, Moriah. Judge Martindell signed that
order. He's a close friend of mine. He won't divulge
anything to Senator Williams, either, so you needn't
worry."

When Royd placed his hand on her shoulder, he startled her, and she opened her eyes to find him gazing
down at her with tender affection. "We're not enemies,
Moriah. In fact, I daresay we're more alike than you
could have possibly imagined. Trust me, Moriah. Let me
help you stop Lester Figgs. If I betray your trust, you can
use what I've just told you against me. Believe me, the
jackals will destroy my name and my business in less
than a fortnight."

Moriah's pulse quickened as she studied his face. The
handsome devil who tormented her for so long was only
a man, a human being with faults and virtues no different from any other. But this man, with bedazzling honesty reflected in the depths of his green eyes, was able to
reveal his past and take the blame for trying to protect
his future. Would other men be as forthright?

When confronted with an ethical dilemma, Royd
faltered, perhaps, but in the end, he made the conscious
choice to take a stand. He risked everything by rescuing
her and providing the help she desperately needed. Was
he merely trying to salvage his conscience or did he have
another motive?

Taking a deep breath, Moriah realized it was time to
stop making assumptions and simply ask him. "Why are
you really telling me all this?"

Royd gazed at her with such intensity that Moriah's
heart nearly stopped beating. "I know all of your secrets.
It only seems fair that you should know mine."

If Moriah's assumptions about Royd Camden had
been a kaleidoscope of contradictions before, now they
were a huge thundercloud that rumbled and rolled
through her mind. Shaken by her failure to judge him
correctly, shame filled her breast and reddened her

cheeks. Tears washed away the contempt and distrust that had hardened her heart against the man who never once intentionally hurt her even though he had many opportunities to do so.

Humbled, she dried her tears and took a deep breath before reaching out and clasping his hand. "I owe you an apology," she offered, shaking her head when he started to speak. "You've done more for me than I probably know. You've also been honest when you could easily have kept your silence," she murmured. "If we're going to stop Lester Figgs, there can't be any more secrets. I have one last secret I must share with you."

♣
Twenty-six

Royd followed Moriah down the hall to the library, his mind racing. *The diary.* Was she finally going to share its contents with him? The candle she carried trembled in her hands, but the look on her face was resolute. When her hand reached out to grasp the doorknob, he placed his hand over hers. "Don't," he pleaded, unwilling to take advantage of her while she was still reeling from the gruesome events of the day. He wanted her to reveal the contents of the diary because she trusted him, not out of some sense of obligation incurred by his confession about his past or her weakness caused by her recent confinement at Willow Valley.

Still defiant, she shook her head and turned the knob. As she opened the door, Royd had the distinct feeling that once they stepped through that door, neither of them would ever be able to hang on to the tentative trust they now shared. Not when she realized later what she had done. Would she resent him? Charge him with deliberately tricking her into revealing the secrets in the diary . . . secrets she had guarded nearly at the cost of her life? No. For now, it made better sense to him to leave the last remaining secret as a phantom without features rather than a fully detailed monster which would haunt them both in the morning.

Once inside the room, Moriah slipped over to the desk and sat the candle close to the final draft of his report which lay strewn in semiorganized piles. After stacking the report together, she carried it over to the table in front of the window and laid it down. She hesitated for a moment, apparently preoccupied as she studied the bookshelves before she moved to a series of volumes Royd could not identify as any more important than the others.

Intrigued, he waited just inside the door, watching with increasing curiosity as she removed the leather tomes and laid them on the floor. Distracted by a fleeting glimpse of her ankles as she stood on tiptoe to reach up to the now barren shelf, his eyes narrowed further as soon as he realized that she was searching for something that apparently had been hidden just beyond her reach.

Taking several long strides, he casually stepped alongside of her and reached into the shadowed void. Grasping a pile of folded papers that had been wedged next to the wall, he handed them to her and turned away to walk toward the table.

Relief, all too apparent on his face, surged through his body. Expecting to find the strips of her leather diary, Royd wondered if the secret she had to share was something different. Something he could bear to hear. Gradually, his heartbeat returned to normal, and he sat down, confident that he would not have to dissuade her from explaining the entries in her diary.

Moriah sat down across from him and placed the folded papers in front of him. The candlelight shining from some distance across the room cast their little alcove into little more than dusk. She looked about, retrieved the candle, and set it in the middle of the table.

As Royd's eyes adjusted to the brightness, she tried to smooth the folds from the papers and shuffled through them, rearranging them several times before she seemed satisfied and laid them on her lap. As last, she looked up, her blue eyes luminous. "Keeping secrets has caused a lot of misunderstandings between us. The report," she said as she laid her hand on top it, "is almost finished. I-I couldn't have dared to gather the facts as thoroughly as you did."

Royd cleared the lump in his throat. "George Atwood deserves most of the credit," he murmured, his eyes focusing on the golden highlights in her hair that caught every flicker of the candle's flame.

"You could have stopped him. You could have cooperated with Senator Williams. You didn't."

Shifting in his seat, Royd stared at the report. "If I had any character at all, I would march that report straight to the legislature myself instead of sneaking back to Hampton and letting you shoulder that responsibility alone."

"Don't underestimate your courage," she said softly. "Neither should you overestimate mine. It's my responsibility. My mission. Perhaps it's why the Lord sent you to me, and why he spared me. I prayed so hard for an avenging angel to help me."

Royd sneered at her support. "I'm quite sure the good Lord made His first mistake if he sent me as His angel."

When Moriah chuckled, his eyes narrowed. "What do you find humorous? The notion that God can make mistakes or the ludicrous idea that I'm some sort of angel?"

"You'd look perfectly ridiculous with wings," she said, laughing. "Now that you mention it, you couldn't be an angel. You have a beard."

"You have Bandit to thank for that rather belated addition to my visage," he said, his hand instinctively stroking the whiskers on his left cheek. Her eyes widened, and it was his turn to laugh. "You wouldn't care to hear how much fun I had trying to lose that critter in the woods, I suppose?"

Moriah bit her lower lip, her eyes pooling with concern that made his heart begin to pound. "What happened?"

"Before or after he mauled my back and gouged my face?"

She clapped her hands over her mouth. "He didn't!"

Royd nodded and burst out laughing. "It's not the crime of the century, Moriah. We reached a compromise. Eventually."

"Compromise?" she croaked.

"We both walked. All the way back to the inn which nearly cost me my room. Blasted critter tried to follow me back to Hampton, too. After a few miles, I finally relented and scooped him into the coach and took him home, which sent my housekeeper into a frenzy. Last I heard she was still spreading rather juicy tales about the whole episode even though she quit without giving me notice."

Moriah blushed, but Royd waved away her embarrassment. "He turned out to be good company, and I realized that he might be able to help you so I brought him along with me to Willow Valley."

"He did help me," she murmured, and her eyes darkened.

"Why do you suppose he's decided to leave now? I thought for sure that you'd have him installed in your suite."

"Not with Moll around. Besides," she added, her expression growing wistful, "he has better company now. I've seen him with a mate."

"That's just wonderful!" Royd uttered with feigned alarm. "The rascal's litters will overrun the property. We'll never be rid of him."

Moriah shrugged her shoulders and grinned as though the idea appealed to her. "I'd like to see the little coons, but I'll be gone in another month. Will you be staying here for the winter or returning to Hampton?"

"I don't have much choice," Royd admitted slowly. "I

can't run my printing firm from this distance." Royd
found the idea of staying on the estate without Moriah
almost as unfathomable as resuming his old life. Now
that he and Moriah were able to talk to each other without any secrets separating them, he found Moriah even
more beguiling.

Secrets.

His smile faded, and he glanced at the papers on her
lap.

Moriah seemed to sense the turn of his thoughts and
handed him the papers. She moistened her lips and lowered her gaze. "Do you remember the promise you
made never to ask about my diary?"

Royd's back stiffened, and his hands gripped the side
of his chair. "It's a vow I intend to keep."

"I didn't trust you enough to let you read it . . . before now," she said, her voice cracking with emotion.
"I've transcribed the coded entries from the leather diary onto paper."

His mouth went dry as she placed the folded papers
on the table in front of him. He stared at her, his heart
nearly pumping out of control. What kind of man did
she think he was? Had she been so isolated from decent
society that she did not know that he would not take
advantage of her distressed condition just to satisfy his
curiosity?

"Keep your secret safe for now," he murmured. "I'm
not sure you're in any state of mind right now to judge
whether or not you can trust me." He handed the papers
out to her. "Hold these until you've had a chance to rest.
Think about what giving them to me truly means. I can
wait. For as long as it takes."

She gazed deep into his eyes as she urged the papers
away and smiled. "I trust you. Read the entries. They're
out of proper order, but I want you to read them all. I
trust you'll do the right thing and help me after you do."

"I don't care to read them now!" he thundered, his

voice echoing violently about the room. "I don't see how waiting a few days will matter."

Moriah flinched, her eyes glimmering with tears.

Ashamed of himself for using such a sharp tone of voice, he realized that it might be the only way to dissuade her from making a mistake. For tonight. Tomorrow she might appreciate his reticence and understand his harsh rejection of her offer.

Visibly shaken, Moriah's face drained of its color. She rose and her hand rested on his shoulder, lingering briefly before she drew back. "I have a right to make up my own mind. I'm not certain why you're reluctant to read my diary, but the information it contains is too important to allow your pride or mine to prevent it from being used wisely." She turned around and walked from the room, her back straight, her steps steady.

Slamming his fist on the table, Royd sent the candle toppling to the side, splaying wet wax onto his hands as he grabbed it before it could set the papers on fire. Dratted female! If she wanted to rile him enough to read her blasted diary, so be it!

Ripping the first page from the pile, Royd held it closer to the candle. As the flame danced and flickered, shadows obscured most of Moriah's carefully penned words. When the candlelight grew steady, his hands started to shake as soon as he read the first entry.

He sank deep into the chair and slowly continued to read the rest, only too aware of the snicker of his conscience that cursed him as a fool for ever believing that the rumors about Apple Knoll were false.

After checking one last time on Rebecca, Moriah returned to her suite of rooms although she had to make her way slowly without the aid of the candle. Physically exhausted and emotionally drained, she was nevertheless too upset by her confrontation with Royd to sleep.

After undressing slowly, she slipped a sleeveless nightgown over her head, letting the soft, lustrous fabric glide into place with a whisper. Tying a ribboned bow in the scooped neckline, she sighed. She turned away from the platformed bed which was softly drenched in moonlight. A gentle, late summer breeze brushed her back as she sat at the dressing table to undo her braids. Staring into the dark, obscured mirror, she combed her hair and let it hang in wavy ringlets around her face.

On impulse, she climbed the turret stairs, grateful that she had left the top door to the terrace open so that slivers of moonlight guided her steps. Once she reached the terrace, she stared out over the walls, listening to the fading night sounds of summer's cicadas and crickets. The trees, swaying majestically in the wind, added a chorus of rustling leaves and creaking branches. Overhead, a galaxy of twinkling stars challenged the moon's luminance while far below, the lush heavy scent of summer gave way to the subtle promise of fall.

Nature's beautiful and orderly passage from one season to the next reminded Moriah how badly she had managed the transition from being a prisoner to a free woman. Instead of starting a new life with her sister at her side and her Christian faith intact, Moriah faced an uncertain future. Alone. With the awesome responsibility of standing up against a system corrupted by a few men who viewed women, especially convicts, as less consequential than the lowest of God's creations. Her faith seemed to falter as often as it was challenged. Worse, she seemed unable to find a speck of forgiveness in her heart for the men who had committed such unspeakable horrors. Lester Figgs, Tamin Jones, Senator Williams. Even Raymond Haskell. All evil men, their souls destined to spend eternity in hell if God had any true sense of justice.

Royd Camden.

A good man who tried to help. A man who was downstairs reading her diary, learning that he had been part of a plot to cover up atrocities against female prisoners. Villainy that would continue until someone had the courage to step forward and demand reform. Why didn't she tell him about the diary entries before now?

Analyzing her motives, she realized that it was more than just fear that he would destroy the information the diary contained. Tears of regret trickled slowly down her cheeks as she admitted to herself that she needed to have a reason to stay near him. If he finally learned the truth about Apple Knoll, would he see her as a hapless victim instead of a woman? Would the primal desire she saw blazing in his eyes disappear? Holding the diary like a shield of armor between them, she was also able to protect herself from her own weakness, her own wicked desires.

God help her. From the first moment he held her in his arms, she fell in love with him. In spite of his faults. In spite of his betrayal. In spite of all that was rational. She loved Royd Camden, and the frightening physical desires she felt for him made her weep.

As the secrets between them unfurled, like the petals of a rose, her love blossomed and deepened. Could she bear it if he dismissed her now? A man like Royd would have too much honor to ravish her virginal body without the promise of marriage.

A sound, somewhere between a sob and a laugh, escaped her lips as she dried her tears with the palms of her hands. Royd's future in genteel society had no room for a wife who was a convicted murderess! Her love for Royd was doomed from the start, but her heart refused to listen.

She almost wished that she had taken his advice and kept her diary secret for a few more days. Maybe then he would have taken her to his bed, and she would have had one precious moment to tuck away like a child hordes a piece of candy. Moriah could have savored the memory of his kiss, his touch, and his loving embrace. For a lifetime.

A sudden gust of wind chilled her flesh, and she made her way back down the turret stairs. She was not sure what she would say to Royd in the morning, assuming he would even speak to her. Perhaps he would simply assure her that he would use the information in the diary at the hearings and send her on her way, a thought that made her regret giving him the diary all over again.

As she emerged into her bedchamber, she closed the door to the turret. Bowing her head, she rested her forehead against the door and closed her eyes. The beat of her pulse was steady, and she wondered how that could be. Her heart was broken.

Royd stood in front of the window next to Moriah's bed. He had not been totally surprised to find her chamber empty, although he still was not accustomed to her habit of disappearing when he least expected it. Instead of letting panic send him on a frantic search for her, he waited for her to return so that he could talk to her. He practiced apologizing, something that seemed to be his specialty when it came to Moriah. He never seemed to do or say the right thing, something that was a new experience for him, particularly when it involved the gentler sex.

Was it because they had started out as such total enemies or was it because every time he looked into her eyes, his mind was bedazzled by the woman?

Time dragged on interminably, and he was afraid that if she did not return soon he would be totally tongue-tied when he finally confronted her. When he finally heard her footsteps as she descended from the turret and stepped into the room, he heaved a sigh of relief.

Royd gazed at her dejected form as she leaned against the door. Her nightgown, colored such a pale yellow that it was almost white, shimmered as she breathed. When she turned around, his mouth went dry, and he sucked in his breath. Awed by her sylphlike beauty, his loins ached with a need he had denied for too long, and he knew that talking to her was definitely the last thing he wanted to do.

Moriah's eyes, large with wonder, locked with his, and she hesitated as a shadow of a smile tugged at the corners of her mouth before it disappeared, and she licked her lips nervously. The rise and fall of her breasts, as her breathing became slower and heavier, teased the lustrous fabric of her gown with the faint outline of her nipples. Shock waves rocked through Royd's body, and his loins tightened.

Neither spoke, but the room filled with a primal energy that drew them together like two clouds gathering for a storm that had been brewing since the day they had met. He approached her. Slowly. His heart pounded with anticipation. When he reached out to lift an errant lock of hair from her forehead, her soft sigh fanned his fingers.

"My beautiful Pale Eyes," he murmured, rewarded with an even better view of her luminous orbs as her eyes widened and flashed with requited emotions that took his breath away.

She loved him. She loved HIM? Despite all that had happened between them?

Awed by the incredible notion that she returned his love, Royd's heart skipped a beat. He had no right to claim the miraculously sensual woman who stood before him, but he could no sooner turn away than deny he loved her with all of his heart.

"You should send me away," he whispered as she stepped into his embrace and wrapped her arms around his waist. He held her close, inhaling her sweet scent as the swell of her bosom pressed against his chest.

"I cannot," she answered, dazzling him with the depth of the emotions that resounded in her voice.

Moriah took his hand and led him to the bed. She stood on the first step of the riser and cupped his face with the palms of her hands. Standing face-to-face, he could see her lips quiver as she issued an invitation that only a saint could resist.

"Love me."

For the first time in his life, he was glad that he was no saint. When Moriah closed her eyes, he traced the outline of her mouth with his fingertips. Her long lashes, damp with earlier tears, cast delicate crescent shadows on her cheeks. Reverently, he kissed the tender flesh of her eyelids and felt her breath warm his throat as she exhaled slowly.

Passion flared as he lowered his mouth to caress her lips. Their first kiss, sweet and tender, burst the clouds of distrust that had shadowed their relationship for ever so long. He deepened his kiss, tasting, nibbling, devouring, until his breath came in ragged gasps. He broke apart, struggling for control as he smiled and shook his head. "Do you know what you're doing to me?"

When she blushed, he placed his lips against the base of her creamy white throat where her pulse throbbed with an urgency that matched his own deep needs.

"Are you going to keep it a secret, or are you going to tell me?" she asked, her voice husky with emotion.

"No more secrets," he said, wondering if there was ever a more inopportune moment to tell her that he was betrothed to another woman. He hadn't quite figured out how he would manage to keep this wisp of a woman by his side, but if angels had wings, he would do it! The irony of his vow made him chuckle, and she kissed him. Hard.

"Tell me what's funny enough to make you laugh," she demanded.

He shrugged, wrapping a lock of her hair around his finger. "I was just remembering part of our conversation earlier this evening."

When she frowned, he teased her lips into a smile with the tip of his tongue. "I believe, madam, that you referred to me as an angel. At the moment, I'm afraid I have rather devilish designs on your person. It seems that—"

She yanked on his beard and pouted. Startled, he drew back and rested his hands on the swell of her hips. "What was that for?"

"I don't want an angel or a devil. I . . . I want you. Only you," she whispered as she placed her finger on his lips. The color of her eyes deepened, reminding him of rare, sparkling sapphires.

Royd cocked a brow, parting his lips to suckle at her fingertip. Her gasp of surprise brought a smile to his lips, and all thoughts of Alexandria disappeared into a problem that could be resolved another time. This moment belonged only to the one woman who claimed his heart and soul.

In the space of two heartbeats, Royd scooped Moriah into his arms and kissed her breathless as he carried her up the last two remaining steps and laid her gently on the bed. He removed his clothes slowly, enjoying every tormenting moment as her expression changed from maiden curiosity to a hunger that sent caution to the wind. Lying beside her, he brought her hand to his lips before untying the ribbon that lay nestled between her breasts. As his fingers brushed against her skin, she trembled, and he kissed her forehead, one hand lingering at the base of her throat as he slipped the gown off her shoulders.

"So lovely," he murmured as he eased the garment away, inch by tantalizing inch, until she lay splendidly naked, a vision of loveliness too precious to be real. His eyes filled with wonder when she rolled to her side, tracing the mat of fur that covered his chest.

Taking hold of her wrist, he turned it over, gently kissing the thick scars. The sound of her gentle mewing made his heart race even faster, and he lowered his assault, nibbling at the soft under-flesh of her elbow.

Moriah shuddered as strange, heart throbbing sensations raced up her arm. Royd's body, warm and strong, pressed against her, and she leaned forward to run her fingers through the cascade of black curls that covered his head. Soft and silky, they were an amazing contrast to the coarse fibers of his beard and the springy hairs on his frame that shivered her flesh whenever they grazed against her skin.

Burying her face in the warm shelter between his neck and his shoulder, Moriah followed his lead, nipping his ridged muscles lightly with the tip of her teeth. His sharp intake of breath frightened her, and she froze, wondering if she had acted too brazenly.

Royd nuzzled her throat and groaned. "Don't stop," he murmured as his hands fondled her breasts and trailed lower to caress her hips and abdomen.

Shyly, she parted her lips and kissed him, flecking the tip of her tongue across his flesh. His body tensed again and the pressure of his hands increased as he rolled her hips toward him. Hot and pulsing, his masculine desire pressed against her abdomen, and she quivered, nipping at his throat as glorious bolts of pleasure seared her passion. Her hips arched instinctively as she sought more . . . ever so much more! When his hands parted her legs and fondled her womanly folds, she gasped as liquid fire spread through her limbs.

His lips trailed kisses up her throat until he reclaimed her lips and sent her mind spinning into oblivion. Breathless, she clutched his shoulders, her body molded feverishly into his.

Royd paused and cradled her face in his hands. Moriah stared deep into his eyes, awed by the stunning reflection of her own devotion and desire to share the ultimate union of body and spirit that mere words could not describe.

One precious moment. The one that she hoped to store in her heart for a lifetime was at hand, and she realized too late that it would take more than one lifetime to understand the powerful love that miraculously flowed between them.

Limbs entwined, hearts and souls joined together, they created a world not for sinners or saints, but for lovers. A touch. A caress. Warm and gentle at first, then hot and bolder as their passion grew—until their bodies joined together and soared to one heart. One spirit. One love.

Redeemed by secrets revealed.

Suffused with an overwhelming desire to stop the hands of time and remain cradled in Royd's arms forever, Moriah welcomed the first rays of dawn with a heavy heart. Nestling closer to him, she kissed the column of his throat. When his arms wrapped tighter around her waist, she sighed. "You're awake."

She was disappointed. There was no time left to study his beloved features one last time before the harsh reality of the breaking day ended their brief respite in a dreamworld reserved for star-crossed lovers like themselves.

"One can only awaken after falling asleep." He chuckled. "I've had precious little of that, love."

Blushing, Moriah raised her head to gaze steady and wide-eyed into his compelling green eyes. "When fate hands us such a brief time together, it seems a terrible waste. Sleep, that is," she added when a question lit in his eyes.

"I love you," he whispered. "We'll have a lifetime together."

Moriah shook her head, although his declaration of love was a haunting testament that she would treasure forever. "We live in a world that has little room for people like me. Or you." Her voice dropped to a whisper. "Once I testify at the hearings, my identity and background will be public knowledge. You've been able to carve out a respectable life for yourself. I won't ask you to give that up for me."

Royd shuddered and hugged her close to his chest, his heavy heartbeat pulsing against her cheek. Tears streamed down her face. "Knowing you return my love will have to be enough."

"Not for me," he argued. "We belong together as husband and wife."

"You would resent our marriage. Eventually," she said softly, wondering if he was moved to take her as his wife out of pity or remorse for taking her virtue.

"Marriage never meant more to me than a means to enhance my ambitions. Until now."

Startled by the cynicism in his voice, Moriah held her breath. His expression hardened, and she felt a tremor race down her spine.

"Marry me, Moriah. I'll ride back to Hampton and sell my business all in a single heartbeat."

"Loving, sweet man, you are the love of my life, but you know I can't let you do that," she gushed, her heart swelling with newfound love. "Even if you did," she added sternly as he opened his mouth to protest, "think about what would happen. The senator would know that you had turned against him, and he would destroy you."

"I don't care anymore," he growled.

"He'll destroy me, too, although I don't have any qualms about facing society's condemnation again. But what about the others? If the senator undermines my testimony by using our reputations against us, all the women who are left at Apple Knoll will continue to suffer. New inmates will arrive. Do you want them to suffer, too?"

Royd's eyes glistened. "Your arguments persuade all but my heart, love. I'm not as noble as you are. I've waited all of my life to find you. I can't let you go."

Moriah smiled and kissed him, her lips moving softly as she spoke. "I didn't mean it would be easy. I'll love you every hour of my life and want you even more. But God has a plan for each of us. We must trust He'll take care of us."

Royd's laugh was bitter. "He's not making it easy, is He? I'm not a saint like you are, Moriah."

"A saint doesn't break His word and yield to temptations of the flesh." Her bottom lip quivered. "It was almost easy to be faithful to His Word living alone in a cell. I never realized the multitude of temptations in the world until . . ." Tears ran down her face as guilt filled her soul.

"You're the wife of my heart," he crooned. "What we shared together was not sinful."

She bowed her head, his breath grazing her cheek. "What we shared is meant for couples who marry and pledge their vows before God."

"Then I suppose I must redeem both of our souls, my darling little sinner. Marry me after the hearings," he said quietly as he lifted her face to gaze into her eyes. "Unless you prefer wasting the rest of your life doing penance and spending eternity in hell."

"Don't be blasphemous!" she gasped, tapping his shoulder lightly.

"I thought you'd accept my proposal," he said, chuckling.

"What about your business?" she inquired, still not certain that he understood what he would have to give up if he married her.

His eyes turned to slivers of green ice. "I'll need time to find a buyer. Unfortunately, I can't do anything until after the hearings or the senator will become suspicious. Give me until the first of the new year. In the meantime," he added, "let me contact George Atwood. He'll arrange for your lodgings in Harrisburg and help you to prepare for your appearance at the hearings. Afterward, you can stay here with Moll and Jack."

Moriah bit her lower lip. "Are you sure this is what you want?" she asked, watching in astonishment as his eyes melted into verdant embers that glowed with an intensity that made her heart skip a beat. He smiled as the glint in his eyes turned decidedly wicked.

"Perhaps you should persuade me," he murmured, shifting his body and capturing her hips between his hands.

A sharp rap at the door sent Moriah scrambling out of bed, draping a sheet around her body. "It's probably Moll. I have to get back to Rebecca."

Royd chuckled and pulled on the edge of the sheet until Moriah toppled back into his arms. He tucked her back into bed. "Saved from my wickedness! Your succulent charms will be reserved until our vows, Pale Eyes. Otherwise, you'd probably take to wearing a horsehair gown. I won't have you blemishing your skin. That's my pleasure," he said as he slipped out of bed and hurried to the door that led through her suite to the sitting room.

With a groan, Moriah plopped back against the pillows as another rap at her door echoed in the room. In the space of a few hours, she had gone from despair to ecstasy, from maiden to womanhood. Without the benefit of God's blessing, she realized again. Dismayed by her rapid fall from grace, she begged for forgiveness, wondering if He knew that her remorse was only half-hearted.

Twenty-seven

The only sound in the library was the soft rustle of papers as Royd read the printed version of the report that Jack had picked up from the village postmaster earlier that day. Moriah twisted her hands in front of her, waiting for Royd to finish. They had spent several days polishing the wording in the report before sending it to Hampton to be printed. Only a few weeks remained before the hearings, and Moriah was filled with a sense of urgency. What if the printed report contained errors? Would there be time to correct them?

"Well?" she asked as Royd finally stopped reading and leaned back in his chair.

"Stevens did a remarkable job getting it finished so quickly. It looks impressive." He toyed with his whiskers, his face pensive as he stared at the pile of printed reports that sat on the table ready to be presented to the legislators at the hearing.

The relief that surged through Moriah faded quickly. "Then what's wrong? I thought you were pleased with the report, especially with the new information from my diary."

"It's powerful, Moriah. Particularly with the facts about Ruth and what happened to you. The rest is hear-

say evidence. At best it will warrant further investigation. For proof."

Moriah sighed with exasperation. "I saved Bandit's
collar so I could demonstrate how the other inmates
contacted me, and I have the leather remnants to document what happened to those women. They wouldn't lie
about what those men did to them!"

Royd picked up the report and held it out to her.
"There's no firsthand testimony here. The fact that you
have used code names instead of the women's real
names or their prison identification numbers makes it
seem like you have invented tales about their treatment,
too. Without a direct statement from the women themselves—"

Moriah slapped the report away, her eyes stinging
with tears of frustration. "You know I used codes in the
report to protect them. The women can't be identified or
step forward. They're afraid. What if the legislators
don't believe them? What do you think will happen to
them?" Her voice grew shrill, and her chest heaved as
she took deep gulps of air. "You can't imagine the terror
and the degradation they'll endure."

Royd flew out of his seat and gripped her shoulders.
"I'm not the enemy, Moriah. I'm trying to help you!
Senator Williams and the rest of the bloody committee
will be far less tactful than I am. Don't you see what's
going to happen? They'll claim the diary is a fraud, and
if they don't say it outright, they'll insinuate that you've
lost your mind. Lester Figgs will be only too happy to
use your transfer to Willow Valley to his own advantage.
The cross-examination will be merciless!"

Moriah stiffened as Royd pulled her into his arms and
embraced her. Using both hands, she pushed against his
chest. "I thought you agreed that I would have the advantage as long as the committee doesn't know about my
testimony in advance. They'll be caught off guard, and

by the time they contact the warden, enough doubt will be raised to make his rebuttal suspect."

"Lester Figgs will be at the hearings."

Moriah's head snapped back and she gazed into Royd's worried expression. "Why didn't you tell me before now?"

"I'm sorry. I didn't want to add to your troubles. I intended to tell you before the hearings because I didn't want you to be shocked when you saw him. Now that the hearings are so close and you're ready to testify, I've been lying awake at night trying to envision this whole scenario. Some of the legislators who attend are good men and will hear you with an open mind. The others, when they attack, will be brutal."

"Brutal enough to reveal themselves," she said firmly. "Then the others will be swayed in my favor."

His eyes softened and he brushed his hands down her spine, easing away the tenseness that stiffened her spine. With a sigh, she melted against his frame and wrapped her arms around his waist.

"I know what you're doing is important, love, but I don't want you to face the committee alone. If not by your side, let me sit close. You'll need a supporter, someone who believes in you."

Moriah trembled. "It's too dangerous. You have to sit with the other investigators. If Lester Figgs sees us together, he'll know you helped me."

"I told you before—"

"No." She lifted her head and brushed his cheek with her hand. "George Atwood will be there. Didn't Jack bring a letter from him when he came back from town yesterday?"

Royd took a deep breath. "Atwood agreed to help. He's offered to let you stay with his parents in Harrisburg until the hearings. He included their address."

She nodded. "He's been a good friend, Royd. May I

write to him? I'd like to thank him personally. I want to write to his parents, too. When do I leave?"

"Too soon." Royd kissed her gently. "The hearings start in mid-October. You should probably arrive toward the end of September to avoid gaining notice."

She smiled and kissed him back before slipping out of his embrace as a dangerous warmth spread through her limbs. "Another ten days of kisses like that and I'll let you talk me out of going at all." She sighed.

Chuckling, Royd pulled her hard against him and took her breath away with a kiss that made her head spin. When he broke the kiss, he grinned. "That's precisely my intention, little saint. If you won't listen to reason and at least let me attend the hearings, then perhaps I'll use your passion against you to make you change your mind."

Blushing, Moriah tweaked his beard. "Cur! You promised to wait!"

With an exaggerated grimace, Royd shook his head. "A promise I'll keep, but I have another one for you. When all this is settled, the beard will be shaved away. It gives you a decided advantage when you want your way."

"You told Ruth you'd keep it," she argued playfully.

"Ruth is too besotted with her new playmate to even notice. I'm the one who should feel betrayed."

"Jack loves the attention. Besides, other than Ruth, no one else would swallow that tale about hidden treasure. Sometimes I think she's even more excited about it than he is."

Royd cocked his head. "He told you about that? He wasn't supposed to breathe a word. Wait till I get my hands on that old goat!"

"Ruth told me," she giggled. "Telling a secret to a six-year-old isn't the best way to keep it hidden for very long. Anyway, Jack sent Ruth to ask me if they could play in my suite today. Do you really think they'll find something?"

"If they don't, Jack will finally have to give up this whole insane idea. He's torn through every other room without luck. What did you tell Ruth?"

"Yes, of course. I may even help," she added. "It sounds like fun."

"You have letters to write," he corrected as he steered her back to the table. "When you're finished, we'll take the letters to town to be posted. Then I have something else planned for the rest of your day."

"What?" she breathed, thrilled by the prospect of spending as much time alone with Royd as she could before she had to leave.

"I'll tell you after you finish your letters," he promised as he placed a pen in her hand. "Write."

Jack sat on the floor in Moriah's dressing room with little Ruth peering over his shoulder as he studied the blueprints. Again. "Nothin' here, darlin'. One last room to check." Scrambling to his feet, he joined hands with his last remaining supporter and walked into Moriah's bedchamber.

As he inspected the walls, moving furniture and drapes, Ruth followed him. Perspiration dripped into his eyes, and he bent down so she could mop his brow. "Thank goodness you're here." He chuckled as she nodded in agreement. "Thought for sure the heat was gone for good. How 'bout we take a rest?"

"Moll said we had to stay till you were done. She's baking a special cake to cel- . . . cel-"

"Celebrate." He laughed as he patted her head. "Can't tell Mr. Royd why Moll baked the cake, though. He'll be in a real temper if he finds out you told her the secret, too."

"Mr. Royd will be real surprised if we find the buried treasure, and he won't care then, will he?" Grinning,

Ruth tugged on Jack's hand. "I bet it's under the bed. I hide lotsa things under mine. Mama gets mad, 'specially when it's taffy. Last time it melted and made a mess."

"What we're lookin' for won't melt, but I don't think it's under the bed, neither." Jack led Ruth to the platform. Kneeling down, he showed her the heavy wooden frame that rested on the floor. "They build this to support the bed. It has to be real strong. Can't push nothin' under it, see?"

Frowning, Ruth furrowed her brows. "Maybe there's a secret door. You found one in Mr. Royd's wardrobe."

"That I did," he agreed. "Led to an empty back closet, too. Guess it wouldn't hurt to check, though." Crawling along the side of the platform, Jack ran his hand along the wood. Finding no seams, he checked the bottom edge and started along the other side. He checked as far as the steps before stopping.

"Nothin' yet," he gasped, his breathing ragged. While he moved to the other side of the steps, Ruth sat down on the first step to watch. "Sorry, little one," he announced as he sat back on his heels. "No secret doors."

"You missed the steps," she pouted.

Shrugging his shoulders, Jack gave in to her and ran his hands over the side of the miniature stairs closest to him. Unlike the frame of the platform, the staircase was intricately carved. Pressing his fingers into the nooks and crevices surrounding the raised wood, he found it solid.

"Now the other side," she demanded when he stopped.

"You'll make a fine wife someday," he grumbled. "You give orders almost as good as Moll." Crawling to the opposite side of the staircase, Jack lost his balance and his shoulder slammed into the side. Ruth jumped up squealing, but Jack smiled at her. "I'm not hurt," he reassured her as he sat down and she plopped onto his lap. "Did I scare you?"

She shook her head, her eyes wide. "The step scared me."

"The step?"

"It moved. I felt it on my . . . my bottom," she gushed as she stared at the step. "Look!"

Jack took one glance at the bottom step and felt his mouth go dry. Lifting Ruth off his lap, he edged forward, his eyes narrowing. He nudged the end of the step with his finger. It slid farther back into the casing of the staircase, and Jack peered into the dark cavity. "Well, if I ain't the fool," he whispered. Then he grinned, hugged Ruth to his side, and let out a howl that made the room shake.

Royd followed Jack out to the stable, grumbling as the old lantern Jack carried cast a weak light ahead of his footsteps. "It's nigh midnight. Couldn't this wait until morning?"

"Nope."

"I'm tired, Jack. Do you have any idea what it's like being stuck on a stool in a dressmaker's for six hours? My back's got more aches than a chicken's got feathers. Now I know why females like to have their garments made one at a time."

"It's not my fault you took Moriah to town for a new wardrobe and stayed to watch. I told you to take Moll and let her do it."

Royd tripped and muttered an oath. "Not on your life. Moriah wouldn't have gotten everything I wanted her to have, and Moll wouldn't be able to insist."

"Didn't have to take the long way home," Jack said as he raised the lantern and nodded toward the stable door.

Sharing a late picnic supper on the way home as the sun set was a private memory Royd would treasure in the months he and Moriah would be apart. "The time when I had to account to you is long past," Royd countered as he opened the door.

Jack led the way, and Royd found his curiosity increasing in spite of himself. Placing the lantern on the floor near the wall, Jack looked around, checking the empty stalls before turning to Royd with a grin that stretched from one ear to the other. "Ready?"

"For what?" Royd growled.

"To admit that I was right."

"You're right about a lot of things, Jack. Would you care to be more specific?"

Jack chuckled as he pointed to a canvas bag lying against the wall where the tack was hung. "I thought you'd never ask. Look in there, son."

"Tack? You brought me out here to look at tack? I have to talk to Moll. You're getting senile, old man. You've probably been spending too much time with Ruth. Is this a new kind of hide-and-seek we're playing?"

"I'm gonna love it when you eat your words, boy. Take a good long look inside. Go ahead," he urged when Royd shifted from one foot to the other.

"After I look, then you'll be satisfied and go back to the house?"

When Jack nodded, Royd turned his attention to the bag, wondering why Jack looked so damn . . . triumphant? His hands started to shake as he undid the drawstring. Lifting the lantern with one hand, he used the other to open the mouth of the bag. His eyes widened as the light reflected back at him. He blinked several times before putting the lantern down. Using both hands, he lifted out the most incredible bounty he could have imagined.

When he was finished, six bars of solid gold were stacked at his feet. In his hands, he held a velvet bag with an assortment of precious stones every color of the rainbow. "I don't believe it," he murmured, his voice husky.

"It's a king's ransom, Royd. Now it's yours."

A lump in his throat made it almost impossible for Royd to take a breath. "Do you know what this means?" he said quietly as he looked at Jack. "Moriah won't have to go to the hearings alone! The world and its parasites be damned! I can give the business away if I choose to. There's enough of a fortune here to buy this estate and ten more like it!"

"Hold on a minute, son. You got to do some serious thinkin' first. I mean, they sure do look real," Jack suggested as he nudged the gold bars with his foot. "Can't say for sure till we have an expert look at 'em. Jewels, too. Could be that the lawyer Brockley hid 'em to convince you to buy the place."

Royd's heartbeat slowed to a dull pace, and he was grateful that Jack had the presence of mind to be so cautious. "Do you know someone who could tell us?"

"Sure. He's in Philadelphia, though. You and me would have to take a trip. Might take a solid week to get there and back. Won't leave much time for you and Moriah."

Royd nodded, his lips forming a smile. "If these are genuine, Moriah and I can be married the day I return. If not . . ." His voice trailed to a whisper. "Did you tell Moll you found this?"

Jack grimaced. "She knew I was lookin', but I didn't tell her nothin' 'bout findin' anythin'."

"What about Ruth?"

"She's sworn to secrecy, but I asked Rebecca to keep her out to the cabin till we get back. Just in case," he added.

Royd looked at Jack skeptically, but decided that he would have to take his word. "I'll saddle Brandy. Pick one of the coach horses for yourself."

"Now?"

"The sooner we leave, the sooner we get to Philadelphia and find out whether or not this is fool's gold and colored glass. I'll leave a note for Moll and Moriah. Unless you want me to go alone?"

"Not a chance," Jack retorted as he lifted a bridle off the wall. "Way I figure it, we got a full week to spend together, and at least twice a day you're gonna tell me how right I was."

"If the treasure is genuine, I'll make that twice an hour!" Royd laughed. He felt almost giddy just anticipating the possibility that he and Moriah would be joined together in matrimony before the hearings even convened. Hand in hand, they would face the committee and force Senator Williams and his cronies to answer for their wrongdoing. Nothing could stop Royd and Moriah from being together.

A dark cloud of guilt shadowed his optimism as he thought of the one lingering secret between them. If he was successful in Philadelphia, he would have to select a very special jewel and have it fashioned into something quite unique for Moriah. That might help when he finally got the courage to tell her that he was betrothed to another woman—a betrothal he did not dare break publicly until after Moriah testified at the hearings, even though he would already be married to Moriah by then.

All he needed was one week.

Moriah tucked Royd's note into her pocket and forced herself to smile. "I'm sure it was important," she said as she pushed away her dinner plate. Knowing that Royd would be traveling to Philadelphia and returning only days before she had to leave made her appetite vanish. The fact that he also left a fair sum of money for her to use for travel expenses in case he was delayed made her wonder if they would even have the chance to say goodbye before she left for Harrisburg.

"He should have waited until morning," Moll clucked. "Jack should have stopped him. It don't make sense to start out on a journey in the middle of the night."

Moriah's hands were shaking as she sipped her tea. "Royd will be careful. Before you know it, they'll be back."

Moll dabbed at her eyes. "With a pocket full of good reasons for not waitin' to say good-bye, or I'll clobber both of 'em!"

Giggling, Moriah sat her teacup down and got up to place her arms around Moll's shoulders. "They'll watch out for each other, and we'll just have to keep each other company."

Moll patted Moriah's arm. "I'm gonna miss you, darlin'."

Moll's sad expression prompted Moriah to wonder if she should use this opportunity to tell Moll that she and Royd planned to marry. Deciding against saying anything since Royd insisted they wait until just before she left, Moriah simply squeezed her hard. As they clung to each other, Moriah's mind dared to hope that her suspicions were correct. Maybe Jack really had found something valuable! Maybe Royd was on his way to finding himself wealthy enough to afford the luxury of buying the estate without having to sell his business first.

They could be married and attend the hearings together!

A glimmer of hope filled her soul, and Moriah vowed to concentrate all of her prayers to that end. Prayer had been powerful enough to send her an avenging angel. Surely God wouldn't mind turning the angel into her husband so he could stand by her side at the hearings.

Would He?

Twenty-eight

The maid shook her gnarled finger at her mistress who was preparing to disembark from the coach. "You can't be doin' this, Miss Alexandria. It's not proper. Your papa will—"

"Hush, Letty, or I'll tell my father to find a younger lady's maid for me," Alexandria hissed. "I have every right to know where my betrothed is hiding. The wedding is only six weeks away! He's supposed to be here with me, but obviously Royd has found something or someone else more fascinating than his future wife!"

"Royd is an honorable gentleman. He won't take your spying on him any better than your jealousy."

Alexandria's laugh was brittle, even to her own ears. "Visiting Royd's firm hardly constitutes a major sin. Stevens is the only one who might know where Royd is. He's not capable of running the business without getting instructions from Royd. I merely want to talk to him and find out why Royd has abandoned me."

Alexandria's eyes narrowed when the maid frowned her disapproval. "Even honorable men take license to stray, but I'll not stand for it!" The idea that purchasing land for an investment was a legitimate reason for Royd to be away was not important to her. Alexandria was jealous of a snowstorm if it meant that Royd's attention was directed away from her. The inconceivable notion that Royd found a parcel of land more important than being with her made her blood boil. She did not dare think he was chasing after another woman, or she would explode!

As the coachman opened the door, Alexandria straightened her bonnet and fussed with her hair. "Stay here," she ordered when the maid attempted to follow her. Despite Alexandria's threat to have her replaced, Letty would be sure to repeat every word Alexandria said to Stevens to the senator when they returned home. Alexandria had no intention of letting that happen. Not even her father could stop her from finding out where Royd was, even if it meant she had to lie to him.

The moment the apprentice ushered Alexandria into Royd's office, she sensed that her female intuition had been correct. Blushing madly, Stevens's mouth dropped open as she sauntered casually near a pile of boxes he was preparing for shipment.

"M-Miss Alexandria, you're not supposed to be here!" he stammered. His fingers shook as he readjusted his wire-rimmed spectacles that had slipped to the tip of his nose.

She laughed softly as she moved closer to him. "It's nice to see you again," she purred, lowering her lashes demurely. Was it her coquettishness or the furtive glance she took at the writing on the top of the box that made him start to tremble?

Gambling on his lack of confidence, she ventured closer to the boxes. "Are these the parcels being sent to Royd?"

Stevens gulped so hard that his Adam's apple bobbed nervously up and down the length of his skinny neck. "You know about the books? Mr. Camden said I was the only one he trusted!"

She flashed a smile that made the young man's mustache twitch. "I'm his fiancée. We have no secrets from each other," she murmured as a dazzling idea popped into her head. "Royd wrote to me and asked me to bring the books to him. I only stopped by to make sure they were ready."

His eyes narrowed as he squared his shoulders. "Mr. Camden didn't mention anything about that in his last letter," he challenged. "His instructions were to send the books in the post."

Sighing deliberately, Alexandria watched with hidden amusement as the man's eyes focused on her breasts. "Royd's letter to me was quite specific," she said, her eyes filling with tears. "I—I can bring it to you, but I must ask your indulgence. Royd is quite lonely for my company, and his words are too sentimental for a lady to share with just anyone."

"I don't know . . . Mr. Camden would have written to me and told me the change in plans."

As Stevens weighed her request, Alexandria seized her advantage. "You mustn't breathe a word to my father. He thinks I'm going to Philadelphia to visit my sister. Royd and I are counting on your help," she pleaded.

When Stevens nodded as though he understood, Alexandria felt her stomach twist into knots. Whatever Royd was doing, he was being very secretive about it. Obviously, it involved her father, and she was determined more than ever to get to the bottom of the mystery. That it probably revolved around Royd's participation in the investigation of Apple Knoll made her mouth go dry. Royd Camden would live to regret it if he betrayed her father, but she would never be able to face society if her betrothal was broken so near the wedding!

Her fingers instinctively curled around the heart-shaped locket that hung from a long chain around her neck. She had to know the truth, and there was only one way to discover it. Royd Camden had better be supporting her father, or she would find a way to convince him to do so. And when she did, Royd Camden would learn that no man lived to play her or her father as fools!

Clad only in a simple, sleeveless shift, Moriah lay across her bed, hoping that a brief nap would buoy her spirits. Her trunks lined the entry of the foyer downstairs waiting until she gave Will the order to load them into the coach. She should have left for Harrisburg days ago, but she did not want to leave. Not without seeing Royd.

She had not heard from Royd since he left so surreptitiously a dozen days before. With the hearings in less than two weeks, Moriah was anxious to get settled with Mr. and Mrs. Atwood to avoid detection by members of the committee. There was still so much she wanted to say to Royd, but unless he arrived by tomorrow morning, she had no choice but to leave.

A bevy of female voices from the hall below made her smile. Moll must have organized yet another chore that required several of the Haskell girls, although she did not often raise her voice like she must be doing now. If Moriah did not know that she would be returning here, she would have been consumed with sorrow at having to say good-bye to all the people she had grown to love in the past two months. Instead, she found the sound of their voices comforting.

Rolling to her side, Moriah stared out through the window and drifted into a light slumber as a band of clouds danced slowly across the horizon. Just as she felt herself slipping into a deep sleep, the door to her chamber crashed open. Heart pounding, Moriah dazedly sat up and stared at an outraged woman who stood just inside her chamber door.

Moll charged in on the woman's heels, her face flushed with anger. "You got no right enterin' Moriah's chamber," she spewed. "I told you to wait downstairs."

The woman dismissed Moll with a haughty smile. "I don't take orders from servants."

"You'll take orders from me," Moll retorted angrily as she started forward.

"P-please," Moriah cried. "It's all right, Moll. I'm awake now."

Moll looked at Moriah over her shoulder, her lips set in a frown. "You don't need to be talkin' to her."

Curious, Moriah ignored the stranger's snicker. "Why don't you take the girls to the cabin and then bring Ruth back with you. I haven't seen her since Royd left."

Moll's eyes softened. "I'll wait till I see her coach leave. Then I'll be back," she sniffed as she stepped around the stranger and closed the door.

Moriah's eyes widened as the woman approached her bed.

"They told me in the village that Royd lived here with his *ward*. I must admit that I'm more than a little surprised Royd installed you in chambers more suitable for his wife or his mistress. You don't mind if I have my things brought up here, do you? This room suits me more than the others."

Scrambling out of bed, Moriah started for her wrapper that lay draped across a chair next to the window. The woman, however, managed to reach it before Moriah did and held it up, inspecting the garment with a curious eye. "Royd always did have exquisite taste," she said icily. She toyed absently with the imported lace collar, her eyes glittering as she stared openmouthed at the numbers tattooed on Moriah's bare arm.

Moriah grabbed the wrapper out of the intruder's hands and clutched it to her chest. Her eyes riveted on the overly tall woman whose carriage and cultured words matched the elegant styling of her coiffure which molded ash-blonde ringlets like a crown on the top of her head. The woman was young, perhaps no older than Moriah, but she was much more beautiful and sophisticated than Moriah could ever hope to be. Her expression, however, was hard and brittle, as though it were difficult for her to be in the same room with someone as distastefully low in the social strata as Moriah. "Who are you," she gasped as the woman started walking around the room like she was taking inventory.

Turning to face Moriah, the woman's dark brown eyes flashed as she returned Moriah's steady gaze disdainfully. "I'm Alexandria Williams. I came to visit Royd. It's been terribly hard being separated from my beloved fiancé, especially with the wedding only weeks away." Her mouth twitched nervously as she approached Moriah and pointed to Moriah's arm. "I had no idea that he installed a *convict* in my bedchamber!"

The room started to spin, and Moriah closed her eyes, trying to take deep breaths of air to regain her equilibrium. Tremors shook through her body, and her heart pounded so fast that she thought it might burst.

Royd never mentioned being betrothed when he was baring his soul and revealing all of his deep, dark secrets. Surely he would have told Moriah something as important as planning to be married! The woman had to be lying!

The woman's cackling snicker made Moriah's skin crawl, and she opened her eyes to glare at Alexandria. "Are you related to Senator Williams?" she asked as she slipped awkwardly into the wrapper and belted it around her waist.

Alexandria's smile was cold as she stared down her nose at Moriah. "He's my father."

Moriah swallowed the lump in her throat as a wave of nausea made her light-headed again. As wicked as Senator Williams was, would he send his own daughter to investigate Royd? What if the woman was lying about being betrothed to Royd? Did she hope to upset Moriah enough that she could find out whether or not Royd was planning to undermine the scheme to cover up problems at Apple Knoll? "You say you're betrothed to Royd?" Moriah asked, trying not to let her voice crack.

Alexandria sneered. "He gave me this as a symbol of his devotion." Slipping a necklace over her head, she held out a heart-shaped locket. After she turned it over, Moriah reached out to hold it still so she could read the inscription on the back. *For Eternity. RC*

Tears blurred Moriah's vision. The silver locket was burning evidence of Royd's betrayal, and she drew back before it singed her flesh. No more secrets. Isn't that what he had promised? But apparently he had lied to Moriah and kept one final secret that made a mockery of the love she had given to him so completely.

What kind of man would profess his undying love and propose marriage to her when all the while he was pledged to another? If his guile made her bitter, the notion that Alexandria would lie in her bed and make love to Royd in the same room where Moriah had lost her virtue shattered Moriah's heart.

Judge not.

Moriah found it difficult to listen to her conscience, but thoughts of Royd began to nibble at her anger. She had misjudged him before, and although she was dismally hurt over his failure to divulge his betrothal, she wondered if perhaps Royd had meant to break his betrothal to Alexandria. Hope replaced anger, and she gathered her wits about her before trying to confront the woman Royd possibly intended to hurt dreadfully by breaking their betrothal. "When did you last speak to Royd?" she asked, her heart barely beating while she waited for Alexandria to answer her.

Alexandria, however, must have been caught by surprise. Her eyes widened before they snapped wickedly. "I don't see any need to discuss my private affairs with a common criminal!" she hissed. "You didn't know I was coming, did you? Bah! He probably neglected to mention me at all! Did you think he had fallen in love with you? Come, my dear. You can't be that naive. Royd invited me to come. *After* you'd left, of course."

"Royd invited you?" Moriah gasped, clutching her fist to her mouth.

Alexandria answered sarcastically. "Of course he did. Why else would I be here? It's just that I arrived a few days early, judging by the trunks I saw in the foyer. They're yours, I suppose."

Moriah nodded woodenly. Cruelly and painfully, all hope that Royd had intended to break his betrothal to Alexandria turned into a searing pain in her chest. How could he send Moriah to Harrisburg early, claiming that it was for her own safety when all along he planned to have an assignation with Alexandria? Here? It made no sense to even presume that he would break his betrothal here instead of returning to Hampton. As much as she tried to have faith in him, to trust in the love he proclaimed for her, and to battle the overwhelming evidence against him, she could not blind herself to his betrayal.

The truth made her tremble.

Her initial anger transformed itself into a deep, soul-wrenching sadness that nearly overwhelmed her. "I was leaving this afternoon," she said dully as she walked over to her gown. "Will you have Moll tell Will to load my trunks?" As she walked to the dressing room, Alexandria startled her by grabbing her arm.

"Where are you going?" she demanded to know.

Moriah shook free of her grasp. "I don't have to answer to you or to anyone else."

Alexandria's face skewed into a thoughtful frown. "You're going to testify at the hearings, aren't you?"

Moriah's back stiffened when the woman blocked her way into the dressing room. "Whatever I intend to do, I don't have to explain it to you or to Royd."

"You little slut! You *are* going to testify! Did Royd help you by giving you his report? The one my father rejected?"

Moriah tilted her chin and refused to be intimidated

into answering. When the woman raised her arm to strike her, Moriah grabbed her wrist and squeezed it hard. "Don't," she hissed, losing all of her natural inhibitions against using violence. "I won't let you or your father stop me. By the time I'm finished, your father and your fiancé will be lucky if they can find a position emptying troughs for pigs!"

Alexandria shoved Moriah, tittering when she stumbled to her knees. "You can't stand up against a man like my father."

"I can. And I will," Moriah said between gritted teeth. "There's nothing your father can do to stop me from helping the women at Apple Knoll who are being mistreated. They're my friends. I won't let them be abused any longer."

"Oh, you're wrong," Alexandria said harshly. "He'll destroy you by using your past to discredit you. What legislator will believe a convicted . . . thief? Harlot? Just what was your crime, dearie?"

Moriah grinned. "Murder. Now get out of my way."

Alexandria paled and moved quickly to get out of Moriah's path. "I'm warning you for the last time. Stay away from the hearings. Or . . ."

"Or what?" Moriah laughed. "You'll have me sent back to prison? I'm sorry to disappoint you, Alexandria. I've completed my sentence. Perhaps you think you can destroy my reputation. I don't have one. Not one that can be any worse than it already is. So you see, *dearie*, there's nothing you can use to threaten me. You have Royd. Be satisfied with that."

The expression in Alexandria's eyes turned wicked. "If you testify, what do you think will happen to your friends at Apple Knoll?" She started to giggle hysterically. "You really are naive, aren't you?"

Moriah's anger turned to fear. "You can't do anything to them," she whispered.

"You're right. I can't. But my father can. He has

friends in very high places. If you are able to get the legislators to believe you, which I doubt, my father will have the women transferred to another facility before the sun sets on the day you testify. And I promise you this," she mouthed as she approached Moriah with her finger pointed at her face, "you won't be able to stop him. Would you like to imagine what would happen to those women?"

Fear clutched at Moriah's heart, but the code she used to hide the women's identities suddenly loomed as a precaution well taken. "He can't do that. He doesn't know who they are."

"You little fool. Why do you think Royd helped you? My father probably has the list on his desk already."

Moriah's mind raced. She had her leather diary, the copy she transcribed for Royd, and the only copy of the report that contained the women's names. Royd did not. Unless he had made a copy without her knowledge, he did not know who the women really were. The printed reports, which were also safely stored in her trunks, contained only the code names. He would not be able to recall the names, would he? She sighed, knowing that she could not take even the slightest chance that he could remember just one. "What would you have me do?" she asked, her voice as dry as her love for Royd Camden.

"Testify to your heart's content about yourself, Moriah, if you have the stupidity to think you can defeat my father. Just don't implicate him. Or Royd. If you breathe either of their names or one word about the other women, my father will make sure that every woman at Apple Knoll is punished severely."

Moriah shook her head. The only way she could be absolutely certain that Alexandria was exaggerating about the senator's power was to challenge him—something that would place Sophie and Iona and all of the others in jeopardy. As much as she wanted to use the information from her diary, she would be forced to keep silent. Her testimony would have to be restricted to her own mistreatment as well as her sister's, but nothing could dissuade her from divulging what had really happened to each of them.

"I'll be ready to leave in an hour," Moriah murmured, hoping she would have enough time to search Royd's suite before she left to make sure he had not made a copy of her transcribed diary. "If anything happens to my friends, I'll hold you responsible, too, Alexandria."

Moriah walked into the dressing room and closed the door. She could almost feel the crown of her Christian faith as it slipped from her head and hung around her neck as a reminder that she had acted more the sinner than the saint.

At this point, she did not care. Saints got their rewards in heaven. She could not wait that long to find justice.

As Royd reached the main house, he spied Will loading Moriah's trunks into the coach and heaved a sigh of relief. He was glad that he had left Jack in David's Crossing to handle a few last minute details for the celebration he planned for tonight. Easing from the saddle, he planted his feet on solid ground for only the second time in nearly eighteen hours. Bone-tired but exuberant that he had reached home before Moriah left, he clapped Will on the shoulders with an apologetic grin on his face. "Miss Moriah will be staying a few days longer. Take her trunks back inside."

"Leave them exactly where they are!"

Moriah's sharp order, issued as she stormed past Royd, made him flinch. Will shifted from one foot to the other as though he were not quite sure which one of them he should obey. He blushed when Moriah placed her hand on his arm, ignoring Royd completely. "I'd like to leave now, Will."

Was he invisible or in the middle of a nightmare? Moriah simply could not be that overwrought because he had left for Philadelphia without saying good-bye or because he was gone much longer than he suggested he might be in his note!

"Moriah?"

The only indication that she heard him was the stiffening of her spine. When she proceeded to walk to the coach, Royd grabbed her hand and spun her around. Shocked by the anger that flashed violently in her eyes and the cold, firm set of her jaw, he dropped her hand and stepped back.

"Before I jump to conclusions, you'd better explain your behavior," he growled.

"You hypocritical, lying bastard!" she hissed as she wiped her hands on her skirts. "I owe you nothing more than this." Before Royd could react, Moriah's hand cracked across his cheek.

His hand shot out, his fingers wrapping tightly around her wrist. Fury raged through his veins, and he ignored her squeal of pain. "I didn't do anything to deserve that," he snarled. "Now I suggest you calm down so we can continue this discussion *inside,*" he added, nodding toward Will who stood only yards away.

"Let go of me!" she snarled. Her cheeks flamed with indignation. "I have nothing to say to you."

"What's wrong with you?" he hissed, releasing her arm.

Her laughter was shrill as she rubbed her wrist. "Other than the fact that I've decided that being a saint is tantamount to being a fool, nothing."

Startled by the cold expression in her eyes, he ran his fingers through his hair. Royd had tried to visualize their reunion, but nothing in his wildest dreams ever prepared him for this! "I'm not sure what I did to make you so unreasonably angry, but I apologize. Now can we please go inside? There's so much I need to tell you."

Her gaze shifted upward, over his shoulder. Pain muddied the color of her eyes to deep slate. "You can't begin to apologize for that," she murmured.

The minute Royd turned around and looked up at Alexandria, who was standing at the top of the turret, he felt his whole world begin to spin out of control and crash at his feet. His hands trembled as he reached out to Moriah. "I know I should have told you—"

"You should have told me a lot of things, but you didn't. Of course, you probably would have told me about your betrothal to Senator Williams's daughter. Eventually. But would you have told me that you plotted with the senator to find out the names of all the women in my diary? Did you plan to make sure that they would refute my testimony? How did you plan to convince them, Royd? The iron gag is most effective although it does tend to leave nasty wounds that take weeks to heal. Rape? Ducking? Which method is your personal favorite?"

Reeling from her outrageous accusations, Royd felt his heartbeat skid to a halt. "You know I couldn't do that," he whispered.

"I know you've lied to me for the last time," she countered, her voice shaking as tears welled in her eyes. "I have no choice but to agree to the senator's demands, or I'll risk the very women I tried to help. I don't care what he does to me when he tries to undermine my testimony about what Lester Figgs did to me and to Ruth. I'll testify if it's the last thing I do on this earth."

Pausing to take a breath, her chin quivered. "I'm sure you'll be there to witness the final act in the wicked scheme to keep me silenced. Just be warned," she added as tears began to stream down her face, "I'm no longer the naïve little saint who trusted you. You betrayed me. You betrayed the women at Apple Knoll who needed your help. I'll have to pray for a very long time to find the strength to forgive you someday. I only hope you can live with what you've done."

Swirling away from him, Moriah climbed into the coach and closed the door. Dazed, Royd answered Will's unspoken question with a silent nod. As the coach slowly rolled toward the entrance to the estate, carrying within it the one woman he dared to love, Royd's heart tightened.

Less than an hour ago, he had asked the minister in David's Crossing to come to the estate tonight to perform the marriage ceremony that would bind Moriah to him for all time. The deed to the estate was in his pocket, along with a note certifying that he had a king's fortune deposited in several Philadelphia banks.

He had finally reconciled his past with his future, knowing that he had enough money to stand up against anything or anyone who stood in his way. He could follow his conscience, accompany Moriah to the hearings, and support her openly. His visit to Judge Martindell was only part of his plan to destroy Figgs and Williams and help Moriah to make her case against them. After the hearings, he and Moriah could build a life and a family together here, financially secure and isolated from the sordid, artificial world of politics and business.

Without Moriah, however, his life was as empty as a night sky stripped of moonglow and starlight.

His hand reached inside his waistcoat pocket and he pulled out a satin packet. Untying the lace bow, he lifted the sapphire-studded wedding band and placed it in his palm. Shadowed, the jewels were listless and dull, but when he held the ring up to the sun, the pale blue stones danced and sparkled as brilliantly as the love he remembered shining in Moriah's eyes the only night they had shared as lovers.

Was their love destined to end in the shadows of secrets unrevealed and clouds of lies and distrust? Or could he redeem her affection and restore the lustrous wonder that filled his life when she was by his side?

Reverently, he returned the wedding ring to its satin

folds and placed it back into his pocket. Turning back to the house, he looked up. Alexandria still stood in her turret throne, a look of triumph evident even from a distance. As he entered the foyer, his mind raced with possibilities, all of which focused on one remarkable woman with luminous blue eyes, a spirit that defied the imagination, and a halo that had slipped just enough to make her human.

When he entered the foyer, he saw the boxes of books he had been expecting, and the question of how Alexandria had found him had a quick enough answer. How she had managed to convince Moriah that he was still helping Fithian Williams was more difficult, but knowing Alexandria, he had no doubt that Moriah was cunningly persuaded into giving Alexandria just enough information to stir her imagination.

He climbed the stairs slowly and made his way to his suite to have a few moments to collect his thoughts before confronting Alexandria. "You're wrong, Pale Eyes. There's one final secret you've yet to discover," he murmured.

Royd knocked on Alexandria's door wondering if she could possibly hear him above the din she was creating. By the sound of it, she was wreaking more havoc than a hurricane that had gone off course and invaded his home! Twisting the doorknob, he was surprised to discover that she had not locked the door. As it swung open, a crystal vase flew through the air, landing short of its mark and smashing at his feet.

Shaking his head, he flashed Alexandria a mocking grin. "Temper tantrums don't become you, darling," he teased.

Alexandria's tearstained cheeks flamed brighter. "How *could* you!" she shrieked as she clutched one of Moriah's nightgowns in her fist and shook it violently in front of her. "You betrayed me with a cheap, no-account whore!"

Swallowing the words he wanted to use to defend Moriah, Royd slumped his shoulders and tried to look penitent. "I was only trying to help your father's case, Alexandria. Things got more complicated than I intended. We never shared more than a few kisses."

"Liar!" she hissed, spittle oozing out of the corners of her mouth. She wiped her chin self-consciously. "You ungrateful turncoat! You plotted against my father with that . . . that jailbird!"

"She told you that?"

"Of course she did. After I made a few well-ventured guesses! I'm not stupid," she spat.

"No. You're overwrought. Unfortunately, you've also jumped to conclusions that wound me deeply," he drawled as he approached her. "Do you honestly believe that I would risk my name and my fortune for the sake of a few convicts?" He smiled, reaching out to take her hand into his. Raising it to his lips, he kissed the back of her shaking hand. "Would I risk losing you?" Purring his voice, he murmured her name. "Have you no faith in me at all?"

Alexandria trembled, her eyes welling with tears. "She admitted you helped her," she sniffed. "What was I supposed to think, especially after I found her here. Living with you!"

"I brought her here to get information to give to your father to prove that I'm loyal to him. Not to betray him."

Alexandria's eyes narrowed. "Why should I believe you?" she whispered, removing her hand and backing away from him.

"Because it's the truth. Moriah had a diary which recorded certain things that could not be made public at the hearings. Unfortunately, it was written in code. When I returned to Apple Knoll to force her to decipher it, I learned that Figgs had sent her to a lunatic asylum to prevent her from testifying."

Royd watched Alexandria carefully, noting the slight relaxation in her shoulders and the glimmer of self-doubt that lit in her eyes. He lowered his voice, speaking seductively. "I knew it was important to find out the names of the women she was going to reveal at the hearings, just in case they completed their sentences before the hearings began. There wasn't time to notify your father. I guess I didn't want to face him if I failed."

"Did you get the names?" she asked, her voice trembling.

"I had to leave for a few days. Moriah promised to give them to me when I returned. Unfortunately, you chose to arrive just before I did."

Eyes wide and nostrils flaring, Alexandria's hand flew to her mouth. Royd suppressed the urge to laugh at her pathetic image and forced himself to look stern. "I suppose you threatened Moriah when she told you she was going to testify at the hearings?"

She nodded, and one of the curls that had come askew during her rampage flopped to the middle of her forehead. "I—I told her m-my f-father would see that the other inmates were p-punished," she stammered.

He laughed softly. "No wonder she was so frightened."

"She was packed and ready to leave for the hearings!" Alexandria charged. "Why would you let her do that if you were really going to help my father?"

"Do you think she would cooperate if I told her she couldn't testify? The reason I left for a few days was to make arrangements with several men who were going to stage a carriage accident. They'll be waiting for her tomorrow," he said grimly. "Not today."

Groaning, Alexandria clutched her chest. "I've ruined everything! Father will be furious with me. What am I going to do?" she wailed.

Royd sighed as he pulled her into his embrace, disgusted that she would be more concerned with her own fate than the fact that he had just told her he had arranged to murder Moriah. He pulled her into his arms and rubbed her back to still the tremors that shook her frame. "You're going to trust me," he crooned. "Let me handle everything. Your father need never know. It will be our little secret."

Alexandria lifted her head and stared at him. "Will you ever forgive me?" she whispered, her lips quivering.

"Once we're married," he murmured, vowing that that event was just as likely as the other.

One question loomed even greater than how he was going to tolerate Alexandria's company until he sent her back to Hampton. It tore through his soul. Would Moriah forgive her avenging angel . . . just one more time?

Twenty-nine

Moriah occupied a chair in front of Dr. Miles Jerome, President of the Pennsylvania Society for Prison Reform, as he sat behind his desk. His head nodded occasionally as he studied the report Moriah had painstakingly prepared to outline her testimony at the senate committee hearings. Careful to omit all references to other female inmates, Moriah included only information about herself and Ruth. After spending the past six days huddled over a desk in the corner of the society's cramped office, located in the retired physician's home, Moriah hoped that her testimony was strong enough.

When Dr. Jerome finished reading, he handed the report back to her as he smiled. "You did a fine job, Miss Lane. The senators should be duly impressed, particularly after the pretentious testimony today."

With a sigh of relief, Moriah relaxed her hold on the sides of her chair. "You promised to tell me what happened at the hearings."

Pushing his chair away from his desk, Dr. Jerome leaned back and crossed his legs as though preparing for a lengthy conversation. "It was quite what I expected, although Senator Williams seemed taken aback that I had replaced Marley Young and announced that the scoundrel had been asked to leave the society. The senator isn't quite sure what I'm all about." He chuckled.

Moriah laughed softly. "I'm not quite sure I am, either. When I first arrived in Harrisburg, I didn't know where to go or who to trust," she admitted. She did not mention her invitation to stay with George Atwood's parents; neither did she tell him that she had spent several days watching the society's headquarters before daring to venture inside.

Moriah only had Royd's word that Atwood was the only man on the investigative committee who was honest. After the horrific events that destroyed her faith in Royd, she was reluctant to trust anyone. When she finally decided to approach the society and ask for help, she was fairly certain that the kind-faced gentleman who sat opposite from her now was not part of any conspiracy. When she learned that he had fired Marley Young, Moriah decided to let that action be the deciding factor which earned him her trust.

"There's no deep mystery concerning my work," he responded. "I have time and energy, both of which required a good cause."

"I didn't mean to question your commitment. I just never expected to be welcomed into your home like a guest instead of—"

"A guest you are, young lady. And an important one, too," he interrupted. "Mrs. Jerome and I enjoy your company. The society needs you. Without your testimony, it's doubtful that anything can be done to prove that the committee's official report is a fraud. This afternoon, listening to Williams and his cronies laud the job the warden's done at Apple Knoll made me ill." His lips turned downward into a frown that left deep crevices in his wrinkled face.

"How many men on the panel support him?"

"Of the other five senators, only Harris. As far as I know. The others seemed interested enough with the report until the business contractors testified. Dull stuff, really. Ellston Montgomery slept through most of their testimony, and Leonard Adams had the nerve to pick his nails!"

Moriah giggled. "I wish I could have been there." Her fear of being interrogated by powerful men in government eroded a bit with Dr. Jerome's humorous description.

"Even if they let females attend, which they don't, your appearance today would have lessened the drama of your entry tomorrow."

A shudder ran down Moriah's spine. The prospect of testifying before the senate committee was daunting. The idea that she would be sitting in the same room as Lester Figgs made her skin crawl. She tried to block out her emotions where Royd was concerned, but the anticipation of seeing him again made her heart beat erratically. "What time do I testify tomorrow?" she asked, resolving to save most of her energy for when she faced Royd and silently condemned him the same way she had the first day she confronted him—with her eyes. Truth to tell, she knew that it would be a huge struggle to hide the love for him that still burned deep in her heart. A love she thought he returned. How could she have been so wrong?

"Late afternoon when the investigative committee brings witnesses forward. Mr. Darlow and Senator Atwood will probably use up most of the morning. I'm not sure if Mr. Camden is expected to make a statement or not."

"Royd might be testifying?" she gasped as her heart leaped in her chest. Could she bear hearing his lies? She must. Perhaps it would be the most effective way to harden her heart against him so that she could begin to heal.

A flicker of sympathy crossed the physician's face. "He led the investigation on Williams's behalf," he murmured. "I hope you don't have to listen to his testimony, but I'm sure he'll be there to hear yours."

Resentment burned Moriah's soul which she would have traded to the devil for the opportunity of discrediting Senator Williams and Lester Figgs with her own testimony. Unfortunately, she could not do that now without endangering the friends she left behind. She remembered Royd's suggestion that he sit by her side, and her naivete, insisting that he should stay seated with the investigative committee to distance himself from her for the sake of his reputation. He relented, and even though she now knew the real reason why, she found it hard to blame him. His reputation was the only thing that protected him from an unforgiving society.

Swallowing hard, Moriah attempted to smile. "You'll be there, won't you?"

He nodded. "Of course. I may not be able to sit beside you, but you know I'll be championing your testimony. As will others. You must have faith, Moriah. The prison reform movement has many benefactors. Some are willing to stand in the public arena; others prefer to remain anonymous. Who is to say which requires more courage?"

Embarrassed, Moriah felt her cheeks grow warm. From the moment she met Dr. Jerome, she sensed that he was a man of impeccable character. She had every faith that he would do as much as he could to mitigate the expected attack on her credibility. She had been totally honest with Dr. Jerome about everything, including the role Royd played, and supplied the physician with both versions of the reports Royd had written.

Alone and without anyone else to help her, she had to trust someone! Dr. Jerome did not seem overly quick to condemn Royd, however, even when she told him about Royd's participation in the cover-up and Alexandria's threats against the female inmates who remained at Apple Knoll.

A man of few words, Dr. Jerome usually kept his thoughts to himself. When he did speak, it was usually a brief comment. While that made Moriah uncomfortable when she first met him, their lengthy conversation tonight made her curious. "Is there something you're not telling me?" she asked when she detected an unusual gleam of sadness in his eyes.

"What? Oh," he mumbled, "not at all. I was just thinking about tomorrow. Forgive me. Old men like myself tend to find their thoughts wandering when they should be more attentive to the present."

Something about the tone of his voice or his quick apology aroused Moriah's suspicions. "Are you sure?"

"Yes, young lady. I'm sure. Now I suggest that you turn in and get as much rest as you can. You have an awfully big day tomorrow. Just remember," he said as he ushered her to the door, "that honesty will always prevail if we have the courage to face it. You'll do very well tomorrow if you tell the truth. Even when it is very painful or it appears that all is lost. Have faith."

Moriah kept silent, knowing that Royd Camden had destroyed much more than her faith.

Only half of her ordeal was over, and Dr. Jerome's parting words echoed in her mind as she bowed her head. She could not look at the panel of six senators who sat behind a massive walnut table which sat on a raised platform directly in front of her as they waited for her response. She could hear the hushed voices of the fifty odd spectators behind her in the formal hearing room. To her right, Lester Figgs and members of the investigative committee sat behind several desks that had been pushed together. Royd sat at one end, Dr. Jerome at the other, like bookends representing the opposing forces of good and evil.

Physically drained at the conclusion of her emotional testimony, Moriah paused to take a respite from the gapes and glares of the panel. She noted with some interest that none of the senators had fallen asleep, and several of them, with the exception of Senators Williams and Harris, actually seemed moved by her words.

She wondered what Royd was thinking. Although she glanced at him when she entered the formal chamber, she could not bear to make eye contact with him. Looking splendid in a charcoal gray waistcoat with an ice blue cravat, he was even more handsome now that he was clean-shaven. Dismissing his promise to shave his whiskers when they married as yet another fanciful lie, she did not fail to notice the fine, pale scars on his cheek. Royd's gaze, however, never left her when she gave her testimony. It burned her skin as though it were a branding iron, hot against her flesh.

The bang of the gavel startled Moriah, and her head snapped up. Senator Williams was staring at her like she was dim-witted. Confused, she looked at the other members of the panel, but they were all looking at her oddly, too. She had the distinct impression that they were waiting for her to answer a question. "Would you repeat the question, please?" she asked after clearing her throat.

Senator Williams smiled irritably. "I asked you to state the nature of the conviction that sent you to Apple Knoll. You do remember why you were sent to prison, don't you?"

Moriah gulped twice, recalling Royd's admonition that her cross-examination would be brutal. "Murder," she replied, her voice clear and calm.

"The victim was your own uncle, is that correct?"

She nodded, but the senator only glared at her.

"Answer aloud so everyone can hear you," he demanded.

"Yes."

Moriah flinched as the spectators' whispers grew more agitated while Senator George Atwood motioned for the right to speak.

"Miss Lane, would you tell this panel what circumstances surrounded your uncle's demise?"

Moriah noted the sympathy in Atwood's eyes with surprise. "My uncle was dying. Very slowly. Painfully. He . . . he had a terrible wasting disease. He asked my sister and me to help him," she whispered.

"How old were you at the time?"

"I was thirteen. Ruth was a year older."

"And what did you do?" Atwood prompted, his voice low and compassionate.

Silence filled the room as Moriah paused for a few moments. Every vivid detail of her uncle's last few hours flashed through her mind. "We . . . we left a bottle of laudanum where he could reach it. Then we all prayed together before Ruth and I left the room. When we returned, he was unconscious. We stayed with him until . . . until he died."

"Did you administer the drug?"

"No," she whispered.

Senator Williams pounded on the gavel to restore order as the spectators started talking openly among themselves. "Your guardian stated otherwise, and you pleaded guilty to voluntary manslaughter, I believe."

"I did," she responded, her chin tilted defiantly.

Williams grinned with satisfaction. "You also stated that you were confined to Willow Valley Lunatic Asylum. I presume the physician there diagnosed you as cured before you were released into the custody of this unnamed benefactor you mentioned."

Startled by his tone, which implied that she might still belong in an asylum, Moriah answered quickly. "No. But I told you I was sent to the asylum because—"

"A simple 'no' will suffice, Miss Lane. Thank you."

Again, the spectators' voices became a cacophony as her supporters debated her detractors. As order was restored, Senator Atwood interceded on her behalf. "I'd like to ask Miss Lane to consider her testimony concluded. With the permission of my fellow senators, I'd like her to be permitted to remain for the testimony that is about to be presented."

The six members of the panel conferred noisily before a red-faced Senator Williams ordered the bailiff to bring an extra chair for her. "Miss Lane can take a seat next to Dr. Jerome," he said gruffly.

Moriah's heart began to race. Thoroughly surprised that others were also scheduled to testify, she changed her seat. When she looked sideways at Dr. Jerome, he returned her gaze with little more than a quick smile before turning his attention to a stack of papers spread before him.

Dr. Jerome rose and addressed the panel. "Gentlemen, as you know, the Pennsylvania Society for Prison Reform is committed to ensuring a safe environment for inmates in county as well as state and federal penitentiaries. As president, I applaud the efforts of the committee, and I appreciate the opportunity to present witnesses like Miss Lane who have the courage to come forward to describe their unfortunate experiences."

For the next hour, Moriah was so mesmerized by the events that unfolded, she scarcely remembered to breathe. First, Reverend Beecham testified. His unwavering affirmation of her good character brought tears of gratitude to her eyes. As he concluded his testimony about the abuses he suspected were being perpetrated against the female inmates, however, tears streamed freely down her face.

Senator Atwood posed one last question. "Is there any reason why you failed to notify the authorities when you suspected the female inmates were being so terribly abused?"

The gaunt minister shook his head, his eyes filled with shame. "I'm an old man," he said, his voice cracking. "Congregations today need younger, stronger ministers to guide them. I needed my place as chaplain at Apple

Knoll. My sister's eyes have worsened these past few years. She's nearly blind now. She depends on me. What would I do if I couldn't support her? She'd last on the streets less than a day."

"Did anyone threaten to have you replaced?"

Reverend Beecham's expression hardened. "The warden."

Lester Figgs rose indignantly, his chair crashing to the floor. "He's so senile he's hallucinating!"

George Atwood shot to his feet. "He's a man of God!"

"Sit down!" Williams bellowed, taking control of the situation from Dr. Jerome. "Senator Atwood, you're out of order. Mr. Figgs, you'll have ample time to defend yourself later. This witness is dismissed!"

Moriah barely had time to consider how much she owed Reverend Beecham for protecting her and how badly she had judged him before a woman, hooded to protect her identity, took a seat to testify. She knew Sophie by her height alone, even without seeing her face or hearing the sound of her long-familiar voice.

Alexandria's threats reverberated through Moriah's thoughts, and Moriah began to tremble. Dr. Jerome squeezed her hand. "Have faith," he whispered before rising to question Sophie.

Dazed, Moriah heard Sophie recount the forced sexual encounters that she had to endure at Apple Knoll. After identifying Lester Figgs and Tamin Jones as her assailants, Sophie told a hushed audience about Moriah's diary which would correlate specific dates and support her own testimony.

Forcing herself to imagine the worst, Moriah envisioned such severe repercussions against the other inmates that she felt dizzy. Chancing a glance at Royd, she saw that he was sitting casually in his chair, his expression bland. He did not even appear to be nervous! *Of*

*course he isn't afraid! He knows Sophie's testimony won't
be able to connect him to the conspiracy!*

Dr. Jerome approached Sophie. "If what you're saying is all true, why is it that you aren't afraid to come
forward? Aren't you worried, knowing that you will be
returning to Apple Knoll?"

"No, sir. I'm not going back."

Lester Figgs rose again, this time more cautiously, and
conferred briefly with Senator Williams. "According to
the warden, you have three months left to serve," the
senator stated confidently.

"I have papers signed by Judge Martindell. Two days
ago, just after the warden left, I was released."

"Who brought you those papers?" Figgs demanded,
ignoring proper procedure by questioning her.

"I don't know," she admitted. "Reverend Beecham
said it was an angel, but I don't care if it was the devil in
disguise. I'm free now, and there's nothing you can do to
change that," she spat. Gasps filled the room as she
stood to her full height of six feet. "No man is ever
gonna touch me again unless I want him to."

"Unless he pays," Figgs chortled. "Dr. Jerome failed
to ask you your crime. Would you like me to share that
information with the senators? It was whoring. Your
third conviction!"

Sophie squared her shoulders. "That's right. At least
the other men *paid* for their pleasure! Or did you mean
to keep a tally and pay me when I was released?"

Outraged, Figgs's reply was drowned out by a chorus
of laughter and sneers. Williams looked pale and disori-
ented, but Royd simply nodded and scribbled notes on a
tablet of paper in front of him. By the time a second
woman entered and took the witness chair, order had
been restored.

Iona's testimony was markedly similar to Sophie's except for her last statement. "I was luckier than Moriah's
sister. The doctor's operation didn't kill me."

Moriah closed her eyes as the room started to spin. The last time she saw Iona was the night Royd had been waiting for her in her cell yard. Heart pounding, Moriah remembered trying to console Iona who was five months pregnant and very, very frightened. Senator Atwood's voice broke through Moriah's reverie, and when she opened her eyes, Iona's head was bowed.

"I didn't mean to tell them that it was Moriah they heard me with that night. They . . . they hurt me so bad!" Turning to Moriah, she started to cry. "I didn't want to tell them," she sobbed before dissolving into tears.

The truth of how the warden discovered that Moriah had been leaving her cell hit her square in the chest. Clutching her breast, she gasped for air. Relief that Royd was not responsible quickly turned to the heart-rending reality that it was all her fault. The guards overheard her talking with Iona, not Royd. Accepting the blame made her tremble, and there was still a part of her that was loyal to Royd and rejoiced that this was one instance where he was blameless. Another part, however, suggested a different reaction. Royd must have known all along that it was Iona's fault, yet he played the role of the martyr so well that Moriah had believed him when he took full responsibility for her clandestine forays being discovered! The pain that filled his eyes when he begged her to forgive him for not realizing he was being followed was just another ploy to gain her sympathy! Her heart fought back. Had Royd cared enough about her to shift the blame away from her to spare her the pain of knowing that she had alerted the guards herself? The part of her that loved him still grew stronger.

Dr. Jerome placed his arm around Moriah's shoulders as Iona was led out of the chamber. "The truth, Moriah. Listen to your heart."

Moriah shook free, attempting to make sense out of

utter nonsense and trying to listen to her head instead of her traitorous heart. When Dr. Jerome recalled Moriah to the witness chair, she wiped her face and walked unsteadily until she took a seat directly in front of the senators again. When Dr. Jerome placed a copy of the printed report in her hands, her pulse began to race.

"Do you recognize this report?" he asked, his eyes locked with hers.

Moriah's heart was pounding so loudly in her ears that she could barely make out his question. What did he think he was doing? Didn't he believe her when she told him that this report couldn't be used without placing the female inmates in danger? Tearing her eyes away from him, she looked at Royd and found his deep, green eyes riveted on her. He looked so confident, so assured, her heart cried out to him to help her.

"Miss Lane?"

She swung around to face Dr. Jerome. His brows furrowed, but she remained silent. "All the senators need to hear is the truth. Do you recognize the report I just handed you?"

"Y-yes," she stammered.

"To the best of your knowledge, is the information in this report true?"

Moriah tried to look away, but Dr. Jerome's steady gaze held her captive. She trusted him, didn't she? Or had Royd's betrayal left her so vulnerable and shaken that she had lost the ability to believe in anyone?

"It's true. All of it is the truth," she murmured.

"With the exception of Senators Williams and Harris, all of the senators on the panel received copies of this report during the midday recess. We met at the society's office where the report was discussed in great detail. Senator Atwood? I believe you would like to make a statement."

Moriah's eyes darted so quickly from one member of the panel to the next that her vision blurred, and her mind raced in so many directions that her head was spinning. A private meeting at Dr. Jerome's? Why? Mrs. Jerome's insistence that they take a carriage ride to soothe Moriah's nerves before testifying suddenly took on implications that took her breath away.

"This is an extraordinary breach of protocol," Williams shouted. "As head of this committee—"

"As of noon today," George Atwood interrupted, "you were removed from this committee, Senator, along with your colleague, Senator Harris."

"Balderdash! You can't do that!" Harris snorted, breaking his heretofore silent presence.

"I assure you, sir, that the other members of this committee were quite insistent. I have been aware of this report ever since Senator Williams rejected it and insisted that Mr. Camden prepare the official version which we all received at the beginning of the hearings yesterday. Dr. Jerome, would you like to continue?"

Heart pounding, Royd observed the announcement he anticipated with mixed emotions. His attention, however, was riveted on Moriah. Dressed in sober brown, which accented her fair coloring and made her pale blue eyes even more luminous, she looked more beautiful and delicate than he had a right to remember. She seemed to be taken off guard by Atwood's announcement. He only prayed she would continue to listen carefully. With an open mind. Before she rendered her final judgment about him.

Dr. Jerome addressed the panel as he stood next to Moriah, his hand on her shoulder. "Gentlemen, as we discussed earlier, I want to assure you that the eyewitness testimony you heard today from two former inmates correlates precisely with the information gathered by this valiant young woman. If necessary, I'm sure we could secure the testimony of the others. The purpose of these hearings was to address a very serious issue indeed. I believe we have made an impressive case that few men would be able to disregard."

"As a committee," Senator Atwood continued, "our first directive will be to remove Lester Figgs as the warden of Apple Knoll. Effective immediately. We are also suggesting a full Senate investigation into the affairs of Senators Williams and Harris. Recommendations for a full criminal investigation by the proper civil authorities have also been made."

Williams glared at Royd. Figgs slumped in his chair. Royd ignored both men, his eyes focused on Moriah's face as Atwood droned on about the events that led to the downfall of the conspiracy to hide the problems at Apple Knoll. Her eyes, wide with amazement, reflected her surprise. Would they shine so lustrously when he finally had the opportunity to speak with her?

The moment Royd had waited for had finally arrived. As Atwood summed up his presentation, Royd's pulse began to pound. He had never been so nervous in all of his life. But then, nothing had ever been this important to him, either.

"For the record, we would also like to commend the efforts of the man who worked diligently to bring this matter to our attention. He personally arranged for the witnesses who appeared before us today and assisted Miss Lane when her situation was very precarious indeed."

Moriah's expression of stupefied amazement as the senators nodded in solemn agreement made Royd's heart skip a beat. She looked like she just could not believe that the miracle that she had prayed for had actually happened. She had won her valiant struggle! Lester Figgs would never, ever hurt another female inmate. Senator Williams and his cronies had been discredited, despite Alexandria's dire predictions of quite the opposite!

Royd expected Moriah to turn to him, and his heart

skipped yet another beat. Instead, she smiled . . . at Dr. Jerome! Did she think that Dr. Jerome, and not Royd, had been able to intervene on behalf of Sophie and Iona as well as Reverend Beecham? Obviously she did, he realized, as she laid her cheek against the physician's hand. When she finally lifted her head and looked at Royd, his heartbeat screeched to a halt.

Sadness and hurt, deeper and more compelling than he had ever dreamed anyone was capable of experiencing, turned her eyes into pools of blue misery. There was no anger. No condemnation. Only grief . . . at love once claimed and lost forever?

Atwood asked for silence before he continued. "Mr. Camden, the committee owes you a tremendous debt of gratitude. I consider it a privilege to have shared duties with you as part of the investigative committee."

As Moriah's head snapped back, Royd stood up and faced the committee. He only had eyes for Moriah, however, and prayed that she would listen to him and give in to the pleadings of her heart. "The credit, gentlemen, belongs completely to Miss Lane. I admit that when I first arrived at Apple Knoll, I assumed that the rumors were false. Miss Lane defied any number of verbal intimidations and physical mistreatment—at great personal sacrifice—to convince me that I was wrong. When I faltered, driven by blind ambition and the all-consuming desire to be accepted into society, she is the one who reminded me of my duty. And she is the one who overcame tremendous obstacles for the sake of truth and justice and jolted my conscience until I acted honorably."

He paused, watching Moriah's face fill with a combination of incredulity and wonder. "Miss Lane taught me to use my strengths to overcome my weaknesses. To have faith." He walked, one slow step at a time, until he stood before her. "I didn't plan to be here today to support her when she testified. I didn't have the courage. I was willing to let her stand alone out of fear that I would lose my good name and my fortune if she failed." He paused, shaking his head. "I can't even take credit for changing my mind. I have fortune enough now that society's acceptance or blame is immaterial to my future. So you see," he murmured softly, "I truly had nothing to lose or to sacrifice. Except my name. For the record," he said, his voice growing firmer, "my real name—"

"No!" she cried as she bolted to her feet. "Please. Stop. Haven't you told me enough to make me suffer for the rest of my life for not believing in you? Don't . . . don't add any more."

Royd barely heard the sound of the gavel as Atwood declared the hearings officially concluded and ignored the flurry of activity on the dais as members of the committee gathered their papers and departed.

"I love you, Moriah," he whispered, afraid to move and take her in his arms for fear she would push him away. "I should have told you about Alexandria. It's all my fault."

Tears streamed down her face, and her body trembled visibly. "I don't deserve your devotion," she murmured. "I failed to love you enough to trust you. I will never forgive myself for the pain I must have caused you."

"Forgiveness is part of love," he countered, alarmed by the resoluteness he saw in her eyes. "You once told me that the past was spent and nothing was more important than the future. I love you, Moriah. Marry me. Share the future with me."

He held his breath as she stared deep into his eyes, her pain so haunting that it nearly broke his heart. Didn't she understand that they had both made mistakes? Would she let those mistakes destroy the love they shared? For one brief moment, he thought she understood.

He was wrong.

She shook her head and slowly turned to Dr. Jerome.

"I'll have my things removed before you arrive home."
Before Royd could stop her, Moriah quickly stepped
into the crowd of spectators and disappeared. Brushing
past Dr. Jerome, Royd felt the pressure of the man's
hand on his shoulder. He stopped, his eyes blinded by
tears that threatened to spill onto his cheeks.

"Let her go, son. Give her time," he said softly.

"I offered her everything. My apology. My love. My
forgiveness. And my name. What more does she want?"

Dr. Jerome smiled. "She wants peace of mind, Royd,
but she'll never find it unless she's able to forgive herself
for not trusting you. If you love her, you'll give her the
time to come to terms with herself."

Royd wiped his eyes with the back of his hands and
straightened his shoulders. The final secret between
them had been a wedge of suspicion and doubt that even
love had been unable to dislodge today. Would it ever?

"I'll be waiting, Pale Eyes," he murmured, wishing
that she could hear him and loving her enough to let her
go. "Please. Come home to me."

♣
Thirty

Church services on Christmas Eve. Men, women, and children. Crowded into the narrow pews, huddled together for warmth. Coat and bonnets. Dusted with snowflakes, sparkling in the candlelight. Faces. Aglow with faith and the promise of God's covenant to be fulfilled with the breaking of dawn and the birth of the Savior. Voices. Raised with renewed hope in God's love and forgiveness.

Except for me.

Moriah looked around the small church as she stood in an alcove near the front of the church. Alone. Hidden by the shadows and shivering. Not from the devastating cold. From an emptiness deep within her soul.

For over two months, she had worked relentlessly from dawn to midnight, blindly committed to the prison reform movement. She had traveled between Harrisburg, Pittsburgh, and Philadelphia, inspecting penitentiaries and writing so many letters and reports that she had callouses on her fingers.

Exhausted to the bone, she fell into bed every night. Sleep, however, eluded her as guilt kept her awake during the only time she had no interruptions. No excuses. Nowhere to hide. In the hushed hours before dawn, she faced her own human frailty and rejected it, crying herself to sleep just before the first light of yet another day.

As the church service continued, Moriah caught the scent of fresh evergreen and stared at the boughs of pine and spruce that decorated the altar. Ever green. Ever faithful. Symbols of God's omniscient and ever-present love. A love that knew no season and never wavered, despite man's weak and sinful nature. A love she no longer deserved.

Royd's eyes were almost the same verdant color. His love was deeper and more enduring than any she had ever known. Closing her eyes, Moriah recaptured the look of devotion in his eyes when he pleaded for her to return to him. He blamed himself, not her. Forgiveness and understanding etched his face as he held his breath, waiting for her to accept the fact that although she had made a terrible mistake by believing Alexandria instead of him, he understood.

And he loved her still.

With a sigh that made her tremble, Moriah opened her tear-filled eyes to a blur of candlelight. She loved Royd so much that it made her ache deep within her heart and soul. Had she lost the right to claim his love? Forever? Royd had found it in his heart to forgive her for not trusting him. But would she ever be able to forgive herself?

Driven by twin demons of pride and self-loathing, Moriah had no rest. No comfort. No faith. She could not pray anymore. Her Bible lay unopened, its cover dusty, its pages unread. Lured by tonight's services in desperate need for some kind of peace, she listened to the minister's sermon with only half a heart as she remembered a Christmas Eve so long ago when she could still pray. And sing. And believe.

She had betrayed Royd's love. She had turned her back on God. Surrounded by so many of God's faithful servants, she was a lonely refugee. For her, there would be no redemption. No salvation. She deserved the suffering and loneliness which wrapped around her heart as the price she would pay for failing to believe in Royd and the love he offered to her. For being consumed with vengeance and spite, despite her alleged faith in God who demanded that His followers forgive their enemies.

The minister's voice deepened as he finished his sermon, rousing Moriah from the depths of self-pity to hear his final words. "For those who are in pain, He brings blessed relief. For those who mourn, comforting love. For those who have hardened their hearts against others or even themselves, He promises all-abiding love and unequivocal pardon. Open your heart and accept His Son as a precious gift. For then you will heal. Or hope. Or forgive. Others. And yourselves."

Stunned by the simple eloquence of the minister's words, Moriah closed her eyes and listened to the sound of her own heartbeat. Did she dare to open her heart?

Did she dare *not* to?

As she accepted herself as one of God's precious creatures—not flawless, simply human—a comforting warmth suffused her. Body and soul. Tears streamed down her face as she fell to her knees, allowing the miracles of faith and love to wash away her sins. And her fears.

For Mary, traveling to Bethlehem had been long and arduous, but she accepted God's plan for her, however unworthy she thought she might have been. Once Moriah accepted God's forgiveness, could she make the journey to David's Crossing and accept the love Royd offered to her, knowing that human love was always as imperfect as the man and woman who shared it?

Royd stood on the terrace atop the turret that adjoined Moriah's old suite of rooms, oblivious to the cold. The Christmas feast had long been devoured, and the gaiety that filled the halls of the estate had slipped into the past with other Christmas memories. He gazed at the land surrounding the estate, blanketed with still-falling snow that captured every shivering moonbeam and illuminated his night view.

For the first time in his life, Royd had glimpsed both the wonder and sorrow of Christmas. Sharing the solemn holiday with so many people he loved filled his heart with emotions that only magnified his grief.

"Moriah."

His chest tightened as he whispered her name. Without her, his heart was laden with loneliness, even though he was rarely ever alone. Being with Moll and Jack, sharing the travails of the Haskell family, and actively working with the prison reform movement filled his days, although thoughts of Moriah always crept into his mind to haunt him at night.

He wondered if Moriah knew that he had converted the estate into a halfway house where newly released convicts like Sophie and Iona found a safe haven before trying to forge a new life for themselves. Reverend Beecham, along with his sister, tended to his new flock with an energy that Royd envied. Did Moriah know that Royd's dream was only half fulfilled without her by his side?

The muffled clopping of a horse's hooves echoed in the stillness of the night. Narrowing his gaze, he scanned the landscape. Who would be traveling alone in the shadows of the night? On Christmas night?

A fair distance down the road, he spotted the lone horse. The animal looked exhausted, his head hanging low and nodding slowly as he took one wearied step at a time. The rider's shoulders hunched against the wind, his hat, coat, and breeches coated with fresh-falling snow.

Royd grew concerned that the rider, who appeared to be a young boy, might be lost. He was heading away from David's Crossing, and there was not another village less than half a day's ride away. Royd turned and walked quickly downstairs. There was no time to grab his coat. He needed every moment to reach the main road before the lad passed by.

A blast of frigid air numbed Royd's just-warmed face as he ran from the house. Ankle-deep snow slowed him down, and when he finally reached the end of the path that connected his estate to the main road, Royd was afraid he might be too late. After crouching down to study the snow covered road, however, he nodded with relief. There were no fresh prints. The horse and rider were still heading toward him.

After brushing the snow from his hair, Royd hugged his arms around his chest for warmth. His throat was raw from inhaling the cold air, and his feet were numb and tingling.

Moments later, the rider appeared as the horse rounded the bend. Royd waited, hoping the boy would lift his head and see him. He was afraid to call out for fear of startling the boy, although he guessed that the horse was too tired to bolt. When the rider passed within a few feet without even noticing him, Royd grabbed the bridle and brushed the ice and snow off the horse's nose and eyes as he brought the steed to a halt. Puzzled, Royd approached the rider slowly. Had the poor lad frozen to death in the saddle? He nudged one of the stirrups, shaking the boy's leg. "Lad? Are you ill?"

The rider flinched, then awkwardly attempted to sit up straight. Royd watched him closely, half expecting him to topple out of the saddle. Instead, the boy's gloved hand tightened on the reins as he lifted his head.

Curious, Royd stared into the boy's face, and his heart began to race as he gazed into those miraculous eyes. Pale blue eyes, the color of a spring sky that miraculously appeared in the middle of a snowstorm!

Eyes shining with a love that made Royd's heart leap for joy.

Too mesmerized to speak, Royd reached out and cupped his beloved's face, his fingers trembling with the fear that she was only a mirage that would disappear before he could touch her. Her breath fanned his palm as she turned and kissed his hand. Tears welled in his eyes as she leaned toward him, her arms outstretched to embrace him.

"Moriah," he whispered as he pulled her into his arms. He showered her face with kisses, tasting traces of winter cold snowflakes washed away by her warm, salty tears. He held her so tightly that he could feel her heart pounding against his chest, and the full promise and power of love redeemed filled his soul. "Welcome home, Pale Eyes," he rasped as gazed into her luminous eyes.

"I must have drifted off," she murmured. "You startled me. I thought you were an angel."

He chuckled as he scooped her into his arms and carried her back to the house, trailing the reins to the horse who followed behind them. "I thought we settled that issue once before, Moriah. I'm not an angel, despite your claims otherwise. I'm just a man. A man who loves you very much."

Moriah snuggled closer. "You look more like an angel now. Your beard is gone."

He stopped and gazed into her eyes. "I made a promise to be clean-shaven the day we married. I never gave up hope that you'd come home. I love you, Moriah. Marry me tonight. I want you so!"

She giggled. "You're right. You can't be an angel. A heavenly creature couldn't possibly be so . . . so lusty! Don't you think we should talk? I owe you an explanation! You can't just welcome me back without wanting me to tell you why—"

"You're here. That's what matters. As for what you *owe* me, madam, that is not suitable for prolonged discussion." He bent his head and whispered into her ear, chuckling when she gasped. Her frustration at finding no whiskers to tweak brought an added blush to her cheeks.

"Royd!"

Laughing, he started back to the house, increasing his pace to a jaunty trot. "Remind me not to grow another beard. It would give you unfair advantage."

"Before or after we're married?"

"Most definitely before. After we're married, there won't be time for talk. I have other plans. Would you like to hear them?"

"Heavens, no!" she squealed, reveling in the wondrous joy of being held in his arms and the promise of a future that would be a far more incredible journey of faith and love if they traveled the road of life together.

Arnette Lamb...
Anita Mills...
Rosanne Bittner...

Join three of your favorite storytellers on a tender journey of the heart—in an extraordinary collection of breathtaking novellas written around the theme of motherhood. Before you finish, you'll have been swept from the storm-tossed coast of a Scottish isle to the epic fury of the American frontier, and you'll have lived the lives and loves of three indomitable women as they experience their most passionate moments.

Cherished Moments

COMING FOR MOTHER'S DAY IN MAY FROM ST. MARTIN'S PAPERBACKS